The Eyes
North Korea Strikes

To Captain Stephen Conway

Enjoy the book!

Donald L. Rosenberry

Bedside Books
An imprint of American Book Publishing
P.O. Box 65624
Salt Lake City, UT 84165
www.american-book.com
Printed in the United States of America on acid-free paper.

The Eyes: North Korea Strikes

Publisher's Note: This is a work of fiction. Names, characters, places, and incidents either are the product of the author's imagination, or are used fictitiously, and any resemblance to actual persons, living or dead, events, or locales is entirely coincidental.

ISBN 1-58982-248-X

DONAKI, The Eyes: North Korea Strikes

Special Sales

These books are available at special discounts for bulk purchases. Special editions, including personalized covers, excerpts of existing books, and corporate imprints, can be created in large quantities for special needs. For more information e-mail info@american-book.com.

The Eyes
North Korea Strikes

DONAKI

Dedication

To the memory of my father-in-law, Takashi Nishiyama, Otō-san to me. He was an inspiration and tremendous presence in my life—arigatō, Otō-san!

FOREWORD

There are several scenarios generally accepted as the possible processes by which the Korean peninsula will eventually reunite: status quo, soft landing, hard landing, explosion, and muddling through. All conclude the integrated peninsula would be under the political, economic, and military control of South Korea.

Status quo is the notion that the situation on the peninsula can be left to itself, maintaining the current arrangement indefinitely. The counterargument is that status quo implies stasis, or no change. Unfortunately, the status quo in the Democratic Peoples Republic of Korea is steady disintegration. Naturally, that would eventually precipitate a collapse of some nature. The resulting integration of North and South Korea in a precipitous way could be devastating to the global economy, many times more severe than the crisis initiated when Thailand floated the Baht in the 1990s.

The notion of a soft landing theorizes the gradual decline of economic capability of the DPRK concomitantly, nurturing a gentle integration of the North and South in a peaceful unification. The antithetical philosophy here is how unlikely it is for the ruling regime in North Korea to abandon what has been its driving force for half a century—regime survival.

The notion of the hard landing theory hinges on a final dramatic economic collapse of the DPRK, with the South left to pick up the pieces. This would be a traumatic event, and though not overtly a military operation, it could well require the full military force of South Korea and its allies to prevent a chaotic rush of the majority population of the DPRK from inundating the South, both physically and economically. An uncontrolled immigration of the starving peoples of the North across the Demilitarized Zone (DMZ) into the South could also easily precipitate an economic collapse in the Republic of Korea as well as create a daunting humanitarian crisis. The global implications would be dramatic and negative.

The notion most feared is the concept of a second all-out war whereby the winner takes all. The West generally presumes South Korea and its allies would prevail, but the human and economic toll would be catastrophic. It is worth remembering that North Korea has more than a million men and women under arms along the border. With the advantage of surprise and mass of size on the battlefield, a repeat of the first Korean War wherein the South and its allies were driven all the way south to a small perimeter around the port city of Pusan is not in-comprehensible.

But the generally accepted notion of muddling through is the one the world can most easily stomach. Under this concept, the world stage ignores North Korea unless, and until, a specific tragedy occurs and is highlighted in the media; then concerned nations "Band-Aid" together a response just significant enough to quell the crisis, returning the North to its pariah status, a perennial target of WMD control and a potential source of assistance to terrorist organizations flush with money and eager to purchase the weapons North Korea can sell.

Don Rosenberry was a student of mine at the Asia-Pacific Center for Security Studies, where he proffered an unconventional, additional possibility and an interesting global response. In *The Eyes*, he brings to life the possibility of the DPRK working the military arm of the power of a nation state in a limited fashion to continue the survival of Kim Jong Il's dictatorship. It is a clever blend of real-world concerns and circumstances, with a measure of science fiction added in, hidden within an entertaining and gripping story. He's done a great job of bringing an arguably academic topic to life in a very engaging and readable drama.

Dr. Stephen Noerper

FEBRUARY 3, 2000, NORTH OF BISMARCK, NORTH DAKOTA

Bitter cold wind greeted Dr. Eugene Dorman as he left the lab facility. He hated the cameras, the long hallways, the guards, the multiple double doors, the metal detectors, and most of all, the case checks. He considered it a tremendous invasion of privacy to have to open every bag, briefcase, and package for someone to awkwardly grope through on his way in and out of the building.

I can't even bring my lunch to work without everyone knowing what it is, he thought. *In addition to the unmistakable feeling that I'm not trusted, it takes a full half-hour to enter or exit from my own lab.* The irritation did nothing for his blood pressure, already a little high. Finally outside, he pulled his beige London Fog trench coat up around his neck, though it never really helped. The wind whipped his exposed face, and the frozen lapel dug into his neck. The surrounding darkness reminded him he'd stayed later than he'd planned yet again. At least the contract security company had made the jump to an enclosed parking garage. The six-story facility was state of the art, and, he remembered with a sudden happy thought, thus far he'd been able to keep the "security Mafia" from making it yet another bastion of stupidity.

Once outside the laboratory proper, I'm free of the security apparatus. On the other hand, he mused, *I might be able to get an enclosed*

The Eyes

walkway built from the garage to the lab under the disguise of a security precaution. I'm already subject to their harassing activities anyway, so it just may be worth it. I'll call Charles tomorrow. He'll be suspicious of my reaching out to security after all my tirades, but it just might work, and it is so cold!

THE LABORATORY PARKING GARAGE

"This is going to be easy, Hassim. The Americans are idiots! They have more security at their shopping malls directed at themselves than at their regional research laboratory. It is truly hard to believe; not only is there very little security at such a delicate facility, its location is announced on huge signs for twenty miles along the public highway for anyone to see. They are blinded in their hedonism and arrogance." Abdul spat the sentence as if trying to get rid of a foul taste.

"Yes, Abdul, but keep your thoughts focused on the business at hand," Hassim growled in Arabic. "What can you expect? For all their self-proclaimed superiority, this is largely a country of ignorant cattle. Most Americans are technical imbeciles, and their ability to change is astoundingly poor. For instance, their standards for measurement are archaic; what is this *mile* they use? Five thousand, two hundred, and eighty feet, of course, but what is a foot? Again, it is twelve inches, but what is the inch based on? They still cling stubbornly to these unique measurements—miles for distance, pounds for weight, gallons for fluid volume, and acres for land area. The rest of the world laughs at them behind their back, but they are so violent that the world also caters to them, creating separate facilities for building material for export to America. My absolute favorite is their temperature scale. The standard

The Eyes

is one hundred degrees, but unlike the Celsius scale, in which one hundred degrees represents the boiling point of water, their one hundred degrees represents the *normal* temperature of a sheep's anus! There's some scientific superiority for you. Still, we must be very careful. Not all Americans are as dumb as the masses seem, and they have their own brand of loyalty—they can be fiercely dangerous." He turned away from his companion and continued his vigilant scanning for the doctor. *Why did they make me bring Abdul along?* Hassim thought to himself. *He is such a fool. It will be a tremendous burden to have Abdul's help in this effort. He repeats the fiery wrath of the pious, doddering fanatics at home verbatim.*

I loathe this country, he thought, *but despite all the things that we who follow Allah know should spell their failure, the United States remains unquestionably at the heart of the world's greatest and most complex science and technology. Where there is such technological capability, the leading-edge weapons of war are created. Ignoring this reality has always been our mistake,* he contemplated. *Religious leaders always overlook the simplest of truths. In their own arrogance, they become victims of prejudicial blindness. If America is, among all her sins, stupid, why then does she possess the world's greatest technology? Why doesn't Allah strike her down? Why do the greatest Arab minds forsake the righteous path and the divine heredity of the Middle East to join with Satan on the North American continent? Yes, never underestimate the unknown complexities in any event. To continue to survive requires holding the divinity of hajj at arm's length to prevent one from becoming blind to reality.*

The moment the doctor stepped out of the lab, Hassim spotted him. *What irony,* Hassim thought, *that this traitor would turn the tide. For once it will be the Americans who have made the fatal mistake of underestimating the enemy.* Hassim would be certain to make this happen.

"Are you ready, Abdul?" Hassim whispered. "We must make this appear completely normal. The doctor shuns security, but you must remember that the security forces do not shun him. They are obligated to protect him with their lives. It must be distasteful for them to have to come to grips with the idea that an Arab is more important than they are. Nevertheless, these are trained security forces. These are men we must believe are as skilled as we are, perhaps watching us just as we

12

watch the doctor. Even without knowing who we are or why we are here, they have courses of action, which will spell our failure or even our deaths if we are not careful and vigilant. To win this day, we must act normal. In each step, imagine the situation is reversed. If we were protecting the doctor, in what manner could they act in our place that would keep us from suspecting anything was wrong?"

"That is ridiculous!" Abdul protested. "You suspect everything and everyone without reason. It is what I hate most about working with you. It is almost as if you respect these heathen animals. No matter; I am ready, Hassim. You handle the doctor. I'll drive his car. It is how we planned it, and one does not change the plan in execution."

"Yes," Hassim responded tersely. *How could you ever understand that flexibility is the key to most successful missions?* He thought to himself. *Abdul did not possess the instincts necessary to respond instantaneously to the unforeseen things a working operative encounters. Because of that, he is as good as dead as an operator in this field; but what does that matter?*

Hassim returned to his business and slowly removed the automatic SOCOM from his pocket and opened it. Even the name of the knife, derived from Special Operations Command, was designed to enhance its sinister nature. The feel of the perfectly balanced knife in his hand was reassuring, familiar. Using such a weapon up close, face to face, was comfortable and honest. *If you are to kill a man, it should be done with such a weapon, the event concluding as Allah sees fit based on the rival skills of the competitors, right from wrong decided man to man. The godless ones kill from afar, too squeamish to see the results of their handiwork. Hiding in their fifty-thousand-pound shells screaming over the earth at or above the speed of sound, they can casually omit from their thoughts and stories the women and babies they've burned to ashes as they crow about their heroic battles on high. But death is not on the menu today.*

Keeping Dr. Dorman alive seemed so wrong—treasonous at least, if not blasphemous. How could an Arab doctor forsake the kingdom of Allah and sell his skill to America? Are the comforts of modern buildings and the attentions of slovenly exposed whores worth a man's very soul? Perhaps to some the answer is yes.

The Eyes

Everything about this mission seemed doomed. Before it had even begun, Hassim was summoned before the elders. It had been a very long session, and Hassim did not like to talk to religious fanatics. During the ensuing "conversation" with the religious leaders, they had made two points very clear: Abdul would accompany Hassim on this mission, and the doctor would make it to his destination, alive. Otherwise, Hassim was also dead. This provided an obstacle Hassim had never had to include in his planning—what would plan B entail should there be a mistake caused by this oaf Abdul? If things went wrong, and for any reason, the doctor died, Hassim would need a plan of action. He had already decided he would not become one of the volunteers for the "experiments"; he knew they were just a waste of time and lives. Better to leave them to the young martyrs-in-waiting. He would use his familiar knife on himself, finally knowing exactly how his many victims had felt as the 154-centimeter, titanium-carbon-nitride blade slid across their throats.

Turning his attention back to the present, he knew that today he would not kill. The blade would only need to be menacing. The doctor would be another "soft" target; any weapon would be enough. It always amazed Hassim that so many men knew so little of hand-to-hand fighting. Americans were the worst of all, with their maniacal passion for guns; they were unable to defend themselves without one. The irony was that most people who owned a personal weapon were unqualified to use it. They were more likely to injure themselves than any assailant.

The doctor neared the entrance to the parking garage. As he had for the past three days, he stopped at the vending machine and grabbed a chocolate bar. Hassim, fastidious as always in his preparation, had purchased the same two days ago in the effort to know more about his prey, but the candy was not to his liking at all. No wonder Americans are so fat, he mused. Sweetness should be saved for relaxing, which is much better enjoyed in a good, strong cup of coffee. Real coffee, of course, not the weak swill Americans drink served in their huge plastic coffee mugs. There seemed no end to the things Americans could degrade. Even so simple a pleasure as a fine cup of coffee, properly served in a small, highly decorated cup, became another victim of America's obsession with size, quantity, and volume. Everything became an issue of more, bigger, or faster—an entire society of hedonists.

OUTSIDE THE LAB AT THE PARKING GARAGE

At the entrance to the parking garage on the first floor, the elevator opened and the doctor got in. Had he been paying attention, he would have noticed that the elevator had come down to him, and that the man inside didn't get off; instead he rode back up with the doctor. He might also have noticed that the man looked Middle Eastern, wore a scowl, and was inappropriately dressed for the weather, but the doctor was too engrossed in removing his jacket and opening his prized chocolate bar. The elevator began again, and the doctor turned subconsciously toward the other man. He was large, with dark features, like his own. Americans would naturally take the doctor's elevator companion's weather-beaten features for age, but he was in reality still in his late twenties. The doctor nodded, and Hassim nodded back slowly. The door opened on the third floor and Hassim walked out first, as planned. As the doctor walked toward his car, he would feel no threat; give no thought to the mysterious man from the elevator. What of it? There were many other cars in the parking lot, and the stranger strode away from him in plain view. The doctor's thoughts returned to his lab and his work. Arriving at his car, the doctor routinely unlocked the driver's side, reached in, and put the key in the ignition. As always, he would start the car and let it warm up while he settled into the car, arranging his briefcase and checking the mirrors and radio. The engine sprang to life, and the doctor walked around to the other side of the car. Just as he opened the passenger door, he felt, more than heard, someone behind him.

"Do not turn around, and do not struggle, Dr. Eugene Dorman, and you will not be hurt." The voice held no discernible accent, but it had an edge that made it abundantly clear that compliance was the only option. The disgust this man seemed to hold for the doctor nearly dripped off his words. "Scream or fight and I will slit your throat right here and now. I care nothing for traitors like you, who change their names to work for the scum slaveholders whom you beg for attention." At this point Hassim held the knife in front of the doctor, giving him all too good a look at the black tapered handle and serrated blade. The doctor stood very still, and the unknown assailant continued, "Very good, Dr. Ibn Il Hosni Muhammad." Hearing his birth name for the first time in so long, and spoken with a clear, deep accent, sent chills down the doctor's spine. He was immediately transported in memory and time to another event.

He had been just a boy when a man had seized his father, also at knifepoint, speaking in English with the same heavy accent. In front of Dr. Dorman's own eyes, his father's neck had been savagely ripped open. In seconds, the man he had so loved and revered lay in a crumpled heap, covered in his own blood. His final image of his father, his head angled back obscenely, attached by only a sliver of skin, eyes still open, was etched permanently in his mind. From that event stemmed his family's long trek that ended in America. Here he vowed to help the United States in its war with terrorists, but it always ate at him that his culture, heritage, his very people were stereotypically terrorists in the eyes of most Westerners.

Abdul now joined Hassim and held the doctor in a vice-like grip. Hassim ripped open the doctor's sleeve, roughly rubbed an alcohol wipe across the side of his arm, and then jabbed him with a needle, completely missing the "cleansed" area, and administered an injection. Dr. Dorman was as concerned the needle would break off in his arm as he was about the liquid being injected into him. He felt an increasing, intense burning sensation spread up his arm and across his chest, and

Outside The Lab at the Parking Garage

suddenly he became very cold. His vision began to fail, and, finally, he had no sensation at all.

THE BED OF A PICKUP TRUCK

The grogginess wasn't as bad as the overwhelming thirst. Every time Dr. Dorman awoke, it was the same. His last memory was always the needle, then darkness. He awoke to find his hands over his head, tied to a metal bar in what appeared to be a very old and rusty pickup truck. The only other things in the truck bed appeared to be duffel bags on either side of him and some boxes near the tailgate, held in place by a modifying bar welded across the back of the truck horizontally. The truck was not insulated, and his hands and feet were racked with pain from the rough cord used to bind him. Despite the intense pain, he was determined not to cry out—it always brought the needle. Whoever these people were, their number-one goal seemed to be to keep him totally quiet. Dr. Dorman's captors made no effort at speech or any other type of contact with him. He had no clue how long it had been since he left the lab that Friday afternoon. Certainly days had passed, but it could easily have been weeks or even months. No, he corrected himself, not months. He could remember being force-fed stale water and some kind of hard bread, but nothing more. On that kind of diet, an extended period would have seriously affected his weight, and for now his clothes all seemed to fit reasonably. I have got to think. What have I done differently lately? What would cause someone, anyone, to want my research this badly? I never had the opportunity to verify the last, apparently successful, experiment, and I've told no one about it. Even Jack doesn't know that we seem to have found a way to cross from a natural nerve ending to a synthetic neural synapse. His mind drifted wearily back to the lab, where he'd spent most of his waking life for the past three years.

For a couple of weeks, he had pursued a new direction on the sensitive business of getting neural excitation past a synapse from a human nerve to a synthetic nerve. The attempt to graph the synapse to a neural trunk had been dismal. The concept of excitatory materials had been exhaustively researched, everything from photographic and photosynthetic to the parthenogenetic response in some frogs, without much success. Theory always seemed to fail in the lab, but this new area of research using old methods in the presence of neonatal fluids had seemed very promising. In true capitalist form, the politically correct public discussion on the use of placental material in research focused on major diseases like multiple sclerosis and Parkinson's disease. In reality, most of the true energy in research for the major pharmaceutical companies was in vanity. The company that developed a working hair growth formula or a lotion successful in reducing the wrinkling and aging of skin would be the next financial wonder child of Wall Street. For Dr. Dorman's sake, the pharmaceutical companies provided chaos theory research. So much money and time examining every facet of a developing possibility for any hint of a profitable wonder pill frequently revealed clues for spin-off material—for the person who could see it. The problem was the incredible speed with which information was developed and published, usually via the Internet. Information overload was a whole new area of research for Dr. Dorman; it was the reason he relented and hired Jack in the first place. Jack was a smart young man. He was computer savvy, and, at least as far as the doctor could tell, almost painfully inquisitive by nature. Dr. Dorman's "handlers," as he liked to call them, had foisted a fresh direction upon him within the world of neonatal research. The handlers were marginally educated scientists who approved Dr. Dorman's budget and *reviewed* his work. To get them off his back, he'd contributed an article to *American Researcher* a few months back on possible effects of neonatal fluids on the regeneration of neural tissue. Jack had collected an incredible amount of research on the subject for him and made the article reasonably painless to write. Thus had begun an unusual chain of events, more like random chance than science that had changed his research dramatically.

Shortly after submitting the article, Dr. Dorman had been sent a small quantity of the fluids he needed for his own work, and he began to hypothesize about some amazing possibilities. Ultimately, what he discovered was way more amazing than what he had dreamed of, and the discovery was completely devoid of all the classic scientific processes. It had been well documented that neural tissue exposed to the growth extract began to exhibit regeneration. The doctor had, naturally, begun focusing his research on that mode of regenerative influence. He worked many long hours on ways to affect the process—faster, slower, more complete growth, anything that would affect actual cell division would be helpful in revealing the mechanism allowing regeneration. In that process, the nearly absurd allowed him to make a major discovery. It always amazed him how major breakthroughs occurred. Penicillin and expanded foam were both ideas nearly lost, but discovered nevertheless through some chaotic sequence of events.

Trivial events a professional researcher would normally try to avoid had been exactly what were needed. Had the camera swivel not been too loose, had the ceiling fan not activated, had the vibration not swiveled the camera filming at high speed, his discovery would have ended up in the trash. But these things had happened, and he had been too tired that evening to turn off the camera after discovering that eight hours of film had been expended on the "wrong" end of the apparatus.

As Dr. Dorman had begun the mundane task of cleaning up, he had noticed the incredible. The remnant tissue wasn't just draped over the synthetic arm; it was actually growing into the synthetic material. Here was recorded proof of living tissue and inorganic matter actually blending. There was even evidence of vascularization in the synthetic material. But had he'd never gotten a chance to tell anyone about it, save one e-mail to Dr. Sanderson, but that couldn't be the reason he had been kidnapped; but then what else could it have been?

The truck came to a stop. Someone opened the cab and got out. Despite the blindfold, he could tell a tarp was moved and he was being examined. He felt a firm hand on his arm, pushing up the sleeve of his now-tattered shirt. Not a word was spoken, just a perfunctory alcohol swipe, and the syringe unceremoniously jabbed into his arm. The pain from it was bearable, but he couldn't help but think the needle was tearing more than piercing his arm. *It's dull, probably been reused*, he thought. As Dr. Dorman drifted off, he kept hoping that it had only been used repeatedly on him. A cold dread spread through his body from the pit of his stomach; he felt himself being lifted from the truck, then, darkness.

ABOARD A PROPELLER-DRIVEN AIRCRAFT

The pain clawed at Dr. Dorman; it felt as if each and every muscle in his body was ripping. As he fully regained consciousness, his situation came crashing back in on him. He was in a truck, traveling somewhere with two men. But no, the steady vibration, much louder engine noise, and greater cold made it very clear he was no longer in a truck. A dark, penetratingly cold cargo hold of some aircraft was his home for now. His feet and legs were numb where they touched the floor. His arms were stretched up and tied to some kind of post fitted with fold-down footsteps. As his eyes adjusted to the dim light, he realized his feet were bound together and his shoes had been removed. If he could get some circulation going, perhaps he could stand up. What he would, or could, do after that was insignificant. Right now, the most important thing in his life was just standing up.

He began by alternately tightening his thigh and calf, first left, then right, again and again. With each effort he was greeted with searing pain. He had been sitting here for a very long time, and his muscles were fighting the reintroduction of blood and resisting his will to contract them. He fought, thinking of the times he had sat too long and one of his feet had gone to sleep. The foot had been unwilling to bear his weight at that time, and the sensation had been unbearable, or so it had seemed then. Now that same feeling extended to everything from his chest down. He knew that what now seemed debilitating could cost him his mobility permanently and perhaps even his life eventually. He would stand up!

Finally his legs began to react to his efforts to move. He pulled hard with his arms against the rope and slowly began to move up the post. His arms too had lost a measure of responsiveness, and the effort to stand took at least twenty minutes. He now leaned against the post as much as stood, and tried to take stock of his new surroundings.

This was indeed some kind of cargo aircraft. The floor appeared to be made of aluminum. There were rows of rollers stretching back to an inclined ramp. On either side of the ramp were small windows in what looked like doors. Similar small windows spaced out along each side of the compartment all the way up toward Dr. Dorman. His post was up against some form of wall with all manners of straps and equipment located along the sides behind some kind of red webbing. The steady drumming of the engines was very loud. He was thirsty, but had obviously been given water, as his shirt was damp and it was too cold to sweat. He was now so ravenous he could barely think of anything else. Had he been able to see himself, he would have been immediately struck by the effects of six days without food. His captors had indeed given him water on a regular basis to ensure his survival, but they were definitely not concerned with his comfort, and feeding him was evidently an effort they felt too demanding. He looked around for anything remotely edible, but there was nothing but a few oily rags, some wooden blocks he correctly guessed were the aircraft chocks, used to ensure the aircraft didn't roll after parking should the brakes fail for any reason, and an oxygen bottle strapped to the wall.

"He is awake!" a man roared above the engine noise. He was standing to the doctor's right, looking past the wall and up into what must have been the cockpit. The big man turned around, but all that could be seen were his eyes peering from beneath the hood. He walked toward the doctor and roughly yanked his arms down from the hook. He half dragged him to the side of the compartment and sat him down on a seat made from the web material found all along the walls of the aircraft. The doctor's legs were unbound from one another, and then unceremoniously retied to hooks set in the floor. The entire cargo compartment seemed ingeniously designed to allow anything to be tied down at almost any angle. His captor walked back to the wall and reached up into the cockpit, leaving him seated, his hands bound together with primitive handcuffs, but otherwise unfettered—the most mobility he had been afforded so far. The mysterious man then approached Dr. Dorman and, just when the doctor expected the needle again, tossed a box in his lap.

"Eat now!" his captor commanded above the din of the engines.

Giving thought to no other desires or complaints, the doctor began awkwardly tearing into the box. He didn't care what was in it. *If it is empty, I'll just eat the box*, he mused. He glanced up to find himself alone. Inside the box were an apple, two partly opened roast beef sandwiches, a chocolate bar, and two cans of orange soda. Dr. Dorman thought to himself that he had never received a finer gift in his entire life. He wouldn't think of anything else until his hunger and thirst were appeased. He ate ravenously. As he drifted off to sleep, he realized his captors had used a different method of administering the drug to him; he approved.

FINAL APPROACH

Dr. Dorman awoke to an all-encompassing, penetrating mechanical scream—the four Allison turboprop engines of the second-hand C-130 he was traveling in. Despite his already doubtful situation, the thought of crashing now superseded everything, and he was gripped with fear. The plane lurched from side to side and was clearly descending. The roar of the engines grew even louder. If that wasn't bad enough, the aircraft seemed to be bouncing through the air instead of flying. He gripped the aluminum frame of his web seating so tightly that his hands actually hurt. For the second time since this ordeal had begun, he was thoroughly terrified.

The aircraft abruptly pitched up. To Dr. Dorman, it felt as if the nose and tail of the aircraft switched places, as if the pilot had initiated a steep climb to clear some unseen obstacle. Then the aircraft smashed into the earth with considerable force; this was certainly not an average aircraft landing. The engines screamed as the aircraft rapidly decelerated. Dr. Dorman forgot about everything except the overwhelming possibility that he was about to perish in an aircraft accident. Then, almost as quickly as it began, it stopped. The engines calmed to a loud but acceptable pulsing propeller beat. The somewhat-quieter engine noise was known as low-speed ground idle, and in comparison to the sounds the engines made in reverse, they were practically quiet. The aircraft ceased its lurching and began the familiar rocking motion aircraft make while taxiing. Dr. Dorman's pulse slowly returned to normal, or as normal as could be expected. Wherever "here" was, he had arrived, and, for now at least, he had survived.

The aircraft turned rapidly yet smoothly, followed by a final whoosh as the four variable-pitch propeller engines shut down. It was at once a tremendous relief and a new source of anxiety. As he appeared to be the only cargo aboard, he reasoned he would now certainly receive attention from someone. He wouldn't have to wait long to discover how right he was.

From the cockpit came the face that had been flitting in and out of his consciousness since the encounter in the parking garage. The man walked directly up to Dr. Dorman, reached down, and lifted him effortlessly. At the same time, he whipped open the menacing knife that the doctor remembered so well. This time the doctor was neither impressed nor frightened. Even bad logic would allow one to conclude it was unlikely he would be dragged through this long traveling ordeal just to be stabbed to death in the back of an airplane in the middle of nowhere. He was right. Hassim sliced through the doctor's bonds, and for the first time in more days than he could accurately determine, the doctor was free. But free can be a relative term, and that was clear to the doctor as well as his captor.

"Welcome home, Dr. Eugene Dorman. When you leave this time, it will be spiritually only." Hassim held his face very close to the doctor as he sneered these words. It was in both their interests that the doctor fear Hassim and obey his instructions without question. While it would likely not seem so to Dr. Dorman, his life was in Hassim's hands, and, ironically, Hassim knew his life was contingent on the doctor staying alive. "You will listen, and you will cooperate. Now you will be taken to your tent. Do not waste your time, or the precious resources you will find there. Eat, drink, and then sleep; you will need your strength." Dr. Dorman started to ask a question, but Hassim had already hoisted him like a sack over his shoulder and carried him down the ramp at the tail of the aircraft. Dumped unceremoniously in a fairly large, dark tent, the doctor elected to take the advice he had been given. He was unsure he would be treated this well again soon. Without questioning the source or sanitation of the food and water, he drank and ate his fill, mindful that in his state, overdoing it could also have a detrimental effect on his health. Then he lay down on the old military-style sleeping bag and drifted off to sleep, this time without the benefit of the burning drug.

APRIL 23, OUTSKIRTS
OF DENVER, COLORADO

Definitely middle class, Jack thought as he surveyed Dr. Sanderson's house and the surrounding landscape. *I've stumbled across the typical suburban scene—two-car garage, a sedan in the driveway, even a white picket fence to complete the image. I wonder if he has two kids, one boy and one girl*, Jack thought as he laughed to himself. The sudden smile surprised him; it had been quite a while since anything had seemed even remotely amusing. Dr. Dorman's sudden disappearance haunted Jack. Not surprisingly, the laboratory security administration was quite sure he had defected back to Iraq. Jack conceded it was probably a natural conclusion—Dr. Dorman was Iraqi, and it would explain his constant and rather public outbursts against security. Nevertheless, Jack didn't believe it. The security folks were always defensive and even hostile toward Dr. Dorman. They felt he spared no effort at thwarting their every move, even humiliating them whenever possible. They would naturally assume the worst. But Jack knew the doctor better. He knew about Dr. Dorman's father, the nightmares, and how and why the doctor hated the feeling of being enclosed and scrutinized by the security staff. Though Jack knew he might be alone in the thought, he did not believe for a second that the doctor left of his own volition. What concerned him was that with the convenient dismissal, there would be no search and no energy expended to determine if the doctor had been killed.

As Jack approached the front porch, he allowed himself to gaze across the flawless green carpet of grass to the neatly manicured flower garden with the tulips and chrysanthemums standing just inside the fence. *For a guy with a reputation as "a brain," Dr. Sanderson sure must spend a lot of time in the yard; but then everybody has a hobby,* Jack thought. He turned his attention to the cherry-stained mahogany door in front of him. He tried to peer through the diamond shaped window, but a thick curtain blocked his view. Ignoring the brass knocker, Jack raised his clenched fist and knocked with three strong raps. Almost instantly, he found himself staring into lovely brown eyes of a beautiful young woman.

"I-I'm sorry. I…"

"No, I'm sorry," she said in a soft, full voice. "I didn't mean to startle you."

"No harm, no foul. I should have been paying attention," Jack recovered.

"I'm Sanderson, Emiko," she said, extending her right hand. "Dad's down in the basement lab, as usual. You must be…"

"Jack. Jack Armstead. Your first name is Sanderson?"

"Of course not, silly. I am half Japanese, and in most of Asia, one's last name is presented first, at least on first meetings and formal occasions. It reflects the Asian emphasis on family first, then self. We've been expecting you. When I read your resume, I couldn't believe it. If half of what you've written is true, you'll make an ideal assistant. I think you could say Dad's impressed. He's read it to me so many times, I feel like I've known you all my life. Please come in."

"Thank you." Jack stepped through the door and into a hallway leading to a living room. His polished black loafers squeaked against the hardwood floors.

"Oh, I'm sorry, but could you take your shoes off? We don't wear them in the house."

"Oh, sure." Slipping off his shoes, Jack thanked the unknown protector of the social misfit that he had selected a new pair of socks for today. "I guess the noise against this hardwood floor would drive anyone batty."

April, 23, Outskirts of Denver, Colorado

"It isn't the noise. In addition to protecting your feet, shoes are supposed to act as a barrier, protecting you from all sorts of nasty material. If you track whatever you may have stepped on outside with you inside the house, you've kind of defeated the whole idea of outside being different from inside. Please don't make me get earthy with the descriptions. Suffice to use one of Dad's favorite epithets, 'You wouldn't want stray animal refuse tracked all over, would you?' You'll get used to it staying here, and you'll never feel the same about wearing shoes in the house again...any house."

Emiko turned and crossed the huge room. Her skirt swung suggestively from her well-shaped slender hips. Jack found himself reevaluating his new assignment. She stopped, opened what appeared from the distance to be the door to a closet, and turned back toward him. "Well, are you coming, or do you plan to just stand there with your mouth hanging open?" Jack veritably recoiled from her words. He felt his face flushing as it filled with heat. He realized he actually *was* standing with his mouth agape. He didn't know which was more embarrassing, her catching him staring, or her knowing he would be staring.

"I'm right behind you." He quickly crossed the room as Emiko disappeared into the closet. He caught the handle just as the door was closing and pulled it open to reveal a long stairwell. As he descended, he noted this was no ordinary basement; it had obviously been rebuilt. The gray concrete walls, noticeably out of place in the well-appointed house, gave way to a large, sterile-white waiting room.

"This is Dad's study. Wait here, and I'll tell him you've arrived." Before Jack could respond, Emiko disappeared through another door at the far end of the room. From the slightly acrid smell, Jack deduced the lab was just beyond that door. While he waited, Jack took in the room. There was a single painting on the far wall, but he couldn't make out what the subject of the painting was, so he walked over to get a better look. The image was unsettling, but intriguing. At first glance, it seemed to be a man with some kind of helmet strapped onto one side of his face. Upon closer inspection, the device clearly appeared to be protruding out of his face and eye. "Nice painting," he thought out loud. "It looks like a blend of man, spider, and toaster oven."

"I quite agree!"

The Eyes

Jack spun around in the direction of the new voice. "Dr. Sanderson! You look just like the pictures in the press. I'm very pleased to meet you." The doctor had a firm yet unremarkable grip, which Jack returned in kind.

"The pleasure is mine. When I read your resume, I was indeed impressed. I figure any resume worth its salt is at least one-third garbage. If yours is even two-thirds true, I am fortunate to have you; whether I need you or not is an agency matter. Add to it the fact that you didn't compile the resume and weren't even seeking a position here—well, we are pleased."

"You flatter me, Doctor, and I guess I am a little nervous. I was just admiring your painting. Is this the end result of your research?"

"Hardly. There have been many attempts to match the biological with the mechanical. Work in prosthetics has probably yielded our earliest and greatest progress. Still it seems we are at a primitive stage given the advances medicine has made in other areas. Prosthetic research has been somewhat successful, however, and has moved us down the road. Unfortunately, we've never been able to replicate the complex structure and function of a working nerve—a problem that has prevented us from truly integrating technology with the human form. That has never stopped the creative side of us from experimenting and dreaming though. Thanks to clever editing and the advantages of computer graphics, we can achieve perfect blending, at least on the big screen. From *The Six Million Dollar Man* to the outlandish characters in *Star Wars*, we have been fascinated with all types of technology-enhanced human beings. This artist's rendition really caught my eye—no pun intended."

"Clever, Doctor. What exactly is it I'll be doing here, and for how long?"

"First of all, call me Alex. I prefer a relaxed environment. Dr. Dorman and I work in the same area. We have been kept separate in the hopes we might accomplish the same result through different paths. Now that he is gone, they have decided, before they really know what happened or where he is, that he is a threat to the program. I disagree with immediately trashing someone's loyalty, but I understand the risks. You are here to feed me anything you two had found that worked, and also to keep me from doing it the same way. Admitting this up front allows us to get past any resentment we might form and to move ahead. To that end, you will be right in the thick of my research, shoulder to shoulder with Emiko and me. My first rule is that you must tell me if you think I'm holding out on you. I have no intention of doing so, but I'm not used to working as a team of three. So, if you don't get the information you need, ask. The short version is you'll be doing whatever needs to be done. Some of it will be downright disgusting. Any time one works with biological research, there are going to be some unpleasant support activities.

"I doubt if you or I really have anything to say about *the terms of employment*, if you will."

"Great, although calling you Alex will take some getting used to. This sounds exactly like what I need following the untimely end of my last job."

"Dr. Dorman is ahead of his time," Dr. Sanderson stated quite frankly. "I always hoped we could merge our research one day. Gene, as he allowed me to call him, works on one method of electrical transfer, while I work another. Together we just may have something, but I doubt we'll ever know. The government does a great job of keeping us in our own little sections. What would make him just up and quit his research?"

"I really don't know," Jack said quietly.

"You can speak freely here, Jack. I have my own devices to scramble listeners, and they work as well as theirs do. One of the few concessions I insisted on when they built this lab was that none of the laboratory or waiting room conversations would be taped or monitored. We have no communication devices down here. There are no phones, modems, or cables. Nothing except a single panic button hard wired to security."

"Well, first of all, thanks for referring to Dr. Dorman in the present tense. I don't know what happened to him, but I hope he is safe."

Dr. Sanderson and Emiko stood quietly, a sad expression mirrored on each face; both thinking the same fate could have been theirs.

"I had hoped the reason would turn out to be earthier, something like finance," Dr. Sanderson started. "It isn't that far fetched really. Science is supposed to be the search for answers—knowledge in its own right as a worthy effort. Unfortunately, the pursuit of knowledge isn't usually very profitable to the researcher. Neither Dr. Dorman nor I could have afforded the laboratories, supplies, or equipment we needed to begin this line of research. Private grants work and are available after you're established, but they always want a predictable payback, and quickly. They dry up when nothing you've done will sell. The political whining necessary to get the rich and famous to support one's research is so offensive that almost any alternative is a better idea. This led both of us to conducting research for the US government. I always believed that for his own private reasons, Dr. Dorman wanted very much to not only work for the US government but to help them in every possible way; he was almost a superpatriot. Of course, his resentment of security personnel is legendary, but not unreasonable given the state security he experienced growing up."

"Your description of his resentment is mild and magnanimous. In fact, he would get really bent out of shape when the security forces got in his way. He was short tempered with them and sometimes outright intolerant, but I always felt he did it to make sure the lines remained perfectly clear between security and harassment."

"Yes, I remember Dr. Dorman never did well with supervision. The government is really not a bad sponsor, but one still has to explain theories and account for time and resources to a lot of educated yet largely unthinking middlemen. I never really knew what lay behind his deep-seated resentment for loss of personal freedom."

Jack proceeded to tell them the story of Dr. Dorman's tragic youth. When he finished, Emiko looked as though she would cry, but said nothing. "I didn't plan to upset you with this whole situation, but now I know I'm not alone in believing something is dreadfully wrong here."

DECEMBER 15,
FORT COLLINS, COLORADO

Lee Wong hated waiting. He looked over at the coffee table; professional hardware journals and today's newspapers lay haphazardly all over it. The headline of a small paragraph caught his eye: "Sanderson on Brink of Biotronic Breakthrough." *This should be interesting reading*, he thought.

"I figured you'd latch on to that headline." Frank carried his portly body through the door and headed for the fridge. "For the life of me, I can't understand why you read that stuff. If you were really smart enough to understand it, you wouldn't be working here for me. Besides, a man that can work with his hands as well as you can isn't supposed to be cerebral. It ain't natural!"

"You're right about that, Frank. If I really had the skills, I'd be somewhere else. Not that I don't enjoy working here. Nevertheless, I read enough when I could afford to go to school to remain interested. Maybe my ship will come in one day and I can finish. At any rate, I'll read this on my next break. Somebody needs to stay with Yin Hee out on the floor."

"You'd be better off reading the *Handyman* magazine; it might help you out here. This is a hardware store you know."

The Eyes

"Frank, you're a good man, but you have the academic drive of a teenager just discovering the opposite sex. Academic biology is so much more."

"Maybe it is, but the only biology I ever needed to learn I learned from my wife—and not in any classroom!" He laughed at his own joke.

"You're a jerk, Frank, and you better keep that to yourself around Yin Hee," Lee laughed. *What an enigma this big friendly galoot is*, Lee thought as he walked through the swinging doors labeled "Employees only." *With his attitude and looks, it's a miracle he has children. But then he has a saint for a wife, and the mechanics of creating children don't really require any thinking parts.*

That opposites attract couldn't be better demonstrated than by the marriage of Frank and Kathleen Jenz. A programmer for a gaming software company, she was still a stunning brunette at forty-something. The longer Lee knew them, the more surprised he was. Frank and Kathleen had a marriage of twenty-one-plus years that was rock solid—Lee had never understood why. Sure, Frank was a good man, but he was obese, a klutz, and about as refined as stone. It was truly a mystery to Lee; but then he remembered that he never seemed to be able to nurse a relationship beyond a couple of encounters in very public places. *Just don't have the touch*, he guessed. But Frank was a good employer, and a steadfast businessman. He took good care of his family, customers, and employees. He'd asked Lee and Yin Hee to work today, New Year's Eve, on the pretext that they were short a few hours. At first glance, one might be offended that he selected the only two single employees—one male, one female, both Asian—but Lee knew Frank too well to be upset. So did Yin Hee. Frank had been careful in his methods, but he was a bit clumsy in his social skills, as his wife gently put it, and it didn't take a genius to know he was trying to find out if Yin Hee and Lee had plans. For their part, neither was upset that he wanted to know their plans, or that they had no plans. An invitation to the Jenzes' place was usually an occasion to remember—meticulously designed and always just plain fun. They served good food and thought of fun games for adults to play without being too risqué, with a generous supply of libations thrown in on Frank's behalf. So at least they could look forward to a reasonably good time while ringing in the New Year.

December 15, Fort Collins, Colorado

Yin Hee was talking animatedly with a large burly man in plumbing. Lee approached to see if his expertise was needed. Yin Hee was a competent worker who handled herself extremely well with customers. Still, since she was just four feet eleven and weighed in at a meager eighty-eight pounds, Lee got nervous when any big guy walked in. It had only been a few years since someone had actually stalked her. It had gone on for months, with the police, as usual, saying that until he did something, their hands were tied. Then on a rainy Wednesday night, the stalker did something. He tried to pick Yin Hee up outside the store without her consent. Luckily, Lee and Frank had been there and ended the incident without delay. Well, it was mostly Frank's doing, Lee admitted when he was honest with himself. Lee himself wasn't much bigger than Yin Hee. She still talked about it on occasion, always careful to split the compliments between the two, and Frank never said anything. The truth was that at six feet four and 275 pounds, the former high-school football player was formidable enough all by himself, even if he was a "little out of shape." On those very rare occasions when Frank became angry, he was terrifying. For his part, Lee had kicked the assailant's ankle out from under him, tripping him so Frank could get hold of his arm. Frank always maintained that they could never prove he broke the guy's arm, but they all knew; the visible bone shard was a reasonable indication. Yin Hee didn't press charges when the guy agreed to never come back, and they never saw him again. Nevertheless, even after three-plus years, the three of them couldn't forget about it. They would never be quite the same again, always wondering what the next customer brought into the store with him besides a mere hardware challenge.

"I'm trying to repair the water faucet in the back of my house," the customer told Yin Hee. "I can't really see anything wrong, but water is accumulating on the floor under our washer and dryer, and I've already turned the water valve to the washing machine off, with no result. So I'm guessing it has to be the main water faucet, although it is outside."

"You're probably right," Yin Hee started. "Is the pipe leading to the outside faucet inside an interior wall?"

"Yeah. I had to see if I could get to it, so I cut a hole in the drywall. When I looked in with the flashlight, I saw the faucet, which seemed awfully long, but with no problems I could identify. That seemed crazy, so I came down here to talk with you all."

"Chances are you have a freeze protection pipe installed, but it may be installed level. The long faucet neck you saw has a purpose. The idea is to have the water shut-off valve located far enough inside the wall that the warmth of the house will keep water from freezing in the pipe. To make sure the faucet doesn't break, though, the pipe has to be angled slightly down so the last of the water will drain out after you turn the faucet off. Does the water come out constantly, or is there more when you turn the outside faucet on?" Yin Hee asked.

"I don't really know," the man admitted. "My wife found the problem. What will it mean if that's true?"

"Just that there's a crack in the faucet, probably on the side you can't see—away from the hole you cut. You may not need to cut a bigger hole if you can get the faucet head removed. We have a reasonable selection in stock, and we're open for another six hours today." Yin Hee smiled sweetly and turned away.

"Thanks, you've been very helpful. I'll go see about removing the faucet, and I'll see you later." The customer turned and walked down the long center aisle and left the store. Outside, he walked casually over to a large, white van sitting in the parking lot. He got in the passenger side, and the driver started the engine and drove off. On the highway, he turned to face the backseat. "All right, I went in and verified she's there. You said it was worth a hundred dollars. I want my money now!" The man in the back looked up; all that was visible were his eyes.

"You have done well for us, friend. We now reward you with much more than money could ever hope to provide—you will have peace," and he shot the large man in the head. "Drive Abdul! We will dispose of this one and get back to the doctor; the next phase of our mission can wait a few weeks." Hassim disliked using the gun, but it had fallen into his hands. It was a locally identified weapon, so the authorities would be looking for someone in the area. In his business, anonymity was a good thing; finding someone else to take the rap was even better. There was no love lost between the elements of the dark.

PYONGYANG, FEBRUARY 27

Dawn at Paektu—a beautiful but very cold morning approached. Kim Chon Ul felt old as he clambered up the trail. "Why do we keep coming here, comrade? It proves nothing. Our people know only what we tell them. They have no means of verifying anything. Those few who watch television see what we tell them, and we've even done a reasonably good job of shutting down the infernal Internet. We both know you weren't really born here; it is just more of the game we play with the people."

Kim Jong Il turned to his closest aid and gave him an icy stare. The general had never believed in juche, or self-sufficiency. He'd never realized how important it really was. *I will have to remove some of this dead weight as things pick up,* Kim Jong Il thought. *I need people who believe, and Chon Ul simply doesn't. Most of the world thinks my philosophy is mere propaganda, never meant for real implementation. They are wrong.* Finally he responded aloud, "You will tell them I have received renewed strength from the Taebeck, as always. That the true struggle to reunite the peninsula will soon begin. We will unify the peninsula as we have struggled so hard to do for these past fifty-five years."

"Why don't we let the mouthpiece, Sonbin, issue another 'signed statement,' as if anyone ever reads the useless tripe they print."

The Eyes

"Be careful, Chon Ul. Change is in the wind. The boughs that don't bend will snap off, no matter where they are on the trunk!" He abruptly backhanded the stunned senior propaganda minister, who fell backward roughly to the ground. The Dear leader turned back to admire his view of the lake. "It is true the words written about me are melodramatic, but our people need something to cling to—I am it!"

"You are what we write about you!" the old man spat. "Without us, people would know you as what you are—nothing! You are a mere figurehead for the great Korean people. Do not pretend to be more than that when you are alone with me like this. I have spent my life creating your image, for us—not you!"

"The words you write are useless, especially to me. My so-called biography, boldly posted on the World Wide Web, reads like very bad fiction. Our people can't read it, and Westerners see through the words."

"No! It is just as your father planned. The world sees you as a mentally feeble old man, clouded in mystery, trying to follow in his father's shoes and clinging to power like a parasitic vine, bleeding the country of its resources for the benefit of a few powerful cronies. That is just as it should be. It allows you to remain quietly poised to make the ultimate contribution to the world—a reunited Korea! Thanks to me, you may do so at your leisure!"

"Well, we agree on that at least. But we are running out of time. The generations are changing. North and South are about to transition into a nation in which every living man, woman, and child has only known two separate Koreas. A united Korea will become another fact to be remembered on the historical timeline for schoolchildren's history tests. Every North Korean and every South Korean has been reared on hate, not just for outsiders, but also for each other. As the light dims in our elderly comrades' eyes, the fire to reunite cools in the nation."

"The right is on our side, and you have the opportunity to motivate the true people of Korea. The traitorous scum puppets of the United States to our south mean nothing! What do we care for them? We care only for the righteous loyal comrades of the Democratic People's Republic of Korea!"

"Our people are starving to death! We feed only those in the 'breadbasket' because they feed us, and, of course, we feed the military. Besides them, our people do what they can to fend for themselves. With our stupid policy of dumping ever-larger quantities of fertilizers on the fields, we've managed to ruin nearly all of them! Leave me; I wish to enjoy the tranquility of this place."

Silently, the old man turned and retreated down the trail. Kim Jong Il was tired of the facade, the clinging to useless rhetoric. It was time to make a move, before the common people found the strength, born of despair and hopelessness, to rise up against their leader. The world thinks the only possible solution is to reunite Korea. The world also knows it cannot afford to reunite Korea. The world, as usual, is led by the United States. They have so-called experts on Korea who write endlessly about the future of the Korean peninsula. In the past, they predicted one of four primary scenarios would unfold: status quo, soft landing, hard landing, and explosion. Now a fifth thought has entered their expert opinions—muddling through. Status quo is wrong from the start. It implies stasis, or no change, yet the status quo in the DPRK is steady disintegration. The soft landing theory implies the gradual decline of economic capability of the DPRK resulting in the gentle integration of the North and South in a peaceful unification. The hard landing theory is hinged on the final dramatic economic collapse of the DPRK, with the South left to pick up the pieces. The explosion concept is the one most feared—an all-out war by which the winner takes all. But the concept of muddling through is the one the world could most easily stomach. Ignore the North until a specific tragedy occurs, then "Band-Aid" together a response barely significant enough to quell the crises. *Each is right, and all are wrong*, Kim Jong Il thought. *But how could the Western pundits know? Most of them have never been here before.* He turned and looked out over the expanse of the countryside as another bitterly cold yet beautiful day opened its eyes.

23 NOVEMBER, OUTSKIRTS OF DENVER

Whether it was superstition or habit, Jack had taken the first room offered to him. It was beginning to sink in that Alex and his daughter had given up a lot for the research facility. This was much less a home than an elaborately concealed laboratory and hotel. It was now afternoon, so Jack wandered back downstairs to get better acquainted with the place. But after extensive wandering, Jack concluded it was a normal house on the top two floors—clearly the lab was the place to be. As he walked down the stairs, could hear Alex and Emiko discussing something in heated voices. He moved closer to the bottom of the stairs quietly, and stood just out of sight.

"And I'm telling you that without more information, there simply isn't enough data here to draw any conclusions at all! But I will say this much—I trust Jack. Yes, I could be falling for a reasonably shallow con job by the agency, but I don't think so. We have had no other contacts from the agency, no additional line inquiries or e-mail scans, unless they have a new software package, and more importantly, no increase in physical surveillance. I believe Jack is not acting; I felt he was genuinely angry about the treatment of Dr. Dorman. I don't really believe the agency had anything to do with it. They could easily have closed up shop here if the project was the problem. I suspect they feel Dr.

The Eyes

Dorman was on the wrong track, but this would represent a heinous new means of dealing with that. I'm concerned, but not about the system. In Gene's last note, he mentioned something I don't quite understand. Maybe together we can figure it out."

"You mean he's contacted you since he went missing? You could get in big trouble over that. The note might even be dangerous to have in your possession. I vote we delete it now using the classified purge program!"

"Calm down, Emiko! It was transmitted the Friday before his disappearance and on a system I don't think the agency even knows about. From the content of the note, either he was having just a regular day, or he was under the most extreme duress."

"What do you mean? What system don't they—or I—know about? We have no privacy here at all."

"I know all of that, and I don't mean to play 'I've got a secret,' but you'll understand when you read the note. Dr. Dorman's message comes across too casual to be written as hasty, last minute words to the world. Let's suspend all the melodrama for now. There may be something important about the biotronics, if I can figure it out."

Jack stepped into the room, trying to look as if he hadn't been eavesdropping—it didn't work.

"And how long have you been standing there?" Emiko demanded. She held him in an icy glare that he knew he would prefer not to witness again.

"Hey, I'm sorry, but no one posted any off-limit signs at the top of the stairs, and I didn't want to interrupt anything."

"I see. So the only logical, noble course of action was to stand just out of sight and listen in. Is that what you would expect us to believe?"

"Emiko, must you be so abrupt? I'm sure there is a reasonable explanation," the doctor said calmly as he turned toward Jack.

"OK, Doc, I admit I was curious to find out if all the commotion was about me, or what I told you about this morning. I swear I wasn't spying on you to see what other info I could gather. I didn't catch all of your discussion, but I did distinctly hear that you had some communication with Dr. Dorman. I'd be most interested in seeing that, if it's OK with both of you."

"I have no problem—Emiko?"

23 November, Outskirts of Denver

"What's the use? He knows we've got it. If he's agency or worse, we're sunk now. Let's go see this message," and she stormed by Jack with a tempestuous flash of her eyes and a serious "don't go there" expression. The only question Jack had on his mind was, did she bump him intentionally or was she just too angry to care?

"Why is she so upset?" Jack asked innocently.

"She is afraid. She has always been nervous, but the disappearance of Gene has increased her fear that I may be next." Dr. Sanderson spoke in a whisper so his daughter wouldn't hear. "Almost all anger can be traced back to fear in one way or another. Think through all the times you've been really angry; then be honest with yourself, and you'll see you were afraid of something. Don't get me wrong; fear is a powerful emotion, and not necessarily a bad one either. It prepares the body and mind for some of the most fantastic displays of human thought, strength, and even compassionate restraint. Emiko is afraid of the current situation, and so am I. Perhaps I will regret deciding so quickly that you are for real, but there is no time for that now. It is time to move on." Ah, the computer is online; it looks like we are finally in business here. And here is his note." Dr. Sanderson pointed at the screen.

> *Alex,*
>
> *May this message find you at peace with yourself and your family. I seem to have stumbled across an interesting event. It always seems so sad that despite our considerable effort and careful academic preparation, the really big discoveries, the ones that shift us to a new level, always seem to be pure accidents, which grow on you over time. Such is the environment from which I characterize the genesis of my newest direction (no pun intended). It is sad that such pure art as our science, an art as innocent as an unborn child, is surprisingly juxtaposed to artificial, even plastic concepts. Hollywood could do no better in its movies. It would be a great waste to lose new breakthroughs. We must get together to discuss this at your earliest convenience. For now, I'll continue my pursuit down this latest track, hoping for new growth in my research.*
>
> *May Allah keep you in his light.—Gene*

The Eyes

"Well, what do you two make of that?" Dr. Sanderson asked with some frustration.

"He certainly never spoke like that around me," Jack offered. "There is a message in there somewhere. We just need to find it."

"I agree," Emiko chimed in. "He seems to be trying to tell us something about his work, and some new direction he was taking, if we can discern it. But why would he need to use all the subterfuge to talk to you if he thought no one else would read the e-mail?" Emiko turned to Jack and continued, "Did you know of any new finding, any new technique he was trying?"

"Well, nothing that he confided in me, but as you may recall, he wrote an article for *American Researcher* on the value of neonatal fluids and tissue to neural propagation research—maybe there is something there. Clearly his reference to 'an unborn child' is some reference to the neonatal research he was working with. But as I understood it, that line of inquiry turned up nothing significant. He just wrote the article because his sponsors told him to. But maybe rereading the article is a good place to start."

"Great idea. I think we have those magazines here somewhere," Emiko said as she began shuffling through the magazines on the table.

PYONGYANG, DECEMBER 23

Today dawned as so many others—the pomp and ceremony failing to hide the ragged condition of the ceremonial costumes and decorative sashes. Everywhere Kim Jong Il, the last bastion of personal demagoguery, looked, he was reminded of the unbelievable reality—North Korea's centralized economy did not lead to prosperity. Nevertheless, that roll of the dice was not his. That pleasure had been his father's. Even if he had the desire to trade his status as a virtual deity, it would not be easy. The world saw North Korea as an entire nation run like a cult, all following an egomaniacal personality desperately trying to hang on to the power he inherited from his father. Even in their most generous moments, foreign media could offer nothing more legitimate than hero worship for his reign. Though he was loath to admit it, he knew they were partly right. He also knew something very basic—their own Maslow had spelled it out quite clearly, though the West was either ignorant of it or chose to dismiss it—the people of the DPRK desperately need something to cling to; for better or worse, he was it.

He would reestablish the DPRK as a nation under his dynamic leadership and unquestioned authority. The key, he reasoned, was to act when least expected, and with violence so spectacular that the battlefield would immediately belong to the attacking forces, his. Everyone assumed that his plan would require technology unavailable within the

The Eyes

DPRK, but that problem, too, had been resolved. The so-called four-party talks had worked exactly as he'd expected. He had already spent four years leveraging the "Madman Tyrant Dictator" moniker into millions in aid and technology for his country, and the world wasn't tiring of this act yet. His latest coup was convincing the world to give the DPRK half a million American dollars in oil every year until the West built the world's most advanced light-water reactors, at a cost of billions. All he had to do was not process uranium, or convince the other countries he was not. Not bad for an economy teetering on total collapse.

The civilized world simply could not stomach the torrent of injury and death a second Korean War might invoke. The images of the last Korean War were still too fresh. Kim Jong Il actually found it amusing that it had required so little to convince the West to provide the very tools he needed to win again. This time the plan was far more comprehensive than his father's had been. Every conflict has to have a trigger; his father had the speech by US Secretary of State Acheson to set up the last conflict. In that particular address, Acheson had detailed the geographic areas in Asia the United States considered a part of its sphere of influence—the Korean peninsula was not included. His father took that as a sign that the United States would not intervene if North Korea acted militarily to reunite the peninsula, and therefore proceeded to attack with Soviet approval. Kim Jong Il often thought it both sad and interesting that that speech, one of the most famous speeches involving Korean history, was nothing more than a trivia question to most of the contemporary world.

Now, fifty-plus years later, the nuclear menace would set the stage for the continuation of the Korean conflict. With the world on edge, fearing the second-ever use of a nuclear device on a population center, it would be easy to take the West by surprise. That would then set off an unprecedented humanitarian effort, which would greatly benefit the people of North Korea and leave him in power. *If I can just trust those I have placed in positions of authority, this will work*, he thought. *I have to do something. We are slowly decaying as a nation state. Our economy has crumbled; our ability to feed ourselves is inadequate. We will only survive if I can get more land, and a means to introduce capital into our economy. The time when we can sit back and wait for handouts from our traditional so-called friends has passed. We must take what we need in the short term, and position ourselves to grow for the future. This plan had been many years in the making, and it was given a tremendous helping hand with the new war on terrorism. Using the philosophy of "the enemy of my enemy is my friend," disparate cells could work together well.*

FRANK AND KATHLEEN'S HOME

Frank was waiting in the living room. He had turned the TV on, and the local news was prattling on about this or that celebration for the evening. It was still early, and the city was bracing for the usual trials of year's end and beginning. He turned and proposed a toast, "To the best of friends; may the New Year bring only great rewards!"

Yin Hee dropped her glass; it shattered against the floor spilling the red fluid in a random pattern. She stood staring past Frank, pointing at the TV with her open mouth covered by her other hand. The screen showed a close up of a man lying in the dirt. Kathleen rushed to Yin Hee's side and watched her focus on the story. Frank had already grabbed the remote and turned up the volume. The announcer continued in his deadpan description: "The middle-aged man was found earlier in the day, dumped by the side of a road with a bullet through his head. The police are looking into the possibility of a drive-by shooting, but have little to go on. The man, identified as Art Schrabb, was a local. The reason for this cold-blooded, heinous slaying is unknown. Mr. Schrabb's identification, wallet, and money were all found on his person, eliminating robbery as a probable cause.

"In other news, the mayor has stated again that the policy against fireworks in residential areas will be upheld…"

The Eyes

"Are you OK, Yin Hee?" Kathleen had her arm around the young lady and could feel her shaking. "What is it? Do you know that man?"

Frank and Lee immediately jumped to the wrong conclusion. "Yin Hee, he can't hurt you anymore; he's gone now," Frank began.

"He isn't the same guy anyway," Lee added.

"No! That man was in the store today! I helped him with a faucet problem." Yin Hee's eyes were wild with fear. She was distraught. Kathleen put her arm around her and took her to the bedroom.

Frank and Lee covered their discomfort by cleaning up the broken glass and raspberry wine cooler from the wood floor. Frank turned off the TV and put on some light salsa music. Frank finally turned to Lee and asked, "Was that guy really in the store today?"

"I'm not positive, but he sure looked close enough to be him. Naturally, Yin Hee saw him best, so she should know."

Kathleen came back out into the living room. "She'll be fine. Let's just give her a few minutes. I'd be shaken up too if I was her. It's scary to know someone you just spoke with is now dead."

In the bathroom, Yin Hee collapsed to the floor. It was happening all over again. Last time, when Frank and Lee had intervened, she had felt their efforts were going to get them all killed, as well as their extended families. That had turned out to be nothing more than a sick, common criminal. This time? Who knew? How could she tell these people what was really bothering her? For all she knew, her "unknown handlers" were watching her. She knew they would come for her eventually, that they knew her every move, and that she'd never really know when she would be "called in" until they contacted her. Her entire family's lives depended on her doing as she was trained, not as she wished.

Early in her training, she had seen what could happen if she did not follow orders. Another young woman, her real name had been Keiko, also stolen from her homeland as Yin Hee was, fell victim to the transplant process, thinking that over time they would leave her alone and her services would never really be needed. She was the first of the so-called deep plants. She made the mistake of trusting a girlfriend and telling her story one evening. Unfortunately, the girlfriend was an agent for North Korea.

The next day she was collected, shipped back to North Korea, and forced to watch as her mother and brother were decapitated. The trainees were then brought in to witness the girl's punishment. They watched as the trainers coldly replayed a video of the girl's earlier indoctrination, when they carefully worked at her mind, getting her to admit in her naïveté her darkest fears. Each of the other girls, now watching in silent horror, knew she had done the same. The girl on the tape had admitted her greatest fear was drowning. She was now forced into a closed glass container. Her feet were chained to the floor, and then the container was very slowly filled with water. It took an hour to fill the container—she drowned before Yin Hee's eyes. It was just another part of the training.

After that, life had settled into somewhat of a routine. They studied the Korean language and English, subjects that Yin Hee excelled in, perhaps too well. They also spent many hours in training in martial arts; but most astonishing to Yin Hee was the focus on throwing darts, British style. Every girl near Yin Hee's age spent hours being coached and practicing throwing darts. When she began, Yin Hee had trouble hitting the board. In time, however, and with considerable help from a very patient instructor, she learned to do it very well. Over time, all the girls became exceedingly skillful at the game, as it was the only opportunity they had to socialize in any way. During dart training, there was no pressure, no screaming or beating from their instructors, only the games.

Compartmentalization, Yin Hee! She scolded herself for drifting off for so long. *It is time to return to the party. It's best not to reveal anything. This might be merely a coincidence.* Yin Hee would know something was amiss if Colonel Song stopped his somewhat irrelevant e-mails. She had come to the conclusion that he continued sending her regular e-mails about things she had little interest in, namely his work, as a means of keeping track of her. If she didn't respond, her handlers might assume she was trying to hide or run away. As long as his e-mails and her responses kept a somewhat-regular schedule, things would be OK. She'd check her e-mail in another day or two to make sure today's event had nothing to do with her.

"I think Frank's right to contact the authorities," Kathleen was saying as Yin Hee stepped into the living room. Everyone instinctively turned toward her and moved closer.

The Eyes

"I'm OK now," she forced a brave smile. "I guess I just wasn't prepared for it. I think you're right; we'll have to tell the police. But perhaps they won't care if we wait until after New Year's? We don't really have any information that is of any real value, and they would probably prefer to take a break now anyway, don't you think?"

"I'm way ahead of you, Yin Hee." Frank put his arm around her shoulders; she was much calmer now, though the occasional tremor still rumbled through her tiny frame. "I just spoke with a Detective 'Ohl Suk,' however that is spelled, who has agreed to interview the four of us next Friday." Turning to Kathleen and unconsciously wrapping his arms around her, he continued, "You too, babe. I guess they just want to be thorough."

Frank and Kathleen began to sway with the music. Taking his cue, Lee walked over to Yin Hee who took the opportunity to shift the attention away from herself and back to the New Year's celebration. No one noticed that Yin Hee had turned white as Frank had explained they would all be interviewed. At that moment, Yin Hee decided this would be a very lucky night for Lee Wong. Even if he had no idea why, he would not protest, and she did not want to be alone.

KILOMETERS NORTH OF
THE DMZ, NORTH KOREA

Construction had been completed for over a week, but, of course, it wouldn't be announced for several months from now. Colonel Kim Ul Song clutched his notebook proudly to his chest. It contained the blueprints, plans, artist's depiction, and progressive photographs of what may as well have been the Taj Mahal. Naturally, the dam had been funded from outside the DPRK, more credit to the skills of the dear leader. But this was not an exclusively foreign project. Proud DPRK comrades by the thousands had worked on it, side by side with engineers from other nations. It was a joint venture, and the colonel was secretly thrilled not only to have been a part of its planning, but also to have been named senior engineer for its operation. He had been a little disappointed in the job because the government had not permitted him to oversee or even visit the dam while it was under construction, but his training had always taught him to have unquestionable faith in the system. Perhaps his wife was right; maybe there was someone who had finally recognized his talent and education.

He had worked hard to learn Japanese as a youth, an effort that did not endear him with most people who were unfavorable toward Japan. Then, years later, when it became obvious Japan had emerged as a technological superstar, some were chosen for a special linguistic course in Japanese. Colonel Song had jumped at the chance, and while hardly fluent, his comprehension and pronunciation were quantum leaps above most of the other contenders. He was easily selected and spent a year with a Japanese instructor. When they were first introduced, he had been told her Korean name, Yin Hee, but she would only respond to "Sensei," or "Teacher" in Japanese. Rather than meeting in person, they spoke through a variety of screens. He always had the feeling that she was sad, but she never spoke of anything but the lessons. Living in North Korea, one learned early not to be too inquisitive. Colonel Song wasn't sure why, but he had begun sending her e-mails while he was in Japan, which settled into a somewhat-regular pattern of correspondence.

Colonel Song wasn't the only student displaying exceptional linguistic ability who Yin Hee trained in Japanese. Hae-Jung Nim was another. In addition to a fastidious work ethic and phenomenal pronunciation, she was stunningly beautiful. Several lesser male students, struggling with the academics themselves, were removed from the program, in part, Yin Hee believed, because they spent a little too much time watching Hae-Jung instead of watching the lesson. She never knew what happened to those removed from her class, but she wasn't optimistic about their future. Although that class had thirteen students, it was primarily the colonel and Hae-Jung around whom it revolved. At various points in the progression over the three years they spent together, Yin Hee found herself looking at the striking young woman with...well, what was it, jealousy? She shrugged it off as yet another side effect of her virtual imprisonment. Somewhere inside though, she knew it was just her gut female reaction to another woman, as catty as that seemed. Now, so far removed from it, she could laugh; hadn't they all become great comrades and friends? No, Yin Hee was smart enough to know that of all the people she chatted with on what was essentially a closed chat room were dangerous people for her.

Yin Hee didn't really know the details of the Web site she visited; it was actually a bulletin board set up to allow a finite number of people to post messages to one another from anywhere that had Internet access. She was quite sure their purpose was to keep tabs on her. Posing as friends, these former students merely plied the obvious link between Yin Hee and them to the government's advantage. As long as she stayed in touch, they would know that she was still there and presumably still ready for whatever mission was in store for her.

It was that logic that kept her returning time and again to the bulletin board, checking for new messages from the two. It was interesting, she noted, that although Hae-Jung's messages oozed femininity, obviously directed at Colonel Song, his messages always seemed generically open. He remained an honest, open, even vulnerable man, just as Yin Hee had thought of him all those years before. He had genuinely been interested in learning to speak Japanese, and had spent a lot of time studying on his own. He seemed destined to do that which he desired most, command a dam. The concept had seemed foreign and insignificant to Yin Hee when she listened to him drone on and on about the detailed workings of a hydroelectric dam. She often thought she'd rather be watching paint dry, but he was so fascinated by it that somehow he held one's attention anyway. Hae-Jung hung on his every word, which he took for genuine interest in his subject matter. How men could be so dense was beyond Yin Hee's ability to discern. From her perspective, Hae-Jung was veritably drooling, and the colonel saw nothing. True, he was a married man, and that could be the explanation, but Yin Hee suspected it was more a fanatical obsession with the concept of his engineering desires that kept him single-mindedly focused on work, despite the obvious and easy-access distraction right in front of him.

Colonel Song, of course, had finished the course; the "final" had been an admissions test for foreign students at an engineering school in Kyoto. He passed and spent the next two years in Japan, continuing his engineering pursuit in the study of dam construction. Hae-Jung had been sent to South Korea where she was to become a TV reporter, specializing in breaking news, special reports, and international affairs, with a specialty in things Japanese. It had struck Yin Hee as odd. Weren't North and South Korea at greater odds with one another than Japan and North Korea? Well, she had her own world to worry about. Whatever it was that the colonel and the reporter were doing on the global stage wasn't as important as staying alive, was it?

The colonel found the Japanese to be quite polite, helpful, and very orderly. He studied hard, worked at what jobs he could find on the side, and managed to accumulate wealth that would have required a decade of toil in the DPRK. He was also smart enough to know he had a problem—how to get the money back home. He met a large number of displaced Korean patriots in Japan, those whose parents had been brought in as virtual slave labor during the occupation. They provided the means whereby he could get the money he had accumulated transferred to his account in the DPRK—he stuck to that plan scrupulously. He was a meticulously structured individual.

Finally it seemed all his scheming and hard work was paying off. As senior engineer of the dam, he could begin to enjoy some of the finer things in life with his dedicated wife. They hadn't had children yet, but perhaps now they would. He was so sure he'd finally made it, and the proof, as he saw it, was his selection for this prestigious position over three candidates with seniority. He should have been more suspicious.

COLONEL SONG ARRIVES

Today was Colonel Song's first day on the job, and although he desperately wanted to survey the hydroelectric generators first, he knew they would have to wait. They were the heart of the hydroelectric dam, and he had become mesmerized in his studies of the nearly miraculous simplicity of these generators. The design was deceptively simple but functional. Efficiency, of course, was a challenge, one that would be debated, as a target of improvement probably forever. The sheer generation of electricity in this manner was pure genius in Colonel Song's mind.

One could almost ignore the cost of building the dam and hydroelectric motors because, by selling the produced energy, the costs would be recouped, though for the DPRK, this would be a future effort. The energy would be absorbed in the effort to simply power the nation first; the economics of the event would have to come later. *The good news*, Colonel Song thought to himself, *is that over time, a hydroelectric dam creates virtually free energy, and the environmental impact for a nation like the DPRK will be more than acceptable.*

The idea that he would be in charge of this dam overwhelmed him, and he was anxious to begin. The generators were supposed to be just a few months away from activation, when the first kilowatts of hope would be created. But for now, he knew he must endure the discipline of protocol and allow the men and women who worked for him to exe-cute their reception plan for the dear leader. He knew it would be a long day, filled with whatever pomp and ceremony they could muster with no resources and no budget.

POLICE HEADQUARTERS, FORT COLLINS

The outer waiting room bustled with the lower rungs of the city's inhabitants. Yin Hee heard the drunks, prostitutes, thieves, and sundry other criminal elements all protesting their innocence, and, to be sure, probably a few were really guilty of nothing more than overindulgence or misunderstanding. She saw none of them as she made her way to Detective Ohl Suk's office. This "voluntary" trip downtown to discuss the events of the previous week had been one of her toughest efforts. She had thought of little else since the party, except the remarkable evening she had shared with Lee.

It took very little energy to convince Lee that a visit to his place might be worth the trouble of an unexpected guest. He had been gracious, even gallant, as he offered her the bedroom while he readied the couch for himself. She had ended that chivalry quickly. She was desperate to find something else to think about. She wrapped her arms around him and kissed him deeply; he hesitated only a second before responding.

She let herself briefly wonder why she stayed so isolated, but she knew why. Then, sadly, she had the rest of the night to wrestle with her demons alone; it had taken Lee less than ten minutes to slip into the happiest sleep he'd had in five years. She wasn't angry. He had always been polite, gentle, and a friend. It was right that they became closer, though she already began to feel guilty about the facade she maintained. Everything about her was not as it seemed.

Now, here at the police station, she was about to come face to face with...what? She didn't know, and that feeling of loss of control was devastating. How should she approach this interview? Was this cop a "contact"? Would she be tasked? If she was tasked, should she acknowledge the tasking? She had to focus. She rapped lightly at the office door hoping beyond hope that no one would be inside.

"Come in," called a voice from inside the room. *Game on*, she thought as she took a deep breath and opened the door.

"Hello, I'm Kwahl Yin Hee."

"Yes, I know. I'm Inspector Ohl Suk Chee. It is so kind of you to come down and talk with us about this unfortunate coincidence."

"What coincidence?" Yin Hee was already off guard.

"Why, the gentlemen that came to your store the day he lost his life. Unless you don't think that it was a coincidence?"

"Oh, of course I do. No, I just didn't expect it to be called a coincidence. It's more like a terrible nightmare or tragedy from my perspective."

"Ah, of course. I see I am once again guilty of failing to realize that not everyone deals with murder as a way of life. At any rate, thank you for coming in. I won't keep you long. I have just a few questions to ask you. First of all, had you ever seen this gentleman before that day?"

"No, never." Yin Hee was beginning to relax. The inspector didn't seem to know anything more about her than any one else she'd met since she came to America six years ago. She almost didn't hear the next question.

"Did he say or do anything that might lead you to believe he was not genuinely just a customer?"

"No, he was just a regular guy who had a problem with his faucet." Her guard was back up. There were too many things one could read in to that question. She decided it was best to move on as smoothly as possible. Yin Hee related what she could remember of the conversation she'd had with the man. Then suddenly her face went pale.

Police Headquarters, Fort Collins

"Yes? What did you remember?" Inspector Chee was an experienced interrogator. Her facial expression clearly indicated she remembered something and that something appeared to startle her.

"Well, I'm not sure, but something about the way he asked my name. Oh, it's so hard to remember those little details." Now she was stuck. With absolute clarity, she now remembered what had made this guy so memorable in a spine-tingling way. With equal clarity, she also realized the last thing she wanted to do was let this detective know what she had remembered.

"Go ahead," Chee was urging. "Sometimes these uneasy feelings or partial memories can be very important." He leaned forward, closing in on her personal space and making her even more nervous. It was a deliberate act. Unsettling the individuals sometimes helps prevent them from shutting down or deciding they had said enough.

"It seems like he asked me if I was Yin Hee, but that is impossible. No…wait, I was wearing my nametag—that's it." She was very convincing. The detective didn't seem to notice that although she forced her body to relax, her grip on the chair never slackened. She knew very well that she had forgotten her nametag that morning. Frank and Lee had teased her mercilessly about it. Whoever the now-dead man was, he had known her name before he walked in the door.

SEINE'S FACTORY,
FORMER EAST GERMANY

Seine's factory had begun as a semiconductor manufacturing company, pumping out silicon chips from an externally produced and reconstructed clean room. It had been wildly popular, as labor was still quite cheap there. The company made the transition to making more sophisticated microchips, for the more technologically advanced and miniaturized electronic device market. Finally the natural progression of miniaturized computer and artificial intelligence devices led them to the medical equipment market. At least that is the way it appeared on the surface. They had collected the best of several nations' top scientific minds, specifically from the former East Block, and added in some true creativity, and an unhealthy dose of genuine evil. Long before the scientific community imagined the downside to implanted health devices for humans, the lead scientist at Seine's had begun production.

The device was a hybrid. The result of the kind of science that cares not for a human as an individual, a thinking, feeling person, but instead uses an uncaring analysis of the human body's means of systemic function. Japanese physicians had developed a means of using the optic nerves of blind patients to transmit electronic images received by artificial receptors. Using the philosophy that vision is the result of electronic impulses interpreted by the brain, they determined that even when the ocular portions of the eye, even the optic nerve, were defective, there was still a way to transmit the same electronic signals into the brain. This research, in its original form, led to revolutionary devices that allowed blind patients the ability to at least detect light from dark—a miracle to the sightless. Similarly, physicians in the United States developed a means of capturing the chemical stimulus that initiated muscle movement in paralysis victims and transforming them into electronic impulses capable of directing computer cursors, enabling motionless people the ability to communicate—truly a gift of deistic proportions. The same methodology could use residual muscle movement in patients who had suffered traumatic eye injury or medical enucleation to manipulate electronic devices. This could allow these patients to enhance their contracted sphere of influence over their physical environment. The brilliant but unscrupulous scientists at the Seine's factory, however, saw an opportunity to blend the technologies and magnify their effect.

How best can one use the human structure as a weapon? Perhaps remove the eye and insert a targeting device, one so sophisticated and rapid that it functions at the speed of thought. One might then attach it to the remaining musculature for movement, and, finally, attach it to the nerve or implant it directly into the brain for interpretation and action. Here is where Dr. Dorman's research had come into play.

The irony is that the good doctor has no idea his work was right on track and dovetails nicely with ours, Dr. Lehnon thought. Dr. Hans Peter Egen Lehnon was not as convinced as his rather easily excited Muslim "partners" in this endeavor. A pioneer in biotronics in East Germany, he was constantly reminded that because East Germany was part of the "Evil Empire" by proxy, his work would never garner the attention of the scientific world—unless he made his work impossible to ignore. The two bumbling idiots from the West, Sanderson and Dorman, were the darlings. They could pretend to have mastered cold fusion, an obvious hoax, and get more press than his life's work had commanded. But that would change, so long as Dr. Dorman didn't bungle his part of the process.

Lehnon was skeptical that a man who had experienced the things Dr. Dorman endured as a child could be easily convinced to join the cause of fighting global capitalism. That was much more the call of individuals who had never experienced the upside of the process. Back in the day, he had seen many operatives handled, and they were rarely lured in by violence threatened or visited upon them. But that was not his problem. His job was to perfect a device, not worry about how it was "mounted."

The new work on attaching a true human eye into the spherical device affords many luxuries of design, Dr. Lehnon thought to himself. Now the metal casing for the eye could be equipped with multiple laser or infrared range finders, allowing the weapon to be targeted with no more effort than merely looking at it. Once that was done, all that remained to complete the package was a single addition, a microchip, already designed and miniaturized, that would take the interpreted electronic signal and use it to power a weapon. More correctly, all that was really necessary was the activation of a controlled electronic pulse that could reach the excitatory threshold of a receiver. Microelectronics could then take over to power a weapon. Preferably, it would be a weapon of significant destructive power that was both man-portable and easily rearmed. Seine's factory, with the help of Dr. Lehnon, had found several solutions to the riddle.

With a near-limitless budget, they had found brilliant scientists from Eastern Europe and the collapsed Union of Soviet Socialist Republic. They successfully leveraged these men's survival instincts and their drive to invent against a created global need for therapeutic ocular devices to gain the scientists' trust. Seine's had duped intelligent men into creating devices of potentially devastating tactical advantage. It was of no relevance to Seine's that the project required the near destruction of the individual outfitted with the weapon. Once this device was implanted in a "volunteer," that person's life was forfeited to the use of his or her body as a weapon. To ensure that the volunteer did not attempt to report his condition to anyone, the weapon was equipped with a lethal dose of poison. The computer chip would inject it directly into the volunteer's bloodstream milliseconds after the last volley of the embedded weapon discharged. These mercenary soldiers could target and destroy nearly anything that could be visually acquired. The mobility of these man-machines, their virtual invisibility as weapons, and the integration of the target designation and weapon function capabilities marked a significant technological advance for the non-nuclear fighter relying on hit-and-run or terrorist methodology.

Dr. Lehnon was villainously proud to have surmounted the only remaining complication unsolved by Drs. Sanderson and Dorman: how to get the electrical impulses, both moving and targeting, to transmit directly to and from the device by controlling the fusion proteins by which neuronal vesicles release acetylcholine into the neuromuscular junction. The best solution, for the efficiency of the weapon, would be to make it a part of the human system, not attached to it. The difference might seem insignificant, but if a weapon could be targeted, retargeted, fired, or terminated at the speed of thought, a new era in fighting would indeed have dawned. After a year's worth of research, and innumerable volunteers, they had perfected a way to get the artificial eye to grow in place. The optic nerve and all the attached muscles were completely functional. It took a little over two weeks' training to teach the host how to use it, but they now had humans with the capability of lethal "upgrades."

P'ANMUNJOM, DMZ, KOREA

Today the dear leader would meet with officials of the "Great Enemy," the United States, but these officials had no idea he would be there. He liked to keep his true intentions as secret as possible, springing his unpredictable actions on his enemies and allies alike at the last minute. Sometimes he reveled in the world seeing just another episode in the long-running series of the "Madman from North Korea." Enigma was his greatest weapon, but today he would throw in some fascination and even a little stability, a variation on the "hide in plain sight" tactic. He would agree to allow families divided in the North and South to rejoin for the first time since the Korean War.

Naturally, his minions had devised rules and selection processes suitably strict, even ridiculously transparent to preserve the "World's Most Paranoid Leader" image he'd so carefully nurtured. From the North, only those individuals who still believed in the regime more than the unity of families would be selected. For the international press, some would be selected who had already passed away, but the world would never know it was all planned that way. It would sharpen the international focus if a few stories about elderly women who passed away at the prospect of being reunited with their long-lost children were leaked. *The saddest part*, he thought to himself, *is that I have to orchestrate every detail myself. How ironic that the man the world con-*

The Eyes

tinues to believe is borderline incompetent, if not actually mentally retarded, is actually personally running every detail of history's greatest hoax.

Oh, the situation in North Korea is true enough, the world's last bastion for communism and the great central government planning concept is indeed in a state of steady, gradual disintegration, but the "doddering fool as head of state" myth is total nonsense.

His father, the great leader, had condemned the country by tying its economy, inseparably, to both China and Russia, never committing to one or the other. In the end, North Korea, like Mongolia, wasn't even a consideration in the economic morass the former Soviet Union found itself in as it collapsed from within. While China remained one of few friendly nations, even her stolid remembrances of the DPRK's assistance to her could only go so far—China had its own problems with well over a billion people to control. North Korea found itself with marginal assistance and a totally dysfunctional economic system. Years of incredibly poor agricultural policies had even destroyed what self-sufficiency had been maintained. Today would be the opening volley in this new war, but only he knew it had started. It would be a delicate dance until things started rolling, and by then it would be too late.

By the time the United States, Republic of Korea, Japan, China, or Russia decide how to react, we will have already won, the dear leader thought to himself. The beginning feint he would deliver today. Then he would travel to the new dam for the opening ceremonies. *Never mind that the dam will never produce a kilowatt of electricity - it is needed for something much more important than that. Eventually the new commander, Kim Ul Song, will discover the real reason for this new hydroelectric dam and he will begin frantically attempting to enlighten me. At this very instant, he is probably readying the ceremonies for tonight's appearance. How disappointing this day will be for him.*

NATIONAL LAB, WASHINGTON, D.C.

The enormous lobby was the essence of ostentatious Washington architecture. It always seemed that unless the ceiling of the lobby was difficult to see from the floor, it couldn't possibly house a service of any real significance. Dr. Sanderson's credentials raised numerous eyebrows, since he was allowed access to the most sensitive areas of the building, yet no one on the security detail had ever seen him. But if *his* credentials bore speculative responses, Emiko's and Jack's were just too much. The trio would be denied access until someone at a higher level could vouch for them. Emiko was quick to grab her father's arm and guide him to a chair in the lobby out of earshot of the security personnel.

"Dad, this is simply not a good time to vent your accumulated frustration at the security forces. They are doing their job the best way they can. After all, you would also be the first to strike at his or her mental capacity if someone unauthorized were allowed access to your research. We've managed to become strangers to our own parent laboratory, and we'll have to live with it. I, for one, find it a modest price to pay for the luxury of spending the majority of my life in a seminormal part of the world."

"That's because you conveniently ignore the roving vehicles, scanning electronic sweeps, electromagnetic interrupter pulses, and the

The Eyes

hundreds of other indignities we live with daily. What is the purpose of all these credentials, badges, and iris and fingerprint scans if at the end we get benched by the "C" team while we wait for the "A" team to arrive?"

"What we don't see, and hopefully doesn't affect us at the cellular level, won't hurt us—so why expend the extra energy whining?" Emiko felt somewhat self-righteous in this exchange. She wanted to maintain a level of professionalism here, for without regard to their current work, if she were to follow in her famous father's footsteps, it would have to be here in Washington. A continuum of the sourpuss reputation her father seemed bent on maintaining wouldn't help at all.

The security shift supervisor, Charles Stevenson, arrived and immediately recognized Dr. Sanderson. "Dr. Sanderson! How good it is to see you again. Sorry for this inconvenience, but as you can see, we've rotated our guard personnel and they have been trained to follow hunches as well as hard facts. All three of you have clearance to go into virtually any research area in the building, which is fairly rare to begin with. If you then add to the fact that security have never seen you enter this building even once, it kind of throws a flag to those trained to be professionally paranoid. Please accept my apologies. Where shall we go today?"

Emiko stepped in. She was determined not to be a mere shadow on this trip, "We would like to start with Dr. Dorman's research material. I understand it is here now." She thought she'd done well to leave out any mention of specific events that would make this true, and thus make her guide suspicious of what they already knew. She was, however, a little embarrassed to have just blurted it out, and subconsciously shifted her gaze to the floor. In doing so, she missed two important nonverbal signs. First, Dr. Sanderson's face had gone pale then flush red at the last sentence from the head of security. He had never been escorted anywhere in this building. In fact, his was the principal research that sold this building! What the heck was going on here? Second, the head of security had snapped his head up at her words, momentarily dropping all semblance of a smile. Just as quickly, everything returned to normal. They proceeded down the hall in trail, with the head of security leading the way.

"Wait here," Charles spoke, almost commandingly, to Dr. Sanderson, Emiko, and Jack.

"OK, that's enough," Dr. Sanderson spat.

"We'll be fine right here," Jack quickly interjected, while firmly but inconspicuously grabbing Dr. Sanderson's arm just above the elbow. Dr. Sanderson immediately understood the maneuver, and though it was difficult, he let his protest drop as Charles walked down the hall and into another office. Then Dr. Sanderson spun around to face Jack.

"I will not be treated like a visiting speaker who has arrived out of sequence in the very research lab constructed around my work!" Dr. Sanderson protested.

"That's just it," Jack replied quietly and calmly. "Why would they put you through this? My guess is there is something they fear you will discover. I think we'd better have a plan. I'll leave right now and go back to the hotel." Without waiting for a response, Jack turned and walked back down the hall.

DESERT TRAINING CAMP

"I need more light! How can you expect me to work under these conditions with any possibility of success? What about your victims? Do you care so little for them that you risk their lives twice: once in these ridiculous attempts, then again by refusing to provide adequate facilities?" Dr. Dorman was shrieking. Partly it was from the pent-up contempt he felt for his captors, partly from exhaustion, but mostly from shear terror. After the first two days in this village, as he called it, he had regained his strength somewhat. And as his body had healed and he had been left alone, his composure returned with a margin of confidence. But then on the third morning, he'd been brought to the "cutting tents" where the experiments were conducted. What he'd seen these men do to one another was worse than many of his childhood nightmares. Knowing they'd so willingly do this to each other left no doubt in his mind about the amount of mercy they would have for someone outside their beliefs that got in the way of their quest.

Dr. Dorman sensed the blow before he heard it, and he heard it before he felt it, but he couldn't move fast enough to avoid the cane across the back of his legs. Though the strike of the stick avoided the ankle and the knee, falling across the meat of the calf, it was applied with such force that he crumpled immediately to the earth. He did, however, manage to drop the scalpel and avoid cutting himself or anyone else.

"Do not make the mistake again of thinking you are important enough to be kept alive, Dr. Dorman. The next blow will be neither as gentle nor as protectively aimed as this one. There are other surgeons in this world." The man growled in Arabic, and his expression was menacing. But Dr. Dorman saw nothing. This man, known to Dr. Dorman only as Hassim, never seemed quite friendly or unfriendly. He was more like an assigned escort. Rough though he was, Dr. Dorman knew Hassim's punishing blow probably saved his life. The ring of men surrounding him watched, smiles carved in their wind-burned faces to see what the doctor would do next. The agony was unbearable, but he knew he must get back up and at least pretend to be sorry. So beyond the strength he thought he had, he stood slowly.

"Impressive, Doctor; most men would not even try to stand. As usual, however, your understanding of this situation is confused by your utter lack of faith. These men are not victims. They were not spirited from their homes and families in the dark of night. They are volunteers. They volunteer for the opportunity to serve Allah. If they die in the attempt, they are martyrs, heroes of the highest order. They do this because they truly believe in our cause. Though we may not see it come to fruition in our lifetimes, we each believe in our hearts that our great-great-grandchildren should be able to live peacefully and prosperously in their own land. They should be free to worship in a safe place without the fear of government-sponsored reprisal or murder. You are merely a tool. That we have many among us who could possess your level of skill is beyond doubt. Allah has seen fit for us to dwell here, where there are few natural riches so coveted by your wasteful new compatriots. You are soft and have grown spoiled; these are the finest facilities at our disposal. You have changed much, Doctor, since you left this land.

"The land does not change so rapidly. It remains virtually constant. You will do with what we have, when we tell you, and you will politely ask for what you absolutely need. There are many here who do not believe we need you at all, and it is they I will turn you over to with your very next outburst. This is also a good time for me to explain that many of us are well versed in this area, and have studied long in this matter.

Thus, we will not be easily fooled. Your failure to give this your best effort will have very unfortunate results for you. This is not Chicago or Washington, Doctor. There is no one to turn to—you will be a part of this. You will be taken to your tent now. Rest as much as you can; sleep if possible. The length of your work hours here will test your stamina to its limit."

"Sleep? And what will you do with this lad? I have not finished the procedure. You can't keep someone anesthetized forever. I…"

"Noted, Doctor! He is not anesthetized; we have no drugs to give him. He will remain here, immobile. We will keep the surgical area clean and moist. I know this one. He will not even disturb your sleep. Now be gone!" And he motioned dramatically to the other men to take the doctor to his tent.

The instruction was obviously not up for discussion. Dr. Dorman's head reeled at the thought of the suffering this young man of twenty would go through postoperatively. The doctor had been invited to assist with three young men today. Each walked silently into the tent and lay down upon the table without a word. There was barely time to rinse away the blood from the previous procedure before the next one began. The patient's eyes shut briefly in silent prayer, and then opened for what they must surely have believed to be the last visual experience of their lives.

Before Dr. Dorman's arrival, some men left this tent without their eyes; most did not leave the tent alive. Dr. Dorman was intent on making at least one change in the procedures right away. He would argue there was little gained from implanting experimental devices into both eyes of the volunteers simultaneously. The results of one implant would be sufficient to prove its value. The winning argument, however, was that by using one eye at a time, each volunteer could be a part of the experiment twice, doubling the "volunteer" pool. The impact of this tragedy was compounded by the doctor's frustration. He knew, beyond any doubt, that the experimental devices he assumed he would implant later would never work. Besides, they weren't so much implanting them as jamming them into the tissue at the back of the eye socket a few weeks after removing the eye. So far, his captors measured success by the number of patients that lived, blinded for life, of course.

The Eyes

Dr. Dorman wanted to tell someone, but there was no opportunity. He had no one to talk to but Hassim. He believed he knew a method that had at least a hope of working—he decided he had to try. Little did he know that his work, in the hands of some less scrupulous but equally insightful researchers, had already resulted in considerable progress.

OUTSIDE POLICE HEADQUARTERS

Yin Hee felt absolutely drained. The inspector had been professional and aloof; then again, he had also been sympathetic and caring. This was the madness of it all. Was he the one planted or sent to "waken" her? There was no way to know, and she dared not trust anyone.

She would redouble her efforts to remain inconspicuous. Tonight she was to have dinner with Lee again, and this time the date would end at the restaurant, she decided. He arrived, annoyingly, on time. He had made reservations at a reasonably posh seafood restaurant she had casually mentioned more than a year earlier. She was discovering Lee had remembered a great deal of what she had said throughout the time they had worked together at the store. She found it a humbling yet special feeling that someone seemed to care about her even in small ways. Perhaps she could allow one person into her life. It wasn't forbidden, though she admitted to herself it was probably unproductive at best and outright selfish at worst.

Dinner was without event, which was not to say that she didn't enjoy it tremendously. In addition to being a seafood restaurant, it was a Japanese restaurant. Immediately after the waiter left the menus, Lee began a long speech, explaining in great detail what each dish was, what it was made out of, and how it was prepared. It was cute, but very frustrating. Yin Hee knew it was her own fault, though; she had told him many times that she'd never eaten in a Japanese restaurant, mostly to avoid a discussion in which she might slip up by saying too much. "I'm not sure if you already know this or not," he was saying, "but there is much more to Japanese food than just raw fish. Unless you think it is too chauvinistic, I'll be happy to order for you."

To her relief and pleasure, he selected a generous "set course" for two—a little expensive, but it included many different kinds of entrees. Between the sake, the joyous taste of the food, and the clever banter that Lee seemed to have no end of, Yin Hee was truly enjoying herself. How could she have worked with this bright, witty, vigorous young man for so long without ever really seeing him? She concluded it was because she kept a protective wall of vigilance wrapped so tightly around her that no one could get in.

They left the restaurant together in Lee's car, and he invited her back to his place. "It's much too early for this night to end," Lee began as if right on cue. "Why don't we go back to my place and watch a movie?"

Just as she had planned and practiced in her head, she declined. "I really had a very wonderful time, Lee," she said and really meant it, "but I think I'd better turn in tonight." She was ready for the inevitable attempt to get her to change her mind, but she was resolute. When he began speaking, she focused on her own thoughts about how to word the second and, she hoped, final declination of the evening. That's when her mind caught up to what was going on. Lee had turned the radio up to an uncomfortably loud level. As she turned to face him, he handed her a piece of paper then held his index finger to his lip, indicating quiet.

The paper had three short sentences typed in bold on it.

I KNOW YOUR SECRET. YOU ARE SAFE. THERE IS SOMETHING I HAVE TO SHOW YOU AT MY PLACE, SO PLAY ALONG.

Her mind was reeling. Lee? How could he know? What was happening? Then it became crystal clear that she really had no alternative.

Outside Police Headquarters

One way or the other, her fate had been decided, and now she would simply have to react as things moved along.

WASHINGTON, D.C., JANUARY

Jack made his way out of the building quickly. He had an incredible feeling that every eye, every camera was tracking his every movement. All the concerns that spin in the mind of the hunted crept into focus almost unexpectedly, sharpening his thoughts and increasing his heart rate. Am I walking too fast—too slow? Do I look nervous, unfocused, or completely natural? Outside, he allowed himself to sigh audibly as he walked away from the building. If he was ever going to get back in, he'd need to know much more about the facility itself, and a careful examination of the outside was a good place to start.

He walked as casually as his nerves would allow. It was depressing. He'd been around the stupid building twice, and with the renewed interest in security that America now employed, he was about to conclude that he didn't have the wherewithal to enter the structure uninvited. Just then he noticed a van drive past him headed for the parking lot at the rear of the building. The van was ornately decorated with the label "Hectors Industrial Cleaning."

Even the cleaning people are affected by the intense security, Jack thought to himself. *No one is allowed into the traffic circles originally built as loading and unloading docks, or for that matter, to stop or park their vehicles less than twenty-five meters from the building.*

The Eyes

Hectors was the same cleaning company used at Dr. Dorman's laboratory. Jack had never given the company any thought; most people don't think much about who is contracted to clean the common areas in big buildings. Nevertheless, he had come to know Carlos quite well in the past year. Carlos was the team manager for the group assigned to Dr. Dorman's facility. The professional courtesy and the meticulous attention to cleanliness and detail that Carlos effused had struck Jack as uncommon. Furthermore, Carlos instilled this work ethic in the workers he employed. As Carlos and Jack got to know each other better, he found that Carlos was actually born in the United States, after his mother had come across the border illegally. Carlos had made it clear that the romantic notion that any person born on US soil or a US-flagged seagoing vessel was afforded the same rights and privileges of any other American was nothing more than a myth. Far from bitter over it, he would tell his stories with a cavalier approach, a pragmatist to the end.

Jack thought this would be a great time to contact Carlos and see how he was getting along.

P'ANMUNJOM

P'anmunjom, one of the most infamous places on earth, permanent population—zero. With the highest per capita armed populace in the world, it was located just twenty-five miles north of the heart of South Korea—Seoul. Here North and South Korea had their sporadic meetings; a requirement of the armistice intended to maintain some communication between the technically warring states.

General Hodge, the US Army commander, was in for a rather interesting shock today. General Shin-Nok, chairman of the DPRK National Defense Commission, was the usual participant in this routinely scheduled meeting. Instead, General Hodge was stunned to see Kim Jong Il himself walk through the door from the North. As the dear leader approached the table, General Hodge stood at attention; proper courtesy to the head of a sovereign nation was imperative.

"Please sit, General." The translator's English was quite good, not a surprise considering for whom he translated. "I'm sorry to have come unannounced. I trust this will not cause too great a problem for you. I have nothing substantive to bring to the table. I just wanted to participate in person for once—a leader's role, don't you think?" The DPRK diplomatic translators routinely spoke as if the words were their own, to convey the image that they weren't even there, that the conversation was directly between the two diplomats. Kim Jong Il's translator confirmed, with a barely perceptible nod, the translation had adequately conveyed the spoken words.

"I agree, sir. Then shall we cover the agenda as written?" General Hodge was no stranger to the delicate dance of diplomacy. He had served much of his career in the POLMIL, or political military, section of the army. His experience in the Pacific included being stationed all over Asia and studying in a number of military schools there as well. He'd been the J5 to CINCPAC, or commander in chief, Pacific, a few years back during his first assignment after promotion to O-8, major general. That put him in charge of the POLMIL section, among many others.

"No, I don't think that will be necessary. All the correct steps have been agreed to in writing. I propose no changes. I do have a request I hope you can help me with, General."

"If I can, I certainly will, sir." *What should I be calling him?* General Hodge thought. *Certainly none of the names we usually use to describe him, and I understand he has not assumed the moniker "Suryong" yet.*

"I would like to have an audience with your boss, USCINCPAC US commander in chief, Pacific." He said it nonchalantly and even looked over at the South Korean interpreter and smiled. He knew very well that General Hodge would be seething at the implied insult that instead of speaking directly to General Hodge, the dear leader requested to have an audience with Hodge's antagonist, Admiral Corping.

One of the anomalies of the US defense structure was PACOM, Pacific Command. The United States, at its imperial best, divided the world into regions, each with its own viceroy known to the military as the CINCs, or commanders in chief. In their arrogance, each CINC is "in charge" of each of these regions, with one exception. Thanks to some very slick political maneuvering in the 1950s, the United States took advantage of the absence of the former Soviet Union to railroad through the United Nations Security Council an arrangement creating a United Nations Command to deal with the situation on the Korean peninsula. Keeping in form with the other fiefdoms it had created, a CINC was appointed for this command, CINCUNC—commander in chief, United Nations Command. What makes the command unusual is that it is a kingdom within a kingdom. A tiny island carved out of the

PACOM area of responsibility, or AOR. As the CINCs are all equal in rank (four-star full generals or admirals), there is considerable enmity over turf and control.

A running conflict deals with the United States Forces stationed in Korea. There is a commander, US Forces Korea (USFK), just as there is a commander, US Forces Japan (USFJ). The issue arises when anything falls within the CINCUNC arena; then the commander, USFK, reports to CINCUNC instead of CINCPAC.

Adding to the emotional mix, USCINCUNC is traditionally an army general, while USCINCPAC is a naval admiral. This is a natural reflection of the oceanic nature of the PACOM AOR and the doctrinal belief that defense of Korea will be necessarily a ground war, or army function. In wartime, ostensibly, cooler heads will accept this delineation as necessary and correct (although during the Korean War the interdepartmental bickering took on Herculean proportions); in peacetime, it was merely another aggravation, with each service jealously guarding the number of CINCs apportioned to it and the resources allotted to it.

What made Kim Jong Il's ploy work best, however, was that General Hodge and Admiral Corping were career-long adversaries. General Hodge had been a linebacker on the West Point football team, and Admiral Corping had played wide receiver for Annapolis. They first met at full speed on an Annapolis sweep left. The collision made the sporting headlines, though this was before CNN and *Sports Illustrated* mainlined the annual Blue-Gray event. Both players nearly lost their commissions over the concussions they mutually sustained, but, ironically, each caught the eye of his eventual mentor in that fortuitous yet ominous split second. The career of each had been spectacular, punctuated by nearly legendary performance and blinding career progression in rank. Each represented his service's benchmark for rapidity to the final five ranks. Now at the near-zenith of their careers, the step from CINC to highest rank, chief of staff of the army and chief of naval operations, was clearly in each of their minds and nearly foregone conclusions in the minds of the people already in those positions. As the mental chess game continued, it was also clear that only one of them would have a realistic shot at the big ring—chairmanship of the Joint Chiefs of Staff. And so the competitive spirit born on the "friendly fields of strife" at their respective academies would continue throughout their entire careers. For today, it would merely help the dear leader distract a worthy opponent.

Keeping his face and emotions in check, General Hodge replied, "I can certainly arrange a meeting with Admiral Corping, as you wish." Then, in his mind, he added, *I have only one boss—the president of the United States.* "On the other hand," he continued aloud, "if this is an issue dealing with Korea, perhaps I can help.

"No. I've dealt with the admiral before on this issue of great importance to East Asia, and I would like to work with the same professional people for the duration." The dear leader stood, turned abruptly, and left.

THE DESERT CAMP

Dr. Dorman awoke in pain, but that had become so normal, he barely noticed anymore. The injuries he'd sustained on the long trip to the camp were healing well, but the new laceration brought on by the single lash across his calf was both sensitive and unnerving. He began to understand how the physical intimidation by his captors would continue with only the implication of continued application. Still, the grogginess had left him, and though he was thirsty, he did not have the parched, near-panic need for water or the famished starving feeling that the combination of neglect and drugs had given him when he was first captured. He also felt a new purpose. If he were to be forced to participate in whatever his captors had planned, then he would do so on his own terms. He had yet to decide if he possessed the dedication to oppose these people with the fervor necessary to make an impact before he forfeited his life.

"Hassim!" He began carefully; the goal was to be assertive without bringing down the wrath of this enigmatic man who'd become his subjugator and only supporter. He had seen Hassim's reaction when he'd crossed the boundary between competent confidence and what was perceived as insolence—he didn't want to go there again. "If I may, I have a request that may help with the work here."

The Eyes

"You can ask, Doctor. You can ask," Hassim growled. His time in the camp was the worst he had ever spent anywhere, but at least while he was there, his time was purposeful and, though he was loathe to admit it, much more comfortable than time spent in the Middle East. Before he arrived in the camp, the assignments he was given were often confusing, vague, even deliberately useless, but at least there was some action, a goal, and some end for which he strove. Here there was only the unending heat, the screaming, and the waiting.

"I can see you have what appears to be a satellite transmission dish camouflaged near the main tent. Is it possible to send an e-mail from here? If so, I have a request I need to send to a friend. My friend is also a doctor involved in synaptic research and has information and possibly other resources that could significantly increase our chance for success here."

"I will take your request to the elders, Doctor, but I advise you that your chances for a favorable response could be greatly enhanced by a serious effort on your part within the conditions and resources available to you now. While our benefactor is wealthy, we are not his only project. He demands the resources he provides be used prudently and productively. Those who have failed to pay heed to his wishes have perished mercilessly. It is actually best that you do not know more than this—information can be a deadly commodity around here. I suggest you report to the operating tent."

Mohammed would be Dr. Dorman's first solo patient, though the doctor couldn't help considering him his first victim. He was determined that the damage and pain to this young man would be limited by his very best efforts as a surgeon. As the doctor moved toward the table, an old man approached him. He'd seen the elderly man before, of course; the man was there every time he entered this operating tent.

"Be careful with the eye," the old man rasped. His countenance was difficult to surmise. His voice and face revealed an aged man, one who'd lived a hard life. Still, his physical movements were smooth and agile. He manipulated the instruments on the table, arranging them with a practiced, effortless beauty rarely seen in a nonsurgical assistant. "Specifically, be careful with the attachment to the optic nerve; it is necessary."

The Desert Camp

Now what did he mean by that? Once I've removed the eye, all this young man has left to wait for is another surgery when a useless mechanical device from the back streets of Germany will be jammed into the eye cavity. Then no one will ever be able to help him see again, he thought. He lifted the scalpel, but something felt odd and he was once again temporarily distracted. He'd held a scalpel almost every day of his adult life for some purpose, but something was very different here. Then it struck him—he was sweating. It was an entirely different beginning to surgery, one he knew he would have to deal with.

He selected the most sterile blade he could find on the tray, as if that was something one could tell by looking. Still, he hoped for the best. Despite the baseness of the camp, there were considerable efforts taken to clean the instruments and the operating room and table, such as it was. While he noted the floor wasn't polished and waxed, and there was no smell of antibiotics, alcohol, or cleansers in the air, there were some clever approaches to keep down the dust, debris, and pollutants.

He had been watching as the medical assistants set up the tent days earlier, and was surprised at the techniques they had used. The sand had been carefully wetted down, a practice not undertaken lightly in an area where clean water was a precious commodity. A tarp was carefully spread out over it and tacked down with long sand spikes in the corners and at the centers of each edge of the tent. Once the tarpaulin was smooth and tight, hot soapy water was sparingly applied and the surface thoroughly scrubbed down. The tarp was then left to dry in the brutal sun. Once it was thoroughly dry, it was lifted and used to cover a wooden floor in the designated operating tent. All in all, with the routine and frequent sweeping of the tent walls, ceiling, and flaps, the room was adequately clean. The mattress used for the "volunteer" to lie upon was also carefully treated. It was wrapped in plastic and set out in the sun, where it was turned every thirty minutes. After several hours, the bottom side of the mattress was beaten regularly. It was wrapped in plastic again just prior to surgery. He found himself thinking that, considering the circumstances, it was possible the supporting staff here took greater pains to keep conditions clean than in the massive "city inside a building" many American hospitals had become. And this was far ahead of the conditions he'd read descriptions of from the American Civil War or the mobile army surgical hospitals during the Korean

The Eyes

War. These tents even had good lighting, a new uninterruptible power supply, and adequate water supplies. Combined with the caring and concerned staff, this was truly much more of a hospital environment than he would have suspected could be provided in the desert so far from "civilization."

Still, the lack of an anesthesiologist and what this meant for his patients thrust the situation back to the Stone Age—it struck him as absolute barbarism. His "job," if he wanted to stay alive, was to demonstrate first and foremost that he had the skills to execute these gruesome surgeries, and only then could he hope to influence the methods by which his captors cared for the welfare of the patient. This would not be easy, as concern for the patient has a different meaning when the patient looks at death as a reward, as long as it is attained in the pursuit of the right path. Sadly for these brave young men, the "right" path here was determined less by the teachings of the Koran than by the clerics reading them.

Dr. Dorman decided he would begin just under the left eyelid. He sprayed water and a light solution of lidocaine he'd found in bottles on the shelf in the "supply room."

The supply room had a large number of such bottles, but the labels were missing from many of them, and no one purported to know what was in them when he politely inquired. And so he left nearly empty handed, save for a few of the partially labeled bottles. He had no idea at what concentration the lidocaine was suspended, or whether its original purity had been changed, diluted, or even replaced with something else entirely. He decided he had to test the solution, so as an experiment, he peeled back the persistent scab that had developed on his leg from the lashing until it once again bled, then swabbed some of the liquid on the wound. The near-immediate cessation of pain let him know the liquid was probably what it was labeled to be, but beyond that he would be guessing.

His even being allowed in the so-called supply room was a major coup. Apparently his tenacious response to the lash had at least earned him some respect from these men who were tied to the spiritual world in thought but had experienced much—an unpleasant much—in the physical world. Regardless of his mental brilliance, he would have to show the kind of ruthless stamina that these desert nomads depended

The Desert Camp

on with their lives if he were to fit in by any measure. A rather large audience very carefully watched every move he made, and always the old man was there. It was time to do—not think.

LEE'S CAR

The trip back to Lee's place was filled with harmless talk about a random array of subjects. Through facial expressions and hand motions, Lee tried to convince Yin Hee that everything would be fine, while they talked about their date to throw off anyone who may be listening. The idea that Lee believed his own car could be bugged was enough to scare her. The talking kept her from panicking, but just barely. They entered the covered parking lot from the street through the guarded gate just like last time, only now Yin Hee felt the guard was staring at her, following her with his eyes. She had to avert her gaze, and tried to nonchalantly check her makeup in the mirror behind the sun visor. It didn't help. She felt exposed, vulnerable, and alone. Lee parked in his designated spot, got out of the car, and came over to her side to open the door. "Let's go, Yin Hee." His tone was neutral. She had no idea if she was in safe hands, or on her way to an unspeakable process of "adjustment."

Inside the elevator, she stood with her back against the far right corner. Having no way for anyone or thing to approach her unseen was slightly comforting. She remembered her Korean captors' lessons on manipulation. Her instructors had droned on about the concept that the means to influence someone were tied to the individual's needs at a specific time in the victim's life. She had the pyramid memorized—

The Eyes

Maslow's hierarchy of needs was the source theory for finding a person's greatest weakness. They stressed that one had to know the individual well enough to know where his or her basic need level really was, not the level put forward to face the world. Interestingly, the individuals most susceptible to recruitment as a one-time or ongoing agent were not those at the bottom of the pyramid. At the lowest tier, the physiological level, an individual could be manipulated to provide information via interrogation and the application of physical pain, a process as old as mankind itself.

Safety, the next tier, was more a safety from war, accidents, crime, and that sort of social fear. People at this level were not well suited for recruitment. It was not until the third tier that the best opportunities for recruitment were available. What humans would do to be accepted, to feel comfortable or safe within a group, was nothing short of remarkable. The basis for peer pressure, the need for social acceptance, was one of the strongest manipulative techniques known to man. Progressing up the pyramid, for the theory requires at least majority satisfaction of the lower tiers before advancement, comes esteem. Many have been captured by the need or desire for more power or prestige, sometimes at tremendous expense to them personally, a cost they know of in advance. The final tier—self-actualization—was of marginal value for recruitment. By the time one had reached the level of the search for self-actualization, it was often something within the person that was sought, not an external reward. How quickly, she mused, she had dropped to the second layer and was headed for the bottom.

Lee moved closer to her and took her hand in his. Was it a reassuring gesture, an act for anyone who might be watching, or a means to ensure she couldn't bolt? She wanted to stop thinking. This was the longest elevator ride of her entire life. Finally they reached the sixth floor; the doors opened and they walked toward his apartment. To her surprise, they walked right past his door and down the hall to the exit near the stairs. While she stood there baffled and confused, he casually opened a door marked "Maintenance" and dragged her inside. She started to scream involuntarily, but Lee clamped his hand over her mouth forcefully. He had a cloth in his hand, and she imagined herself being drugged; she felt herself fading out. Then, to her surprise, she noticed he was releasing the pressure, and she could hear him saying something quietly.

"Yin Hee, are you OK? I'm going to let go of you, but don't scream. I said you are safe, and I meant it. You are safe for probably the first time since you were brought here to America." His voice was calm, warm, and caring.

"I-I-I don't know," she stammered. *Was it possible?* she thought, *Could he truly care about her and know what she was?* Then she slowly disintegrated into a sobbing ball of a thousand fears, emotions, and questions. For his part, a somewhat-relieved Lee was content to just hold this now-fragile young woman. He, too, had many questions, but they would have to wait.

CAMP CASEY, SOUTH KOREA

Lieutenant Colonel Drierdan looked north. He'd been in Korea for seven months on this tour, making him one of the "old guys." In addition, it was his third tour in Korea. He was experienced and respected. A US military academy graduate, he was good to his men. A ruthless zealot for the physical fitness of every member of his unit, including himself, he lived with his men in the mud. His had a singular purpose—to be ready should the forces to the North decide, for whatever reason, that they had another shot at taking the peninsula. He was sure from his detailed study of the first Korean conflict, and his understanding of the DPRK political mantra, that the enemy still had the same essential strategy. If there were to be another war, it would be conducted with North Korea sparing no effort at driving the conflict all the way down the peninsula to the ocean beach. The lieutenant colonel was sure they had learned from the last endeavor that failing in the initial drive and allowing reinforcements the time to appear on stage was a death knell. That was the reason over a million North Korean men massed at their southern border, trained and ready for the order to attack.

Camp Casey lay within a valley, just eleven miles south of the demilitarized zone in the village of Tongduchon. Should the North attack the South, Lieutenant Colonel Drierdan's unit would be one of the first to encounter them. Owing to that probability, and given that a bored soldier is decidedly an unhappy soldier, he had argued long and hard for the resources to increase his men's training, and in addition to embellishing an already fine reputation, he succeeded. His men spent easily twice as much time in the field now as did their antecedent comrades.

Lieutenant Colonel Drierdan thought often about forces he would fight if it came down to actual combat once more on this tortured peninsula. Most Americans, and, for that matter, most military personnel, thought of the North Koreans as emaciated, poorly trained suckers whose terrible misfortune of birth forced them into service in a poorly trained, disorganized military organization whose main strength lay in numbers. Lieutenant Colonel Drierdan knew better. The North Korean People's Army (NKPA) soldier of today was better fed, educated, motivated, and equipped than his predecessors who fought in the last Korean conflict. He would likely be seventeen to twenty-one years of age and would serve in the army for nine years. He was probably from the city, and was educated, indoctrinated, and motivated by a much more controlled and regimented society than the US Forces. Everything he knew of the world had been provided and possibly manipulated by the state-controlled information and education systems. He would physically be considered wiry by Western standards, but was far from being in poor health. He would probably be muscular and kept in top physical condition through a serious regimen of strenuous workouts. As a result, contrary to popular belief, the NKPA soldier was known by his military adversaries as a fierce fighter in all terrain and weather conditions. His stamina and courage would make US Army leadership proud. His capabilities of strength, daring, and endurance would make him a significant threat to whoever would face him in combat. An excellent and well-trained fighter, he was not to be easily discounted. The US public, jaded by conflicts dealt with in a seemingly simple manner via long-range high-tech weapons, harbored the self-deluding belief that the North Korean Army could be easily dealt with. Fortunately for the lieutenant colonel and his men and women, the North Korean soldier did have some significant weaknesses, and it was Lieutenant Colonel Drierdan's job to make sure his troops knew them.

Camp Casey, South Korea

The first thing Lieutenant Colonel Drierdan had to impress on his troops was a respect for the forces they would face. Relying on the technological superiority of their own equipment, a philosophy almost inherited in the US armed forces, could spell death on the battlefield. He had pointed out relentlessly that in survival school, one is taught that without a lethal M-16, a US soldier could still fashion hunting devices from any number of inanimate objects. Even a well-thrown rock could kill, and death from a rock was just as permanent as that from a million-dollar, optically self-guided, airdropped cruise missile. The human body is a reasonably fragile container, so the fact that North Korean forces used archaic weapons compared with those of the twenty-first-century US Army was not necessarily a winning equation. After all, the Geneva convention was established as a result of the devastating effectiveness of World War I weaponry.

The focus for his men and women was the NKPA soldier himself. Although well trained, motivated, and intelligent, he was most likely over-drilled and trained by memorization. He was also significantly over-supervised. This translates into a soldier who knew his basic job devastatingly well and was motivated to fight to the death, but did not effectively handle change in battle strategies or battlefield anomalies. Whether from fear of or a genuine belief in the chain of command, a NKPA soldier would rarely act decisively without orders or precedent to guide him. This was the margin of error the American soldier would have to exploit. The lieutenant colonel carefully and repeatedly explained to his troops that it was very important to decapitate the enemy forces early, and keep the battle fluid and rapidly changing whenever possible. There was also a great possibility that taking out NKPA leadership could be very effective in defeating NKPA troops. This was the philosophy all US Forces worked with; it gave their military a target.

DSRJ HEADQUARTERS, YOKOTA AB, JAPAN

"Here's another one." Carol turned and handed the printout to her partner. "This is the sixth time we've had a report like this. I can't believe the department is not paying more attention to it." She was exasperated, but that wasn't unusual for her. Though admittedly passionate about her job, she knew that her flair for the melodramatic did not help her professionally.

After all, the truth was that the vast majority of information intercepted by these listening posts was absolutely useless. The sheer volume of information made it impractical to even attempt to record it all. Added to that was the underlying fact that the vast majority of human communication was quite mundane. With the use of sophisticated computer programs, key words could be targeted, in effect, screening out much of the chaff. But even though that may have simplified the process, most of the information necessary to protect the United States and her vital interests was discussed in languages other than English. This complicated the process considerably because now a team for each language had to interact to build the keyword matrix. Then there was the obvious problem of trying to predict what words ought to be highlighted.

The Eyes

With all of this as entering arguments, it was perhaps understandable that reports of unusually high quantities of concrete sighted near the DMZ might not make it into the president's morning briefing.

Fred was already shaking his head. "C'mon, Carol," he replied, "don't start this garbage again. The first time you brought it up, I couldn't have been happier that most of the people here at Yokota have no idea what we do. Just imagine how much flak I'd take from my neighbors if everybody knew how excited my shift got over reports of concrete dumped near the DMZ. Let it go—it's nothing. Maybe they are trying to reinforce their highway system. Why should we care? They've done a billion unfathomable things. Maybe they're trying to prime their economic pump, starting with construction." Fred had taken an earful the last time he let Carol present a half-hour speculation about the purpose of the concrete. Colonel William had been willing to bring the issue up to his boss. His boss was not amused.

Colonel William worked for the chief of the Department of Defense Special Representative for Japan (DSRJ). Although a civilian, he was the senior official at Yokota, despite being collocated with the air force lieutenant general commanding United States Forces, Japan. Normally quite reasonable, he had drawn the line at wasting time on frivolous matters. The concrete might be an anomaly, but without corroborating information, the team was wasting their time guessing about every potential bizarre effort by the DPRK.

"OK, humor me." Carol needed to be careful here; she didn't want to compromise the value of all their efforts over one thing, but she honestly believed it was important. "I won't put it in the report this time if we discuss it here and now, then document our efforts."

"Done." Fred started abruptly, "You start. Why should we care?"

"OK," Carol began evenly, "but you have it a little bit backward. We should be asking ourselves why we shouldn't care. This is the sixth report of concrete trucks lined up miles long near Cho Mya. They show up at dusk and work through the night. When you consider that this location is within fifteen miles of the DMZ, I think we ought to be more than a little curious." Carol tossed her auburn hair as she looked from Fred to Stan Wadell. She didn't see a lot of support in their expressions. "Look, what reports is North Korea putting out about construction in this area?"

DSRJ Headquarters, Yokota AB, Japan

"Great segue, Carol." Fred was always ready to debate. "I've been monitoring very carefully, and they have made no statements at all. I think this is all a little far fetched, and not worth your time."

"I couldn't disagree more, Fred. The fact that they've said nothing about this makes it even more suspicious. The propaganda machine is always ready to spin every event for some gain, be it political or economic, and silence speaks volumes. I think we ought to get this information some more attention somehow."

"OK, I'll run it by the guys in the Korea watch at the Defense Intelligence Agency (DIA) as a heads-up. Will that satisfy you?" He was getting more than a little perturbed over this issue.

Sensing the irritation in his voice, Carol smiled her most beguiling smile and said, "Oh, Fred, you spoil me," and she batted her eyes flagrantly.

"You're such a clown!" Fred chuckled and dutifully took her disk with what he knew would be a well-written analysis of the event and its possibilities.

He turned toward his screen to send the message. He addressed it to Bob Cochlen, a longtime friend with a real penchant for all things Korean. He was an incredibly studious officer, and he had studied the Korean language for years, despite graduating with remarkable comments from the Defense Language Institute's Korean course in Monterey, California. If anybody could make sense of this, he would be the guy. Not to mention that he was a close enough friend to resist the urge to ridicule Fred's team for not catching the significance of the event, if it was significant.

Bob,

We've been tracking some interesting things that have been going on in the dark up north. There's nothing we can really put our fingers on, but it seems kind of odd. Thought I'd share considering we are all on the same purple team. I've enclosed a package one of my interpreters has put together. She isn't a trained analyst, but she has good instincts and her heart is in the right place. What do you guys make of this?

Fred

THE DESERT

Here we go, **Dr. Dorman** told himself, *and this had better be a Heisman award performance.*

The eye is a marvelous gift, he reflected, *far more complex than any camera ever made by hand. Set inside the orbit, it is at once exposed, yet protected. One's natural tendency to protect the eye is so strong that one will automatically put other body parts at risk in the effort.*

He struggled to go through his mental "pregame" ritual, which normally would include a thorough review of the anatomy of the eye, assisted by the ubiquitously accessible, graphical assistance computers provide. He realized the error in taking the Internet and its fundamental ease of use for granted. Now he would need to rely on his memory, and he wasn't an ophthalmologist by trade. *Externally, the eyelids were first, but they would be turned back and held in place, requiring no incision. Moving them aside would include the tarsal gland and the superior tarsus for the top eyelid,* he thought to himself. *This would expose the palpebral and bulbar conjunctiva, where the first incision would be necessary.*

Dr. Dorman began the incision quickly, eager to get the procedure under way. He would carefully cut the conjunctiva, again spraying lidocaine on the tissue. The young man didn't move. He looked straight ahead at the ceiling with a fixed stare.

The Eyes

The doctor was amazed and beguiled. What could one focus on while a perfectly fine eyeball was being removed, plunging one into darkness?

The incision began at the inside corner of the eye and traced a neat arc up and to the right, after pushing aside the tarsal gland and the superior tarsus. Dr. Dorman's assistants, ever ready, moved in swiftly to wipe up the minimal blood, as he instinctively turned to the equipment tray for a second scalpel. Remembering he had all the tools he would get, he turned back to his patient. The next incision was through the inferior conjunctiva after cutting through the inferior tarsus and gland of the lower eyelid. He then asked for the enucleation spoons. The returned blank stare let him know, once again, that the equipment tray was more sparsely equipped than he'd like. Looking for himself, he found what he thought were appropriate pieces of equipment, but quickly ascertained they were nothing more than retooled dinner silverware; they would have to do. The assistants moved back out of the way with catlike agility as he turned from the equipment tray to the patient. Using the surprisingly clean "enucleation spoons," he slid the lower conjunctiva out of the way, forcing the spoon above the orbital septum and into the adipose body of orbit above the maxillary sinus. The eyeball now rested on the spoon, but was still connected by the inferior and superior oblique and rectus muscles, the levator palpebrae superioris muscle, and the suspensory and other ligaments. He turned back to the equipment tray for the scalpel again; he would have to use the same one throughout the surgery—another first. With each momentary pause, the doctor took to look for equipment, the many assistants would take hold of the young man's head, applying pressure around the eye much in the same manner one would grab a stubbed toe to alleviate pain.

The young man was completely immobilized by cloth restraints but registered his pain by violent spasms and occasional groans. A fluid that smelled strongly of alcohol was forced down his throat. It was a poor anesthetic at best, despite the many Western films' depictions that would have one believe drunken men feel no pain. For these volunteers, however, it was a banned substance, and this unfamiliarity would hopefully elicit a greater reaction. It was hardly a substitute for proper anesthesia, but perhaps, at least, a distraction.

The Desert

Dr. Dorman began separating the tissue above and below the eye, working toward the muscles, which he began to score meticulously. Suddenly, the young man, subject to this brutal bodily invasion, involuntarily spasmed—reminding the doctor of the need for speed. He abandoned delicacy and sliced through the muscles. All that remained now was the optic nerve and vascularity itself. Pulling forward gently with the enucleation spoons, the eyeball was forced against the bony opening in the skull, like a grape being pushed into a soda bottleneck. With a very quick movement, he severed the optic nerve. Finally he inserted the upper spoon, and with a sickening squishing sound, pulled the eyeball from the socket. Almost immediately, the removed organ was taken from his hands by the old man who had so skillfully assisted in the surgery. The old man turned and placed the eye in a sterile pouch, which he then placed in a cryogenic canister.

In an instant, Dr. Dorman felt his furor rise and he forced himself to quell it. The fact that the containers, which would be used to transport the removed eyeball, were better and obviously much more expensive than any of the tools used to remove it spoke volumes. Naturally, the company that would receive the organ would provide the precious cargo with free casing. Perhaps, the doctor thought, this company could be imposed upon for better removal equipment, but he had no time for such thoughts now.

A very rudimentary plastic prosthesis was offered, and Dr. Dorman, though surprised to have the device, smoothly inserted it in the now-sightless cavity. He pulled the conjunctiva back over the prosthesis and sewed it in place. As he turned to place the suturing equipment back on the tray, the crowd of able assistants released the young man from his restraints and carried him from the room. He was sweating profusely, but uttered no sound. Dr. Dorman felt exhausted too, and now understood very well why the surgery to remove the eye took up most of the day. Despite what he considered a long and tedious surgery, unnecessarily lengthened by his having to attend to every detail, there were smiles all over the room.

"This one will live," the old woman in charge of the cleaning team proclaimed. From the look in her eyes, and reflected around the room, it appeared to be an outcome all too rare. Dr. Dorman reached to lift the vessel containing the removed organ. The woman holding it hesitated,

The Eyes

then smiled and handed it over to him. As he examined the container, the older man, his lead assistant and the one who had infuriated him at the beginning of the surgery, spoke again.

"Very well done, Doctor. You are truly more accomplished than I, even gifted as many say. Does it disturb you that the eye will be sold?"

Dr. Dorman hadn't expected the question, and now he would carefully weigh his response. Given that the surgeries and their purpose were beyond the knowledge of everyone in the camp with the exception of clerics, selling the organ was probably the most pragmatic thing to do. Why discard an eye, when someone else could make use of it, and certainly would be willing to pay cold hard cash for it? He had no illusions, however, that those profits would be spent on better surgical instruments or anesthesia. More likely, it would fund food and weapons, and perhaps training camps elsewhere.

"No," he finally replied, "one must do what one can." The old man nodded and held out his hand for the container. As Dr. Dorman handed the vessel across, his heart dropped as he noticed an American flag etched on the bottom. *How ironic that this eye would be sold to an American*, he thought. *But that is where the money is after all.*

As if reading his thoughts, the older man said, "Perhaps the American will gain more than just physical sight through this eye, and begin to see the world as others do."

As Dr. Dorman pondered that thought, the tent flaps opened, and the next young man was carried in, whereupon they began to strap him down—it would be a very long day.

CHO MYA

Ah, finally I get a chance to see the inside of this dam, Colonel Song thought. His desire to see the giant hydroelectric power generators had increased throughout the day, and it would be hours before the "dear leader" arrived. There was plenty of time to indulge himself with the one thing he'd been looking forward to for over a year since he was informed of his good fortune in landing this assignment.

"Sir, I think you should stay and oversee preparations for his arrival," Captain Youhn began. "It is a very rare and great honor that he…"

"You have been stalling and hounding me all day, Captain!" Colonel Song yelled at his second in command. "I will not be herded, today or any other day! I am in command, and I will make the decision as to what I should attend to and when I should do it! It is your job," he continued more calmly, "to make my job easier. Now escort me to the generators this instant."

The captain lowered his voice almost to a whisper and said, "Sir, I understand your desire. I'm not trying to make things more difficult for you. Believe me, you don't want to see the generators right now. Please trust me. You will soon see that I am your most loyal officer. I am loyal enough to try to keep you out of trouble, regardless of the personal risk." The captain stood at attention, yet his fear showed through. He knew very well that his commanding officer held sway not only over his career and work conditions, but over his life as well.

As much as Colonel Song hated to put off his visit to the generators, something told him he should listen to this captain. Caution was always good advice, and the generators weren't going anywhere. There would always be tomorrow, and whatever the problem was, he couldn't do anything about it today anyway. Today's biggest concern would clearly be the visit by the head of state.

"Very well, Captain. I'll hold you to that pledge, I assure you," and he smiled. "Let's go make our presence known to the men and women under our command." While Captain Youhn relaxed, Colonel Song thought about what had just happened. This was the very first conversation he'd had with anyone since he arrived. Certainly there were words spoken, but nothing beyond what was absolutely necessary to prepare for their distinguished visitor's imminent arrival. Even that seemed a little odd, as everyone seemed remarkably well versed, as if they'd been through this many times before.

Colonel Song followed Captain Youhn back up and out of the dam. The area on top was very large, and the helicopter-landing-pad Maltese cross was clearly marked at one end. Time and again, he stopped and shook hands with his men and women, but none would say more than the absolute minimum required courteous responses to his inquiries. No one replied with a "Welcome" or "Good luck" or any other normal salutation. It seemed like very strange behavior; but then he thought, *I am their commander, and I always feared my own.*

After what seemed an eternity of dry runs, adjustments, and reruns, the colonel finally heard the familiar "whoop whoop whoop" unmistakably announcing the approach of a helicopter. *An hour late and he's arriving from the South,* the colonel noted. *Well, no matter. The visit of the dear leader is at hand, and men's careers have taken drastic turns over just such an event.* As the helicopter touched down, Colonel Song adjusted his cap one last time and strode confidently forward toward the red carpet that led up to the helicopter. Actually, it continued underneath the vehicle, as the pilot had set the craft down five feet forward of the mark, to Colonel Song's great irritation. *That will be one of my first phone calls after this is over*, he thought. The pilot must know this is unacceptable. As he neared the helicopter door, it opened abruptly. The senior security personnel preceding the dear leader pushed Colonel Song back quite indelicately. As he fell backward awkwardly, he realized there would be no career highlight today. There would be no photograph of him and the dear leader shaking hands and smiling.

His men had brought the lone functioning microphone to the platform. It was unceremoniously taken from them and handed back into the helicopter to the waiting Kim Jong Il. The old man was speaking in a faltering voice as Colonel Song righted himself. He read a prepared speech about the dam's significance to the fight to reunite the peninsula under the Juche ideology, all without even disembarking the aircraft. It was over in less than fifteen minutes; the rotors were turning before the formation had made it through half their marching sequence. Everyone suddenly stopped and faced the aircraft as it lifted off. From the air, Colonel Song knew, his men would look as organized as a soccer game ten minutes after the last whistle—he was livid.

He turned to Captain Youhn and said, "Dismiss them all; we'll begin again tomorrow. Then have all the officers meet me back at my office." He walked off, still shaking his head as he relived the entire day's wasted energy and practice—how could any leader do that to his faithful men? This was a bad day indeed.

LEE'S APARTMENT BUILDING

The room looked very little like the apartment Yin Hee had been in the other night with Lee. That seemed so long ago now. This apartment was smaller, and had only one small window in the back that was covered with thick, drab, dark drapes. The most striking feature, however, was the utter lack of furniture. The floor was covered in bland-colored tiles. Immediately inside the door were multiple utility equipment racks standing eight feet tall. Each rack had between four and ten modules with wires running in and out of them, and several had lights going on and off, giving the impression of a telephone switchboard or a central hub for a local area network.

"Most of it is fake," Lee said as he followed her gaze. "Originally this was another apartment. We rented numerous apartments here from the original owner, who used to work for the agency. Since that's a fairly obvious ploy, he sold the apartment complex to its current owner. She knows this room only as a maintenance room. As you can see, we've gone to considerable lengths to ensure anyone who might be curious enough to enter also believes the story. In truth, the room is where I, and others I would guess, send and receive encrypted messages from central. We can discuss the rest of the details at your leisure, but right now I need your cooperation."

The Eyes

"Cooperation? I don't even know who or what you are! How dare you drag me up here with all your cloak-and-dagger garbage! I'm out of here! Never speak to me again!"

"Noriko Suzuki, calm down! When I said I know who you are, I really meant it."

Lee's use of her birth name stunned her and dispelled any doubt about how serious this situation was for her. If she was being activated or recalled, this was it, and how she acted now could determine whether she lived or died.

"I know things look bad," Lee was continuing. "This couldn't have happened at a worse time. After our last engagement, you must truly find me a scoundrel of the worst sort. For what it's worth, I had no intention of getting that close to you—it just happened."

She wasn't listening; she couldn't. This was just too much pressure. Was this yet another test? Was this man posing as an American agent, but working for the DPRK, just to see if she would start talking and condemn herself, or was he for real? Lee was just standing there, looking at her. There was no clue, no more information.

"You have to trust me," she heard him saying distantly. "Your life could be in danger, and it may have something to do with that guy killed across town after talking to you in the store." Without thinking or saying another word, he walked over to her, put his arms around her, and looked directly into her eyes. The honesty of the moment told her all she needed.

It may be a mistake, she thought, *but I am so tired of this game.* She took a deep breath, disengaged from Lee and began.

"OK. I'm here, and as ridiculous as this is, I trust you. What happens from here on is in your hands. You know my name. What else do you know?"

"I know you were born in Niigata, Japan, and that fifteen years ago, you disappeared from the beach waiting for your father to return from fishing. You were just thirteen years old then. I know it's of no consolation, but we were within half a nautical mile of intercepting the minisub that took you. We can only speculate on your first four years in North Korea, but thanks to your father's dedicated efforts to find you, we knew where to look. The Democratic People's Republic of Korea has a sophisticated network in place, but they are kidding themselves about the West not knowing anything about them at all. When the application for your trip here arrived at the American embassy, we reviewed it as a matter of course. The distinctive scar you bear on your forehead, from a fall aboard your father's boat if I remember correctly, was the best clue we've ever had. Then your mother and father graciously provided DNA from a lock of your hair preserved from your childhood, which we were able to match with another hair taken from you during the bureaucratic dance that led to your permission to come to America six years ago. I was selected to shadow you before you arrived and guided you toward the job with Frank at the hardware store, and, no, no one else at the store has any idea whatsoever about either of us. But let me do this right. I know there are many things you want, and have a right, to know. Yes, your mother and father are well, and are likewise aware you are well. It has been tough on them not to contact you. I have taken the liberty of keeping them updated regularly—with certain obvious omissions." She smiled as he blushed. She was beginning to feel comfortable for the first time in many years.

"I don't suppose I'll be able to see them, will I?" Her face revealed she knew the answer, and Lee began to feel comfortable as well.

"Not for a while, but I promise you that you will be with your family once again when this is all over. The trouble is, we don't quite know what 'this' is. I wish I could let you make just one phone call, but you know, I know, and they know that it would be dangerous to jeopardize all three of you, as painful as it is to have to wait. They are very healthy, in fact, remarkably so. As you can imagine, you are an important person for both the US and Japanese governments. For the United States, you represent a window, albeit one way, into parts of the DPRK espionage system. The same is true for Japan, but you also represent insight into the abduction of Japanese citizens by the DPRK. It is a subject near and dear to the highest levels of the Japanese bureaucracy, especially since Empress Michiko has taken the issue as a personal quest." Then he changed his tone of voice back to that of a confident agent. "Now I need to tell you what has transpired since we last spoke. We haven't yet figured out exactly what it means, but in this business, one deals a lot in educated hunches and we think you will be a part of this somehow. He led her to the back of the apartment and sat with her on a couch where he handed her a sheet of paper. This appeared yesterday in the SIPRNET file."

"What is the SIPRNET?" she asked

"It stands for the Secret Internet Protocol Router Network. It's kind of like a private Internet for classified information."

She took the paper from his hands. It looked a lot like an official e-mail, but all the routing information was either blacked out or obviously cut off.

INFORMATION NOTICE: NUMEROUS INCIDENTS WHEREIN SIGNIFICANT AMOUNTS OF CONCRETE AND OTHER BUILDING MATERIALS WERE DELIVERED WITHIN THE CAUTION ZONE NORTH OF THE DMZ. TO DATE, THERE HAS BEEN NO PUBLIC ANNOUNCEMENT OF CONSTRUCTION IN THE AREA. CLOSEST AREA OF KNOWN CONSTRUCTION IS THE HYDROELECTRIC DAM AT CHO MYA. THUS FAR, THE VOLUME OF CONCRETE WOULD EXCEED THAT NECESSARY TO BUILD THE DAM ITSELF. ALL AGENTS DEALING WITH KOREA IN ANY FASHION ARE REQUESTED TO SOLICIT INFORMATION POSSIBLY RELATED TO THIS EVENT AND PASS SUCH IMMEDIATELY.

Yin Hee read the message three times, then slowly turned and looked at Lee. "I'm afraid I haven't the slightest idea what this is about—honestly," she began. The sound of fear crept back into her voice. "I have heard a lot about the dam, but that's all."

"Don't worry about that; I didn't expect you to." He said quietly as he sat down next to her on the couch. By not pursuing the thought process on the dam, Lee had made his first mistake. He took Yin Hee's hands in his and looked into her eyes. "It wouldn't have meant anything to me except that part of the country is where your 'school' was. That's one coincidence. Then the strange guy who comes in to talk to you gets whacked. That's two. I don't believe in more than one coincidence so close together. It's not healthy. In my experience, even one coincidental event in our business needs to be fully checked out. There isn't anything on the bum who was killed except that he was a laborer who took whatever job came along to keep himself fed. He didn't appear to have any underworld contacts, and the gun that he was shot with belonged to a street gang member on the far side of town.

We were going to contact the gang member, but local police had already noted his gun was stolen the night he was killed. Oddly, his killing did not appear gang related, but instead seemed professionally enacted with a knife. Considering the size and strength of the victim, and his reputation for violence, one might have had questions about how someone could get close enough to him to slash his throat cleanly. But with law enforcement stretched thin, and this thug not having a family to complain about his death, the investigation didn't last long and had no final resolution."

Yin Hee took a deep breath and said, "There is more information about that guy than I told you." She paused, waiting for Lee to give something away, some indication that she was about to perjure herself, but he just sat there, giving her the time and space she needed. She decided to continue. "He knew my name before he came in the door that morning. I didn't realize it until I was in Inspector Ohl Suk Chee's office and he asked me to retell the story of what happened. As I did, I remembered something that had struck me as odd that day. When the man had approached me, the first thing he asked me was if my name was Yin Hee Kwahl. I didn't think much about it, since we all wear those stupid nametags, but then he looked at his hand as he said my name. If you remember, you and Frank gave me hell later that afternoon for forgetting my nametag. That's when it all came into focus. The guy looked at his hand because he'd written my name there; the way a high-school kid writes a friend's phone number on his hand. He was looking for me, but, obviously, he didn't really know who I was. Does that mean anything to you?"

"Maybe," Lee replied. "It sounds like he was trying to find you for someone else. These other people decided to get rid of him so that he couldn't identify them. You told all of this to Inspector Ohl Suk?"

"Absolutely not!" she said with finality. "I don't trust that man as far as I can throw him. I'm not sure what it is about him, but it is decidedly unpleasant."

"Excellent. I'm not sure why, but I don't like him either. I'll be running a thorough check on the good inspector. My initial check seems to have come up clean, but there are still a few things that don't add up. He's only been in the United States a couple of years, yet he immediately took over as chief inspector. His transfer here was by his own request, though his family remains in Hawaii."

"I get the distinct impression he knows much more about me than I'd like him to," Yin Hee admitted. "Unfortunately, there is no way for me to find out without asking, and that is one thing I dare not do." She shivered as she said it, and Lee put his arm around her.

"It's time to go. I don't want to risk someone discovering this room is in use. Are you interested in staying here tonight?" He asked it a bit too quickly, and began turning red as he realized how eager he sounded.

She put her arms around his neck, and kissed him deeply. "If I'm going to trust you with my life, I might as well trust you with my body as well," she giggled.

Lee gave her butt a gentle squeeze and whispered, "I'll protect both with my life." Then he stood up and began guiding her toward the door.

"My, but you agents take your work seriously," she teased him.

"I'm off duty now," he replied as they stepped into the hallway and he pulled the self-locking door shut behind them. The short walk to his room was silent. As he opened the door to his apartment, their eyes met. Both of them had mirror image ear-to-ear grins—they would enjoy this night as neither had enjoyed one before.

HEADQUARTERS, PACIFIC AIR FORCES

"Admiral, the J2, J3, and J5, and their staffs are waiting for you in the conference room," said Colonel Cannen. The *J* designated a joint position, meaning the person filling that job could be from any branch within the Department of Defense. It also made it easier to address them this way than by saying, "The Pacific Command's director of intelligence, director of operations, and director of strategic plans," while maintaining the order of authority. "As added incentive, sir, the coffee of the day is chocolate macadamia." Admiral John Corping looked up and smiled—it didn't happen often. He had good people, and his executive officer, Colonel Ralph Cannen, was one of the best. It didn't hurt to have these people around him when this meeting dealt with a dispatch from CINCUNC in Korea.

"Gentlemen, we have received an invitation to meet with Kim Jong-Il himself. I understand he delivered the request in person to Dave at the meeting," the admiral announced.

"What the heck was General Hodge doing at that meeting? I thought he had a two-star to handle that for him?" asked Brigadier General Curt, the one-star deputy J2. "Boy, I'd love to know what CINCUNC thinks about this." The grin on his face meant he already knew both the answers to his own question, and how much Admiral Corping was enjoying this.

"Well, Curt," the admiral began as he walked to the head of the conference table and poured himself a glass of water, "when this is all said and done, perhaps it will finally be clear to everybody that when it comes to the Pacific Command, there is really only one commander in chief. The time when America and the world needed a separate CINC for the Korean peninsula has long since passed. It is one more of the legacy problems the cold war left us. This bizarre structure has been a pain in our ability to organize, train, equip, exercise, or even inspect ourselves for fifty years. But that's enough of that prattle.

"I called this meeting to gain some information. What you need to tell me is why the crazy old coot wants to talk to me. I want each of you to look at everyone you've got working anywhere on the peninsula with an eye on how something we're doing might have interested their leadership. Pay particular attention to anything we've started within the past year or so. Wherever you go with this, be very careful that it stays quiet. Treat everybody as suspect; pull the information but don't let anybody know what we're really looking for or why. You'll have to be fairly specific in your questioning. What I don't want is all of you calling the ROK and asking these same questions in a general way. That will be sure to create a problem. Questions?" There was a confident silence around the room as the admiral polled each with a sweep of his hand. After he'd looked at each member of his staff, he stood and they popped to attention. "Very well, we'll meet again tomorrow at…" All eyes turned to his exec for the answer.

"You're free at fourteen hundred hours tomorrow, sir," Colonel Cannen stated after checking the wireless PDA he used to keep the admiral's fluid schedule updated.

"Then fourteen hundred hours it is. Let's get back to work!" and he strode out the side entrance that led directly to his office. The rest of the men filed out the hall entrance to the conference room and headed back to what would now be a very different schedule for the next twenty-eight hours.

SEOUL

Hae-Jung absolutely loved the apartment. But then, why wouldn't she? While it was modest by Western standards, it was something seen only in the dreams of the young in the DPRK, reserved only for the political elite. Now, she almost had it all—a television, a computer with Internet access, even a car, which she had yet to learn how to drive. She'd been in Seoul less than six months, and thanks to her short skirts and rather casual attitude toward physical relationships with people in the right positions, her career and personal life were on the fast track to luxury. Her very first week at her new job showed her that her new life would be as fascinating and comfortable as she had hoped.

As a woman, she accepted without qualm that her primary role would be as eye candy for the more experienced male reporters who dispensed the important news and stories, as well as the primarily male viewing audience. She began as the assistant to the weather broadcaster. Her primary function was to stand on stage and look good, at which she was a natural. The studio handled the wardrobe for her, but she got to select the outfits, and with an all-male support staff, the shorter she liked her skirts, the happier they were. They all got along fine until she started catching the stares coming from the news producer, the first man who could realistically affect her job for the better.

The Eyes

She decided her business relationships would start lasting into the off-duty hours.

Kim Yeounjin was tall for a Korean man at six feet, and with his average build, he was considered handsome by most. He had never married, not intentionally, but more from his fanatical pursuit of his career.

As with most careers, journalism offered many opportunities to overwork one, to the detriment of one's personal life. Yeounjin had taken all of those opportunities and was, not surprisingly, a rapidly rising star. At just thirty-one years of age, he was way ahead of the curve. With that came the kind of power that can make a young man's mind swim. He had it all: the great bachelor's pad, the fine sports car, money, and a powerful job that let him mix it up with the nation's high rollers. If it was important, it happened in Seoul. And if it happened in Seoul, Kim Yeounjin would cover it.

A pretty young woman wasn't that big a deal to him or the station. Like most television news crews, there was a viewing doll, as he thought of them, on every shift. He'd heard this new girl was different, though, and he'd made a point of watching her on television several times before coming around to grace her with his presence. After all, in the pecking order at the station, she had three bosses before she got to him, so he couldn't let it seem as though he was interested right away. Still, she did have an incredible allure about her.

For Hae-Jung, he looked better than she had anticipated which she considered an unexpected bonus. She'd have slept with him either way, but nice-looking people were a better choice, as long as they meet the one absolute prerequisite—they had to be in a position of power that she could manipulate to her benefit.

For their first encounter, he had been typically brutish, demanding, coarse, and even dismissive as he dictated the time, place, and, the cad, even the duration. She didn't worry, though, because she knew it would only take that one time to start turning the tide in her favor, and she played the game fatally well. Men wanted their women innocent yet nasty. The key was always the same. She had to convince the man that he was in charge, all while directing every facet of the encounter, before, during, and after. So far, she had managed three raises and a company car, and had moved through all the eye-candy positions, from the pointer for the weather map to the marginally functional "Special Bulletin" sections.

Now she was included in all international features, especially anything with a Japanese tint to it. Very soon, she would be meeting with the newest member of the Japanese diet, a decidedly pro-Korean man. It didn't really matter, though. By getting very close to him, she could provide terrific information to her handler for transmission north, preserving her position here. The added bonus was the scoop of every other news agency with the personal interview she would get, enhancing her value as a newswoman, which could mean another raise. Life had so many sweet things to offer, and now she meant to sample them all.

THE NATIONAL INSTITUTES OF HEALTH LABORATORY

Charles reappeared as Dr. Sanderson and Emiko walked to the end of the viewing room, but he was not alone. The two men at his side were enormous and looked like extras in a bad boxing movie.

"Hello again, Charles," Dr. Sanderson stepped forward and shook his hand. It was a calculated gesture, meant to signal a decrease in hostility. "And who are these gentlemen?"

"This is Roger Davidson, and that is Charles Stanton," the head of security gestured to each behemoth in turn. We call them Rock and Jock as an internal credit to their college sports careers. They are part of the research team now." Both men were grinning and now chuckled out loud, but said nothing and offered no handshake or greeting. They simply stood there, carefully keeping themselves apart with their hands free.

"Pleased to meet you," Emiko stammered. She felt obliged to say something as both men were leering at her. At this point, she was seriously reconsidering her choice of attire. Why did she always have to make a statement that a woman can be smart and still fashionable at the wrong time? Her red and white plaid wool skirt was respectable but at a little shorter than mid-thigh, not exactly demure. Neither man returned her salutation.

The Eyes

Dr. Sanderson smelled trouble. *These guys look as much like scientists as a ballerina looks like a cowboy*, he thought. "What are the chances I could get a look at Dr. Dorman's documentation?"

"No problem." Charles turned to the one they called Rock and continued, "Escort our colleagues to the presentation room, if you would. I'll be right there with the documentation."

They continued down the hall, entering the presentation room, which looked like a standard briefing room. It had the requisite large table in the center with chairs for thirteen people, and a slew of chairs lining the walls, with the "cheap seats," as they were often called, lining the back wall. Emiko and Dr. Sanderson sat on either side, at one end of the table, while the two goons, as Emiko thought of them, stood near the door. It was becoming increasingly obvious they were not members of the elite research team the facility housed. Charles entered from the side door and sat at the head of the table between Emiko and Dr. Sanderson.

"Here are the files from Dr. Dorman's office. Feel free to peruse them at your leisure. He was a talented and gifted scientist. Is there anything in particular you are looking to verify?" His countenance seemed nonchalant, but his facial expression gave away a determined need for something, some piece of information.

"Not really. If you can keep a secret," Dr. Sanderson leaned forward and lowered his voice in a conspiratorial form, "we're just trying to find out if he made any progress in areas that could help our research."

At this, Charles actually laughed out loud. "So this whole thing is a fishing expedition to see if you can make faster progress from his work? I'm surprised, Dr. Sanderson. Your reputation leaves one believing only the scientific method is good enough for any line of research. Please, be my guest. Take your time. I'll leave you to your analysis. Gentlemen, can I see you in the hallway," he said to the other two so-called scientists. Then to Emiko he said, "They missed the morning meeting, and I need to help them catch up." As he stood, he smiled and walked out into the hallway with Rock and Jock.

As soon as he left the room Emiko turned to her father, but was immediately silenced by the nonverbal finger to the lips to indicate quiet. Her father then quietly passed half the files to her and indicated that she should begin reading them as if all was well. Then he said a bit theatrically, "These look authentically like Gene's work. Of course, we have no way of knowing if these are all the documents, since Jack felt ill and left, but then, what would the institute have to hide from us? Well, if you do find anything interesting, this is the wrong place to discuss it. After all, absent the apparatus and cultures, it would be folly to draw any conclusions. Our best bet is to attempt to identify a line of pursuit that we can engage in next time we visit."

Emiko knew very well the purpose of her father's soliloquy. This was a briefing room, and with the security needed in a facility like this, it was likely their conversation was being overheard, and probably recorded. If either of them discovered anything, it would be best not to make any indication of it until they were again in the safe confines of their own lab. Each went through the files and then swapped piles and repeated the process. Neither said anything about what they were reading that could be indicative of a discovery.

As she opened the last folder, however, Emiko noted a lightly penciled entry between the rows of figures that consisted of a single word—video. In accordance with due prudence, she worked very hard to make no outward expression of any kind, simply finishing the document and closing the folder. After a little over an hour, Charles returned to check on their progress.

"So how is the analysis going? Have you found anything interesting?" Gone was the austere expression or the overt interest; he had returned to his nearly disinterested jovial self.

"We've found absolutely nothing, Charles. If I hadn't known Dr. Dorman before this, I would accuse him of overtly wasting time. But thank you very much for showing us his work. I rest easier knowing he was not ahead of us after all. You know how competitive those grants can be." Dr. Sanderson and Emiko stood and walked to and through the door.

Turning, Emiko suddenly asked, "Did Dr. Dorman videotape any of his experiments?"

Dr. Sanderson quickly continued, "We'll show ourselves out, Charles. Thanks again for your time." They started to turn back down the hallway they had come from. Like statues guarding a sacred place, Rock and Jock closed off their path.

The Eyes

Emiko's question changed Charles countenance permanently. "I don't think so, Dr. Sanderson. We have a few questions we need to ask you, and we could use your help in evaluating Dr. Dorman's work." He was grinning as he turned to Emiko, "And you, my sweet, will be remaining with us as well."

At that point, the goons grabbed each of them and herded them down the hallway past the work areas to the dormitory section normally used by the interns and the occasional scientist who got too carried away with the work and forgot the time. Dr. Sanderson shrugged out of Rock's grip long enough to confront Jock, who was forcefully pushing Emiko down the hallway.

"OK, the charade is over. We know what you really are, but I assure you, we can walk down the hallway ourselves. I know the security of this facility, so we're unlikely to try anything ridiculous. How about taking your hands off of us, and just telling us where you want us to go? I don't think we're much of a threat to you two."

Jock looked over at Charles, shrugged, and let his hands drop. Emiko immediately spun and aimed a slap at him, but her Dad had already taken hold of her wrist.

"That won't help us at all, Emi-chan," he whispered soothingly. "Let's just play along." He turned to Charles and demanded, "Well, what's the game? Where are we going and what are we doing? Do you have Dr. Dorman held in here somewhere as well?"

"That will be enough, Dr. Sanderson." Gone was Charles's ever-present grin, now replaced with a very stern glare. "We've been waiting for you to arrive. We have reason to believe that your research and Dr. Dorman's is being used to help enemies of the United States. You're here to tell us how. If you cooperate, this will be neither painful nor long. If not..." He left the sentence hanging. "You will stay here, Dr. Sanderson," and he opened one of the many gray painted identical doors lining the hallway. "The rooms are not opulently appointed, but they are easily as good as most hotels. Make yourself comfortable." With that Dr. Sanderson was unceremoniously ushered into his room and the door was closed. Emiko was herded farther down the hall to the opposite side. Charles opened the door and then left her with the taller of the two goons, the one called Rock. He watched Charles depart, and then walked into her room with her in tow.

"Well, we're home, honey," he laughed as she stood there glaring at him.

"Very funny. Now get out of here!" she shouted at him.

"Hmm. You sure have an odd way of looking at things. The way I see it, you aren't in much of a position to be making any demands at all. You have been given to me to, uh, care for, so if I were you I would rethink your attitude." Then he walked very close to her and whispered, "I can be a lot of fun if you're up for it."

She replied with a resounding slap across the face. He moved faster than she thought he could as he captured both her hands and put them together. Taking them in his powerful left hand he held them together straight up over her head. He used his right hand to explore her breasts and abdomen, and then pulled her hands down, doubling her over at the waist. He bent her over the back of the chair. Then he ran his hand up her leg under her skirt.

"How lovely," he grunted, "and powder blue is my favorite color. How did you know?" He left his hand on her butt and sneered, "A good slapping arm indicating upper body strength, and a great butt. It's truly sad that I have other pressing engagements, dear, but I assure you, I'll clear some time from my busy schedule for you later. Just keep percolating, honey. We'll pick this up again later." He turned and walked out the door, leaving her bent over the back of the chair.

Well, that didn't go so well, she thought to herself. And then she immediately dismissed the issue. She had more important things to worry about than one idiot with too much testosterone. Oddly, she found herself concentrating not on her dad, but on what may or may not be happening to Jack through all this. Did he make it out of the building? The answer would have to wait a while.

COLONEL SONG'S OFFICE

Colonel Song was fit to be tied. *What kind of ceremony was that?* he thought. This has to be the strangest first day on the job he'd ever heard of, much less experienced. First he was treated like a leper by all but one in his new command, and then he was thoroughly humiliated by the dear leader himself. He remembered Captain Youhn's promise of fealty and decided to keep the others waiting while he had a brief private chat with his exec, in case there was even more to this charade than he'd already been slammed with.

"Come in," he barked to the waiting captain. "Have a seat and relax, and I really mean that." Colonel Song knew that regardless of the situation's outcome, he'd need allies somewhere, and this was his first shot at one. "OK, exactly what happened here today? I've been around long enough to know when I've been set up and then slapped down. I need information. I need to know what is really happening. I got the distinct impression that most of the people here have seen this sort of thing often enough for it to have become more than routine, almost boring—is that true?"

Looking over his shoulder, Captain Youhn began in a hushed tone, "Colonel, there is much for you to discover here. Complicating your efforts is this information: we, all of us, have strict orders to delay you in your search for truth as long as possible. Now please hear me out."

The Eyes

The captain held his hands up in a protective gesture, and Colonel Song sat down again. "Don't press too hard too fast. Everyone here is well aware of your background and expertise. In fact, many of us have been holding on to that for some time as a means to retain some sense of sanity. This, too, I will explain in time. Right now it is vitally important that you know many of us are truly here to see you, and us, succeed. Sadly, there are others whose agenda is drastically different. I've discovered much, but I have no way to validate the information. You are just starting right now, gathering information from your perspective as a commander. Perhaps together we can decipher the entire puzzle.

"Use this first session to get a feel for the officers. I don't even know who is a friend and who is here to report on us. There really isn't time to explain now. Rest assured all the officers are expecting some kind of raucous butt chewing for what happened out there. It may be the most important performance of your career. As I told you before, I will be here to help, and I won't let you get into trouble if you'll just trust me. I sense that you have a keen interest in this facility and its purpose and potential, unlike any other commander we've had. I'm eternally grateful, but this isn't the time for the rest of them to know it. At the very least, try to seem more interested in the political affront of today than in the workings of the dam. You'll live longer, and I can start tomorrow with helping you discover what your assignment here is really all about."

Colonel Song was visibly upset, but maintained his cool. "Let's go meet my loyal following," he said with no discernible change in facial expression.

The officers jumped to attention as Colonel Song entered the room and moved to his position at the head of the table. He turned, making no eye contact with any individual officer, and began to speak in a deep, emotionless, baritone. "I want to know who was in charge of the state visit, prior to my arrival, and I want to know now."

An awkward silence ensued, during which he took the opportunity to look at each officer in turn. He used a practiced, slow steady gaze, locking onto each officer's face and exploring it for clues. Finally he got to an officer standing in the back of the room. His nametag read Kim, and as Colonel Song looked at the officer, he noted the officer was glaring back at him. This one clearly felt no threat. This would be a problem, Colonel Song realized. If a major felt no threat during an obviously heated session with his commanding officer who was two ranks above him, something was wrong. One of three scenarios could account for it: he had nothing to do with it and was upset for being lumped together with the perpetrator or he wanted this new commander to fail for some reason or he answered to someone above the commander's grade. Silently and intensely, Colonel Song met his gaze, unflinching, asking the silent question, Do you know? Finally the officer nodded.

"I was in charge of the ceremony, sir."

"Then you have no right to sit here with these professional officers!" Colonel Song decided that he would select this officer for the brunt of his anger. He surmised this major was not exactly a team player anyway. "I have never seen such a debacle! Did you even check in with headquarters to see what it was the dear leader had in mind? Did it occur to you that it was a fairly tremendous waste of manpower to have the entire population of the dam waste an entire day in preparation for a parade of no significance?"

Of course, Colonel Song knew no information would have come; the dear leader's schedule was too sensitive to talk about over the unsecured phone systems. Besides, in truth, the dear leader never kept to his plans anyway, so trying too hard to time things was even more of a waste of time. The best one could do was to be prepared early for his arrival. Still, it was an opportunity to let the real officers understand that their new commander felt strongly about working when it was necessary, and just as strongly about not working when it was unnecessary.

"I assure you," the major used a calm, steady, almost condescending tone, "things went exactly as the dear leader's staff wanted them to go."

"You are dismissed, major! You will report to your quarters and remain there pending further instructions! For now, I'll talk only to your deputy, as you are in grave danger of being relieved of duty." Colonel Song stood as he spoke and pointed at the door.

The decision was swift and irrevocable, and was clearly not in the major's playbook—he had no response. As the major stood digesting this onslaught, he began to think through his strategy. Surely the colonel knew he was overstepping his authority, didn't he? But what if no one had told him where his authority ended? Panic swept his face at the realization that despite his supposedly special position, he was quite alone right now. The colonel seemed to know much more than he should, but how was that possible? *That cursed executive officer! We should have taken him out much earlier*, the major thought to himself. *It had to be him.*

If he were truly relieved of duty, it was tantamount to a death sentence. In the Korean military, if you have no position, you are a detriment to the service. Why should the people feed someone for no reason? A bullet is much cheaper than three meals a day, and the authority to carry out such personnel trivialities rests with the commander—Colonel Song.

"Sir, I can explain." Gone was the confidence and brashness of a few moments earlier; there was clearly fear in his voice.

"I believe I have dismissed you once, Major. Do not make me repeat the order!" Colonel Song stepped forward toward the major, a very threatening gesture since physical rebukes commonly occur in the DPRK.

Silently and quickly, the major walked out the door, yielding a last plaintive glance at Colonel Song as he left. Immediately, the commander turned to the officer nearest him, "Lieutenant, go with him and see that he remains in his room tonight."

"Yes, sir. Shall I…"

"I will not explain or repeat every order I give. I have given you a task. How you do it is your challenge!" Then he continued in a calmer voice, "Now, Lieutenant, do you really need more help with this?"

"N-n-no, sir!" the young man stammered. Then he saluted sharply, spun on his heels, and left. The expression on his face said he couldn't get out of the conference room fast enough.

SEOUL, SOUTH KOREA

Hae-Jung was excited. She had seen the film file on Hideo Ishikawa many times. He was, in her personal opinion, quite a hunk. Sure he was Japanese, and because she was not only Korean but from the Democratic People's Republic of Korea, that should have made him far too evil for her to even consider as a human being, much less a companion. But she didn't really buy all that nationalistic garbage, anyway. She had made a decision long ago that she would not live her life that way. She hadn't been given much, but what she had, a great body and an open mind, she planned to use to her maximum benefit. Certainly South Korea was on a different plane of existence than North Korea. The luxuries available here were plentiful and very satisfying. Still, there was more to be had, so she worked in television and thus had seen the hedonistic pleasures one could attain, if one was smart enough. All one needed for admission was money, and men held the money. How convenient for a woman, she often thought. She had found that the great equalizer, the greatest capacity for the redistribution of that ill-gotten wealth, was every woman's to exploit. She needed only the strength, dedication, and will to try.

Hae-Jung was ready to take the next step from television power to political power. This new political powerhouse from Japan, Mr. Hideo Ishikawa, was natural prey. He was young, powerful, with a reputation

The Eyes

as a lady-killer, and to her advantage, he had almost a fetish-like appreciation for things Korean. It was a combination she planned to manipulate to the greatest extent possible. In addition to scooping all the other networks by hobnobbing with the powerful here in South Korea, she hoped to parlay this visiting dignitary into a ticket to Japan. Yes, she had her assignment and it didn't include international travel, but then her handler hadn't been off the peninsula, and he was far away right now. There was also that annoying go-between, obviously another DPRK agent in the South, Jun-Gae Kim, who always seemed to feel that living in Seoul should have been his exclusive right, and detested anyone else, including Hae-Jung, for intruding into his territory.

Jun-Gae Kim arranged all their meetings with annoying little e-mail messages rife with sexual innuendo, as if she would waste her time on a moron like him. In the power world, he was smaller than she was. It was enough to make her actually enjoy the equally boring e-mails from Colonel Song droning on about his dam. She was supposed to be forwarding any e-mail from the colonel, but as a news reporter, and a darn good one, if she said so herself, she could tell there was nothing significant in anything the colonel had to say. When she chose to answer his e-mails, it was with the firm thought that if she ever got stuck back to the North, it wouldn't hurt to have a career colonel in her pocket. He had resisted all her physical advances, which surprised her at the time, but she was convinced that no man could resist her indefinitely. If she needed him, he would help her. She wondered if he wrote the same type of e-mails to his wife, but the address block always had only two entries, hers and that sniveling Japanese instructor. Then again, his wife probably didn't have access to the Internet or e-mail anyway.

Hae-Jung's job was to become a credible force in the television news industry, a deep plant, as it was known. Well, television is television, news program or entertainment show, it's all virtually the same; give the viewing audience whatever it takes to get them to tune in. If that required showing a little skin, so be it; but she knew that it was scandal, or even better, the rumor of scandal, that got the viewing ratings up and kept them there. This dovetailed nicely with her chosen lifestyle. Now she had an assignment that closed the loop. She was to "befriend" Mr. Ishikawa, and encourage his continued aid in helping Koreans in Japan and, more specifically, to work hard on his recent bill.

Seoul, South Korea

She could care less about the political details. It had something to do with a large number of Middle Eastern men working in Korea. *How tedious*, she thought to herself.

DSRJ, JAPAN

Sitting at the console with the headset on one ear, Carol looked over at Gabe, who, as usual, was amusing the rest of the team. Today he was doing a sidesplitting imitation of the boss, Colonel William, at the peak of one of his tirades on vigilance.

"I know we expect much of you," his voiced scratched its way out in perfect likeness to the soft-spoken, deep-voiced, crusty colonel, "but the hardest thing we ask is for you to stay vigilant. I know you are all professionals, and we pay good money to get the best—you. Still, it gets pretty tough to maintain a state of perennial preparedness. Everything you hear requires your absolute attention. Every conversation you intercept could mean someone's life. By God," and then Gabe raised his voice to a shrill, screeching pitch, "if you overhear someone pissing, it could mean the United States' one chance to take out the kind of regime that threatens the very fabric of our culture!" At this point the entire watch was cracking up.

"For God's sake, Gabe, give it up. You're never going to get on Leno anyway," Carol forced out between fits of laughter. "He's never been quite that bad, anyway."

"You have to admit I've got him down though," Gabe bragged. "He was almost that eaten up after the fiasco with the Chinese embassy."

The Eyes

"Hey, look at Art. I think he just hurled coffee all over that immaculate suit of his."

"Come on, Gabe. I told you not to do that while I'm drinking. I just hope one of these days he walks right up behind you when you're doing it! It'd be poetic justice, though I'd probably still spray my coffee all over the place." Art Morrow was always a sharp dresser, so wearing a cup of java was a big deal that would mean another trip to the dry cleaners. A big man, he originated in Mombassa and naturalized when he was just seventeen years old. He went to Hawaii Pacific University, where his solid six feet four inches and 240 pounds were wasted on the basketball court because the school didn't have a football team. He hadn't lost much of his athleticism, even while tied to the desk these past three years. "How are we supposed to concentrate with you goofing off all the time?"

"Yeah, I love you too, Art." Gabe then motioned for silence and pointed at Carol.

Carol's face had gone cold as she stood holding one hand up, palm out to motion everyone to be quiet. The room became still. Clearly she was focusing on something serious, and had put the other earpiece back over her other ear. Art and Gabe returned to their consoles and tuned in to hear the transmission. After a few minutes, everyone took off his or her headsets. "Well, that is going to elicit a few questions," Carol began.

"It looks like we all better settle in for a while," Gabe added, now acting all business-like. "If I heard that correctly, we have another huge delivery of concrete, enough to pave Death Valley!"

"Great," Carol replied, "but I really think it is time for us to do more than just report what we've heard. What are they doing with that much concrete? It is unlikely that they are building a tunnel with it; they already have tunnels in that sector. It is also unusual to transport this stuff so openly. They can't be trying to keep it a secret, not with a convoy that large! So what do you brilliant analysts think?"

"We get paid to report, not analyze; that's for the geniuses in Langley. But just for fun, I don't mind running this one down. Let's start with what we know. Carol, can you run down the data you've collected to date please?" Gabe asked.

"OK, assuming you aren't doing this for entertainment's sake, here's what I've pieced together so far. Each of the dispatches has a unique source and receiver and we have confirmation of all but the last two from secondary sources, thus ruling out misinformation, at least preliminarily. First we had reports of enough concrete going in to pave a rather lengthy road; the cover story was the Rodong Sinmun release on the completion of the construction of a dam. Fine, but we then have two more reports of similar, if not larger, shipments of concrete to the same place. Using the Internet for an unscientific research source, the amount of concrete delivered to date is over twice the amount used in the total construction of the Hoover Dam. Rudimentary analysis of satellite photography of the area shows reasonable construction of a dam, but no evidence of what happened to the additional concrete. One photo shows the construction of an enormous slab of concrete, but its purpose is unidentified. Then we hear the "dear leader" has personally visited the construction site four times in the past six months. The last time he showed that much interest in a site, we discovered one of his nuclear refining processing plants. According to the sources I've accessed, all his visits were the disingenuous, publicity-type visits, with little or no interaction between him and the people at the dam. That too is disconcerting. Now we have a report of enormous cranes set up all night around the dam site, with visuals indicating a structure proportionally as large as the vertical assembly building at Cape Canaveral going up over the lake. The official line from North Korea is that the structure is to protect the water from contamination, either natural or man-made. That's it in a nutshell; what do you make of it?"

"Not much," Gabe began. "I'm sure I'm not alone in doubting the rationale for a forty-five-foot-thick piece of concrete to protect one body of water. Carol, you've convinced me. Now I'm beginning to see what you mean about this being out of the ordinary. Although I doubt this is of a nuclear nature, there is something very fishy going on here, and I'm afraid with all our attention focused on terrorism in the rest of the world, our Langley analysts may have missed this one. Draft a brief in ESP format, and I'll personally take it to the boss. He can add it to the file he already sent to Langley. Maybe it's time to ask for some kind of initial read on that first report as well. We need some answers here."

"Can do, boss." Carol was happy with the result, but she wasn't a real fan of the Electronic Staff Package (ESP). Sure, every staff officer knows the packages are designed to fit the information needs of management with the electronic transmission medium, but they felt just as stilted as the older hard copy staff packages. This was going to take the better part of this evening to put together; but then she was the one who kept saying this was important.

NATIONAL LAB, WASHINGTON, D.C.

Inside the national lab, Charles returned to the room where Dr. Sanderson and Emiko waited. Though obviously aware of Jack's departure, he made no comment about it.

"This way, Doctors," and he winked obscenely at Emiko. "We've arranged for a tour for you of the area where we've quarantined Dr. Dorman's work. Naturally, you'll have to observe from behind glass, as we haven't fully identified the contents of all of the doctor's experimental material."

They proceeded down the hall Dr. Sanderson knew so well. They had obviously isolated Dr. Dorman's material in the Category V quarantine area, which was sectioned off for the most virulent and dangerous biological material. Either the lab truly did not know what he was working on, or they were putting on one heck of an expensive show for their benefit, or perhaps as a cover—but for whom? Though Dr. Sanderson chaffed at the indignity of being escorted around as if he were a suspicious late-night shopper who'd caught the attention of a security guard, he remained silent, much to Emiko's relief and surprise. At least they could pass on the donning of the space suit–like protective gear, which would have been required if they were to enter the room where Dr. Dorman's work was neatly laid out. As they looked on from afar, a faceless spaceman-looking lab attendant pointed out each apparatus and culture, complete with a monotone, mechanical narration describing the lab's best guess at what was being studied.

"It appears that Dr. Dorman was working on a basic sodium/potassium ladder like one finds in muscle tissue. His notes indicate that this was his current tissue of choice and that this first apparatus was apparently dedicated to the methodical recording of the excitatory threshold in varying ionic concentrations. This is a group of samples," the faceless man continued, "and is the reason for the extra care in handling this material. None of these are labeled, and, frankly, we haven't had the time to run a full analysis of them. Next, we have a new phase of his research, which apparently was begun for the neonatal tissue article he published recently at the request of some of our greatest supporters. Not much here. It even looks like he was a little careless with this one. But if you've read his article, you know his heart was never in this part of his research. Apparently, even his own research wasn't enough to convince him of the value of neonatal research as it impinges on synaptic propagation."

Everything he had said after "Not much here..." was completely lost on Dr. Sanderson. Emiko picked up on her father's famous trance-like focus and engaged in a little subtle top cover.

"Do you mean to say the doctor wasn't careful in his research, or that he was intentionally ignoring this part of the research because he had already concluded it wasn't worth the trouble?"

"Well, honestly," the white-coated lab assistant drawled in what had to be a Mississippi accent, "I don't think he gave a proverbial rat's ass about this experiment. All the rest of his work was fastidiously clean, well kept, and meticulously documented. This one looks like he let a high-school National Science Foundation student run it with little oversight. The apparatus was loosely connected, and some of the fluids had even spilled over the connecting rods. In response to your question, he'd concluded this wasn't worth his time."

Ah, lab assistants, Emiko thought, *always trying to show they have the skills and the information to be a top-level researcher.* She remembered the environment well, and genuinely felt for this unidentified assistant. Her time in the barrel, as they called it, was no picnic emotionally or physically. It was a primary factor in two of her decisions about her career. First she vowed to treat the myriad assistants she

National Lab, Washington, D.C.

would associate with over time with the respect they deserved. They eventually would, after all, be the primary source for full researchers. Even more surprising in her mind was how after being treated that way, researchers would perpetuate the cycle with their own assistants. The second decision that came from her treatment as a lab assistant was the decision to work in her father's lab, despite the obvious comments her working for her famous father would, and did, elicit.

"Well, you are obviously well read and very observant. Thanks for your time and the tour." *That ought to sit well with him*, she thought. *After all, he is doing a good job, and he was more observant than many others in his position would have been.*

COLONEL SONG'S OFFICE

Colonel Song wasn't really sure why he sent the e-mails. Perhaps it was just a way for him to get his thoughts out in a logical manner. Whatever the reason, he always felt calmer after sending them to his colleagues. Knowing they weren't really a part of the NKPA made it easier to write in a casual way, and that had a soothing impact on almost all of his thoughts.

Friends,

My first day of duty here at the dam has been something less than an uplifting experience. The dear leader himself was to arrive and address us as a team, but it didn't work out quite the way I had hoped. His visit was less than perfunctory, totally scripted, and devoid of any meaning for the people working here to build and operate this great dam.

In addition, there seems to be something strange going on here, but I have yet to figure it out. It is almost as if this whole dam is just a ruse, but the sheer size of it seems to defy that logic. Why, when there is so much need, would we expend so many resources for the sake of show? No, I don't believe that for a moment. I will get to the bottom of this, you can be sure. I'll stay in touch.

Colonel Song

USPACOM, HAWAII

At precisely 1400, Admiral Corping strode into the conference room. "OK, who wants to go first?"

The J2, Major General Barns, stood at once. "Bad news, boss. There really isn't anything going on anywhere that would account for something this unusual. There is the regular preparation for the Ulchi Focus Lens combat exercise and the long-range planning for the other annual exercises, but we haven't so much as brought up the phrase "Team Spirit" yet this year. We did get some information from the folks over at DSRJ. It doesn't seem all that earth shattering, but it is a bit odd. I'm having the guys run it to ground now."

"Well, let's hear what you know so far; perhaps the combined wisdom here in the room can help." The admiral leaned forward in his chair.

"Well, we have reports of an enormous amount of concrete going to the dam site near the DMZ. I don't have reliable estimates on the tonnage or volume, but the folks at DSRJ seem to think it is well over the amount used in the construction of the Hoover Dam. Now remember, these are our listening post folks who are doing a great job of thinking, not just recording and passing along information. The site chief was hesitant but concerned that someone with greater expertise would discover this couldn't be true, casting doubt on all their reporting. Apparently, it has been happening over a long period of time. It might not have surfaced if the "dear leader" himself had not visited the site personally at least four times in the past six months. That is all the information I have right now. I'm working with the National Military Command Center to see if we can find out if there are any corollary reports and to see if we can get one of the satellites to fly over and focus in on that construction site. Once we get something, I'll get it to the civil engineering folks for their spin and the POLMIL folks to see what they make of the visits by Kim Jong Il."

Admiral Corping sat quietly for a moment, then turned to his civil engineer. "I know you don't have much to go on, Stan, but any thoughts on the excess of concrete going into that site so close to the DMZ? Could it be more tunnels?"

"Well, sir, it could certainly be tunnels. But since we already know they have tunnels in that area and they know we know they have those tunnels, it defies logic to go to all the trouble of trying to build new ones. I'm not saying that it isn't happening, but combining it with the summit meeting they've proposed, something just doesn't add up. I'll be very interested to see what the satellite photos reveal, if anything. In the meantime, I'll get my construction guys working on it. We were sending another of those joint contact teams out next week anyway, so adding South Korea to their itinerary won't cause any alarm whatsoever. If any of you have members who might be helpful in this endeavor, let my exec know and we'll build them into the team. The timing is perfect as we don't send the country requests for diplomatic visas out for another seventy-two hours, except for those going into Mongolia, and as for the others, they can wait in South Korea for that portion of the trip."

"OK," Admiral Corping wrapped up, "let's get a team together to see what we have here. I'd like a copy of the team makeup and the itinerary of their trip, but nothing fancy. Don't wait for me to make any decisions either. I'm just curious about whom we will need to add. I already had the concept brief for this from POLMIL, and unless there are any changes aside from these additions, the trip is still approved and funded." He stood and walked toward the door where his always-worried-looking executive officer stood waiting to pre-brief him on the next meeting in his event-packed day.

SEOUL, SOUTH KOREA

The director of the Korean Central Intelligence Agency, Kim Cheun Do, was worried. Certainly the Korean version of the US CIA needed permission from no one to act, but this field operation had taken an ominous turn. He turned to his deputy, the only female member of the KCIA and, as a longtime lover, the only person he really trusted. "Kora Lee, it is one thing to establish a deep plant in the DPRK; we have many. But now that he has gained their trust, they are trying to use him as a deep plant in the United States. The repercussions of this double twist could be extreme. How is it they have an agent in the United States whom we know nothing about? How did they get him in?"

"From what I have heard, it is a she; her name is Yin Hee, Cheun Do" Kora Lee replied smiling. "That is probably half the reason. It seems we Koreans have trouble believing women can handle risky assignments. They aren't so squeamish in the North. If Ohl Suk's job is to be her handler in the United States that seems a relatively mild issue."

"No. If the United States finds he is there and handling a North Korean deep plant, it will appear to them an act of treachery. I just don't know what we can do about it." He sloshed down the rest of the sake and poured another glass.

The Eyes

"Well," the petite young women cooed as she walked over to him, "we could always try the completely unexpected. We could tell our counterparts what we know about her and ask them to work with us. You men always look for the hardest solutions to straightforward problems."

"That's probably because we have to try to figure out how to deal with women," he laughed and pulled her toward him. "My first reaction is revulsion, but most of your suggestions have turned out quite well, so I will mull this over. Ohl Suk is one of our best; perhaps sharing is the right answer."

NATIONAL LAB, RESIDENT HALL

Dr. Sanderson was not amused. In his mind, this turn of events certainly complicated the "whodunit" in Dr. Dorman's disappearance. It seemed far from a mystery to the authorities there in Washington. With that thought came an instantly uncomfortable consciousness about his own, Emiko's, and Jack's prospects, or lack thereof, for a viable future. So far, no one had come to speak with him or interrogate him, but he could sense that something was still happening down the hall, where Emiko had been taken. Fear welled up in his throat as he leaned against the door trying to decipher the noises he heard. There was an abrupt silence. He could see through the peephole that one of the goons was walking back down the hallway, past his door, chuckling aloud. While he felt his bile surfacing in anger from the frustration of his impotent state, he concluded ultimately that nothing too horrible could have happened; not enough time had passed. Just as quickly, he concluded that he was just rationalizing because there was little he could do about it anyway.

The room Dr. Sanderson was in was not designed as a prison cell. It was originally designed for interns and other researchers actually welcomed by the institution, so the furnishings were really quite comfortable. As he walked through the two-room suite, he found the furnishings better than the average hotel. He discovered a plush king-size bed, a thirty-five-inch television with endless channels and movies, and a phone on the desk by the bed. Obviously, he thought, it won't work. Nevertheless, he elected to see if his captors had failed to disconnect it. He was stunned to hear a dial tone when he picked up the handset. He immediately hung up. *Now, how do I call room to room*, he thought to himself, *and what room is Emi-chan in*?

A PUBLIC PHONE,
WASHINGTON, D.C.

"Carlos? This is Jack, from Dr. Dorman's lab. Remember me?"

"Hola, que tal, amigo? Of course, I remember you! How are you and what do you want? You wouldn't call on trivial little Carlos just to check on his life's progress." Carlos was fairly direct, though the happiness in his voice gave away his mock annoyance.

"OK, you got me. I could be a little better at staying in touch," Jack replied meekly. "But you are right; I need your help. Where in the world are you? Cell phones make it difficult to tell."

"I'm moving up in the world, amigo. I'm in Washington, D.C., the nation's capital! Now the toilets I clean are very important toilets! You know, if this keeps up and I keep working really hard, I might get a shot at toilets in the Pentagon or even the White House!" His laughter was infectious. "What can I do for you, Jack?"

"I'm also here in D.C. I came out with, well, let's just leave it at that for now. Why I'm here and how it all came to pass is a long story—where can we meet? I need to talk to you but not on the phone."

"OK, 'Mister I've-Got-a-Secret.' How about that Italian restaurant, La Portas, on Duke Street? I can meet you there tonight at about six?"

"Perfect, Carlos. Dinner's on me!"

"Of course it is, amigo."

NATIONAL LAB, WASHINGTON, D.C.

Dr. Sanderson decided to take a gamble and dialed zero. After four rings, he heard a young woman's voice, "Front desk, how may I help you?"

Hoping beyond hope the rooms were subcontracted like everything else in the building had been, Dr. Sanderson assumed the most casual tone he could muster, given his increasing excitement.

"I just checked in with my daughter, but we took different paths to our rooms, so I don't know what room she is in."

"No problem, sir. We have only one woman scheduled for arrival. She's in room 109, just down the hall from you, but I'll connect you to her room so that you can see if she's there rather than walk down the hall for nothing. In the future, you can call other rooms directly by dialing seven then the three-digit room number."

The phone rang again.

In Emiko's room, she just stared at the ringing phone. Should she answer it? Who knew she was here? For that matter, why did the phone work at all? In the span of three rings, she concluded that answering the phone provided no risk, as she was a captive anyway. Not answering would probably just annoy the person on the other end.

"Hello," she said softly.

"Emiko! Are you OK?" There was relief, anxiety, and anger all mixed together in Dr. Sanderson's voice. "Dad! I'm fine. How did you manage to…?"

"We can discuss that later. Has anyone told you what is coming next?"

"No, but one of the goons threatened me with his company later this evening. But don't worry. I'll be ready, I assure you. His interest seemed decidedly personal, not part of whatever we are here to do. Has anyone hurt you?"

"No, Emiko. No one has been by to talk to me at all. Let's hang up for now. Perhaps this telephone oversight will continue. To reach me just dial 7-1-0-0 and it should ring here in my room, or so the operator said. If it doesn't, I can't see how the attempt would make our situation any worse. If that goon comes back for you, don't do anything foolish that would cost you your life. I'll call if I find out any more."

The phone went dead, and she thought about her dad's advice as she hung up the receiver. Well, some indignities are probably worth my life, but I will not be treated like a piece of meat without it costing someone something. Even as she thought it, she knew she'd have to be more lucky than strong to have any impact on that behemoth. So like the practical lady she was, she dismissed the thoughts and decided to take a bath. At least the rooms were well appointed and comfortable.

Dr. Sanderson walked over to the desk and sat down. He took a notepad and a pen out of the top drawer. Absently, he began doodling while he tried to reason out what was happening. He decided he needed to focus on what he'd found in the Dr. Dorman notes. He was sure Emiko had also seen the penciled word "video" in the margin of the spreadsheet page next to the growth median line. There had been another file, but all it contained were photos of the apparatus, not the experiment, and no videotape at all, so he had dismissed them. Perhaps there was something in those pictures he needed to see again. He decided that he'd push to be given another opportunity to review the files and request the original list of items taken from the lab. So far, their treatment had been only rude, not threatening, and Jack had warned Emiko and Dr. Sanderson as much from his own experience with national security at Dr. Dorman's lab.

EARLY MORNING,
COLONEL SONG'S QUARTERS

"Sir, Captains Youhn and Jung with Major Kim as ordered," Jung announced once they returned to Colonel Song's quarters. As the colonel opened the door, the two captains looked at each other and left.

"Well, Kim," the colonel began in an even tone. "What do you propose I do with you now? You've clearly sabotaged a visit by none other than the dear leader himself. With that as a backdrop for my first day here, I hardly think there is much I can gain by keeping you. I believe there is little alternative to having you executed this evening in front of everyone—do you?"

"Sir, I-I-I," Kim stammered, and then steeled himself. It was over for him unless he did or said something dramatic. "I believed you already knew." There, he'd committed himself now.

"Knew what, Major?" The colonel held him steady in his gaze. There was no turning back for the major at this point. It appeared to him that he had been set up. His life would now be forfeited either way. All he had left was to stall for time.

"Well, by now you are surely aware this is not really a hydroelectric dam. Yes, it is a dam, and a very large one at that, but it has no working parts. If you let me, I'll show you. I can also tell you who is here to help you and who is here to see you fail. I, however, need your word that I will not be executed."

"You seem to be in no position to dictate demands, Kim! I have no way of knowing whether or not this is just a continuation of the spiteful plan you began during the ceremony. What I do know is that I have done nothing wrong in my career, which makes it a little difficult for me to believe that I have been deliberately set up to fail for any reason. As far as I know, I have no enemies on staff. I have nothing but an insolent major with a story about some huge conspiracy unraveling on my watch."

"I think not, Colonel. First, you have already spoken with Captain Youhn, so you have to know something is up. Also, you're talking with me, and that convinces me you are at least intrigued. I, on the other hand, have no choice but to gamble; my life hangs in the balance."

"If you are telling the truth, then you know you will be killed by whoever set this up, anyway, so what is the point in postponing the inevitable?" The colonel turned and fixed his gaze on the major again. He could see that the man was sweating and seemed to have lost his attitude altogether. He was either a very good actor, or really believed he was using his last chance to save his own life.

"You would be surprised how strongly one wishes to remain alive when you can see death so close at hand, Colonel."

"Very well. You will work closely with and, need I say, for Captain Youhn. That alone will seem a grave punishment, and you will forfeit your major's rank, but not just yet. I need outward symbols to remain intact until I have a better understanding of this development. After lunch today, you will arrange for me to see the dam's hydroelectric motors, or the areas where they are not. And, Major, one small slipup and I will shoot you in the head myself, on the spot. Is that clear?"

"Yes, Colonel. You are in for a very full, interesting day to say the least." The major saluted, turned sharply, and departed the colonel's quarters.

PYONGYANG, DPRK

The dear leader needed to take some action. The news on the minia-ture army of Arabs was that they were finally coming along—a good sign. The world will wonder why we did not use our own soldiers for the invasion of the Republic of Korea; surely they would be harder to identify. He smiled as he thought that the answer was so clear that most would not fathom it for a long time. It was one of the ironies of the global situation. With all the conflict in the Middle East, specifically against the United States, there was still a significant loophole in world interaction. It turns out that even while travel between Japan and the United States, two seemingly inseparable allies, still had restrictions, this was not so between Iran and Japan. While an American had to have either a passport or a military ID and orders, any Iranian citizen could travel to Japan unchallenged. With the ever-widening gap in economic standards between the two countries, the number of Iranians traveling to Japan in search of economic gain was reaching alarming proportions, at least in Japanese eyes. In Roppongi, Akasuka, and even in the classy Ginza district, with some of the most expensive real estate on the planet, groups of Iranians gathered in parks and ethnic restaurants and stores.

The result was a large population of Middle Eastern men in the streets of Japan. Every attempt to control, corral, or deport them was met with the legal backlash that discrimination and intolerance always awaken. For the authorities, it was a security nightmare.

It was this loophole Kim Jong Il would exploit. The Arab volunteers would have their eyes removed in the desert and have the weapon systems installed in Germany; then the men would travel to Japan. When enough had collated in Japan, part two of the plan would begin.

It was fairly simple, and the groundwork had been laid years earlier. A group of these Middle Eastern immigrants would be afforded a tour of South Korea, in an effort to help both parties. Perhaps the men could find steady legitimate work in South Korea, so the logic went, and perhaps South Korea could use the help of these relatively skilled laborers. The concept had strong support in the Japanese diet, and had received a reasonably warm response from South Korea.

The Japanese diet member had been carefully selected. He had, on his own, decided the plight of expatriate Koreans in Japan was an issue he could exploit for political gain. He was the perfect patsy. A self-important jerk, he also had the arrogance that being a handsome, powerful single male made so predictably manipulative. All the Japanese government had to do was match him with the right female operative and it would be just like joining the Japanese diet outright. The ideal operative was already in place in Seoul. She was the female mirror image of the senator's ideology—arrogant, self-important, and interested first and foremost in self-promotion. As a pair, these two would be frightening. Fortunately, their identical motivations made them safe. They would each spend all their time trying to use the other, to their mutual destruction.

As long as the timing was right, the plan would be executed on all fronts simultaneously, preventing anyone from discovering the nature of any one event until far too late. The biggest controversy was over how many were needed for the operation. Safety would dictate at least one technologically enhanced man per target. Jong Il wanted overkill. If one can destroy a target with one hit, and the target is critical, then use two or more independent strikes to make sure it is killed. These volunteers expected to give their lives in this event—may as well use them all. There wasn't much left for them in this life anyway; longevity wasn't one of the studies performed in the development of these living weapon systems.

HEADQUARTERS, US FORCES, KOREA

Brigadier General Hackwill was finishing his presentation. Actually, it was more speculation than fact, but that was what he'd been asked for.

"So as you can see, General, the only thing going on anywhere near the DMZ is the final construction on the dam at Cho Mya. My guess is Jong Il wants to discuss PACOM's aid visit with the admiral. Why he would think a naval officer would know anything about land construction just shows how little he knows."

Sitting at the head of his conference room table, surrounded by his staff, General Hodge was reflective. He ran the kind of meetings that fostered real conversation, and he needed some advice from his staff this time. He began carefully.

"When I sent the dispatch to Undersecretary of State Guillen, he responded within an hour; so you know the State Department is jumping on this one. Unfortunately for all of us, no one seems to know what is going on."

"When and if he makes this semi-summit with the admiral, or the admiral and I, if I can swing it…" General Hodge paused for the chuckling he knew would come, "then it will be the second time in three months that Kim Jong Il has had a public meeting. That is more external contact for Kim Jong Il than he normally makes in a year. He's contacted the West before, but this is the first time he's done it unannounced and without first contacting Chinese authorities. I don't really know what is going on. It could be either of two extremes, or it could be nothing. If we are at the edge of some threshold, and North Korea is going to act in some fashion, we'd better be ready for anything. This is the time to buckle down and get our people ready. I need you all to be on this every minute. Even getting ourselves ready could send the wrong or precipitating signal to the DPRK. For the time being, I want us to try not to take any overt action of any kind. We don't want our ROK compatriots to think anything is happening, because we don't know if it is. On the other hand, it is time to get past the perennial peacetime training mentality and convince our men and women that readiness is now a real priority that could save their lives."

"Sir, we are fortunate on the timing in one way, the scheduled tunnel sweep," General Drake stated professionally. "I'll have more of our folks join the group this time just for information gathering. The ROK asked for greater participation last time, so this shouldn't raise any eyebrows. Since we always ramp up the readiness issue during these sweeps, we can do it surreptitiously."

"OK. I'll be back in four days, if the air force can keep those jets flying." Everyone got a chuckle out of that except Major General Charles McBride, the Director of Operations, or DO. The lone, or token, air force officer on staff, he took infinite abuse over the condition of the C-135s dedicated to CINC travel. Considering their purpose was to convey the most senior military leaders, it seemed outrageous to be flying aircraft that were forty years old. Maintenance for upkeep of the small fleet was tasked to its limit all the time. In addition, because of the distances in the Pacific Area of Responsibility, or AOR, backup aircraft had to be pre-positioned all over the theater every time one of the commanders traveled, lest they become stranded. Sadly, for many of the nations to be visited, commercial airlift simply wasn't a possibility. Besides, those in the CINC positions were what are known as directed-use travelers. Because of the sensitivity of their responsibilities, they had to be capable of receiving extremely secure transmissions from the National Command Authority every minute of every day, and flying was no exception. In fact, the rules read that it required a waiver from the secretary of defense for a CINC to fly in anything other than the specially outfitted aircraft.

"They'll fly," Major General McBride laughed. He'd long ago gotten used to being picked on. "When do you want to depart? I'll get in touch with PACAF and make sure the schedule works."

"I don't get to choose," the four-star general grinned. "The PACAF staff has already told me when I'll be leaving. I sure thought by the time I got to be a four star, I'd be the one deciding when I went somewhere and where I would go, but I guess that was wishful thinking." The room erupted in laughter. The truth was his schedule hadn't been under his to control since the day he pinned on the rank of colonel. What little personal time he had belonged to his long-suffering wife of thirty-four years. Amy had been an angel through all the moves and separations.

"Yes, sir, I'll make sure we get a positive launch from PACAF and have command post track the mission. If we can't control the flights, the least we can do is keep you informed of the progress in real time."

"Thanks, Chuck, I'd appreciate that. Amy will be going with me this time. What a surprise, eh? Funny she never wants to go when I travel here in Korea, but let me pass through Hawaii, and suddenly she just has to go somewhere."

At least now, most of the time when he traveled, she could officially accompany him. For this trip, Amy had decided she'd go as far as Hawaii and take a vacation from the bitter Korean winter while her hubby doddered off to Washington. Their only daughter, Jillian, was a starter on the Hawaii Pacific University volleyball team. A chance not only to watch her play, but also to spend some time with her would be a real treat for the general's wife. She had been very pleased with this surprise trip, and she had let him know it.

SPACECOM HEADQUARTERS, PETERSON AFB, COLORADO

The satellite was to track from north to south from pole to pole along a great circular pathway. It had already tracked over the former Soviet Union, down across Mongolia, China, the Korean peninsula, and Okinawa before heading south of the equator. The focus lay on the area just north of the DMZ, but the photographs showed nothing remarkable. At that point, the cameras zoomed in for some incredible photographic images of what looked like a normal dam. This pathway would be monitored every other day, and the photos would be carefully compared for changes and any sign of activity out of the ordinary.

As the photos were laid out on the table, the ones depicting the rest of the earth were set off to one side. Major Erin Ma began trying to make out the approach azimuth of the satellite as it was tracing across the Korean peninsula. To get a better feel for the unusual perspective, she went backward through sequenced photos. As she made out the outlines of Lake Baikal and then moved south through the Gobi, she came across a very-well-lit area in what should have been an isolated part of the desert, just across the border from China.

China and Mongolia were part of her area of analysis. With her Chinese heritage, the region was also of personal interest to her. What she was looking at now appeared to be the beginnings of a fairly large community. It was significantly unusual since the inhabitants in that part of the world usually had access only to campfires, while this was clearly an electrically lit facility. She decided to pull out imagery of the desert from the past two years to see if she could determine when it had been set up. She'd have to settle for only a few images per year, since this part of the desert had little in the way of interesting features worthy of surveillance. After a little over an hour, she had discovered that the community in the desert was less than eighteen months old. The total lack of neighboring civilizations or nearby man-made features increased her curiosity. She decided to include the anomaly and a very brief summary with the photos of the dam. Whoever was asking for the special sweep of the area might be interested in the new inhabitants.

LA PORTAS RESTAURANT

Jack arrived fifteen minutes early after taking a very circuitous route. Carlos was already at the bar, enjoying a Corona and watching the locals, well, some of the locals, the female ones to be exact. Jack walked over to him.

"Hola, Carlos! Good to see you again." The two gripped fists in a handshake. "Shall we move into the dining room?"

"With all do respect, Jack, why don't we just grab a table here in the bar area? The scenery is much more to my liking." His grin told Jack he hadn't changed much.

"Fine, Carlos. But I do hope you'll be able to focus on the conversation just a little. Let's take that table by the wall. You can see the whole room, and I don't have to worry about anyone behind me."

"Man, you've really gotten paranoid. I always thought you were the cool-headed one. Let's go. I'll kill this one, which is also on you, and we can start fresh." He gulped the last quarter of his beer and put the glass on the bar. "Barkeep, we'll be moving over to that table. Can you have a waitress come visit us? If it's OK, we'll eat here in the bar."

"No problem," the barkeeper responded as he motioned to a slender young woman who appeared too young to work in an establishment that served alcohol.

"Thanks," Carlos responded. "By the way, I'll have another Corona. And you, Jack?" He was grinning at his friend, knowing it was he the bill would come to at the end of the evening.

"I'll have a glass of the house Chianti," Jack replied. Carlos's easygoing demeanor was infectious. It was a relief to be with someone who he'd known before all this had begun. As they waited for the waitress, Jack filled Carlos in on the strange disappearance of Dr. Dorman, Jack's move to Dr. Sanderson's lab, and why they had come to Washington. As he started explaining Dr. Dorman's work, Carlos interrupted.

"Whoa, my man. You haven't even asked me about the important toilets yet. Slow down a little; I'm having trouble keeping up. Let's order. I'm starved, and here is our lovely waitress now. I think I'll have the focaccia bread with the olives and hummus for an appetizer, and then I'll have the mahimahi for dinner. Also, I think I'm ready for a glass of you house chardonnay. Jack?"

"I'll have the same—sounds great. Does that come with a salad?

"Yes, sir. What kind of dressing for you?" she said with a smile.

"The vinaigrette for me. Carlos?"

"I'll have ranch, please."

After she left, Carlos reentered the conversation. "OK, so you're telling me that Dr. Dorman is gone, but you don't think he went home to the Middle East?"

"Correct, at least not willingly. He had a horrible childhood experience. His father was killed in front of his eyes, by the government, I presume. Then he and his family took a long journey to America. I can't see him suddenly returning to those roots."

"OK, then what do you think happened to him?"

"Well, until we got here, I thought someone may have kidnapped him for his research. But now I'm not so sure it isn't us, meaning our own government. After all, when I left Emiko and Dr. Sanderson, things were looking pretty intense."

"In what way?"

"Well, I left them at the main lab because it looked as if we weren't going to be allowed to leave on our own if I waited any longer. The head security dude, some guy named Charles, looked like your typical bad guy from a movie, complete with seedy mustache if you can believe that. I won't know the outcome of their visit to the lab until later tonight when they are supposed to return to the hotel. But if all went well, you'd think they would have called me. Come to think of it, I may need your help on this too. We are supposed to meet at eight tonight at the sports bar across the street from the Marriott. It would look more natural if I'm not just sitting there alone watching the door. Do you think you can find it in your heart to accompany me? If they aren't going to return, chances are someone is waiting for me at the hotel."

"Sure thing, amigo. You just said you'd need my help in this as well; what else do you have in mind?"

"I'm going to need access to the main lab, but I can hardly walk in, show my ID, and expect things to go smoothly. Do you think you could get me on one of the crews?"

"Gee, I don't know, Jack. It takes a lot of training and dedication to do the kind of job we at Hectors put forth as a quality product." He had said it with a straight face and conviction, but at this point his poker face vanished and he and Jack cracked up. "I'll take you in myself. That way if you screw up, I can cover for you and say you're a trainee. Are you thinking about doing this sometime soon, like tomorrow?"

"I don't know, Carlos. It won't be necessary at all if Dr. Sanderson and Emiko show up at the hotel."

"The look on your face tells me that it's not likely, so let's plan on it for tomorrow morning. Amigo, you are staying at my place. It's not too small; I even have an extra bed!"

"You are too much, Carlos. Thanks!"

FRANK'S HARDWARE STORE

Lee entered the main floor of the hardware store and began his usual routine inventory for next week's order. He started in the back of the store where the true hardware items were: nuts, bolts, wire, plumbing, electrical supplies, and the sort of things that simply always had to be in stock. The front of the store had the bicycles, lawn mowers, and other items slightly harder to spirit away in a pocket or under a shirt. It was tedious—every size and quantity represented a separate entity. Thank goodness he had convinced Frank to update the store to the bar code system. It used to take three days to do the order. It still took the better part of a day, but at least it wasn't all hand written.

Frank didn't trust technology, but when Lee showed him he could manually review every item he was ordering on screen from the desktop in real time, Frank's desire for a new toy overcame his resistance to change, and the system was installed. In the year since they did so, only one item had been ordered in error, and that was because they forgot to clear the item while demonstrating the system to Frank.

Shortly after Lee started the inventory, a patron entered the store activating the familiar "ding" of the optical security bell. Lee paid little heed; this customer would have to be Yin Hee's baby. After a few moments, the customer wandered back to where Lee was working and asked, "Do you work here?"

The Eyes

"Yes," Lee answered pleasantly, "how can I help you?"

"I'm looking for a small air-pressure washer. Do you carry them?"

"No, I'm sorry, we don't yet. Though the owner is trying to figure out which brands will be most effective for us to carry. Do you know which brand you're looking for?"

"No, I don't. Thanks anyway." The young man left, and after he walked out the front door, Lee took a quick look around. "Yin Hee?" he called out. *Well, she is really playing quite the little minx, isn't she?* he thought. After a moment or two of more serious looking, he started to become concerned. He headed toward the back of the store. "Frank, did Yin Hee come back here?"

"Not that I saw. The women's restroom door is open, so she isn't in there either." Frank stated it just a little too casually for Lee.

True panic gripped Lee. "She's gone!" he shouted.

"Calm down, lover boy," as Frank grinned at him, to Lee's horror. "You two didn't think you were fooling anybody, I hope. She probably just headed next door for a soda or something. I'll take the floor, and you can go check if you like."

"Thanks, Frank. And we'll discuss this 'lover boy' thing later." Lee headed down the center aisle to the front door.

"I can't wait!" Frank laughed after him. *What a goofball*, Frank thought. *How did Lee think anyone would miss the way he has started to drool like a fool every time Yin Hee smiles.*

Shaking his head, Frank turned his attention to the rather impressive progress Lee had made preparing next week's order. *I hate to admit it*, he thought, *but this system is as cool as it gets!* He then placed the mark on the screen just as he was taught. The vender and Lee thought they'd fooled Frank, but he knew the mark was a spacer so Lee could always know where Frank had taken over for him and could quality check his work. *Damn*, he thought, *no respect at all!*

Yin Hee struggled with the handcuffs to no avail. After the two cops had dragged her out the front door and into the waiting police car, she had become convinced that screaming would not help her. To the average person on the street, it would appear that another shoplifter was being taken into custody. How could she expect to generate any assistance from these people, when they would all believe, without question, that she must have done something wrong or she wouldn't be taken into custody?

Seated in front of her, driving slowly while puffing on a Marlboro, Ohl Suk gave no sign of what was happening or why.

Safely separated from the panic-stricken woman in the car by the steel mesh of the cruiser, he had the luxury of time. She had no idea what was going on or was to happen to her, and he felt no great need to explain anything to her. She was simply a tool, after all, and one that had caused him considerable aggravation in his estimation.

Yin Hee tried to stay alert. Finally she gave in to the increasing darkness. In a way, as she sat back and sank into the ever-deepening abyss within her mind, she thought how much more pleasant this was than the never-ending terror of waiting for this day to arrive—she drifted off.

HEADQUARTERS, PACOM, HAWAII

Admiral Corping called Colonel Cannen into his office. "What do you think is going on?" he asked as he smiled at his executive officer. "General Hodge has suddenly dropped all signs of cynicism toward me. He even set up the trip to Washington from start to finish, and he hasn't played any cards that I can see."

"Boss, I think that just adds to the gravity of this event. You got a classified e-mail about ten minutes ago that emphasizes Washington's concern over this issue. Apparently, they have no more idea what is going on than we do. I suspect General Hodge has decided this is bigger than the friendly competition between the two of you—I think he's right. I've been trying to fathom what would cause this unprecedented meeting between Jong Il and a US military admiral. North Korea rather routinely dismisses the United Nations Command as an insignificant body with no authority, but why would PACOM be a better substitute? I really can't say I've thought of anything terribly significant, but you have some folks who might be able to help us out."

"Who might that be?" The admiral had to admit that he too was at a loss for what would drive the DPRK to ask for a meeting at his level instead of their usual demands for a summit or at least a meeting with the secretary of state.

The Eyes

"The folks at the Asia Pacific Center for Security Studies. You set it up, and we've spent a considerable amount of money manning it with local area experts. I believe there is a professor of Korean Studies on staff; perhaps the civilian insight might be helpful this time. Naturally, his analysis will answer to his predisposed conclusions, but we've turned up nothing so far."

"Great idea. When can we get him up here?" Admiral Corping liked the school. He met every class in person when he was in Honolulu during their three-month sessions.

Colonel Cannen grinned, "He'll be here in about twenty minutes, sir. I'll bring him to your office when he gets here. Your calendar is free until then." He walked out of the admiral's office whistling.

"Sometimes you really scare me, Ralph. Do you know that?" Admiral Corping shouted after the colonel as he left the room. He then turned back to his computer screen to send out a few more Electronic Staff Packages.

"Admiral, Dr. Woods is here to see you," Colonel Cannen announced.

"Please send him in." Admiral Corping stood and walked toward the door. "Dr. Woods, how kind of you to come all the way up here. How are preparations for our next class coming along?" He shook the younger man's hand and motioned for him to have a seat on the leather couch. Dr. Woods wore a conservative suit and carried himself with confidence.

Colonel Cannen had already placed a pitcher of ice water, glasses, and a small array of sodas on a tray on the coffee table. "Please, help yourself," the admiral said as he sat down in the matching leather chair next to the couch.

"Thanks, Admiral, I will. The next class will be simpler than the last because we've had to cancel it for funding reasons. This isn't the proper forum for bringing that up, and I'll get hell for it later, I'm sure, but you did ask, sir. What can I do for you today?"

"Oh, that's right. We have the issue of paying for all the temporary duty expenses and travel of the visiting students to work out. With luck, I'll even remember not to mention you when I address it with the director. At any rate, I presume you have heard that Kim Jong Il has requested a meeting with me?"

"Yes, sir, I have heard that. It's the kind of information you might expect to travel quickly."

"Well, what do you think that madman wants to talk about?" Admiral Corping knew that would elicit a strong response, as Dr. Woods was rather vocal in his assessment that the West simply didn't read the dear leader correctly.

"First of all, you already know I don't buy into the "madman" theory. I've heard many of the stories, but nothing that would pass any real scrutiny. The honest truth is that we don't know very much about him. What we can ascertain through his actions, however, indicates a shrewd politician. One who plays the hand he's been dealt carefully, albeit theatrically. He has managed a considerable amount of international influence for heading a nation with precious little to sell to the world. I have developed a theory, along with some of my colleagues that may be of interest at this juncture. You must understand, however, this is nothing more than counseled conjecture—a guess."

"Guesses are very helpful in the absence of data, Doctor. I'm starved for some line of thought to take with me to Washington. We are the US first line of contact and defense in reference to North Korea. I don't have much to tell Washington right now. Let's hear your thoughts." Admiral Corping withdrew a pad and pen from the table and waited while Dr. Woods drank some water.

"Well, sir, for some time now we have been reviewing the various theories regarding the ultimate transition from today's two-Korea situation. I won't bore you with a recap; I know you get them from us and from your planners on a regular basis. Our new effort was an attempt to step out of our comfort zone and look at what we haven't been considering. Everyone is familiar with the notion that history repeats itself over time. The East German–West German transition has baited the world for Korea to follow suit; yet so far this has not occurred. Despite both North and South Korea's vehement assertions that reunification is a primary goal, and even with the United States, China, Japan, and Russia singing a supportive refrain, the sad truth is that no matter the conditions, a sudden change resulting in consolidation between the two Koreas would be catastrophic to the global economy. The very first thing that would have to happen would be to reinforce the DMZ, not to keep two warring nations apart, but to stem the human flood from the

183

The Eyes

North to the South. Short of a brutal wall the world is unlikely to allow or support, the effort would fail and South Korea would be inundated with North Koreans seeking a better life. Being homeless in South Korea would be an improvement over most North Korean existences today. China wouldn't escape the onslaught either. The bottom line is we really hope things will just muddle along pretty much as they have for the past half-century. That too is problematic because it is a very unlikely future, if not impossible. With a consistently contracting economy, little outside contact, and an ever-shrinking resource base, North Korea is a tinderbox of possibilities, none of them very pleasant. But what if their leader isn't a madman? What if he has a strategy that will allow him to take over the peninsula? After all, without any regard for the damage an attack on the South would cause, the prize would be a much better overall situation. Of all nations on earth, North Korea would be least affected by a global economic meltdown." Dr. Woods leaned toward the admiral and continued, "You realize we are only speculating, but we thought you should hear this, even if it is neither pleasant nor the mainstream thought process."

"Are you suggesting, Doctor, that Kim Jong Il might be planning to start another war, and in the same breath try to assert he isn't mad? I find that very hard to swallow." Admiral Corping jotted down a few notes and then looked up. "What would be the precipitating factor, Doctor, if your theory were to have merit? Is there something we should be looking for that might give us an indication?"

"That is a much more difficult question, sir. I would continue to look for the same signals we now anticipate for impending action, but the trigger is likely to be an internal switch, and therefore unknowable externally. I'm not suggesting you take this back to Washington as our assessment of what will or even may be happening. I'm recommending only that you take the thought to the president and see if the combined resources of our intelligence and the State Department's might be able to either dispel the possibility or start looking at it differently. Clearly, something is going on, and this might well be the only sign we get; prudence would suggest greater attention to the peninsula. I can only offer my advice, but it might be worth elevating the military readiness and protection status of our forces both in Korea and in Japan. Naturally, the balancing act is doing so in a non-provocative manner, which

Headquarters, Pacom, Hawaii

I leave to you and your qualified staffs." Dr. Woods stood, knowing the busy schedule the admiral kept. "I won't keep you, sir. If you want any of this described in greater detail, just have Colonel Cannen contact me."

Admiral Corping stood and shook the doctor's hand. "Thanks for coming and for the theories. I will take them back to Washington. Before that, though, General Hodge will be here in a few days. He and I will be making this trip together, and, yes, as a team this time. Could you come by for a discussion session with us? He may have some insight from his people that you and I don't have access to, and, of course, he met with the president personally not long ago."

"Of course, Admiral. Just have your folks let me know when to be here." Dr. Woods nodded to Colonel Cannen and walked out into the front office. Waiting there was General Minter, COPACAF, as the Commander of Pacific Air Forces was known. The doctor couldn't help but wonder how these men had any kind of personal life whatsoever.

DR. SANDERSON'S ROOM, WASHINGTON LAB

With some trepidation, Dr. Sanderson answered the ringing phone. Having decided compliance was his best defense for now, he had showered and amused himself watching television for the past two hours. Knowing Emiko was at least being left alone was calming. Now it looked as if things were about to begin again. "Hello, Dr. Sanderson here," he spoke into the handset.

"Ah, Doctor," Charles voice came through loud and clear. "It is time for us to meet again in the conference room. I have something to show you that I believe you will find...interesting. Your rooms will be unlocked remotely so that you can join us. Don't do anything foolish, now. We'll see you both in a few minutes." The dial tone announced the end of the call.

Dr. Sanderson walked toward the door and tried to open it, but it was still locked. An audible click announced the door was open, and he went into the hall. He turned and looked for Emiko.

In Emiko's room, the phone rang as well. It was the one they called Rock, her nemesis. "Hi, honey. I'll be right up. I hope you still have that fiery spirit; I have some time to indulge you now." A few minutes later, the door opened and he strode into the room. His reaction was quick enough to deflect the blow, but the chair splintered across his arm and shoulder.

"Well, that is going to leave a mark," he sneered. He walked over to Emiko and wrapped his huge arms around her, pinning her arms to her side. "I guess we'll just have to do this the hard way," he grunted as he lifted her off the floor and dragged her to the bathroom.

Once inside, he kicked the door shut and immediately let go of her. She spun around and landed two punches to his midsection. Then she spun around again to catch him in the head with her elbow, but he was ready and caught her arm. Though he could easily have broken it, he merely stopped her arm and used his massive frame to push her, surprisingly gently, against the wall.

Immobilized, she started to scream then he covered her mouth with his huge hand and quietly but firmly demanded, "Just listen! I don't need any more pain. I had to get you in here because it is the only part of your room without a microphone and a camera. I'm here to get you and your father out safely. We need your help. We have suspected for some time now that there is a serious problem with our security personnel. It is the only common denominator we could assess between your lab, Dr. Dorman's lab, and this facility. It was a long shot since these folks undergo the most serious scrutiny, but when Dr. Dorman disappeared, there were just too many inconsistencies. None of us believe the 'he defected back to his homeland' story line, but the security group, which was subcontracted to save money, as you might expect, was convinced that was the answer. Somehow, it has something to do with Charles Stevenson, but we don't know what the connection is as of yet. What's worse is that there is an even larger plan unfolding here, and many believe Dr. Dorman, you, and your father are in the middle of it without knowing it. What about that other guy, Jack is it? Where did he go, and how well do you know him?"

"I don't know that I want to tell you anything just yet, but I assure you that I trust Jack very much. If he were working with this Charles character, he'd never have acted the way he did. Call it women's intuition, but he is not a part of that team, or yours, I would guess."

"You're right there. I've reviewed his treatment by the security personnel after Dr. Dorman left, and it seems to me like someone was trying to either set Jack up or use him as a convenient scapegoat. Charles and the rest of his group don't usually play very nicely with others.

"Now you have the toughest challenge ahead of you. You need to maintain that same level of defiance toward me that you had before this talk, compounded by whatever they think happened in here right now. In addition, you can't overtly tell your father anything and you must play along with Charles. Try to keep me and Jock separated in your mind. I'm sure we sort of look alike, but he isn't part of our team; in fact, I'm not sure he can think straight enough to understand the concept of a team. He is exactly the kind of person that gives us big guys a very bad reputation."

"And one you use very effectively," Emiko responded as she smiled at him. "Sorry about the chair and the fists. I'll be able to do my part, but for your information, someone has something from Dr. Dorman's lab that has conveniently not been documented. Perhaps there is a videotape of some kind. My father and I think part, if not all, of the answers are on that tape."

"Thanks, I'll let the guys and gals know and get them cracking on it. Now, I have to undo my trousers and walk out of here so that everyone can believe what the stereotypes insist I must be like. Dishevel yourself, if you can, and follow me in a few minutes. I'm supposed to leave your door open for you. Good luck!"

"And good hunting!" Emiko replied as he walked out of the bathroom. *God, this just keeps getting more and more weird*, she thought.

She left the bathroom with her clothes in a mess and her hair and makeup smeared all over her face. After straightening her clothes and brushing her hair, she walked out the door into the hallway.

"Dad! What the hell is going on? What can they possibly expect us to know at this point? I don't even think we've seen Dr. Dorman's data yet." She ran down the hall and gave him a hug.

"I don't know what to think, Emi-chan. I can't tell who is legitimate and who is playing a game here. I can't even really tell if they are the bad guys, or the good guys who think we are the bad guys. Either way doesn't bode well for us. The best thing to do is to remain calm and see what happens next. You were summoned to the conference room again as well?"

The Eyes

"In a cryptic sort of way, yes. I was told there was something I would be interested in seeing demonstrated in a few moments." She hugged him again and as he held her she whispered, "We're going to be OK. One of the two goons is on our side. Don't react; just follow my lead." She released him and stood straight. Taking her hand, they walked down the hall toward the conference room.

Dr. Sanderson's mind was reeling. From Emiko's information, he correctly concluded that the goon who had taken her down the hall was friendly, while the oaf who herded him around was part of "they"— whoever that was. For now, all he could do was play along.

They entered the conference room to find Charles grinning at them from the podium. "Welcome, Doctors. We'd like to share a bit of video we just found among Dr. Dorman's things. A pity we didn't find it earlier; perhaps there is something here that will help you help us find the good doctor."

He sat down at the end of the table and motioned for someone they could not see to begin the tape. What they saw absolutely dumbfounded them. There was the apparatus they had seen earlier in the lab. It looked, for all intents and purposes, like a regular reflux condenser process used to separate various chemicals in solution. But that wasn't what they were looking at, and they both knew it. Dr. Dorman was busy placing neonatal fluid in the first vial, as the label clearly indicated. He had apparently decided for this experiment to drip the neonatal fluid across the amino acid solution as it was slowly heated, but why? The movie showed Dr. Dorman as he adjusted the various vials and heaters. The center vial was the shape of a banana, with the top of the glass apparatus open. He had another triangular-shaped vial in which he poured sterile saline solution and a suspension of powdered plastic—the material used as synthetic skin for some burn patients. Next he positioned several stainless steel rods with various materials over the vial and in turn immersed each one in the solution. Finally he turned the pipette valve to allow the neonatal fluid to run down the tube and into the solution a drop at a time. Dr. Dorman then stepped off camera. The film stopped and the lights came on.

"Well," Charles asked, "what do you make of that?"

"Is that the entire film?" Alex asked without further embellishment.

"No, the film goes on for more than six hours, but it shows nothing more that is important."

"Why don't you let Emiko and me decide that for ourselves. I think we should watch the whole thing, unless, of course, you already know what happened to Dr. Dorman." Alex was tired of the being treated as a prisoner, and had already decided enough was enough. This wasn't the gulag, and if they had something evil they wanted to do, well, bring it on.

"Very well, Doctor. We'll try this again tomorrow, starting at five hundred hours, so you can go back to your rooms and relax. As far as I'm concerned, this is all a waste of time. You two are free to roam the floor as you wish. It isn't like you're going to get out of here anyway. But remember, I want your answer by thirteen hundred hours tomorrow."

Charles stood and strode imperiously out the door, leaving Alex and Emiko with the two goons.

Alex wondered how it had come to this, where a security officer seemed to be in charge of the entire laboratory. Perhaps Gene had been right all along. At least it appeared their incarceration was being reduced to house arrest, not lock down.

"C'mon, Emiko, we know our way back to our rooms. You two can entertain yourselves anyway you like." Alex stood, expecting some conflict with the two guards, but they just stood there, waving them off as if they didn't care at all. The doctors walked back to Emiko's room.

"Well, what do you make of all of this, Emi-chan? First they start to show us something, and then they shut it down. I don't get it."

"I don't know either, Dad, but I think there is something on that video that will give us a clue as to what has happened to Dr. Dorman. Unfortunately, I'm not sure that will help us figure out what else is going on around here. I've been trying to think of anything either Dr. Dorman or we have been doing that would cause any excitement at the governmental level, but nothing comes to mind. Even if our research progress on excitatory transmission was finished, what could they use it for?"

"Well, I must admit that I think the answer is in the military-industrial context. Once we find a way to allow the mind to control any non-living tissue device directly, whether it is an artificial eye or a computer terminal, the military applications become endless. Imagine a fighter aircraft being able to target and fire its weapons at the speed of thought. We have nothing even close to that now. But combine it with current technology, and you can target a missile, fire it, and then leave it to reach its target by itself—an updated version of the "fire and for-get" computer-generated targeting we already have. Only by accomplishing these things at the speed of human thought will you greatly increase survivability. So if Dr. Dorman made any progress in that regard, I imagine many nations and their militaries would be extremely interested."

"So that is what we're looking for, something that allows the mind to control inanimate objects?"

"Not necessarily, Emi-chan. It has been quite a while since Gene went missing. It is possible that what we will see will be only the rudimentary first steps. Keep your eyes open for anything that would make you think there was an interesting line of inquiry to follow."

"Dad, if we find anything, then what? Do we tell that clown Charles or not?"

"I'd say we might as well. There isn't anything more he can do to us without breaking the law, which he may already have done, but violence doesn't seem likely to me at this point in time, agreed?"

"Reluctantly, yes. Still I'm not so sure about the other goons he has working with him. Will you stay and watch TV with me for a while? I don't feel like being alone right now."

"Sure, honey. If you like, I'll sleep here too; there are two beds here and it isn't as if there's anything pressing I need to deal with right now."

"Thanks, Dad, that would be great. I'll set the alarm for four."

They started to watch television, but with the stress of the past few days and the relaxation of feeling secure again with each other, they fell asleep within fifteen minutes.

THE SPORTSTER,
WASHINGTON, D.C.

Carlos and Jack drove in Carlos's car, which looked a lot like the old car mounted on top of the advertising pole in front of the Sportster bar. The car on the pole, however, was painted in NASCAR colors, complete with advertising slogans, while Carlos's car was solid metallic blue.

"Hey, good choice, amigo," Carlos started. "I always wanted to cruise into this place. It has quite a reputation for the big screens and good Tex-Mex cuisine. Unfortunately, I never think about it until one of the really big games, and then it is wall to wall with people, not my bag."

"I know what you mean," Jack intoned. Carlos parked the car and they walked toward the front door. There was a huge plate glass window just to the right of the entrance where the patrons could be seen waving and shouting at the huge multiscreens on the opposite wall. You could hear the whistles and screams from the parking lot. Clearly distracted, Jack was already scanning the tables through the windows before they walked in. He hardly heard Carlos but thought he'd said something, so he turned and asked, "What's that, Carlos?"

"Jack, my role in this was to help you look less conspicuous. You'll have to start by changing your approach. No problem looking, but it's normal to wait until you're inside. Also, you need to smile. You look like an IRS inspector tracking down a deadbeat taxpayer."

Once again Carlos had disarmed him, and Jack found himself genuinely laughing. "OK, Carlos, you're right. Why not go in and just have a beer. I don't think they're going to make it anyway."

"Well, don't draw any conclusions from that either. As you saw on the way over, traffic can be really bad, and getting a cab at the lab isn't going to be that easy either."

Jack and Carlos were seated next to an obnoxiously loud group of young men who were equally interested in the game and the table of four women seated a few tables farther down. It gave them cover for discussions, but they had to speak louder than they would have liked given their purpose. They had arrived more than a half-hour early, so both settled in to watch what turned out to be a rebroadcast of a Washington Wizards game. Jack continued to scan the crowd, while Carlos watched the door.

Carlos had never met either Dr. Sanderson or Emiko, so the best he could do was watch for what looked like a father and daughter couple also looking for someone. He was pretty sure they were just wasting their time, but Jack was obviously convinced the effort was worth it. Carlos was right, of course; they would have been better off just enjoying the game.

THE FARMHOUSE

When Yin Hee awoke, she was in a room that could easily have been a prison cell. There was no furniture, no toilet, no light, just four concrete walls and a concrete floor. As her eyes adjusted to the minimal light let in by the caged window near the high ceiling, she realized this was some sort of storage facility. She was laying on a nondescript piece of oil-stained carpet, the type people lay down to keep their car engines from leaking fluid on their garage floor. She stood up to take a more thorough assessment of her confines.

Walking toward the walls and then around the room, she found it larger than she had first surmised, probably fifteen meters square. The first wall she came to was nothing more than a concrete slab, gray, rough, and considerably dinged up—likely the impact of careless or industrial use of heavy machinery like forklifts. Half way up the next wall, there was a rectangular steel plate inset in rails. Clearly this opening forming a window, was actuated from outside; the rust seemed to indicate it had not been used in some time. Still the lack of spider webs or other insect infestations kept the status of her room a mystery. The third wall was a replica of the first. The last wall housed what could easily be called a door, to her surprise. It had no door handle, but it had an inset depression one could get a finger hold on to slide the door from right to left.

The Eyes

She placed her hand on the door, then withdrew it and went back to the comfort of the oil-stained carpet. Whatever was to come, she would need her strength, and she wanted nothing more than to shrink away, to fade like the light and become invisible, and therefore safe. She dragged the threadbare carpet over to a corner, sat with her back to it, and wrapped herself in the protective cape, which, only hours earlier, she would have avoided stepping on barefooted. There she passed the next few hours in quiet solitude, still waiting, still terrified.

Eventually, as the light from the tiny window began to fade, Yin Hee decided she would have to do something. Inevitably she would need water, food, and even more pressing, a bathroom of some sort. Gathering her courage, she stood up wrapped in the stained carpet and limped to the door. She was neither injured nor feeble, yet her internal dread of what lay outside made it impossible for her to walk with any confidence. Slowly, inexorably, she made the distance disappear, one step, then another. Her legs felt like they were mired in mud; then, finally, she was there. Holding her breath, she leaned close to the steel plate and laid her ear to it. She heard no sound. She was tempted to knock on the door and see what the sudden noise would elicit, but immediately decided that bringing attention to herself wasn't her best plan. She gripped the indented handhold and pulled.

Amazingly, the plate slid almost silently into a pocket in the wall. Not only was the door designed to slide on ball bearings, it was well lubricated and moved freely. As it disappeared, she looked out into the pitch-black darkness. She was frightened at first, but quickly felt somewhat reassured. After all, if someone were waiting outside, they would probably be in the light. She stepped tentatively into the dark, again her eyes began to adjust to the even greater dimness and she sensed she was in some kind of hallway. She put out her hand and felt wood. If this was a corridor, she imagined there must be a light switch somewhere. Feeling first along the left wall then the right, she came across an uncovered plastic switch. She flipped it up, and a corridor of bulbs burst into luminous brilliance. Involuntarily, she closed her eyes. Slowly she reopened them to find a hallway with cheap wood paneling ceiling to floor stretching out a few hundred meters in front of her, with a door at the other end.

The Farmhouse

There were no photographs or paintings on the walls, just a few horseshoes at varying heights. She walked slowly, but much more comfortably down the hallway to the door. A compatriot light switch awaited her on the left side of the door. She took hold of the door handle in her right hand, and with her left she flipped the switch, plunging the hallway back into darkness. Seeing no light escape from around the door, she simultaneously turned the doorknob, opened the door, and turned the lights back on. In front of her was what would pass for a living room, complete with a couch, recliner chair, ottoman coffee table, and even a television. There was no one waiting for her here either. The light from the hallway behind her illuminated the room adequately for her to find lamps and turn them on. She then turned out the hall light and shut the door, locking it from the inside.

Looking around the living room, she could see she was in a small farmhouse. The windows were covered with plain, off-white, cotton drapery. Sweeping them aside with one hand, she looked out at an unkempt yard with equal parts dirt and weeds, interspersed sporadically with tufts of grass. A long, gravel driveway stretched away from the house. There were no vehicles in sight, and shrubs and trees claimed the area beyond ten meters from the front porch. Whatever road the driveway led to was beyond her vision from the window.

There were two doors leading out of the room she now stood in. One clearly opened to the outside; the other looked like a closet door. Opposite the main entrance, the house opened to a dining room, and farther in she could see the cabinets and sink of a kitchen. The kitchen seemed like the best place to start, so she went in. It was a pretty average-looking kitchen, just a rectangular room open on two ends. The layout was quite bland; the sink and dishwasher, with the standard white tile countertops, were on the outside wall of the house, with a window above the sink facing the backyard, and the wall behind or opposite had the stove and a side-by-side washer and dryer. Above them were some plain white cabinets mounted on the wall. Beyond the kitchen was another smaller hallway stretching down to two more rooms. Both doors were wide open; one led to a bathroom, the other a bedroom.

She felt safe and secure after looking in each room and finding it also empty. After using the bathroom and washing her hands and face thoroughly, she returned to the kitchen. She found an envelope on the kitchen counter with her name hand written on it. Inside she found a single sheet of paper with a lone typed paragraph.

You have been activated as you were told you would be. You will wait here in this safe house for the next few days, when an agent will arrive with your instructions. There is adequate food and drink in the refrigerator. Do not leave the house or attempt to contact anyone; you are being watched.

And just like that, she thought, *it begins.* Resignedly, she walked to the refrigerator and opened it. As the letter promised, there were ready-made meals of various kinds. They were all the frozen, ready-to-microwave types; someone had tried to make her stay a little more comfortable at least. Looking around, she noted the small microwave on the counter. Opening the cabinets, she found clean dishes, and in the drawers, silverware. She grabbed a bottle of iced tea and turned toward the living room. She decided to make the best of it and went in to see if the television worked. She flopped down on the couch and palmed the remote from the coffee table. Suddenly it dawned on her that the doors might not all be secured, so she made one more pass through the small house to ensure every door was locked. She also rechecked every closet for signs of someone waiting to surprise her. It took a while, because each door she opened required she still her nerves. Finally she was convinced she was truly alone as the note implied, and returned to the living room couch, the remote, and the television.

Pushing the power button brought the monotone of an evening news broadcaster. It surprised her how comforting it was to hear another human being again, albeit from the television. She was about to change the channel when she noticed a phone sitting on the end table to her right. Thinking about the unnecessary hours she spent in the room at the end of the hall because she was too scared to try to leave the cell, she decided to try the phone. *Fool me once, shame on you,* she thought as she picked up the handset. Putting it up to her ear, however, she found that there was no dial tone. There would be no simple phone call to Lee to get her out of this situation. She heard something outside and decided she could at least look to see what it was. She crossed the living room, opened the front door slowly, and looked out. Dusk was waning, so she could see very little. She decided running was probably not going to help her. She assumed she had heard a car passing in the distance, but it was of no concern. The note on the table had relieved her because, despite its cryptic content, at least she was still considered an asset, which also probably meant Lee was legitimate, and that she was safe for now. It was amazing how often she found herself assessing her own safety lately. Closing the door, she made sure to lock it and sat back down to take in the news. Still her mind wandered. She wondered what Lee was doing. By now he had to know something had happened to her, and hopefully he had some capability to do something to help her.

ON TOP OF CHO MYA DAM

After lunch they met atop the dam. There were four of them: Major Kim, Captain Youhn, Captain Jung, and, bringing up the rear, Colonel Song. They headed immediately for the access stairs to the main maintenance room. As they approached it, Colonel Song addressed Major Kim.

"Hand your weapon to Captain Youhn; you won't be needing it anymore. I will allow you to carry it only after it is unloaded and disabled. Captain Jung, can you have that taken care of please? Now let's continue inside."

There was no reason for Captain Jung to respond. Not complying was not an option anyway, and the Colonel was clearly anxious to continue. This was the first step into the bowels of the huge facility. The door opened smoothly, revealing a very dark staircase. Each member of the team carried a flashlight, another rare commodity here, but necessary since lighting was a precious resource and the very reason the dam was supposed to have been created. It took over forty-five minutes to reach the main floor.

During the last fifteen minutes of their descent, they experienced an eerie green glow that seemed to be growing, rather than just increasing in intensity. It gave one the impression of entering some kind of radiant gaseous swamp. Finally, as they declined the last twelve feet, the tube they had been climbing down opened up. They now stood on the working floor of the largest enclosed space in the Democratic People's Republic.

The colonel just stood staring in awe, saying nothing. He had been warned, but this was still emotionally trying. He had hoped to be looking into the heart of a great machine that would save his country from the inevitable collapse the rest of the world hoped for it. Instead, he saw huge mechanical devices, pulleys, gears, and internal combustion engines of a primitive but massive scale.

"OK, somebody start talking. Why aren't there any hydroelectric motors here?"

Major Kim began, "For starters, you have to stop thinking about the dam proper as some means of controlling the water flow through the dam, either for irrigation or to harness power. There are certainly means for the water to flow through the dam, but that is for the benefit of the satellite photographs that are routinely examined by the United States and England, among others. The dam was designed to be a fully operational hydroelectric dam, and then everything invisible from the outside was simply not built. Certainly the design is such that the working parts can be installed, but that would take a while. The current purpose of the dam is to hold the water in the lake, which gathers behind it. While these lakes are used for recreational purposes at most dams, we have other ideas in mind. Our lake has solid sidewalls and it will be covered. What you have essentially is a huge can with a lid, and a removable bottom. The bottom can be detached relatively slowly or explosively fast. The reason we will remove it instead of just destroying it with explosives has to do with what the water is for, which we'll get to later. This piecemeal project has taken twenty years, as the needed parts were included in other major design projects funded…externally, shall we say. These added pieces were acquired from their original projects and consolidated at various sites until the shell game ended with their relocation here."

"Why would engineers from other nations build extra pieces for these projects? Surely they would know the pieces were unnecessary and reject the additions." Colonel Song was a practical, logical man.

"Sir," Captain Youhn offered, "it has to do with how nations give things to other nations, particularly the DPRK. The politicians making the decision to give a project to the DPRK are rarely experts, whether it is a bridge, dam, school, or whatever. Their piece of the puzzle is to make it look like a solid humanitarian gift for we evil North Koreans. The parts for a big project are rarely manufactured by a single company. Most Western nations wealthy enough to take part in overseas development or charity are capitalist nations. The politician's greatest concern is that the money used for the projects in our nation gets distributed where it is needed the most, in his or her constituents' pockets.

The final process was to finish the internal engineering work ourselves. The genius of this dam was in getting several nations to actually build the massive structure, then chasing them out to finish the internal components ourselves. The dear leader stated the design and locations of the hydroelectric motors was a national security risk owing to the ability of the United States and its puppets to attack the dam once constructed. If they knew everything about the dam, it would become a target, a veritable weapon of mass destruction in their hands. In one of his finest performances, he even threatened to destroy it to keep it from being used by our enemies."

Kim reentered the conversation. "So since the physical dam was built with its unique lake bottom, we've been working to finalize the weapon."

Colonel Song's features sharpened, "What weapon?" he nearly shouted. "You can't mean we really intend to destroy this dam! Regardless of the intent, this dam still represents the possibility for true change."

"No, sir," Captain Jung finished this part of today's adventure. "The dam is the weapon."

CONFERENCE ROOM, NATIONAL LAB

They showed up in the conference room nearly ten minutes early. Just as they expected, there was coffee and water, but they had overestimated; there was no food.

"Well, this isn't exactly one of your guest lecture conferences, Doc," Jock offered, proving once again that if you're stupid, you should never pass up the opportunity not to speak.

"Whatever," Emiko offered. "Let's get the video started shall we?" As if on cue, the video came to life and the two researchers settled in for a long, boring special presentation. Interestingly, Charles was nowhere to be seen. They spent the next four and a half hours fighting to stay awake. Occasionally, they would even poke each other like little kids in the backseat of a car on a long trip just to stay alert. Then, just as they thought this might actually have been one of their more brain-dead ideas, it seemed as though the camera had started to vibrate. They had been left alone for the duration of the film—clearly Charles must have felt this was a waste of time—so they were slightly more comfortable whispering to one another.

"What do you think is causing the vibration, Dad?"

"My guess is a ceiling fan, one of those air movement devices all the labs have that come on randomly. I'm more fascinated that the camera seems to be moving due to the vibration. It may be what Dr. Dorman was getting at when he made his cryptic comments in his e-mail to me about discovering things by accident. It is time to focus carefully, Emi-chan."

As they watched, the camera painfully slowly continued its vibrating migration. It agonizingly pivoted around on its stand, until it obviously came into contact with something and stopped. All they could see now was the wrong end of the apparatus, and Alex thought the effort had been a waste of time. Then, suddenly, Emiko inhaled sharply, snapping Alex back to focus on the screen.

"What is it, Emi-chan?" he whispered.

"Dad, look carefully at the apparatus itself. There, where some of the fluid and tissue spilled onto it, the tissue is growing into the plastic! It isn't just growing on it; it's growing into it! There even appears to be capillary vascularization in the plastic. I've never seen anything like it!"

"Well, if that is what Dr. Dorman had been referring to in his notes, then he was indeed flirting with danger. The question is, who could have known about it besides Dr. Dorman and Jack?" Dr. Sanderson sat back in his chair for a moment. "I'd really like another look at that part of the tape, but I've changed my mind about telling Charles anything at all."

"Why? I thought you said there was very little he could do to us here anyway." It wasn't that Emiko wanted to tell Charles anything, but she wasn't following the reason for her dad's change of heart.

"Well, Emiko," and he leaned closer toward her so that he could whisper softly, "one of the things that is possibly the same at all three laboratories is the security staffing. As you recall, they are also contracted out. Certainly if they have anything to do with Gene's disappearance, we could disappear just as easily. We need to find a way to get in touch with Jack again somehow. I wonder what he's been doing for the past couple of days."

They were allowed to return to Emiko's room unescorted. Together they walked over to the computer on Emiko's desk and turned it on. The monitor flashed on and after the long boot-up sequence, they double-clicked the Internet Explorer icon. To their joy and amazement, the screen showed the Google search page, a clear indication that they had an Internet connection. Their first search was a dead end as they tried to find excitatory threshold research and kept coming up with references to their own work.

"Why don't we start with a check on Dr. Dorman's unclassified work and see what else we can find?"

"I doubt that will get us very far, but rather than both of us sitting here and getting into an argument over it, why don't you use this one and I'll use the one in my room, OK?"

"That's a great idea, Dad. I'll bet you I find something first!" she said as she laughed.

Dr. Sanderson went back to his room and fired up the computer and settled in.

The information he had found was at once enigmatic and disturbing. First of all, he had found there were other scientists in Germany working in the same field and claiming extraordinary success in encasing the human eye in a light metallic shell and reattaching it to the body. The purpose of the shell seemed intentionally vague, but the Web site mentioned computer-enhancement capabilities. When he followed that chain of thought to search for eye or ocular research, he discovered a very unusual article claiming a large and steady stream of human eyes from China to the former East Germany, and from there to all Western nations.

What caught his attention, though, was the mention of research on human interface with machines. It seemed crude in the article, but this wasn't a science journal, just a zealous media reporter on the Web. His claims that a Dr. Lehnon had successfully blended a human being with a projectile device were disturbing. Dr. Sanderson wasn't sure yet, but there could be some problems developing in the field of biotronics. Worse still, he didn't really know who to talk to or, for that matter, who to trust.

When the phone rang, it startled Dr. Sanderson back to reality. Checking his watch, he was actually surprised that he had spent almost six hours surfing the Web.

"Hello?" He expected it to be Emiko, but it wasn't. Charles's voice came on the line.

"Dr. Sanderson, please ask your daughter to join you and come down to the dining room. It is entirely possible this has just been a big mistake, after all. We'd like you to have a meal here on us, of course, and then we'll be escorting you out of the building. If you need any assistance with your travel plans, please just let the front desk know you are authorized to charge this entire trip on the laboratories' travel account. I won't be joining you as I have a few things that require my attention. I hope you'll understand."

"Certainly, Charles. Thanks for your generosity. We'll see you the next time we're in town." But the line had already gone dead. Dr. Sanderson stood and walked out of his room to go and get Emiko.

THE DESERT CAMP

Not a single patient had died since Dr. Dorman's arrival, and so after a full year, he had a day off at last. More importantly, he had been told he would have a full case of anesthesia and the help of an anesthetist starting tomorrow. Today, however, was a surgery-free day. He would also be allowed to draft his e-mail, though whether it would be sent was still anybody's guess. He'd been thinking about what to write to Dr. Sanderson for a very long time—day and night it seemed, though he was sure he was getting his fair mount of sleep after standing on his feet more than twelve hours each day.

The enucleation process was becoming more and more efficient, so he could take care of each young man within ten minutes. Accounting for the time to take one eye out and strap in the next patient, he was harvesting an eye every forty minutes. His only breaks were during his captors' call to prayers, which occurred somewhat regularly five times a day. They pretty much left him alone then. Ironically, the call to prayers had been his most fearful time in the camp. He assumed they would begin to consider his lack of Islamic faith more during those periods. Instead, everyone seemed to feel their religion was personal and worth more than the effort to harass him for not believing as they did. So after a few months, it became his greatest period of rest and solace. Accounting for breaks and meals, he was roughly averaging fourteen procedures per day—over 5,100 since he had arrived a year ago.

His evenings were pretty much his own. While few had anything to say to him, he was allowed the run of the camp, and no one was menacing or even rude toward him any longer. He had managed to impress his captors enough for tacit acceptance. That was good enough for him for now. He was smart enough to know his very survival depended on these people believing he was of great value to them. He had no idea how many of these procedures he was supposed to perform, and that concerned him.

They seemed to place little value on postoperative care, as the young men were loaded up and transported out of the camp three days after their surgery, despite the doctor's voiced concerns. He had managed to discover they were being shipped to Europe for further surgery, which he suspected was to install something in the eye socket.

Another issue weighing on his mind was where Hassim had gone. He hadn't been around for the past three days, and despite his callous handling, he had represented some protection, in Dr. Dorman's mind at least.

Nevertheless, the doctor had some time today to finally craft the e-mail to his friend, which he hoped would help his old comrade figure out what had happened and what Dr. Dorman's new research might be used for.

> *Alex,*
>
> *May this message find you at peace with yourself and your family. I am at peace, the peace of the traditional lands. Though I was unaware through most of my travels, I find myself with my original peoples, and have need of your help. If it is within your capability, I need information on the neural jump capacity of polyvinyl in the presence of neonatal solution with excitatory stimuli. Previous results grew dramatically, though the end was near. It is apparent that the presence of neonatal fluid alone is inadequate to stimulate growth. Following logic, some form of excitatory stimulus must also be present, lest the growth become uncontrolled in the nature of cancerous tumors. It is almost like a*

The Desert Camp

movie. It would be a vital link to find the methodology of such stimulus; it would allow for the development of growth in otherwise-inanimate tissue. My efforts follow the Japanese research of a similar nature regarding light transmission through neural excitation. It is such with the eyes.

May Allah keep you in his light.—Gene

Now if he could get the message transmitted to Alex and Emiko, perhaps there would be hope of their discovering what was going on, where he was, and maybe even how they could get him out of here.

PACIFIC COMMAND HEADQUARTERS

"General Hodge, have you met Dr. Woods? He is our Korea specialist serving with the Asia Pacific Center for Security Studies here in downtown Honolulu."

"I'm pleased to meet you, Dr. Woods. What a tough tour of duty. How are you handling it?" General Hodge said as he chuckled. Coming from the freezing Korean peninsula to Hawaii made the latter truly seem like paradise.

"I'm managing," the doctor replied with a smile. "How is Seoul? Have you had much snow?"

"Touché, Doctor. No, it's been a reasonably mild winter so far. I'm here to check your crystal ball on what is going on north of the DMZ. Any ideas what they are up to? We've been trying to piece something together, but haven't gotten very far, I'm afraid. I've brought my resident expert on the DMZ tunnels along for a quick briefing on what we think we know about them. Captain Hert, you have the floor."

"Thank you, General. North Korea uses tunnel operations as a central part of their overall concept of waging war. The primary purpose of these tunnels is to move, undetected, large numbers of conventional and nonconventional forces with limited fire support behind the United States and ROK initial line of defense along the DMZ. These forces will act as part of an invasion force. The successful placement of large numbers of troops with supporting firepower behind our lines without our detection at the onset of hostilities would be without question a major tactical advantage on their part. Despite all the technology at our disposal, we are only able to locate the tunnels themselves. The capability to find tunnels beneath the surface is state of the art and highly classified. Clearly this is the kind of technology oil companies would love to get their hands on, but to give away our sources and means has, to date, been ruled more significant to national security than to finding new oil fields. At this level, I can share that the oil fields in Alaska were not found exclusively through the good work of the folks at Exxon, though the hints were delivered surreptitiously enough that most of their field researchers probably believe it was an independent find.

"We have found and documented three large tunnels under the DMZ, and we suspect there are as many as seventeen others. The detected and mapped tunnels are impressive enough to demonstrate to us the significance of tunnel operations to North Korean military strategy. We detected the first tunnel in November of 1974. It was only three feet below the earth's surface, but measured six feet by six feet and was constructed utilizing prefabricated walls and lines. The size of the tunnel is large enough for the movement of significant supporting firepower for troops. It is located a few kilometers east of P'anmunjom. The second tunnel was detected in March 1975. It was built 196 feet below the earth's surface, also measured six feet by six feet, and was dug through solid granite. It is significant to note that the tunnel had been completed for some time before it was detected, despite satellite surveillance. Tunnel two is barely a kilometer west of P'anmunjom, a location of special surveillance. We detected tunnel three in October 1978. This tunnel is 246 feet below the earth's surface, measures six feet by six feet, and it, too, was dug through solid granite. It is half way across the peninsula."

Dr. Woods spoke next. "That matches well with our assessment of the purpose and intent of the tunnels. Specifically to the question of what else the concrete could be used for, we have no definitive answer either, General. But we have a few guesses. We have long suspected the development of the dam at Cho Mya has more purpose than its purported use as a hydroelectric dam." The doctor sat back in his chair.

"What makes you think that?" General Hodge asked. "Our folks have been monitoring the construction of the dam for years. With the exception of the extra concrete, there doesn't seem to be anything unusual, neither weapons nor fuel of any kind so far."

"General, this is going to be a bit shocking, but we aren't looking at the possible uses for the dam, but rather evaluating its use based on the DPRK propaganda."

Admiral Corping jumped in at this point, "That seems a bit ludicrous. They almost never say anything true in their public announcements. How will that help us?"

"Sir, we are using the negative to disprove the positive. As General Hodge said, no one has been able to identify any weapons or fuel or weapon systems being brought to the dam at Cho Mya. That might lead one to believe that they are just being overly cautious in building a hydroelectric dam of significantly robust proportions, but there is a significant omission. There have been no hydroelectric motors or equipment ordered, purchased, or transported to the dam. For all the effort and money involved, it seems there has been a rather significant oversight, wouldn't you agree?"

Admiral Corping and General Hodge looked at each other. General Hodge spoke first, "Who else knows about this?"

"Just the staff at APCSS and me. It is something I picked up on this morning when I asked the guys to go over their impressions of the dam. It occurred to me that no one had any information on which type of hydroelectric technology was going to be used, or what donor nation had provided it. I then ran a quick check on the donor nations' exaggerated claims of help to the DPRK over the past five years, and finally an Internet check of nongovernmental organizations' assessments of donor nation assistance. All were devoid of any hydroelectric motor technology. That is something the donor nation would hardly omit from its global reports on international aid contributions. I could be wrong, of course, but I also hardly believe North Korea is capable of building its own equipment for a dam of this size and scale. What makes it difficult is that all the attachments, power transmission plants, and the equipment to install the motors were donated, and we know they arrived and were installed. That's why no one observing the construction of the dam would be willing to make a big deal out of the missing parts. Things like this are pretty hard to verify from a distance."

"Well, looks like it is time for a call to Washington. Let's give them some time to work up an assessment before we get there," Admiral Corping looked at his exec.

"Admiral, I think it's time for some consolidation of effort here," began Col. Cannen, "we're starting to fragment. General Hodge, you said you are planning to send a team to China to speak with the embassy. Admiral, we are sending a team to South Korea to make inquiries on this issue with their counterparts, and today I got two separate area clearance requests. One was from DSRJ to visit USFK and the UNC, and one from the DIA to visit DSRJ. I don't know if all these issues are connected, but it might be worthwhile to have these teams meet here, and have a conference at the APCSS. Dr. Woods, you have been having conferences quarterly until this quarter when we predicted the funding would be difficult, correct?"

"Yes, quite true. In fact, our commander was saying yesterday he would approach the admiral once again to see if he could reinstate the funding for the seminar this quarter. I could discuss it with him this afternoon and set up a US-only conference for this quarter. We have already sent a message to the many countries in PACOM that the cancellation affects, explaining our inability to fund their participation this quarter. It won't raise any eyebrows to have a US-only conference this time; they would all assume the costs could be more easily distributed this way, as US participants are always unit funded, a topic of frequent discussion at our conferences." Dr. Woods made some notes.

"How quickly could we arrange all this?" General Hodge inquired. He was slightly distracted by the concept of a few days off with his wife and daughter in Hawaii.

Colonel Cannen answered, "I'm certain I can get all of them to convene here in forty-eight hours, since the dates of travel for these disparate teams overlapped to begin with. That's how it came to my attention. Especially entertaining was the request for the visit to DSRJ at the same time DSRJ was trying to visit USFK." They all laughed.

"Thanks, Ralph let's make this happen. I'll call the State Department now and let them in on the generic issues in case they want to play too. Dave, care to join in the conference call?"

"You bet, John." They all stood together, shook hands and went their separate ways. Admiral Corping and General Hodge walked toward the hallway to the next room where PACOM's secure communications equipment was located. As they got to the door, General Hodge stopped and turned to the admiral.

"John, I appreciate the cooperation on this. I know we've been at odds on many things over the years, and I actually had to make an issue of shutting that down with my staff. It's time to bury all that."

"I couldn't agree more. It really isn't our baby to work through anyway; this system evolved politically. Our job is war and peace. Who knows, as this pans out, we might both get our original wish—the politicians may be forced to rethink this issue and its structure. The funny part is, as we get closer to that possibility, I start to worry about how much worse they might make it!" He laughed with General Hodge, and they shook hands again as they walked into the communications room.

The enlisted men in the room were infected with the joviality. From their perspective, this might just as easily have been the two football players walking into the locker room.

"Ernie, how are you today?" the admiral began. "I need to speak with the secretary of state, right away. It needs to be a secure conference call. Can we do that?"

"Yes, sir. I'll get her on the line." These young men and women, for their relatively minor positions in the pecking order of government, nevertheless routinely made contact with the powers that move the nation and the world. It was an exciting yet exhausting career field, and the smallest mistake could end a promising career. After all, it was pretty easy from positions of power as high as ambassadors and State Department officials to treat the communications specialist as little more than debris. Admiral Corping, however, wasn't one of those individuals. He was particularly adept at making sure that members of his team knew how much he appreciated their contribution to the execution of the PACOM mission. In turn, the usual vitriolic banter found in many staff agencies was absent here. It was proof that when leaders respect their followers, the respect of the follower's increases for their leaders. When they were genuinely appreciated for their hard work, it was easier for these young men and women to see and appreciate the scale and scope, not to mention the incredibly demanding schedule, USCINCPAC endured day in and day out. The fact that every single member of the communications unit, which was on duty twenty-four hours a day, seven days a week, had personally spoken with USCINCPAC showed the amount of time he spent in the communications center. "Admiral Corping, the Honorable Lisa Hunter is on the line," the corporal announced, and then turned back to his console. Naturally, it was impossible to not hear what was going on, but it would be a mistake to listen to the conversation. The corporal's role now was to monitor the communications connection, tweaking it when needed to make sure contact was never lost. Whatever he heard of their discussion he had long ago learned was only a part of what was going on. The lower left corner of the big picture as they always joked among themselves. It was a professional attitude that kept the communications staff functioning at peak efficiency.

"Ms. Hunter, this is John Corping, and I have Dave Hodge with me as well. How are you this evening?"

"I'm tired, John. It's been a very long day, and I had planned on calling you tomorrow. What's up?" It was after 10:00 p.m. in Washington, another of the inconveniences of global affairs.

"Sorry to call so late, ma'am, but we think we need to take some pretty quick action. The DIA has made a request for area clearance to visit DSRJ in Japan. At the same time, DSRJ has made an area request to visit USFK. I had already made the decision to send a team to Korea and China, and, as you know, General Hodge and I were about to visit you in the next few days. My staff pieced all this together, somewhat accidentally, and we've concluded that all this activity is likely the result of the same precipitating activity. I've made the decision to have all these teams meet here in Hawaii under the guise of a quarterly conference that the Asia Pacific Center routinely holds. As we make preparations for this, I wanted to solicit your assistance in smoothing the waters with the DIA and let you know what we're doing. The Korean peninsula is obviously the focus of all this and it's probably a good time to get all our smart folks together in one place. Naturally, we invite either you or anyone you think would be helpful to join us as we try to discern what is happening out there." He then paused to see what reaction he would get.

"John, that's a great idea. I can't tell you whom I'll send off the top of my head, but be sure I'll send someone. How soon is this conference?"

"Ma'am, we're trying to convene it in forty-eight hours if possible."

"I'll have someone there. Good night."

"Good night, ma'am." Admiral Corping hit the button on the triangular-shaped speaker in front of him. "And just like that," he intoned, "the ball game begins." They all stood and left the room.

As they walked out, Admiral Corping turned to the general and said, "Dave, why don't you take your lovely bride and that daughter of yours and use my cabin at Bellows for the next two days. You don't really have time to go back to Seoul, and I'll get the communications guys to hook you up with whatever you need to stay in touch with your staff. We have a sort of mini–command center out there that I use every century or so when I get time off."

"Thanks, John, I think I'll take you up on that. What do I need to do to set that up?"

Colonel Cannen stuck his head in the door and said, "Not a thing, sir. Your wife and daughter are waiting on you, and the car is already out front. Enjoy yourself!"

General Hodge looked at Admiral Corping, but before he could say anything, the admiral said, "I know. Sometimes it's just scary. I'm beginning to think of him as Radar from the *M.A.S.H.* television series. Have a great two days. The recreation center has everything you could want. Remember, that beach is documented as the best boogie board beach in the world."

KIMPO INTERNATIONAL AIRPORT, SOUTH KOREA

She expected the media crush for the Japanese government representatives' arrival, but it annoyed Hae-Jung nonetheless. With all their energy and enthusiasm, they'd be lucky to walk away with a telephoto shot and borrowed tape-recorded banter from the Japanese diet member. She had to merely tolerate the insanity and then get in the Kai luxury sedan, which would whisk the two of them off to a pleasant dinner, a private interview, and whatever she decided to serve for dessert.

This whole Internet thing was marvelous, she thought. Not only could she e-mail the politician, but she could also include her photo. That was the key to getting through the layers of protective bureaucracy. The very next day, she was in touch with his people, and two weeks prior to his arrival, her private interview had become part of the official agenda.

"Ishikawa-Sama," she began, using the most formal form of address.

He cut her off, speaking in very good English, "It is Hae-Jung, isn't it? I prefer you call me Hideo; this is to be an informal dialogue. You speak English and so do I, so let's keep in that neutral language; then neither of us has to struggle with the other's native language—fair enough?"

The Eyes

"That suits me very well, Hideo. Shall we pass on the formal interview until after dinner? I'm sure it has been a long day for you so far."

"If it pleases you, we can conduct the interview portion back at the hotel suite. I'd like that very much." Unconsciously, his eyes swept over her from foot to head.

"Perfect," she cooed. Then she moved from sitting across from him to sitting next to him and snuggled up against him. He put his arm around her and she began to imagine where she'd go first when she arrived in Tokyo.

INSIDE THE DAM AT CHO MYA

"Do you take me for a fool?" Colonel Song was beginning to doubt all three soldiers, and he subconsciously reached for his pistol.

"Sir," Captain Jung pleaded, "I can explain. You see it isn't actually the dam that is the weapon, but the water behind it. Until the dear leader chooses to use it otherwise, this dam will in fact continue to be fitted for hydroelectric power generation. It will be used for irrigating the fields near here, just as it does now. And, beneath the covering concrete lid, it will continue to be a source of recreation for those who can use it. But its primary purpose is to be a weapon. As you know, measured by the water it retains, this dam now stands as the second largest in all of Asia, behind only the Three Gorges Dam in China. You also know that water is the most destructive force on earth, capable of more damage than even nuclear weaponry, without the long-term effects, of course. This project was so carefully designed and executed that we actually believe that not the United States, Russia, China, or any of their allies even suspect its unique capability."

"Which is?" Colonel Song prompted impatiently.

"Devastation, sir." Captain Youhn chimed in again, once again eager to get the story out. "To simply, quickly, and absolutely annihilate the puppet government in Seoul and regain that city, the heart of Korea, in a move to reunite the peninsula."

The Eyes

"Rubbish!" Colonel Song spat. "We have more than one million soldiers between here and Seoul. I won't believe the dear leader would sacrifice them all in this effort. And if we attempted to move them out of the way, the United States and South Korea would know it long before the first soldier left the DMZ. By the time the force was moved to safety, emergency earthen levies would be built large enough to force the water to be diverted from the city. Who came up with this idea, and why would anyone believe it could work? All I really see is that we have years more work to do before this dam does what it is supposed to do. It will give us something we can use ourselves and that we can perhaps eventually even sell to our wasteful brethren to the south. To believe anything more is folly. Let's move on." The colonel turned and walked in the direction of the bases of the huge cogs suspended overhead.

"Patience, Colonel," Kim insisted. "We can show you how this will work. As you know, we are in the construction phase for the cover for the dam's surface. If you look at it from the air, or space, for that matter, it does indeed seem to be a protective cover for this now-precious water supply. Luckily, since everyone thinks the dear leader is mad and paranoid, no one really questions it. Laugh at it, yes; question it, not really. It represents the ability to continue to use the dam once the water has been lost, or the capacity for reloading, which will become clear from the mechanical room up ahead."

They walked on somewhat in silence. Occasionally one of the captains would point out places that had been built up for various connection points for the eventual hydroelectric motors, but otherwise they were quiet and deliberate in their progress. Arriving at the lift some forty minutes later, they entered one by one through a wide door. The lift was obviously designed for heavier objects and was frustratingly slow in its movement. They arrived in a mechanical control room. The technology looked surprising modern, and opposite the entrance was a series of rather large windows. Beyond the windows, one could see the floor of the lake. As the colonel walked in, everyone popped to attention, his presence having been announced piercingly by Captain Jung.

"Well, since there are no motors to control, what is it exactly that you do in here?" Colonel Song was determined to run this place, regardless of its designed purpose or state of completion.

Inside the Dam at Cho Mya

"I am Mr. Oh." He was a distinguished looking man with silver hair and wore a white smock that could easily be for surgery or a clean room at a production plant. He stepped forward and bowed. "I run this shift, Colonel. We simultaneously monitor and balance irrigation flow output, dam fill, and the safety of the underwater construction, which you can see on the monitors above the windows. As the sun climbs, if the turbidity of the water permits, you will also be able to watch the construction through these large windows. This is a very large dam, new to us and most of the world, I think, so we also monitor the maintenance of the dam through the seismic detectors installed at 1,100 places around the dam."

"Seismic detectors? Are we so afraid the dam will collapse that we can't rely on the international seismic system?" The colonel immediately liked this calm, professional man before him. Without any reason to or not to, he trusted his judgment and words almost at face value.

"The seismic detectors augment the global system for measuring earth's seismic activity, but many of the instruments installed on this dam are for measuring the dam's heartbeat, as I like to call it. With any structure this size, there is innate movement, somewhat cyclic, augmented by the mechanical movements caused by air-flow devices. There is other activity that affects the dam as well: valve and pressure changes made to influence water flow, and, of course, the ongoing construction. We are still establishing a baseline that will serve as a starting point for the monitoring program. It will measure movement and describe any statistically significant change via warning lights and detailed reports. For any large movement beyond what we select as a threshold, it will sound a rather impressive alarm throughout the complex to warn people to leave the dam and hopefully allow some to escape. I doubt anyone in here has much chance of escape, but we do have the consolation of knowing that if anything can be done to prevent a malfunction or worse, it is from here it will be accomplished. Do you have any other questions, Colonel?" he asked as he moved forward to stand next to his new commander.

"We have anxiously awaited someone who has studied dams and understands what they are and how they work. Our previous leadership, though dedicated, always treated the dam as merely another facility in a chain of progressive career steps. We are at your service and always have time to answer questions. I would ask only that we relax some of the formalities as these men and women are on shift and working; vigilance is necessary at all times. Shall we take a quick tour?" Mr. Oh gestured toward the far side of the console. "Have a seat, sir, and we'll begin."

"Before that, Mr. Oh, there are a few things I'd like to make clear." Colonel Song relaxed a little as he settled in. "I do know the basics of how a dam works, so let's keep this to the unique aspects of Cho Mya. You are an engineer by trade or training?"

"The answer, sir, is both. Early in my career after training in Europe, I worked on the construction of six other dams, two here in the DPRK, three in the south, and one in Russia. I have degrees in electrical and mechanical engineering, but it is the training of working to construct and then run the dams that qualifies me for this job." Mr. Oh started to sit, then looked up at the colonel a little embarrassed.

"Please, do sit, Mr. Oh. This could be a while." Colonel Song was now looking at the eight monitors above and to his right.

They would spend the better part of the next four hours discussing the dam's internal operations.

THE SPORTSTER

"Well, amigo, it's been over an hour since they were supposed to meet us here. I didn't actually think they'd make it, but now I have to find out what is up at the hotel. How should we go about checking it out?" Jack stood and walked to the register to take care of their tab. Carlos followed, and then went past him out into the night.

As Jack came out and walked toward him, Carlos pointed across the street and commented, "Seems like a lot of security for a regular hotel, don't you think?" Jack followed his direction and saw not less than six security and two police vehicles stationed in the Marriott parking lot.

"It is a little too much of a coincidence for me. I think we had better make our inquiry from a pay phone and see what happens. How about if you make the call?" Jack suddenly laughed and said, "I'll be waiting for you safely in the car."

"Thanks, I'll be watching for you to burn rubber while the SWAT team takes me out in a phone booth. Let's try to remember who's helping whom here. Why don't we go back to my place and call from there?" Carlos suggested.

"The same reason we don't just use our cellular phones." Jacks face turned serious, ">From a pay phone, if they try to track us, we can just hang up and bolt. If they find the pay phone later, no problem. We just have to make sure the pay phone isn't somewhere we usually would go, or around a lot of people."

"You mean witnesses," Carlos added. "I think I know just the place, and it's even safe to go there after dark!"

"Bonus. Let's roll." Though Jack didn't think things were going well, he also didn't believe anything too bad could happen unless he didn't get back into the lab within the next two days; then it could turn ugly. But with Carlos's help, he'd be back inside tomorrow morning and he could check on Alex and Emiko himself. Somehow that was relief enough.

Carlos had selected a bank of phones at a metro station. So many people used them that one person remembering another was a long shot at best. Their luck improved further as no one was there when they arrived. The courteous front desk at the hotel put Carlos through to first Emiko's then Alex's room, but there was no answer. When he inquired about Jack, there was no drama, just a ringing phone that was never answered.

"Well, Jack, neither of them is at the hotel, and they don't seem too concerned about you in general. Let's go get some sleep and start out bright and early tomorrow." Carlos started his car and they drove to his apartment. They had a beer as they watched the evening news, which mentioned none of the people Jack was concerned about, and then the two of them retired for the evening.

FRANK'S HARDWARE STORE

Lee was immediately aware that something was seriously wrong. He had walked through all the stores in the shopping center, with no sign of Yin Hee anywhere. He walked back to Frank's Hardware store, and just as he opened the door to go back in, he overheard a young girl telling her mom something about a shoplifter arrested in the hardware store. He turned to the mother and daughter and, trying to appear calm, he approached them.

"Hi there," he began. "My name is Lee and I work here in Frank's Hardware store. Did I hear you say someone was arrested here not long ago?"

The girl stepped behind her mother but poked her head out and said the words Frank did not want to hear. "Yes, a woman was arrested for shoplifting. The policeman took her away in his car in handcuffs."

"What did the woman look like? Was she big or small?"

"She was pretty little," the girl said as she slowly stepped from behind her mother. "She looked really sad."

"What did her eyes look like?" Lee asked her, knowing the answer already.

"She had pretty eyes like yours." The little girl then smiled at him.

"Oh, thank you, very much. I guess I better get back to work." Lee walked back into the store feeling tired and upset. He knew he couldn't explain anything to Frank and would likely have to wait until 2:00 p.m. when he got off work to contact the agency.

"Well, did you find her?" Frank asked. He was concerned both that Yin Hee wasn't with Lee and that Lee looked distraught. Without waiting for the obvious answer, he continued, "Look, Lee, I can handle the store today. Why don't you see if you can figure out where Yin Hee went? I'll see you tomorrow."

"Thanks, Frank, I really appreciate this. I hope she just had a headache or something," he mumbled as he turned and walked out the store and headed toward his car. When he got there, he grabbed the satellite cellular phone and punched in the emergency code.

"What is it, Lee?" The female voice of the operator was cool but caring.

"Yin Hee has been taken, probably by Inspector Ohl Suk under the guise of his investigation of the murder that took place a few days ago. Can you check to see if he went back to the precinct? Also can you track the movement of a squad car that came by Frank's Hardware within the last hour?"

"Roger. We were already aware of the squad car; it headed east out of town, then returned to the precinct. We'll check the movement of Ohl Suk and get back to you as usual via voice message. Out." And the phone went dead.

Lee had little idea what else to do, so he decided to drive east out of town on the main thoroughfare. It was a long shot, but it gave him something to do while he waited. It was fortunate for him that all squad cars have tracking devices installed so that if they are stolen, an increasingly popular crime, they can be easily tracked by satellite. Ohl Suk's car was no different; the problem was getting the data. It would take just under six hours to get the information Lee so desperately needed. He had pulled into a rest area and spent the agonizing time trying to ascertain what might be happening here. Was it a coincidence that after he approached Yin Hee openly she went missing? When his phone rang, he nearly dropped it in the flustered effort to answer quickly.

"Lee," he answered.

"We have the address. It appears that Ohl Suk was involved in the pickup of your charge, but he returned immediately to the precinct and has had a regularly scheduled day since then. Nevertheless, the squad car drove to a single dwelling twenty-five miles east of town. No one was booked into custody by him, and no shoplifters were booked by anyone today. It appears to be a blind drop off. How far away are you?" Her professional countenance was reassuring and helped Lee focus.

"I've driven past the residence. I should be able to get there within twenty minutes, however. The real question is, should I?" It was an honest question, but one he did not really want answered. In all probability, Yin Hee was reasonably safe, and their collective best interests would be served in staying near her, but not interfering yet. Unfortunately, that is the one thing he wanted the least, leaving her vulnerable and involved. These missions had very small margins for error. Being near might be reassuring to him, but not to her. But the most frightening reality was that unlike all the heroes on the silver screen, in real life the person closest to the target had the best shot. Whoever was now controlling or handling Yin Hee had her fate in his hands. A preemptive move, without considerable planning and coordination, might kill her instead of saving her.

Bringing him back to reality the voice repeated, "Lee! Are you there?"

"Yes, I'm listening, sorry." Lee was sorry; he couldn't afford to be taken off of this assignment due to his emotions.

"You're right about not storming the place, but we have no indication of any movement anywhere near the grounds. You are directed to approach from the west, leave your car out of sight, and make the last mile on foot. We have no reason to believe anyone can place the two of you together outside the store environment, so if you come across anybody, remain calm and just walk away. There is a Korean community nearby, so you will actually have a believable alibi until you arrive at the house. Approach tactically. You don't know if she is there or if she is alone. And, Lee, remember, this is not an extraction. We have to know where this is heading and what is going on."

"Copy all, moving now." He hit the end button on the phone and pocketed it. Immediately he withdrew it again and selected its silent and vibrate-only functions. It had a global positioning system upgrade that made it a cinch to track whoever had it. That, he knew, could save his life.

The Eyes

The dark was both the greatest enemy and the greatest friend, depending on the circumstances. Tonight, he was grateful for overcast skies and the setting of the sun. As he approached the house, he had a strong desire to drive past it for a quick view of the various approaches, but he knew that every opportunity the occupants of the house had to see him decreased his chances of success. A dirt path heading into a patch of trees provided the cover he needed to hide the car. He turned off all his lights and sat on the side of the highway for a second to make sure no vehicles were approaching from either direction, then very slowly pulled the car off the road.

While speed was his desire, he was acutely aware that a dust cloud lingering in the night air beside the road was as telling as a neon sign that a car had pulled off the road out here. He parked the car and killed the engine. From the backseat, he pulled his backpack with his field equipment. It was nothing elaborate—he was no navy seal—but it had dark clothing, specifically a dark blue sweatshirt with hood, and some basic tools, including a multipurpose tool and a generic Swiss army knife. It also had a halogen flashlight outfitted with a red lens, which he palmed for the trek to the house.

The hiding place for his car was considerably closer than a mile from the house, but it was the beginning of the only significant foliage in the area. Everywhere else had been cleared for the development of the farmers' fields. He moved steadily below the trees and bushes, careful to remain low and out of sight. After nearly twenty minutes, which felt like three lifetimes to Lee, he emerged from the underbrush. In front of him appeared a fairly plain farmhouse, ranch style with some kind of silo attached by an enclosed walkway. It took everything he had to resist the urge to sprint to the window and look inside. He would do this right, beginning with a full 360-degree sweep of the area from the protection of the untended growth surrounding the house. Maddeningly slowly, he began, focusing to keep his thoughts on observation, not what might be happening inside the house.

Inside, Yin Hee was watching the rest of the evening news, while finishing the microwave Mexican meal she had heated up for herself. *I might as well get a shower and get some sleep*, she thought, and took yet another look around the house. She thought of trying to barricade the doors, but realized the futility of the effort; she would have to ride this wave to the end, so rest was probably the best idea. There were ample towels, shampoo, soaps, and even bath beads in the bathroom, and to her surprise, a selection of women's jeans and tops in varying sizes in the bedroom chest of drawers and closets. Clearly this was meant as a waiting place, not a termination facility. The shower idea succumbed to the comfort of a bath, so she started the water and headed back to the kitchen. *Might as well see if they have some tea*, she thought. *It will be soothing after a hot bath, and I'm not sure I'm going to be able to sleep all that well tonight.* She found a variety of teas, and selected a Chai tea bag.

Back outside, having fully encircled the building, Lee was convinced there was no one watching the house. If she had been dropped off here, her captors were relying on either someone with her or her own fears to keep her inside. The possibility of electronic monitoring was still strong, however, so just knocking on the door would be a poor tactic. Just as he decided to approach the living room window, the light went out inside. Someone was there; the question was, who? Lee waited until he saw a light emanating from the back side of the house, and made his way around to it. There was a small, frosted window about five feet off the ground that indicated this was likely the bathroom. *Great*, he thought, *now I can hide under the guise of being a pervert if it isn't Yin Hee.* He approached slowly, until he was standing right beside the window. He could hear water running; clearly someone was drawing a bath. That increased the odds to him that it was at least a woman, and with his optimism perhaps Yin Hee was here, but would she be alone? He used the multifunctional tool to pry the screen off the window, which he quietly laid on the ground. Using the small screwdriver, he carefully levered the window. It began to slide and he was grateful it appeared not to be locked. Agonizingly he pried the window open a millimeter at a time. Still the window groaned from lack of use. The water was still running, and he could only hope it masked the sound. Finally he had the window open about an inch. That was enough for him to use the dental mirror from his pack to check out the room. From the lingerie he saw draped over the sink, he was now certain that the person drawing the bath was female, and his pulse quickened. Now he would wait, but he was in an exposed location. He grabbed his

The Eyes

backpack and tools and retreated to the tree line. His signal would be when the water stopped.

Yin Hee walked back to the bedroom. She took off all her outer garments, wrapped a towel around herself, and walked to the bathroom. The whole room was a bit steamy from the hot water, and it felt good to be really warm. The ceiling fan was a bit noisy, but not unreasonable. She hung the towel over a hook on the wall and turned the hot water off and the cold water on. *The best way to draw a bath*, she thought. *Just hot water at first—that way if the hot water heater capacity is small, at least you get all you can from it. For the run-down look of the rest of this place, the bath is actually pretty nice.* She walked back to the bedroom and switched on the small TV. The sounds from the TV were helpful in distancing the loneliness of being here in isolation. She walked back to the bath and plunged in her hand. It was hot but not scalding, so she turned the water off. Stepping toward the mirror, she wiped away a circle of condensed steam. The image peering back at her looked familiar, but different at the same time.

"Stress isn't very good makeup," she said aloud as she turned the sink taps on. She leaned over and began scrubbing the day's woes off her face.

In the trees outside, Lee heard the bath water stop and silently stood. He crossed the distance to the window silently, carrying only the dental mirror. Once in place, he raised the mirror to the small opening in the window. Directly across from him, he saw the heart-shaped butt of a woman bent over the sink. His heart lurched. This was a butt he knew well; it was Yin Hee's. How to get her attention without causing her to have a heart attack was another matter, but he decided he would need to be direct. He stood and calmly but firmly spoke through the opening. "Yin Hee, it's me, Lee. Don't scream."

The instruction was wasted breath. Standing in a bathroom naked except for a pair of panties in a strange house was hardly the way a woman wants to be found. As she grabbed for the towel, missing badly, her eyes swung to the window and she noticed it was open a small crack. After the brief scream, her mind had enough time to process the words and not just the unexpected sound.

"Lee?" she managed. "Is it really you?"

"Yes, come open the window quickly."

Frank's Hardware Store

She practically jumped across the room and quickly tried to open the window. It was stuck. Together they forced the reluctant metal to slide out of the way. Lee climbed in through the window, and then crouched to the floor, drawing Yin Hee with him. They held each other silently for a brief heavenly moment. Then he released her and began to speak.

"Are you alone?"

"As far as I can tell, yes. It is a small house attached to some kind of storage silo by a hallway. I think I've been in all the rooms and no one else is here. What is going on?" she asked urgently.

"We don't know. By now, I hope you know I had no idea this was going to happen. You just disappeared from the store; what happened?"

"Well, I was standing by the register when a man in uniform came in. I didn't recognize him as a policeman until I walked up to him. I asked him if I could help him, and he said his bicycle lock was jammed. He asked if we had any bolt cutters for chain, and so I took ours outside. The minute I stepped outside, Inspector Ohl Suk grabbed me and put handcuffs on me. People started to stare at us and gather around, and the other police officer told them I was being arrested on suspicion of shoplifting. Naturally everyone backed away, and they forced me into the car. Lee, you have no idea how scared I was. I didn't even know if you had put them up to this. I'm afraid I passed out on the way here, and then I woke up in the silo. Stupidly, I stayed in there for hours when I could have walked out at any time."

"I'm not sure most people would ever have walked out of there, Yin Hee. Where did you find the courage?" He was genuinely curious; she had a way of surprising him again and again.

"Well, I'm afraid it doesn't have much to do with heroism. I needed a bathroom pretty bad, so I had to do something," she giggled. It was like music to his ears. She was OK for now. "But there was a message. I'll go get it."

"Don't bother, just tell me what it said." He held her hand and wouldn't let her go even to get the message.

"Well, basically, I am now supposed to wait here until I'm contacted with some kind of task. That's really all it said. It gave me no other instructions, and there seems to be enough to eat and drink. For the time being, I think I'm still on their good side." She seemed almost casual about it.

"Perhaps, but I'm still concerned that they left you in the storage room. Why not bring you in here where they obviously meant for you to wait?"

"I've given that a lot of thought as well. I think it has to do with my training. First they wanted me to remember that they control me. Whether I am safe or not, is their prerogative. Second, and the part I forgot, was a basic lesson—never torture yourself. If I had remembered that, I'd have been in here and a lot more comfortable much sooner. They want me to pick up the pace, get the edge back for whatever it is I'm supposed to do. The missing piece is Ohl Suk's role. It was he who collected me from the store, and I expected him to be the one to give me my task, but instead all he did was drop me off here. I'm not sure what is going to happen next."

"Are you sure you can handle this?" While he knew she was the best chance to ferret out what was going on, he was genuinely concerned for her safety and well-being, physical and mental. "If not, I'll get us both out of here right now."

"Absolutely not," she exclaimed adamantly. "I know of many dozens of Japanese the North Koreans have abducted and dragged to their country. It has to stop! Injustice exists all over the world, I know, but we have to attack it one piece at a time. Most of my life has been stolen by the DPRK. I owe my parents the effort to do what I can to finish this for all of us. Knowing you are who you said you are, and that you are trying your best to help me, will make this bearable." She grabbed Lee in her arms and held him close. "Now you have to go. There is no phone here, so we'll have to play it by ear on contacting one another. I will assume you can see where I go, and I'll try to be as conspicuous as I can if I must move around."

He released her and reached into his pocket.

"Put this on your watch." It looked like any of the stylish interchangeable faceplates used on women's watches. "It is a passive homing device; in other words, it makes no emissions unless interrogated by a special radar bandwidth. That way it won't appear on any device sweep or set off any detection field. If, however, we were to lose contact with you, this device could be detected by satellite if we absolutely had to use it."

He leaned forward and kissed her, then opened the window, took a brief look around, and climbed back out into the night. Yin Hee went immediately to the bedroom and switched the faceplate. Then she came back into the bathroom and got in the bath. Now she could actually enjoy it.

USPACOM HEADQUARTERS

"Ladies and gentlemen, I think you all have a pretty good idea why we're here. The president of the Democratic People's Republic of Korea has invited me to a one-on-one meeting with him. He has yet to define an agenda, location, and time or rule in or out other participants. So far, we have had precious little serious information on anything new that is happening or is about to happen on the peninsula that could explain this unprecedented step. From the travel requests floating about recently, it occurred to General Hodge and me that this was a good time to get everybody together and see if we can't put at least a few pieces of this puzzle together. What we propose is to let all of you spend the next two days getting to know each other and trying to hammer out your guesses as to what the blazes is happening in North Korea. This is the most important thing on either my or General Hodge's agenda for the foreseeable future, so we are here for you. We don't want to burden your discussions with formality or conflict, so we will spend our time just down the hall with protocol trying to figure out how this thing should be handled. You should know we have been given access to, and the unconditional support of, the president's entire administration. Any question you arrive at, any assistance you need, we can get. We will come and go at your meetings, and we are hereby suspending all formalities. This entire floor is now a working command center, so I don't want the room called to attention on anyone's arrival or departure. I suspect I'll know if the president were to arrive, so, short of that unlikely event, let's get to the bottom of this if we can. Does anyone have any questions for either of us at this time?" Admiral Corping was doing all he could to engender a camaraderie that he knew could spell the difference between success and failure in the staff's analysis.

After the inevitable around-the-room introductions and short speeches on who represented what, it was time to get down to business. Colonel Cannen had taken the assignment as facilitator for this diverse group enthusiastically. It was a chance to be in the room when real progressive thought created policy, from his perspective. It was history in the making, as he liked to think of it. He had carefully laid out a schedule based on the participants and their specialties. He hoped he had built a timetable wherein each presentation would feed the next and come to a conclusion greater than the cumulative individual parts.

The meeting began with Carol making her presentation from DSRJ on the types of concrete convoys, the number of vehicles, and the times of day they were spotted. One additional piece of information she had developed was the amount of time the vehicles remained on site. The significance was unclear, but with each convoy of the same size, the amount of time on site increased greatly. Her speculation, and she was very clear it was a personal guess, was that the concrete was being moved somewhere, farther and farther away with each convoy. Again, she couldn't ascertain any further meaning to this anomaly.

Next came the folks from US Forces, Korea, whose primary information was that the training status of the forces north of the DMZ simply hadn't changed at all. They had PowerPoint slides detailing every aspect of the ground and air forces' movements over the past year, with an expanded portion detailing all the troop movement and air sorties of the past month. The bottom line after a two-hour presentation was that there was no pattern interruption to the North's military training schedule. The reigning philosophy was that if the DPRK were planning to attack the ROK, there would be a significant downtime for aircraft and troops, in which they would perform final repairs and upgrades to aircraft, and a final equipment issue and check for ground forces. In addition, there would have to be an accompanying logistical movement of food and supplies forward, as well as a repositioning of their armored vehicles in order to physically breech the DMZ itself. Absolutely none of that had occurred to date. Still, as is the way with intelligence analysts of every ilk, they didn't rule out the possibility that the North was simply going to blow off the rational precursors and initiate hostilities in an attempt to leverage surprise over preparation. As Colonel Cannen pointed out to the amusement of everyone there, they had spoken for two hours to carefully explain that the DPRK was either going to attack or not. It was as frustrating as hearing the Hawaiian weather forecast, which almost never varied. It was always warm and sunny, with a chance for windward and Mauka (mountain) showers, code for "there is a chance of showers in the area, but no way to know where or when they will happen."

The POLMIL contingent asked if they could defer until after lunch, hoping to discuss their ideas among themselves before coming up with a presentation for the group. Colonel Cannen agreed, as theirs was the most speculative of all the presentations. Following the POLMIL contingent, the APCSS folks would present, and last would be the CIA and DIA presentations. Colonel Cannen had deliberately held these two for last in an attempt to give them the benefit of all the other laymen's views of what was happening. He hoped it might shed greater light on the very highly classified data these two worked with regularly but couldn't really share with the whole group.

From the discussions he overheard on his way back to the conference room, it was apparent that not everyone was thrilled with the culinary prospects near USPACOM headquarters. He was hardly surprised. About the only thing available was the standard "food court" kinds of meals—pizza, a local Oriental buffet, and fast food hamburgers. In an effort to appease the masses, he made an announcement as they reconvened.

"For those of you who are so inclined, we have arranged for a stylish bus to take you down to an area on Honolulu Bay where there is a Gordon Biersch, Fernando's Mexican food, and, dare I say it, Hooters restaurant in one small area. It's a lovely place where you can watch the sunset over Honolulu Bay, with pretty decent food, and drinks of your choice. Naturally, we'll have transportation back to your hotels afterward. For those who want to go out or stay in on your own, we will also have wheels to take you straight back to the hotel from here.

The Eyes

Is anyone staying somewhere besides the Hawaiian Hilton Village?" After a few seconds with no response, he nodded. "I thought we'd gotten everyone together. Well, with that bit of administrivia handled, let's reconvene and begin with the much-awaited POLMIL folks. You have the floor." He took his seat at the table and waited for the POLMIL representative to get up to the podium. The speaker was Lieutenant Colonel Helen Zamlow.

"Thank you, Colonel Cannen," she began. "We don't have a lot of slides to show you, but would instead like to go through what we perceive is an unusual pattern of contacts from the DPRK to our folks in various places in Asia. We'll also discuss what we've discerned about President Kim Jong Il and his diplomatic efforts over the past sixteen months. At the outset, it is important to remember that what we have developed is somewhat like circumstantial evidence. We are drawing a conclusion based on the actions of the working functionaries well below the ambassadorial and political levels. Literally, it is like watching a civil engineer repeatedly request a bridge in a certain area and concluding there must be a military reason for crossing the river or gorge in question.

"First and foremost, it is important to understand that the huge amounts of concrete delivered to Cho Mya Dam were requested in a combination effort between the PACOM construction team, the Japanese Overseas Development Agency, and several nongovernmental organizations that have helped the DPRK over the past several decades. To us, then, the movement of concrete does not appear to be that unusual an event, given that they made all the requests publicly and through regular channels. In fact, at least two of the convoys carried concrete provided logistically by the State Department through USPACOM. Having heard the presentations this morning, though, we have discussed several possibilities, but we don't have the technical expertise to evaluate the feasibility of these rather, how shall we say, unusual ideas. Colonel Cannen, we don't want to disrupt the flow of organizations you've established, so perhaps we should save these provocative guesses until after everyone has made their initial presentation, and we move to the discussion phase."

Colonel Cannen, by way of response, turned to Dr. Woods and asked, "Are you ready to make your statement?"

"Yes, sir. What I have isn't very long, but it does have the excitement of being somewhat alarming, combined with the unfortunate downside of being unconfirmed. Without going through a great deal of buildup that I suspect almost everyone else here has already observed, I'll cut to the single piece of information that has created somewhat of a buzz at our center. Simply put, despite our best efforts to track them down through all channels available to us here on the island, we have been unable to determine what kind of hydroelectric motors are installed in the Cho Mya Dam, if any. Given the propensity of donor nations to take public and voluminous credit for donations to the Democratic People's Republic of Korea, it struck us as odd that no nation has claimed to help them with the single most important functioning part of a hydroelectric dam. It defies logic, and we have made precious little progress in explaining it."

As Dr. Woods spoke, both the CIA and DIA representatives sat up and leaned forward. James Forman the representative from the CIA spoke first, "Dr. Woods, are you saying that the dam, now nearing completion and long touted as the energy panacea for the breadbasket of North Korea, may not be a hydroelectric dam at all?"

"Actually, we have no way to verify that is the case, but since it became a focus for us at the direction of Admiral Corping, we have been able to identify the donor nations for all the other parts for a working hydroelectric dam. That includes the very expensive pieces necessary to mount these kinds of motors. But try as we might, we cannot find anyone claiming to have helped the DPRK with the motors themselves. Parts of a dam, especially this size, are extremely expensive, and would take a very long time to build. In fact, they are so critical to an effort of the proposed size and significance of the Cho Mya effort that it would seem virtually impossible to keep it a secret even if a country were trying. What do you make of it?"

The CIA agent leaned over and whispered to the DIA representative, then turned back to Colonel Cannen.

"Sir," he began, "we could get up and give our standard babble, as we had planned based on the secretary of state's instructions, but the combination of information we've heard so far today stirs some very distinct problem areas of a significant nature. I'd like to forgo the DIA's presentations and ours, and get with USCINPAC,

USCINCUNC, and their respective Special Security Officer, and secure communication back to our respective headquarters and the Departments of State and Defense. I believe we need to establish a Special Compartmented Information classification for this event, get all the individuals here in the meeting approved, and discuss this in earnest. It is only half past noon. With the admiral and the general's assistance and push, we should be able to reconvene by two o'clock. In the meantime, I have some information to check on, including getting a team working on confirming, denying, or establishing Dr. Woods' discovery as fact. I suspect the information each of us brought here has evolved a great deal over the course of this morning. If I might suggest, and if the facilities permit, each group should spend the next hour discussing among themselves their speculations on what is really happening in light of the cumulative information we've come upon so far."

Colonel Cannen nodded assent, motioned for the staff sergeant to go and get the two CINCs, and then asked, "Before we brief the big guys and then break, is there any other piece of information anyone would like to toss out now as we all head for our separate internal conferences?"

The DIA representative raised his hand and was recognized by the colonel, "Please, step up to the microphone."

As he walked up to the podium, Bob began his discourse. "I'd like to thank all of you, even at this early stage, for bringing together fresh perspectives on issues we have been watching with little insight over the past six months to a year. As I watch this chaos come together and bring light to dark corners, there is an anomaly we've been tracking for quite some time, which may or may not have anything to do with North Korea. It has been nearly a year now, but a leading research scientist and doctor went missing from one of our national laboratories. His field of research was specific, determining or developing a method to produce a neural impulse across a synapse, with the added complication of attempting to do so from living tissue to a synthetic material. I wouldn't bring it up here, but recently complicating the events of this missing doctor is the appearance of a Korean man posing as a police detective, who suddenly disappeared after contributing to the forcible abduction of a North Korean deep plant, who is actually a kidnapped Japanese citizen, whom we have been watching for some time. He went by the name of Chee, Ohl Suk. Before he arrived in Denver, he was stationed here on the island of Hawaii. Before that, he appears not to have existed. I'm not asking for your help in the case, just your thoughts, should they in any way impact your areas of concern."

General Hodge and Admiral Corping entered the room, and almost everyone resisted the urge to snap to attention, some more successfully than others, which elicited a smile from both CINCs. Once they had taken a seat, Colonel Cannen took the podium and gave a lucid summary of the morning's presentations. He then let Agent Forman make his case for the establishment of an SCI. Both of the senior leaders agreed with the concept, and then asked what they had decided to name the SCI.

It was protocol that, just like major military operations, SCIs had a specific name given to them for easy reference. While it seems like an easy task, coming up with these names was often a cumbersome chore rife with opportunities for ridicule. Clearly names like Northern Madman or Rice Weasel might seem terribly appropriate, but simply wouldn't pass the diplomatic test. After all, some day these, too, would be declassified. Ultimately, they settled on what seemed a bit like an oxymoron: "Healing Sword." It was an effort to capture the concept of a largely military effort to reduce tension on the Korean peninsula. They recessed for an hour.

OUTSIDE THE FARMHOUSE

Outside, Lee keyed the phone pad again. "Yes, Lee," the controller responded, "what have you found?"

"Yin Hee is here and she is alone. She has agreed to continue with the mission. What other assets do we have?"

"Right now, Lee, you are it. There is virtually no indication of any movement in your area, so I'd settle in if I were you. Of course, you can, and should, call for assistance if anything else should happen. For now, just sit tight." The female voice was final; he was on his own for now.

Despite his great desire to go back in to Yin Hee, he knew he needed to return to his apartment, get his equipment, and return to settle in. It took him only fifteen minutes to get back to his car and less than a half-hour to return to his apartment. There he gathered up what he thought he would need to observe and monitor Yin Hee's safety, including his Glock 20 pistol. A relatively new handgun, the Glock 20 chambered fifteen rounds per magazine. The Glock pistols were becoming standard equipment for anyone in need of truly reliable hand-held firepower. He took a shower, changed his clothes, and headed back to Yin Hee. How ironic that he would spend the night outside watching the lights of the house, and she would spend the night inside, both holding the other in their thoughts and, eventually, their dreams.

The Eyes

The night passed uneventfully and much more comfortably for Yin Hee than for Lee. The morning was little different, and Lee made no attempt to contact Yin Hee.

THE HILTON HOTEL, SEOUL

"That was a fabulous dinner, Hideo." Hae-Jung really meant it. She had rarely seen such attention fawned on one man. As his lady, she too was treated with the exact deference she hoped to make a permanent part of her life. The Hilton was another treat she had yet to experience, especially the VIP suite on the top floor. She tore herself from the spectacular view from the veranda and crossed the room to perch on the couch across from the king-sized bed.

"Shall we get to the interview now?" She took out her stenographer's pad and a small tape recorder.

The diet member smiled, paused from removing his tie, and reached into his briefcase. He withdrew an eight-page article typed in hangul.

"Here is your interview," he said. "Why don't we dispense with all this stuffy formality? Is there anything specific you needed to ask or tell me, or will this suffice?"

"Well," she said as she began removing her blouse, "I would sure love to see your bill on sending the Iranians over here pass into legislation and get funded."

"Consider it done. If it isn't too presumptuous of me, why don't you come over here and show me how grateful you can really be." And he grinned from ear to ear.

The Eyes

"Just try to stop me." She returned the grin as she slid to the floor and crawled across the plush carpet to the bed.

SECURITY CONFERENCE ON KOREA, USPACOM

When they reconvened, all present spent the first thirty minutes signing their appointments to the new SCI, and confirming under oath that they understood the implications of their participation in the SCI and the restrictions on their ability to discuss what they would hear and talk about.

CIA Special Agent Forman began the discussion by confirming that they too had not found any indication that hydroelectric motors had ever been delivered to, or installed in, the dam at Cho Mya. He revealed the CIA now had a team focused on this one location, and asked Carol if her team could provide their report in electronic format.

Bob from the DIA then indicated he already had the report at his office and had directed his people to get a copy of the entire file over to the CIA.

"While I'm up here, assuming we are now in a more or less free-form format, I'd like to hear the speculations Lieutenant Colonel Zamlow alluded to this morning. We have a guess ourselves, and would very much appreciate her bringing up her ideas first.

Colonel Cannen started to speak but was drowned out by the unexpected voice of General Hodge, who had sneaked into the conference through the back door.

The Eyes

"Please, let's get the guessing started. I think I can safely speak for Admiral Corping and myself when I tell you that we are holding an empty bag concerning our appointments with the State Department, and then with the most mysterious leader to date in this century. Colonel Zamlow, you have the floor. I'll shut up now, and please just forget I'm here."

"Thank you, sir. Well, here goes. Based on the information we've been given, and that has been presented here today, it seems to us, as laymen, that the North Koreans are branching off from the tunnels already in that area to reach new destinations, extending them, or reinforcing them. Granted we have no hard data, nor do we have any real concept of why they would be doing this, but that is the result of our no-holds-barred brainstorming session. The most important question is why? What if they were planning to take advantage of USFK's benevolence thus far to enlarge the tunnels for a major underground invasion? The reinforcement part, which we think would require considerable concrete, would make the DMZ passable even for very heavy vehicles at any time of the year. They would no longer be restricted to seasons when the ground was either frozen or semifrozen. It would give them a year-round window. Anyway, that's our unscientific two cents worth." Helen sat back down.

Bob stood and walked to the front of the room.

"We have an equally bizarre set of ideas, developed by a sharp but incredibly shy analyst. He made me promise not to mention his name, so on behalf of our teammate, here goes.

"One of his ideas is that they are using all the extra concrete to develop a missile launch facility inside the dam. And if that isn't scary enough, his second idea will really get your attention. He thinks they may be building a channeling tunnel to use the dam water to flood areas in South Korea. Just as the POLMIL folks have pointed out, we have no hard data, and no on-site eyes to confirm or deny these concepts; they are pure speculation." Mr. Cochlen sat down and took in the room, which had become eerily quiet.

Special Agent Forman stood and addressed them all, "What we have discovered here is that what may be absolutely nothing could potentially be a deadly new technique for fighting wars. We will now…"

Staff Sergeant Pickering knocked on the door. He held a Top Secret/Special Security Compartmentalized Information message from CIA headquarters for Special Agent Forman. "Come in," Agent Forman called from the podium. Staff Sergeant Pickering walked into the room.

Stiffening involuntarily upon seeing General Hodge in the back, he apologized, "Sorry to interrupt, General, but this dispatch for Special Agent Forman just came in and is marked Immediate."

"No need to apologize, Sergeant. Thanks for bringing it down to us." General Hodge spoke on behalf of everyone in the room, "We may get many of these urgent messages, so let your folks know to bring them in right away, regardless of how they are marked."

"Yes, sir." Staff Sergeant Pickering replied then spun about and left. Agent Forman elected to read the message to the room:

> *SA WOODS,*
> *Reference your inquiry into hydroelectric motor movement globally over past eighteen months. There has been negative movement internationally on any equipment the size necessary for such a dam. We have word within the past two days that officials at the Cho Mya Dam are inquiring into sources for eight large hydroelectric motors, but the lead-time for producing them would exceed two years and, to date, no donor nation has acted on the tentative requests. As an aside, imagery of the dam is now available.*

"Well, I'm not sure that this helps or hinders our analysis, but it does seem to take some of the pressure off if the DPRK is actively pursuing the motors."

"Perhaps," Dr. Woods interjected, "but it still seems extraordinarily unusual to wait until the dam has already been built to start working on ordering the most significant parts. I hope we would still include these concerns in the proposed presentations for General Hodge and Admiral Corping. I believe it is important to keep all the possibilities on the table, at least until we can find a source that can verify the purpose and use of the dam."

General Hodge spoke up again, "Please make sure you record all of these thoughts. We will share them with Washington and ask for a thorough analysis of each. We'll also be trying to find the right means to ask specific questions of the North Korean delegation, if this meeting with Admiral Corping takes place, which may be the trickiest part of all of this.

Colonel Cannen tells me tomorrow's agenda is to write up your findings. Please include the electronic version so that we can disseminate it in Washington. Again, we are specifically asking for your ideas and speculations, as well as any recommendations you might have on lines of inquiry or circumstantial evidence that might help us decide what, if anything unusual, is going on.

AT THE FARMHOUSE

Abdul arrived at the farmhouse mid-morning. Driving past it four times before pulling into the driveway, he hadn't found anything out of place around the area, and though he was informed there would be no problems, he was cautious as always. With the gravel driveway, it was unreasonable to expect his arrival to be undetected. The normal response by anyone inside would be to come and take a look. Anything else, like several people looking out, or no one checking, might indicate a trap. His knowledge of people was confirmed when he saw a slender hand pull back the curtains to take a peek at the intruding vehicle. Slowly, he opened the car door and extracted a packed backpack from the backseat and strode toward the front door. While he could easily have forced his way inside, he chose merely to ring the doorbell. Yin Hee opened the door tentatively.

"Who is it?" she asked quietly.

"Who I am is not important," Abdul said as he walked into the room. He dropped the backpack on the floor and pointed at it. "Everything you need is in this backpack, but there is more you must know. I will be watching your every move. If I even think you have decided to do other than as you are instructed, I will make sure you are dealt with very harshly. It will be the kind of pain you have never even imagined." He sneered at her, but she did not react.

The Eyes

"Do not try to threaten me." She held him in an icy stare. "You know nothing about me or what I have already been through or can imagine going through, so save the histrionics. Are all the instructions here in the bag?"

"Yes," Abdul's reply was a bit less terse now. He began to think there might be more to this young woman than he knew, but he wasn't sure if that made him more or less uneasy. "I will go. The car out front is for your use. I will make my way on my own." Even as he spoke the words, Yin Hee felt the panic swelling. Where was Lee? Would he be discovered? As quickly as the feelings came she quelled them. Lee was a professional. He would be safe.

"Very well then, goodbye," was all she said as she walked back to the front door and held it open.

Abdul left without another word. He would make it the quarter-mile down the road to his own car, then circle back and settle in to watch the house.

Yin Hee stood at the door momentarily and watched the direction the man went. Fortunately, he seemed to be heading directly back toward the road. While she was dying to open the backpack and see what her assignment would be, she felt an even greater need to speak to Lee. She knew he must have seen the car arrive, but with it still in the driveway, he might not yet know the man had left.

Lee had watched the man leave by the front door on foot. His heart raced, but he knew better than to respond. All he could do was wait until Yin Hee contacted him.

Yin Hee went to the side window and watched without touching the curtains as Abdul walked out of sight down the road. She ran to the bathroom, yanked open the window, and called Lee. Cupping her hands over her mouth in an attempt to control the sound's direction, she shouted, "Lee! Hurry!"

Lee bounded from the trees to the window, staying low and moving as quickly as he could. "Who is he?" Lee demanded a tad jealously.

She caught the sentiment immediately and coyly responded, "Why, are you concerned?"

"C'mon, Yin Hee! We don't have much time. Unless I miss my mark, he will be back very soon to see what you do next. At least that is

what I would do. Do you know him? Have you ever seen him before?"
Lee was professional, but his concern spilled over into his voice.

"Lee, calm down! I have never seen him before. He is merely a contact. He left me with a backpack that I have not yet opened. He said it contained all the information I would need to do my job. I agree with you that he'll probably be back soon to keep an eye on me. In fact, he told me he'd be watching me every minute, which is why I called you over."

Lee reached into his own backpack and retrieved three items. He handed her a plastic bag, a baseball, and a piece of paper.

"What am I supposed to do with this?" she asked.

"Write out what you want or need me to know, put it and the ball in the bag, tie it closed, and then throw it out the bathroom window toward the trees. The better your throw, the safer this becomes." He leaned through the window and kissed her. "Be safe, Yin Hee. I'll be near." He turned and jogged back to the tree line.

Yin Hee brought his gifts into the living room and sat down on the floor with the backpack containing her instructions between her legs. Slowly she unzipped the pack and looked inside. There were two envelopes, some identification badges, a diskette, some kind of recording device, and two small plastic containers that folded in half, forming what looked like an old-fashioned cigarette holder. The skull and crossbones on the outside of the containers kept her from opening them. Instead, she opened one of the two envelopes. It had the number one written on it—the second envelope was marked with the number two. She made the jump on which she was supposed to read first.

> *You have been activated as you were told you would be. There are a number of things you must now do in preparation for your mission. It is important that you follow each instruction very carefully and calmly. The slightest variation in your voice or composure could spell our failure, and you know what that would mean for you and your wonderful family. You will find in the pack a recording device. It may look simple, but it is a very delicate piece of equipment. When you record the session we have placed in the second envelope, the recorder must be carefully mounted on the en-*

The Eyes

closed tripod and placed on a table or counter for stability. It will be recording your voice and your iris scan at the same time. You will read the script exactly as written, but with your most comfortable tone and demeanor. It is important that you be able to repeat the performance nearly identically in the future. It will be necessary for you to make the recording three times. Do this when you first awaken tomorrow morning. For now, simply leave the rest of the enclosed material and relax for the day. You will not be bothered. The man who contacted you is not a threat; he does not know it, but he is being monitored constantly so that he does not get in your way.

She immediately went to the window to see if the man had reappeared. Finding no one, she took the keys to the car and went outside. She walked around the car to the driver's side, opened the door, and got in. Only then did she realize she was holding her breath. *Calm down,* she told herself. Pretending to familiarize herself with the car, she carefully scanned the visible areas near the trees and bushes. It appeared that for the time being, she was alone. If she was to spend this last night here, she might as well enjoy it, she concluded. With that, she got out of the car and opened the trunk. It was empty, so she closed it and walked around it back toward the house. Since she had not been told to stay inside, she elected to walk around the outside of the house for the first time. This, she believed, would give her the best idea of whether she would or would not be alone tonight. She moved casually from place to place, checking out the wild flowers, looking things over, and just being out in the sun. When she got to the back of the house, she walked directly toward the tree line and then continued along it. She hadn't seen anyone yet and was beginning to wonder if Lee had left, when she heard him from above. Nestled in the branch of a tree, like some leopard, Lee whispered, "What do you think you are doing?"

"Finding you, of course. The note leads me to believe I will be fine, at least for tonight. I think you should come inside. The man who came for me didn't have a key and came alone. With you inside, we can discuss what is going on and what is going to happen next, among other things," and she smiled for the first time since this chapter of their lives had begun.

"OK, you continue your walk around to the front, and if he is watching you, I should still be able to get in through the back window, as long as you leave it open, that is. Hurry. If someone is watching, you are highlighting this area. I'll meet you inside. Why don't you go start the car? You forgot to do that while you were checking it out. That might be considered a bit odd. Perhaps you should even turn the car around so it faces out of the driveway. Doing so will definitely focus attention on you, giving me time and enough noise to hide behind the house. See you soon!"

Yin Hee didn't respond, but continued her seemingly casual trip around the place, remembering to talk to herself every so often, just in case someone was watching her through binoculars.

Abdul was doing just that. He had returned moments after Yin Hee left the area where Lee was hiding. He now watched carefully as she walked casually around the side of the house to the front. She got in the car and started it. As she backed up, Abdul had to move to keep out of sight. He cursed himself for not bringing the car closer. If she took off, it would take him forever to catch up. Well, the best he could do for now was see which way she was headed, so he entered the trees and worked his way back down the ravine toward the entrance to the driveway.

Yin Hee caught a glimpse of Abdul's movement in the side-view mirror. Noting that he appeared to be heading toward the road and away from the house, she elected to push the charade for as long as possible. Feeling the relief of knowing where he was, she backed the car in a circle and headed slowly down the driveway, checking left and right as anyone who was scared might do. When she got to the end of the driveway, she got out of the car and took a long look down both stretches of the street.

Abdul stayed covered, wrestling with the idea of stepping forward and confronting her. She wasn't supposed to leave until tomorrow. Just as he thought better of the idea and settled down, she got back into the car, and backed slowly up the driveway to the house. *Smart girl*, he thought. *Perhaps this will work out after all.*

The Eyes

In back of the house, Lee had heard the engine start and dropped out of the branch in the tree he had selected. He had originally thought to leave his pack behind, but reconsidered. If he had picked this area to watch from, chances were eventually the other man would find the same vantage point useful. Lee walked quickly, deliberately, and quietly to the bathroom window at the back and crawled inside. He went to the bedroom and put his backpack in the closet, after withdrawing his silenced Glock. He then carefully moved from room to room, checking the locations and security of the windows and the doors. He was careful to keep low, lest his shadow fall across one of the openings, exactly what he had been looking for hours earlier to keep track of Yin Hee and her visitor. Lee heard the car backing up the driveway and wondered what had possessed her to drive all the way down to the road in the first place. Hearing the engine stop and the car door open and then shut again, he slipped back toward the hallway out of sight of the front door. The last thing either of them needed was for him to startle her. If she made any kind of noise or sudden reaction, it could alert an observer that she wasn't alone anymore. The door opened and she walked in confidently. She then shut the door and locked it, turning as if to go toward the window.

Lee whispered from the hallway, "Don't go to the window. If he is out there, you don't want him to think you care one way or the other."

Yin Hee turned on the television with the remote then walked toward Lee's voice. "Oh he's out there, all right. He followed me with his eyes down the driveway; I thought that would make it easier for you. Of course, that's assuming he is alone. From his mannerisms yesterday, I would conclude he is used to working by himself. I certainly wouldn't want to work with him. Now you stay here while I secure the bedroom and bathroom windows. There is a walk-in closet where we can examine the rest of my package without worrying about being seen, provided there are no hidden cameras." She said giggling. "That could prove embarrassing later tonight."

"Yin Hee, you're killing me." Lee shook his head. "Show me the way to this mysterious closet. By the way, is there something to eat around here?"

"I'll grab some chips for you from the kitchen," she said laughing, then stopped abruptly when she realized she needed to be careful about how much noise she made. She walked into the kitchen, grabbed a bag of Tim's Cascade Style Chips and two iced teas, and headed for the bathroom to make sure the blinds were down and the windows were locked. Then she headed for the bedroom, motioning for Lee to follow. She pointed at the closet as she entered the bedroom, and then while he waited inside, she tidied up the room, moved some clothes around, and slowly moved toward the windows. She saw Abdul walking crouched between two bushes heading for the same tree Lee had been in. She closed the curtains, and then walked back to the living room to get the backpack. She turned the volume on the television down just a little, mostly so it wouldn't mask any sounds she and Lee needed to hear. Then she returned to the bedroom closet.

"Well, I hope you're cozy in here," she giggled again as she settled down on the floor of the carpeted closet. She wrapped her arms around Lee and kissed him. "It is good to feel somewhat secure again. As long as I'm with you, I feel like whatever happens won't be so bad. Facing things alone is just too tough." She kissed him again.

"Well, I agree somewhat. At any rate, we also have to worry about how to get me out of here, but we'll handle that later. We do have two advantages, however. I'm armed with both a silenced pistol and a partially secure satellite cellular phone. The drawback is response time. There is just no way to know how long it would take for help to arrive if we needed it." Lee was being brutally honest on every count. Their best chance for success was to assume they were on their own. "Let's see what's in the bag."

After carefully removing everything from the backpack and aligning the contents on the floor, they found an interesting combination of items. First, something Yin Hee hadn't noticed before; there were six thousand dollars in one-hundred-dollar bills, and one thousand dollars more in twenty-dollar bills stuffed carefully into the zipper pouch in the front of the backpack.

"Looks like funding isn't a real problem here," she commented dryly.

The rest of the items included the two plastic containers with the skull and crossbones, the recording device, a cellular phone, several security badges with her photograph already digitally imprinted, complete with raised surface holographic markings, and two very unusual looking diskettes. The diskettes were about the size of the standard zip-drive diskettes, but they also had the raised holographic markings on their front and back.

"What do you make of all this, Lee?"

"Well, why don't we find out what's behind envelope number two?" He tried to sound like a game show announcer, but it wasn't a very good impression.

Still they both laughed as he opened the second, larger envelope. The first things they noticed were the two close-up glossy color photographs. One was of an older-looking distinguished man, the other a younger woman, probably half Oriental they thought. Their names were printed in bold black at the bottom of each picture. They were Dr. Alex Sanderson and Dr. Emiko Sanderson, respectively.

"She looks too young to be his wife, so I'm guessing they are father and daughter. Do you know them?" asked Lee.

Yin Hee studied each photograph carefully, and then concluded aloud, "No, I have never seen either one of them. What else is in the envelope?"

A letter folded in three spilled out of the backpack. Lee picked it up and began reading it.

These two individuals are your targets. You will leave today. By now you have completed the recording. At the end of the driveway, turn to the right and drive straight ahead to the interstate. Head east and take the signs that point you to the airport. You have E-tickets to Washington, D.C., on Delta Air Lines. In Washington, at the Dulles Terminal, you have an SUV reserved at Hertz. Drive to the Marriott Suites where you also have a reservation. You will be contacted at ten in the evening and given your mission. Once you accomplish your mission, in the pandemonium that will follow, you will be helped out of the building the way you came in. Once you are out of the building, you will be free forever. You may go anywhere in the world you choose after this mission. As far as we are concerned, you will no longer exist. But fail in this, and there will be no place on earth you can hide.

At the Farmhouse

"Well, they seem pretty sure you'll do whatever they want, don't they?" It was half statement, half question; Lee was still unsure what Yin Hee had been through in North Korea. What he did know about was enough to make anyone fold.

"Don't worry about me, Lee," Yin he spoke softly, but seriously. "What the North Koreans failed to take into account is that we Japanese will never give in, much like the American Indian refused to be enslaved, the Japanese spirit is strong. That is why I was so astonished that I was ever allowed to leave their land. Now that I know I have some assistance and the possibility of safety for my family, I will do only what is necessary to help you find out what is happening here. Still, I'd be lying if I didn't admit that I am terrified. They did a very good job of scaring all of us to our very core." Yin Hee was evidently determined to finish this for good.

"You may have to play along to the very last detail, Yin Hee. It may be your life or theirs. That is a burden I don't want you to have to carry; nor do I want to lose you. We'll have to find a way for you to complete your mission without getting hurt and, for that matter, hurting anyone else in process. In the meantime, let's get this recording finished— might as well do it now."

"I think it should wait until tomorrow morning, just as the instructions said. Why don't we get comfortable?" She leaned over and kissed Lee, and he knew the recording would wait until the morning.

PACOM HEADQUARTERS

No sooner had the two generals left the building than Bob Cochlen was summoned to the signals deck. The close resolution imagery of the top and faces of the dam were ready; time to check for signs of a capability to open the top of the dam. He sat at one of the desks and opened the envelope. The photographs were amazingly clear, and the detail made one wonder how they could really get this kind of resolution from something orbiting the earth. He spent almost an hour pouring over every aspect of the dam and its nearby areas. He found the enormous concrete slab interesting but not threatening. The rest of the dam showed no signs it was hiding anything. It looked just like every other dam he'd seen.

The analysts' take on the photos was pretty much the same, with a few guesses about the concrete slab being a possible landing and launch pad instead of the "cover" for the water, but that still didn't sound any alarms or trigger an alert.

As Cochlen finished with the photos, he noticed there were other pictures added to the brief intelligence summary. As he read through the analysis, he wondered why it had been included with the photos of the dam, but he had to admit that a city built within the last eighteen months near the Chinese border was intriguing, if nothing else.

INSIDE THE FARMHOUSE

"My name is Yin Hee. My name is Yin Hee. My name is Yin Hee. I am from Korea. I am from Korea. I am from Korea." The taping of these mundane sentences took Yin Yee three tries because it was difficult to speak the phrases identically enough for the sensitive recording machine, especially without blinking. Of course, Lee breaking up with laughter after each take didn't help the process either.

According to the instructions, the thrice-repeated phrases were entered into a logic matrix, which then statistically averaged the vocal tones, pitch, and tenor to give a virtually flawless coding pattern. It was state of the art and prevented anyone from recording another person's voice to foil the recognition capability.

Finally finished, it was nearly time for Yin Hee to head for the airport. They agreed that since they hadn't been interrupted the previous night, and no one seemed to be anywhere near the farmhouse, save the one Middle Eastern man now sitting underneath the tree out back, Yin Hee could drive off and leave Lee in the house. He now knew where she was going, and they could both assume she'd be safe until she got there. Then after he watched her tracker follow her, he could leave the house and make his own way to their destination, Dulles Airport. Lee had asked her to call the airport to confirm her E-ticket, and in so doing, determined which flight she would be on. Together they decided he should get on an earlier flight, just in case someone from the store could place the two of them together.

Lee remembered to call Frank and Kathleen; they deserved some sort of answer so that they wouldn't worry, and so that they wouldn't start making noise about Yin Hee and Lee being missing. Since Frank already suspected something was going on between them, the easiest thing to do was to simply appeal to Frank for some time off together. Frank couldn't say no to that, especially while standing next to Kathleen. Lee would have to remember to keep Frank informed, however, should the event continue. Ultimately, the agency might have to brief Frank and Kathleen on some of what was happening just to keep things calm.

Yin Hee left at around noon, though her flight didn't leave for many hours later. This was mainly so she could give Lee time to catch the earlier flight. No sooner had she started the car and driven down the driveway than the man ran from his position under the tree and down the road in the other direction.

Lee exited through the back door after carefully wiping down everything he thought he might have touched. He managed to get the window closed, but obviously he wouldn't be able to lock it from the outside. So as a last thought, he went back into the house and unlocked all the windows except in the bedroom and living room. If anyone were checking, it would appear that Yin Hee hadn't bothered with any of the window locks. Once back in his car, he immediately contacted the agency to brief them on the status of events. With their help, he had a bit of an advantage in travel arrangements and security screening, so it was fairly simple to get on the earlier flight. In fact, it would be the first time the agency had set him up with a first-class ticket. They also managed to get him into the room adjoining Yin Hee's at the hotel. This was turning into too comfortable an assignment. He kept pinching himself to be sure it was still real. When his car phone rang, he nearly lost control of he car.

"Lee here," he said after pushing the overhead button.

"Lee, we have identified the two target individuals as the researchers working on neural transmission. You were correct about them being a father-and-daughter team. So far, though, no one has been able to find any connection between him or her and Korea. They aren't assigned to the lab in Washington, but they are visiting there now. Whoever is handling Yin Hee has a very current information network. No further questions were asked since we don't know who is working with whom. Be careful.

"We are now working on getting you into the Washington laboratory. As soon as you find out when she has to be in the building, let us know. Fortunately, the building is for multiple uses, and we have people in the facility, though probably not in the same sectors she'll be going to—we'll stay on it. Enjoy your flight, but remember you are in a precarious situation, as is Yin Hee. We will have an information package dropped by your hotel room tonight."

Later that day, when he walked into the lobby, Yin Hee was being helped at the counter, receiving a large manila envelope from the front desk. He walked past her and up to his room. First he carefully checked the door to her room for any sign of mischief, but there was nothing out of the ordinary, so he entered his own room and waited. A little later, he heard Yin Hee in the hallway and confirmed it by looking through the peephole in his door. It dawned on him that it was going to be quite frustrating, being right next-door to each other but not being able to talk.

In her room, Yin Hee walked over to pick up the phone and order something from room service, when she heard a light but persistent knocking. She walked back to the door and looked out the peephole, but no one was there. Then she heard the knocking again, but it was coming from behind her, from inside the room. It was then she noticed that one of the doors in the center of the room wasn't a closet door. Her room and the room next door were set up so that the adjoining door could be opened up and the rooms could be configured as a two-bedroom suite. Hesitantly, she opened the door expecting to find the man she had met back at the house, perhaps with more instructions. Instead, she opened it to find Lee's smiling face.

"Lee," she squealed and rushed into his arms. "How wonderful! This is turning out to be like some kind of vacation instead of the nightmare I've been dreading most of my life!"

"I'm happy to see you too, Yin Hee. I wanted to make sure you knew I had made it. I wasn't sure if you saw me at the airport or on the drive over. I was going to have dinner for two brought up from room service, but it occurs to me that you had probably better order something yourself, just in case there are individuals in the hotel watching you. I'm fairly certain I represent no one significant to anyone here, and it was sheer luck that these two rooms open up this way. Trying to arrange this sort of thing would have been cause for alarm. I guess that old saying 'better lucky than good' really applies here."

Yin Hee smiled and walked back into her room. They both closed their door, but didn't bother locking them. Room service would have to be very perceptive to notice.

After dinner, they settled in Yin Hee's room and watched the news on television, snuggled up together on the couch. Neither spoke very much. Both were watching the clock. At 9:00 p.m., a knock rattled their peace; it came from Lee's door so he scrambled into his room and quietly closed the adjoining partition. He went to his hotel room door and opened it without peeping through first. It was, as he expected, a package delivered from the front. The box was wrapped to look like it was delivered from a local sneaker store in the mall, complete with its return address and logo. He signed for the package, tipped the bellboy, and closed the door. Opening the box, he found a sealed envelope with the agency's daily briefing, which he immediately opened and began to read.

Lee's eyes focused on the third page, a paragraph on Japan. It described a growing concern over the increasing population of itinerant Middle Eastern men on the streets of Tokyo. These men largely lived as a homeless community, and as their numbers grew, they became an increasing visible problem, more so in Japan because of its virtually homogeneous population.

The brief identified a new figure on the political front, a young man and a member of the New Socialist Party or Shin-Shakaito. Mr. Hideo Ishikawa had a plan to ameliorate the problem. He was most famous for his support of the expatriate Koreans living in Japan and had a vigorous appreciation for pretty young women.

The plight of second- and third-generation descendants of Koreans brought to Japan during the Japanese occupation of Korea was complicated. While they were allowed to become Japanese citizens, they bridled at the thought of becoming citizens of the nation they felt enslaved their ancestors. At the same time, they had no intention of leaving Japan, and, as a practical matter, really couldn't return because many of their families originated in what was now North Korea.

Mr. Ishikawa had built his career in part around fighting for greater rights for the disenfranchised second-generation Koreans. His latest plan would benefit Japan and Korea, as he touted it. The idea was to take a large group of these itinerant Middle Eastern men to South Korea. There they would split into groups and tour the major cities while sharing their individual skills with businesses in the hope that they would match skills with labor needs, a win-win situation for all.

Japan was more than willing to fund such an endeavor, so it was a popular concept. The DIA had taken notice, however, as these men had passed no scrutiny upon entry to Japan, and now they would be headed for the Korean peninsula, where some thirty-six thousand US soldiers, sailors, and airmen were stationed permanently.

Lee finished reading the brief and put it back in the envelope, which he then placed in his backpack. He opened the partition door and found Yin Hee had drifted off to sleep on the couch, so he sat down on the matching chair and continued to watch the evening news. Yin Hee woke up about ten minutes before ten, jerking upright, obviously startled and temporarily confused about where she was. It all came back to her quickly, and she was calmed by Lee's presence.

"Well, good morning," Lee said chuckling. "Your timing is perfect; you should be getting your instructional call at any moment now. Do you think I should be back in my room, just in case they decide to come by in person instead of using the phone?"

"No! Lee, please stay here. If someone knocks on the door, you can just walk back to your room and close the partition. Fifteen seconds is all that takes."

"OK, but if that happens, don't forget to close your side too." As he finished the sentence, her phone rang. They both walked over to the table and she reached for the handset.

She looked at Lee and he nodded, so she picked up the phone and said, "Hello?"

"You have been activated. Do not speak. Just listen carefully to your instructions. So far you have done well. Tomorrow morning at exactly nine hundred hours you will be downstairs and outside the front door. A van will arrive to pick you up. You are a part of a cleaning crew known as Hectors Industrial Cleaning Service. They will be expecting you, though they will not know you. Get in the van and introduce yourself. Be as casual as you can. Talk normally and be friendly, and they will suspect nothing. When you arrive at the lab, you will be refused entry upon your first effort. Do not be distressed. It is part of the plan. The security chief will be called, and he will ask for your diskettes. If you have done your job, you will be allowed to enter after a fifteen-minute to half-hour wait. Remain confident and sure of yourself. If asked the purpose of your visit, you state you have business in the recreation area. Once you arrive at the laboratory, you will go through a security checkpoint where your personal effects will be x-rayed, just like at the airport. Don't worry; nothing in your pack will set off the sensors. By now you have probably determined that the plastic case holds a set of darts. But these are not just any darts, which is why they are sealed and have safety markings. The darts have been filled in Germany and are perfectly safe to handle, as long as you do not touch the tip. Your job is to throw one dart at each of the targets. Due to the nature of the fluid, it makes no difference where you hit them, as long as a single dart point hits each of them somewhere. With your skill in darts, there is no reason for failure. They will collapse soon after; by then you should be headed back toward the entrance. You will be allowed to pass through. Once outside, your life is your own. Go wherever you want; use the cash you've already been given to start your life somewhere. Don't worry about the cameras and being identified. We have people on the inside to take care of that. Good night." And the phone went dead.

"So just like that, I'm supposed to kill these two people? I can't do it, and I won't do it!"

"Yin Hee, maybe you don't have to. Just play along with them and perhaps we can identify who is their inside person or persons. In the meantime, I'll have the agency track down this company and also let them know that security at the national lab has been compromised. Why don't you crash now. I've got a few phone calls to make. I'll join you later."

"Don't be too long, big boy." Yin Hee winked at Lee, got up, and headed for the bathroom and a shower.

Inside the Farmhouse

"Never fear, I'll be here," he said while laughing and went back to retrieve his phone and get things started for the next day.

Just as he began to leave, she asked, "Lee, did you bring your laptop? I noticed the hotel has an Internet connection, and I should check in with my friend, Colonel Song."

Lee stopped cold. He turned to her and asked, "Do you mean to tell me you are still in contact with a colonel from the DPRK? How do you stay in contact?"

"I told you," she began, suddenly finding his mood had changed dramatically and inexplicably. "I'm not hiding anything. I told you about the semiregular e-mails I've been getting from him since I was his teacher long ago. I use a standard Yahoo e-mail account. We stay in touch every other week or so. I always thought it was a way for them to keep a feel on my mental state. If I trust him and start complaining or saying the wrong things, they will find out and do whatever it is they think they need to do. I'm always very careful, and my e-mails to him are usually very short."

"What does he write about?" Lee walked back toward her, now clearly interested. His mind was on fire. He remembered she had told him about the e-mails on the night he had revealed he was more than just a hardware store employee, but he'd been too wrapped up in the events of the night to adequately weigh the significance of her information.

"Well, you're asking me to remember a very long e-mail trail, but most of the time, he just tells me about his job. Even when he was in Kyoto studying, his e-mails were about the engineering aspects of dams. Now he is in charge of that new one—what's the name? Cho Mya? Anyway, all he's told me about it so far is that Kim Jong Il visited it and the visit was a disaster, and that the dam is defective, or not working or something."

"Do you keep his e-mails?" Lee was leaning forward.

"Not usually. I suppose some of them are on my computer back home, and some are still in the system, although I think they get automatically purged every so often. Why are you so interested all of a sudden?"

"I don't know for sure, but I have read several intel pieces from that area. Our government needs information from there. Perhaps your contact can help, but we would have to be careful. This isn't my area of expertise, so I'll have to 'up-channel' this one."

"Whatever." She had decided to let him handle all the cloak-and-dagger stuff from here on in. She was probably in as deep as she could ever get anyway; too late to be squeamish now.

"I think I'd better make the call to the agency now. This kind of information needs careful consideration. Just remain quiet; no sense giving anyone the idea we are together." He took out his issued satellite cell phone. "Lee here. Yin Hee has her instructions. She is to gain entrance to the main laboratory for the National Institutes of Health by joining a cleaning crew with the company name Hector's Industrial Cleaning Service. Apparently they are in contact with someone at security in the laboratory. As her instructions indicate, she will initially be held up, but then will get clearance to enter. We need someone there to identify who responds to her initial rejection. That person is likely the contact, the accomplice. Her assignment is to kill the two doctors we identified by hitting each of them with a single ceramic dart filled with nerve agent. Any suggestions?"

"Of course, Lee. Why don't you get some sleep. We won't be able to get you into the lab, but we'll have agents inside. Tell Yin Hee to do what they ask. We'll protect the two doctors."

"Are you saying she should go ahead and throw the darts?" Lee was incredulous. "These darts are filled with sarin, for crying out loud. If they spill onto the floor after they hit the target, the whole area could be affected. Many people could die!"

"Lee, we'll be ready. Yin Hee needs to do exactly as she was instructed if we are to determine who is involved and have any chance of catching them. Tell her to throw the darts. But, Lee, don't be stupid. Tell her tomorrow morning, if you plan to see her early, that is," and the voice on the other end of the line giggled.

Lee could feel himself blushing but simply said, "Roger that. Oh by the way, I think I need a secure conversation with someone back there—whoever is working the concrete issue." He knew he shouldn't try talking around classified information, but he didn't have time to fool around.

"We'll work on it. It will probably be easier now that you're in Washington. We'll let you know."

Inside the Farmhouse

"Lee out." He went back to Yin Hee's room to find her sound asleep on the bed. He climbed in beside her and after a while, drifted off to sleep himself.

They awoke without the benefit of an alarm at just after six in the morning. Right after their room service breakfast, Lee turned to her and began.

"Yin Hee, I spoke with the agency last night. It is their desire that you simply comply with the instructions as given. I know you don't want to do this, but they assure me they will be able to protect the two targets."

"Lee, they aren't targets. They are people. Living, breathing human beings, and they are family. How can you expect me to kill a family?"

"But you won't. They'll be safe. The agency assured me again and again."

"Lee, I don't think you get it. If I throw the dart, it will hit them. I don't miss. And even from across the room in bad light, I wouldn't miss."

"Perfect," he said as leaned over and took her hand. "That's exactly what we need you to do. Please just think of them as targets; the agency never fails either. If they say the doctors will be safe, then they will be safe."

Lee walked back to his room. He was beginning to think this was going to be his last assignment no matter how things worked out. *I've got some money saved up*, he thought. *We can just move to Hawaii and start over. The agency owes me enough to help me get started out there in police work or something. Get a grip, Lee!* He came back to reality. *This isn't the time to fall apart. I've got to get into the building before Yin Hee does. That way I can be there to help if things start to go south.* He packed up his things and walked down the hall to the elevator. He got in and pushed P1 for the first-level parking garage and then waited. After the usual eternity, he got out and walked to his rental car.

Lee had the map to the laboratory, but he really didn't need it, he had been over the route in his mind hundreds of times. He knew where he would park and how he would approach the lab. It would take nearly nine minutes to get from the parking area to the front of the building. He decided he would drive there now and walk toward it. He would wait for the arrival of the Hectors van by standing at one of the many

275

metro bus stations just down the street, and then head for the entrance. If he timed it right, he might make it into the lab at the same time Yin Hee did.

CARLOS'S APARTMENT

The next morning Jack awoke to the sound of Carlos singing in the shower. He got up and walked out into the living room/kitchen area to find Carlos had set out a variety of cereals, a couple of microwave breakfasts, and had peeled and sliced an apple.

About then Carlos appeared in his robe and said, "Dude, you better get your rear in gear. We've got to leave in about thirty minutes." Then he disappeared into the bedroom.

Jack opted to shower first; then realized he'd have to wear the same clothes again, so he got dressed and stepped back out of the bathroom. He grabbed a few slices of apple and waved off the rest.

"I'll grab something there. It's a laboratory; it has to have food. They probably have a pretty decent cafeteria, and if it's like any of the others I've been around, once you're in the building, they don't care what you do. Thanks for the apple. I'm ready when you are. By the way, keep your day job—your singing stinks."

"I see you have no appreciation for the arts. Well, no problem. We can work on that. OK, let's go. We'll be driving the van today. My cool wheels will have to wait here."

Carlos ran a thorough inventory on the van, and then they took off. I have one more stop to make, another greenhorn cleaning professional to babysit. I get all the good stuff."

The Eyes

"No sweat, Carlos. I'm here to learn. You teach and I'll follow. Are you sure I'm going to be OK with the security?" Jack remembered his last shot at getting into the lab had brought the chief of security, which was what had started this whole mess.

"You are no problem," Carlos sighed. "I'm a little worried about this new rookie. Maybe it's a blessing though. If we have trouble with her getting in, the focus will be off of us, and you can just hang loose and act bored."

"Great. If she draws Charles's attention, he'll recognize me, and then we're smoked."

"Don't worry about it. I work with these guys all the time; they'll let the rest of us in while they work on her. It happens regularly. You really are paranoid these days." Carlos was confident, so Jack let it go.

They stopped at a hotel and a young Asian woman got into the van. She introduced herself as Yin Hee, and explained she was new to this and appreciated the opportunity. On the way to the laboratory, they picked up two more crewmen and headed for the facility. Each unloaded a set of cleaning devices and carts and then entered the building. As each came up to the security checkpoint, the security officer ran them through the iris scan, fingerprint, and voice-recognition booth, and then had them and their carts pass through two metal detector devices and a chemical scanner.

Jack was amazed as he passed through without any problems whatsoever. As expected, the new recruit didn't pass through, and so she had to wait for the chief of security. Jack stayed as far away as he could from the activity, but he couldn't help noticing that Charles had a markedly different response to this young lady than he had to Alex, Emiko, and Jack when they had arrived at the lab a few days ago. Charles personally took her identification diskettes and allowed her to pass through without scanning her cart or belongings. While it seemed very odd to Jack, he wrote it off. She was a lot better looking, after all. Perhaps Charles was human after all.

Neither Jack nor Yin Hee noticed that her backpack was thoroughly searched by Carlos's other two men. They handed her the pack, and she and Charles walked around the scanners to the far side. The rest of the crew set about their daily schedule, and Charles assured Carlos that Yin

Carlos's Apartment

Hee would be joining the rounds within a few minutes after the identification information was verified.

Jack and Carlos headed for the top-floor laboratories. They would work their way down from there and meet on the overnight quarter's floor around four in the afternoon. With luck they would quickly find Emiko and Alex and figure out what to do next. Now that Jack knew he could come and go in the facility with apparent ease, he felt confident he could help his friends, if they needed it that was. But that would have to wait. They had work to do now.

It didn't take them long, and they were ready to head downstairs to the fourteenth floor. Like many buildings, this one didn't have a thirteenth floor. They were now within forty minutes of getting to the living quarters. Finally, they had finished all the rooms on the floor.

Carlos walked toward Jack and said, "Let's first go downstairs, park the carts right in front of the freight elevators, and just walk through the floor. We'll be able to get a feel for whether they are even in their rooms. If not, we're going to have to kill some time, or even skip the floor and come back."

DIA HEADQUARTERS

"Sir, my name is Sam Philips. I'm with the European section. I understand you have some questions about Dr. Lehnon. We've been tracking him for some time now. There has been a tremendous amount of material flowing into Germany and making its way to Seine's laboratory, where Dr. Lehnon works. What we found most interesting about your briefing was that you mentioned in your opinion on Dr. Dorman that he was probably in a desert training camp. I can assure you there are no facilities of that nature that we don't know about in any of the Middle East countries, even Syria. Since the wars in Afghanistan and Iraq, we have a much greater presence and, of course, easier access to the skies. We are no longer tied to satellite coverage, which the training camps used to know very well. They would routinely cover anything they didn't want us to see because they knew when the satellites would be in their area. On the other hand, we have a reliable source indicating there is a significant flow of viable human eyes coming out of China. Does the possibility that the doctor could be in China seem unfeasible?"

"To be honest, I just don't know, but I do know there is a camp in the Gobi that wasn't there eighteen months ago. We had one of the satellites sweep the Gobi. We don't normally cover that area, so our cartographers automatically sent us those images for preliminary analysis.

The Eyes

One of my people found a rather large buildup in the Gobi. It was large enough that we spent more than a few minutes speculating what it might be or mean."

"Well, Bob, we have just rerun the images you sent us and you are right. There is a very large camp set up about three hundred kilometers northwest of Hohhot, which lies in Inner Mongolia. This would place the camp right next to the border between China and Mongolia. It is a fairly large camp and thermal readings indicate power sources for specific tents. We have no one on the ground who can verify what the site is for, but we do have reasonably good relations with Mongolia. I took the liberty of asking our deputy ambassador to China, Colonel Rich Hester, to help out. He handles Mongolia on a part-time basis from his assignment in China. He will get a ride down near the area with Major General Bataciqan. They get along well, and the Mongolian general likes to hunt from his helicopter. He was also very interested since he views the abuse of the territorial integrity of Mongolia as a very serious violation of international law. They will make the pass this afternoon.

ULAANBAATAR, MONGOLIA

"General, as always, it is such a pleasure to visit your beautiful country. Will you be demonstrating that keen eye of yours today?" Colonel Hester knew that before General Bataciqan took to public life, he had been an expert horseman and archer. His skill in the festivals was near legendary. The colonel had been honored with an invitation to one of the festivals a year or so before, and the site of the twelve young men riding the horses at a full gallop, hanging off the side, and firing arrows pass after pass dead into the center of the target brought a fuller understanding of the devastating skill the much maligned Mongol hordes must have had.

The general had humored the crowd with a few passes of his own, and despite his virtual antiquity compared with the other contestants, he was bested by only a few. He was still a strong competitor and an avid sportsman. He had been educated in both Russia and the United States, and had a doctorate from Harvard in international relations. His English was extremely proficient, as was his Russian, Chinese (two dialects), and, of course, his native Mongolian. He was often asked about his favorite experience in America. Without pause, he always responded with "the ubiquitous invitations to a Mongolian barbecue." Now that he had risen to a position equivocal to the American secretary of defense, he spent most of his time in negotiations with national representatives from all over the globe. His primary concern was in finding a way to fund growth in this great nation. The Mongolian people had suffered a long history of subservience to invading nations. Off and on, China had control of Mongolia, and then Mongolia would successfully throw them off only to have them return again. Finally the Soviet Union had overtaken Mongolia. This was perhaps the most devastating of all. While Russia had built the majority of the capital city of Ulaanbaatar, they had also occupied seventy percent of the intellectual positions of the nation. The Russians largely dominated the medical, academic, and political positions. So ubiquitous was the Russian presence that nearly all Mongolians still spoke Russian. Then the Soviet Union collapsed. There was no transition period; they just left. Suddenly Mongolia found herself free, but free with few educated or experienced enough to run a country. Mongolia had an air force, but none of the planes were airworthy and no one knew how to repair them. The Soviet Union had pillaged most of the valuables from the nation, most notably their religious icons. A huge golden Buddha had been taken to the Soviet Union and melted down for the gold during the occupation, as the Russians prohibited all forms of religion.

But all that was history now. General Bataciqan looked to the future, and he had a plan. Currently air defense in Mongolia was extremely primitive. Capitalizing on the incredible dryness of the atmosphere, herdsmen were trained to watch the skies. Any aircraft, even as low as five thousand feet, would generate a contrail in the cold air. Once a contrail was spotted, a herdsman would ride to a border patrolman, also on horseback, who would ride back to his outpost. Once there, Morse code would transmit the information to Ulaanbaatar. Controllers in the capital would faithfully plot the contrail on a huge map of Mongolia in grease pencil. The problem, General Bataciqan would always assert, was that the only thing that could be done next would be to throw rocks at the airplane. What he envisioned was to get another nation, preferably the United States, to donate some of its antiquated radar systems. If Mongolia could prove to the international Civil Aviation Organization that it could control its own airspace in real time, then it could start charging airline flight fees, like every other nation in Eurasia did. This income would jump-start their economy. It was a plan with considerable promise, and Colonel Hester supported the general in his efforts as best he could.

Today would be a treat for the colonel. He didn't often have the time to visit Mongolia, and to see it from the general's helicopter was always special. The general had remarked that almost all Americans visiting Mongolia fell in love with the countryside. Rich agreed. Once you turned your back on Ulaanbaatar and headed out into the country, it was truly a sight to behold. Rolling hills as far as the eye could see interrupted only by the occasional gathering of the traditional gers. These circular tents were a marvel unto themselves. They could be erected or brought down in a matter of hours by experienced tribesman, and were solid enough and warm enough for the people to survive in the open even during the brutal winter months. The Mongolians had learned to live in concert with the land and the animals, and, in fact, there were more animals per capita in Mongolia than anywhere else in the world. The herd was dependant on the tribe, and the tribe was dependant on the herd for its very survival. It was a truly symbiotic relationship between man and animal communities. There were also many wild animals in Mongolia, and it was these the general loved to hunt from his helicopter. Anything he killed would be field cleaned on the spot and given to the nearest tribal group they could find. It was quite a scene to watch a helicopter descend into a field and to witness the gift of the kill to the tribesmen, who accepted it without consternation. The juxtaposition of the tribal people, living literally off the land, and the appearance of the helicopter was nothing short of astonishing and a grand example of the flexibility of the people.

They flew southeast from the capital, with the general maintaining a steady description of the land, the herds, and the peoples as they passed. After a while, the general turned to Rich and asked, "What do you want me to do if we find a camp? I can certainly have it surrounded and taken, but I suspect that would not necessarily be helpful now."

"You are very insightful, General. We need to establish that there is a camp, and then find a way to determine who is running the camp or who is in it. To be honest, I don't have a good plan on how to do this. We suspect the men running this camp are from the Middle East; thus, none of the local languages will be adequate to help us determine what we need to know." Rich always felt it best to give the general the straight situation, as he was a gifted strategist and usually very helpful in sorting things out.

"The language isn't a problem. I have people I can bring up here who will appear to be herdsmen who are well trained not only in the languages of the Middle East, but in the tactics of the freedom fighters from the desert." He smiled knowing the freedom fighter remark would get Rich's attention.

"OK, General, point well taken. One man's freedom fighter is another man's terrorist. Nevertheless, it can't be good for Mongolia to have these folks setting up camps in your territory, regardless of their intent."

"Precisely why I asked what you would like us to do. For our part, we could just annihilate the place and all would be fine. We have no need for squatters who bring their enemies with them. Mongolia is in the business of growth, so alliances with people who build training camps secretly in the desert aren't a high priority. Ah, look there." The general was pointing forward and down.

Straining his eyes, Rich could make out some disturbance in the otherwise-pristine surface of the flowing desert sands. Something large was there, and there was movement within it, as was evidenced by the dust cloud surrounding the area.

"Thanks, General. If your pilot can identify where we are on the map after our return, that is all I need for today. How long do you think it would take to get your people here?"

"They could be here in hours. Just say the word. By the way, do we intend to extract the American?"

"To be honest, I hadn't thought that through. If he's here, I presume he would want to be freed, but I have no information from my government about whether they are willing or desirous of attempting such a rescue. It seems ridiculous to think they wouldn't want him brought out alive, but I'd still better check with Washington."

"Very well, Colonel. Sure you don't want to have a go with the rifle?"

"Yes, General, I'm sure."

EMIKO'S ROOM, WASHINGTON NATIONAL LAB

"Emi-chan, let's go. They are letting us out of here." Alex opened her door, but she wasn't anywhere to be seen. He walked into the room and through the suite. When he found the bathroom door open and no one inside, he suddenly had a very bad feeling. He turned and started to walk back down the hallway. All he could think of was trying to find where they might have taken her. He decided to start his investigation in the dining area, which was adjacent to the recreation room. Maybe she had grown tired of the Web search and had gone down to the recreation center on her own. Her concentration was good but her patience was thinner than his was, and she normally didn't like to interrupt him while he worked. *Yeah, that had to be it*, he thought. *She must have gone out exploring. Charles, Jock, and Rock had started treating them better, so she probably felt she had the run of the place. She's probably playing pool right now.*

Just then someone grabbed his arm and dragged him into the janitor's closet. He felt a hand over his mouth; he couldn't move.

Then he heard Jack's voice. "Alex, calm down and we'll release you. We just couldn't afford to have you shout right now; the second goon is headed for your room, and we need him to go away." Alex nodded his head and the man holding him let go. "Alex, this is Carlos.

The Eyes

He's a great friend of mine. He used to work at the other laboratory facility with Dr. Dorman. He got me in here."

"Where is Emiko?" Dr. Sanderson sounded very concerned.

"We saw her heading for the dining room, escorted by the other of those two muscle-bound morons we met when we first arrived. What's going on? What happened to you and Emiko after I left?"

Alex tried to run down what was happening, but gave up. He knew he wouldn't be able to concentrate until they got out of the lab facility.

"Look, I need to go down to the dining room as they asked me. If Emiko is headed that way, there is still a chance they actually intend to let us go. If we do anything else, they may become displeased with us. Why don't you guys meet me down there, but wait here for a while so it doesn't look like we are together."

Alex then opened the door and walked out, slightly more comfortable knowing Jack and Carlos were down the hallway. He headed for the dining room. When he arrived, he saw Emiko sitting with Rock over at one of the tables. She didn't seem the slightest bit distressed, and that made him feel much better. She looked up and waved him over, but she didn't smile—what did that mean? What the heck was going on here? He walked over and sat down with Emiko and Rock.

"Emi-chan, what is going on? Why didn't you let me know you were coming down here? You nearly scared me to death. Charles called and told me to get you and have you join me for a meal here; then we are free to go." Alex looked over at Rock and said, "Emi-chan thinks we can trust you; so be it. Are we really going to be let free?"

"That's what I came to find out. I heard them talking about it earlier today, but it is a drastic change in plans for Charles. And since we don't know whom he really is working with or for or even why he's interested in you two, I thought I'd better come along. Why don't you two just go through the line like you normally would, and I'll wander around and look obnoxious like I normally would. When you're done with your meal, if nothing problematic has happened by then, go ahead and head out just as Charles promised you could. I'll shadow you until you get to the front desk. You're safe there as virtually everyone at the desk works for us on the DIA security team."

"Why would the DIA be watching this facility?" Emiko's eyes were wide as she started thinking it through.

"We'll have time for explanations and much more after we get you both out of here. Now go eat, though I suspect that's going to be a little hard to concentrate on."

Rock stood and headed toward the recreation room. The recreation area and the dining area merged in a big open space with the tables shared between them. It was possible and comfortable for those with less-than-gourmet eating habits to grab a burger and a beer and then throw darts or play pool during their meal.

Dr. Sanderson walked over to the counter and ordered a cheeseburger, fries, and a Miller Genuine Draft. For her meal, Emiko ordered a chicken Caesar salad, which she expected she would do little more than pick at anyway.

While they were in line waiting for their food, Alex stood very close to her and whispered, "Emi-chan, don't react to what I'm about to tell you, OK? Pretend I'm talking about the food."

She nodded, pointed at the chef adding the Swiss cheese to his hamburger and nodded again.

"Jack is here in the building. He is safe and will be down here shortly. You cannot let anyone see you acknowledge his presence. He is no more than a cleaning crew member—got it?"

She nodded again, but her face had brightened considerably.

"He has a friend with him and they will be shadowing us out of here, if they don't get caught themselves. Do you think I should let Rock know?"

She shook her head and said, "Not unless he comes back. Let's get our meals; they're about ready now." She sure seemed a lot more interested in the food now. Alex sat watching his daughter wolfing down the salad and even helping herself to his fries. It was amazing how she could suddenly feel so secure, when they were in the midst of all of this. She looked up and as her cheeks blushed, he knew Jack had made it to the recreation room.

"Before you say anything, I can see in your face that he's somewhere behind me. If you're done with your meal, I suggest it is probably as good a time as any to see how this is going to pan out. Shall we head for the front desk?" She was already standing and gathering her tray and dishes. The quickest way out was through the recreation area, which was OK with both of them as Rock was on one side and Carlos and Jack were on the other, both trying to pretend they weren't watching Alex and Emiko. Casually, they strode past the tables and into the recreation room. Suddenly Alex put his hand up to the back of his neck, and keeled over on the floor. As Emiko turned in reaction, she felt a sharp prick just below her shoulder, and then she dropped to the floor beside her father.

ULAANBAATAR

Colonel Hester made the secure call to Washington from the embassy compound. "Bob, this is Rich. We have found a sizeable camp in the Gobi. The question is, what do you want us to do about it?"

Bob had anticipated the question but didn't have a good answer. "Do you have any ideas, Rich? We're a little thin here."

"Just one. I don't know how well it will go over in Washington, but here it is. General Bataciqan is willing to take out the camp, and in the process get Dr. Dorman out, if he's there and alive. What do you think?"

"Would he need cooperation from the United States?"

"No. In fact, now that the general knows the camp is there, my suspicion is they will take it out anyway. The only question is whether or not we want the doctor rescued, which would complicate the operation."

"I'll give the approval for the backdoor request then. I know it will take a few days to set things in motion, so if anything comes up, I'll call. Keep your satellite phone on."

COLONEL SONG'S
CONFERENCE ROOM

"Major Kim, Captain Youhn, and Captain Jung, you have done well today. Now I would have you explain what the new construction is really about. Clearly, the only thing left for the dam is the installation of the hydroelectric motors. Major Kim?"

"Sir, the remaining construction is twofold. They are preparing the sides for acceptance of the concrete safety cover, and then they will complete work on the removable base. It needs to be removable so the water can flood the tunnel constructed beneath it." Major Kim stopped, and the room became quiet as the realization of what that meant seeped into Colonel Song's thoughts.

"Who constructed the tunnel? When was it constructed? Where does the tunnel lead?" Colonel Song was sitting ramrod straight and holding each man in his steady gaze one at a time. He did not seem angry; he now needed to accept what was happening, learn all he could, and determine the next step he should take. It was now clear what the dam's dual purpose was. "Youhn?"

"I don't know for sure who built it. As I understand it, the portion beneath the dam was built from the south, a dead end left for some time, perhaps years. Once the dam was complete, the tunnel was finished beneath the steel plate. To my knowledge, none of us here at Cho

Mya has ever seen the tunnel as the steel plate has never been moved. Major Kim?"

"No, I have never been in it either. But I don't think the same teams that built the other tunnels constructed it because this one needed several things the others didn't. The primary requirement in this tunnel was strength on all surfaces—top, bottom, and sides. Second, to maximize the devastation, the tunnel would need to gradually narrow from its beginning, beneath Cho Mya, to its termination." Major Kim stopped.

"Well, don't hold me in suspense, Major. Where does the tunnel lead?"

"Colonel, it terminates beneath Seoul." Kim smiled; he was probably the only one at this facility that knew the answer.

"So our theory is if the plate can be moved, the water from the dam will flood Seoul and the army camp, and that ensures we can take back South Korea? Doesn't anyone remember the first war? We had the puppets to the south and their friends trapped in a small area all the way in the southernmost port of Pusan. We held 96 percent of Korea, and then were driven back north of the 38th parallel. The difference between our force capability and theirs, excluding shear numbers, has greatly expanded since then to our disfavor. Is there a plan to shore up our fighting capabilities first? Is there a timetable for when this dam will be used in this effort?" The colonel again looked at each man; they, in turn, were all shaking their head. Jung answered for them all.

"Sir, those questions are for the dear leader and his staff to determine. None of us would be privy to such high-level discussions. I'm not sure I'd want to be," he added finally.

"One last question for today, and then we'll call it a wrap. You mentioned early on that even after being used in this fashion, the dam could be reused, or reloaded. What do you mean by that?" Colonel Song was growing visibly tired, and his mind was reeling from the day's revelations.

"I can answer that," Captain Youhn said. "The top cover, which will be strongly attached and could be used as a runway, helicopter landing pad, truck park, or formation field, is designed to be the same shape and size as the bottom of the lake. The connection points are actually long guide rails along the sides of the lake, which stretch from above the water line to the water bed. That way, as the water level rises and falls, the cover can move as well. The real reason for the guides, however, is revealed when one looks underneath the cover. Inserted into it is another steel circular plate identical to the one now covering the tunnel. When that bottom plate is moved, it actually rotates out of the way on a large, circular track. As the water floods the tunnel, the cover will be dropped. Spikes built on the bottom of the lake outside the diameter of the plate will separate it from the concrete cover and allow it to settle back in place at the bottom, closing off the hole and temporarily concealing the attack. The river and diverted waters will then refill the dam. This will increase Western intelligence efforts to discern what happened, while the dear leader continues with his plan. The mechanism beneath is designed to allow for multiple uses if needed. If it isn't needed, we still have the functioning dam." Seeing that the colonel seemed to accept all this new information, the captain returned to his aid role. "Shall I have your dinner prepared?"

"Yes, I have much to digest this evening. We'll meet again in the morning. I want to see what plans, if any, are in place for obtaining hydroelectric motors. Dismissed. We'll meet in my quarters tomorrow at 0830."

WASHINGTON NATIONAL LAB, RECREATION ROOM

Yin Hee nearly fainted. As the two victims fell to the floor, she knew they were dead. Lee had failed; or worse, he was part of the scheme. She wasn't sure who had seen her, or if anyone had.

Earlier in the day, she had carefully selected the table by the dartboards. She had been waiting for several hours, and whiled away the time by throwing darts, but making sure she threw them very poorly. It wouldn't do to attract attention. At one point, the entire room had become empty. She took the opportunity to remove three light bulbs from the overhead system. If anyone noticed, she could just pretend to be the one in charge of replacing them. >From this dark spot in the room, it had been easy to identify the two targets, as she had decided to call them. When she tossed the two darts, one after another, she didn't have to look to see if they had hit their mark—she never missed. All she could do was pray Lee and his people knew what they were doing, but now it seemed unlikely. She had been duped, and now she was a murderer.

By the time the first target fell, she was already out the door and on her way down the hallway toward the front desk and freedom for the first time in her adult life. She was terrified and exhilarated, the combination of which made her light-headed. All she could think of was the front desk, that final cursory security check, and then she'd be out of the building. It was all she could do to keep from running. She quickly walked down the hall around the corner, down the escalator, across the lobby, and then toward the first metal detector. It was unmanned, so she walked through it briskly and confidently. She could see the second escalator at the other end of the hallway. Down that escalator, through one more metal detector, this one with someone there to make sure everyone still had his or her ID badges with them, and she would be out into the lobby. While there were still plenty of uniformed security officers in the front area, they never moved unless someone created a ruckus or they had reason to suspect something.

Yin Hee's biggest fear was that someone would alert the front desk that the two doctors had been attacked. She was tormented inside. How could she have done this? But then, how could she have not? Lee assured her they would be fine, but she knew better. She had hit both of them with darts full of sarin nerve agent. They were probably dead before they hit the floor. Tears welled up in her eyes as she continued on. When she got to the bottom of the escalator she saw the man at the checkpoint looking as bored as one might imagine the person tasked with such a mundane job would become. But as she showed him her badge and he nodded and waved her through, she observed one of the security officers talking with a uniformed guard near the front door. Her panic welled up inside her as she headed resolutely toward the door. She could feel every beat of her heart, and it sounded like water rushing over a dam in her ears. Her breathing was rapid, shallow, and getting faster by the second. Ten feet. Six feet. She had her hand on the door, and she pushed it open and...nothing.

She walked out into the sunshine and felt the weight of the world dropping off her shoulders. She felt like screaming and running aimlessly through the streets of the city. More than anything else, she wanted to fade into the crowd and disappear for the rest of her life. Walking calmly, she decided resolutely not to look back over her shoulder; she would do that after she had crossed the next street. Now she stood with the group waiting en mass at the corner, waiting the seeming eternity until the light turned green. The little, white walk man appeared on the far side of the street, and like cattle herded to slaughter, they all began to cross together. Just as she reached the other side, she felt someone take a firm grip on her right biceps, and almost simultaneously someone grabbed her left biceps. The sheer size of the hands told her she would be going wherever they wanted her to go.

The one on her left said, "Just stay calm and keep walking."

They guided her across and down the next street into a parking lot where a black van with no windows waited. The back door opened and they pushed her in. Just as she passed out, Lee pulled her to him and then gently laid her in the backseat.

The van drove back to the National Institutes of Health laboratory where, to Lee's surprise, a full CIA complement had the building surrounded.

THE GOBI

They looked like a ragtag troop of misfits. Their uniforms were tattered and torn and, on this crisp October night, had they been in America, they might have appeared to be in poor costumes for a Halloween party. But they weren't in America; this was the Gobi desert. These were real soldiers, with a serious mission. They might not have the latest equipment, certainly no high-tech armament, but with their horses, bows, arrows, and frightening daggers, knives, and swords, they were well armed nonetheless. This was a team specially nurtured to enhance their natural abilities. Using skills honed since they were just boys in sportsmanlike competition, they were a formidable attack force. Mounted and very well informed, this night would be very difficult for those designated as their targets.

Since the early days and the Mongol hordes of the past, these proud and fierce warriors were not known for their gentle nature. For tonight's mission, as far as they were concerned, only one human being needed to be kept alive. Whether or not he was removed alive was partially up to him. If he struggled or made noises that would jeopardize their ultimate purpose, his dead body would be handed over in the morning; however, if they could find him and he cooperated, he would remain alive. Everyone else in the camp would perish. Their ilk had burdened the country throughout time, and then departed unceremoniously, leaving behind the rusting shell of their presence. The opportunity to remove some of them was a task to be relished. Unfortunately, removing invaders was a historical responsibility of the nomadic peoples, and they had centuries of experience. This type of raid was, by its nature, brutal and swift.

A single pair of advance scouts would attempt to find Dr. Dorman. Khasar, whose name means "terrible dog" in English, and Bataar, whose name translates to "hero," were two of the best. The Gobi desert, as it is known in the West, is a redundant name. *Gobi* is the Mongolian word for desert. While there are the classic mountains of sand, they are but one part of the six hundred by one thousand mile area known as the Gobi.

The night was cold, even for early fall in Mongolia, which meant it was well below freezing. The Mongol warriors and their mounts were used to the severe conditions found here, and the half-moon with completely clear skies translated into nearly perfect conditions for a raid. They had ridden for four and three-quarter hours in silence; the only sound was the muted crunching of horses' hooves as they pounded the arid sand.

Now the men and their steeds waited, catching their breath and resting as the two scouts moved in complete silence and near-invisible garb over the last thousand meters to the camp. Theirs was the only truly difficult part of this mission. They had been told they would find the foreign doctor in the thirteenth tent, almost the dead center of the middle row. Clearly, this doctor was important to the camp to be placed so centrally. But finding the tent and the doctor was only the first part of the task. Then they would have to wake him, verify his identity, and convince him to go with them, all without causing undue disturbance. If there were others in the tent with the doctor, they would never wake up.

The first two sentries were dispatched with such speed one would have to have been anticipating it to know something had happened to them. Their bodies lay where they fell. As Mongols approached the tent city proper, they came across two more guards. These two were more alert and were actually doing their jobs. Still, death comes quietly in the desert, and two well-thrown knives finished the defensive postings quickly.

The Gobi

They moved in silence, timing their efforts with the wind so that tent flap movement or the chasing of debris through the camp would mask any inadvertent noise. Had anyone noticed their approach, the attackers would have been indistinguishable from the other residents, until they spoke. Neither Khasar nor Bataar had any intention of talking to anyone besides the American doctor, whose tent they now stood before. Nodding silently, the two men rushed into the tent in a synchronous silent flurry.

Before he could begin to gather his senses, Dr. Dorman again felt cold steel against his neck. He was not frightened this time because he believed his assailant was someone from inside the camp. If that assumption were true, the person with the knife would be killing himself if he harmed the doctor in any way.

"Doctor?" the intruder demanded quietly.

"Yes," he managed to say as the intruder relaxed his grip slightly.

Without further communication or ceremony, Khasar lifted the doctor over his shoulder and left the tent. He did not appear that big, but he had no difficulty carrying the doctor swiftly out into the cold night air and away from the camp.

Dr. Dorman felt safe yet frightened because he had no idea what these men wanted. They took him into the desert, and when they had arrived half a kilometer outside of the camp, they put him down to walk. One of the men handed him a sheet of paper rolled up and tied with twine. He untied the string and began reading the document. It had the appearance of an official communiqué, complete with the seal of the embassy of the United States. As he read it, tears welled up in the doctor's eyes. Apparently this horrible chapter in his life was coming to a peaceful end. The letter said these men were working on behalf of the government of the United States to repatriate one Dr. Eugene Dorman to the United States of America. He couldn't remember the last time he had been so relieved in his life.

As with any mission to rescue someone, the one thing that is most memorable to the individual being rescued is the coldness of the people executing the mission. Academically, it makes sense that since they are placing themselves at probable great risk to save one individual out of many, and usually someone they do not know and whose identity they have only minimal time to verify, that they would be quite cold in their approach. Much as with escaped POWs who find their way to sympathetic partisans in war, the victim is and must be treated with great suspicion.

The rest of the army arrived slowly, easily one hundred strong, and not a word was spoken. Just as Dr. Dorman was wondering how so many individuals could coordinate a confrontation of this size, the attack began. In seconds, he understood. When the result is the death of everyone in the camp, there are fewer details to discuss. The methodical manner in which the Mongol warriors went about the business of annihilation was frightening to behold. Four men rode between each row of tents, two per side. With sharp hooks attached to spear shafts, they rode along snaring each tent as they went. With the power of the four horses, the tents were easily ripped from the ground, exposing the confused inhabitants of each tent in succession. These hapless individuals were swarmed by a larger force of warriors, equipped with all manner of blades. In seconds, the sand was stained red with blood.

With no one left alive, the whereabouts of Dr. Dorman now became information that could be manipulated. The operative question was, who would want to manipulate it? The appearance of these rescuers, obviously not indigenous to the Middle East, combined with the paper from the American embassy, allowed Dr. Dorman to make some rapid, accurate reassessments of his location. He elected to remain quiet and calm, and wait out the razing of the camp. It took less than thirty minutes to eliminate the place he had known as home for the past nineteen months. Interestingly, he felt pangs of sorrow for many of the people who arguably were his captors, especially those who had helped him through the surgical procedures he had performed. They had not really been enemies, just people doing what they thought had to be done. He rode silently through the night with his new compatriots, to wherever his next adventure would take him.

SEINE'S FACTORY IN
THE FORMER EAST GERMANY

Once the German researchers had recognized the missing link in the use of neonatal fluids research, brought to them by their agent watching Dr. Dorman, the rest was just a matter of time. All the experiments using electricity, temperature, pressure, amino acids, and even viruses to stimulate growth where none had occurred before had failed. Through sheer luck, from Dr. Lehnon's perspective, Dr. Dorman had found that vibrations, in theory, recreating either the pulsing of blood from the mother's heart or the rhythmic movement of the ocean in the prelife primordial soup, turned out to be the factor that allowed neonatal fluid to work its magic. It took remarkably little time, from a research and development standpoint, to recreate and then control this phenomenon. Having an established working relationship with China proved fortuitous. The country's one-child policy made an abundance of neonatal fluid and tissue available if one had the connections and the money to acquire it.

When the Middle Eastern patients arrived, many were still in shock. Obviously, the conditions of their original surgery were somewhat less than ideal. Dr. Lehnon could not fathom why the fools had insisted on keeping Dr. Dorman in the camp with the volunteers. Nevertheless, something had to be done about the toll the surgeries were taking on the young men. While few actually died, their condition required weeks of recovery before the rest of their transformation could begin. Because of this, Dr. Lehnon had insisted on providing anesthesia and assistance to Dr. Dorman. The patients could then be more rapidly put through their changes.

Once in his care, Dr. Lehnon would begin with the relatively mundane orthopedic surgery. The selection of which arm to use was predicated on the hand favored by the patient. Naturally, the side demonstrating the greatest hand-eye coordination would be the obvious choice. Once the correct appendage was identified, the radius of that arm would be removed, to be replaced by an artificial bone, which was lightweight, stronger than the original, and most importantly, hollow.

The US Army pioneered the type of weapon the researchers had selected. The FGMP-14 high-energy weapon, a heavy support weapon of TL 14 armored infantry, served as the model. There were significant drawbacks, however. The trooper employing the weapon had to be stationary and in one of the approved firing positions to allow the soldier's battle dress to compensate for the recoil. The homopolar generator had to be worn as a backpack; and while it allowed two hundred rounds of fire before reloading, it was bulky. The power pack consisted of the HPG and the gyroscopic recoil compensator. Also, the weapon was capable of firing only every five seconds to allow for the firing, cooling, and recharge phases. The total weapon length was eighty-four centimeters including the firing unit, the support unit, the stock, and the magazine. In addition, the FGMP-14 was linked to the HPG backpack by a heavy-duty cable, a crude arrangement that had to be refined.

This weapon was powerful, however, and would punch through almost all infantry armor. Seine's had made dramatic improvements in all the physical areas, pushing miniaturization to its limits. In order to allow the entire unit to be embedded inside a human body, there were some areas of compromise. The 1.4 megajoule (MJ) power dropped to 0.8 MJ, a substantial tradeoff. This was the cost to avoid the size of the required rotation disks and magnets in the originally conceived device. What this meant in terms of tactics was that the weapon could not be expected to punch holes through armor, even with two hits. But the strategy for which it would be employed was unaffected by this loss, as the targets would all be relatively lightly armored and filled with the most explosive material known to man—gasoline.

Once the firing tube was mounted on the individual's arm, a further procedure drilled out the bones of the wrist and index finger and inserted a flexible ceramic mesh tube while allowing for movement of the hand and fingers. The individual would never regain the original dexterity of the appendage, but most attained reasonably normal movement with dedicated therapy. The computer encasing the artificial eye would control this entire mechanical apparatus. Targeting was a combination of the body's complex neural mechanism for hand-eye coordination and the miniature gyro stabilized detection circuits mounted on either side of the eye casing. Using a rudimentary artificial intelligence algorithm, the two inputs allowed targeting that would make an Olympic sharpshooter green with envy. It was an expensive device, but deadly accurate and invisible as far as spectators were concerned.

The drawback to the effort was an inability to test fire the weapons once they were installed. To circumvent this problem, the soldiers were fitted with lasers attached to their index fingers, which were activated the same way the final weapon would be—through thought.

In order to keep the technology out of the hands of opposing forces, it was necessary that the weapon self-destruct immediately after use. Naturally, with pieces embedded in the eye, body cavity, and arm, it was likely the death throes of the soldier who had fired the weapon would be very loud during the self-destruction phase. To prevent the soldier from drawing attention to himself, the weapon automatically released a tiny amount of cyanide poison just seconds prior to the self-destruct sequence.

This was the real reason the teams would be released as a hunter-killer partnership. The role of the second party, not outfitted with the weapon, was to collect the body of the equipped soldier.

One in every fifty soldiers reacted poorly to the implants. While it was an affirmation that the process wasn't all that clean, it mattered little to the doctor. He could use these anomalies as well. These individuals provided the baseline for speed and accuracy of firing. One at a time, to avoid rumors, they were culled from the group and separated. They thought they would see a doctor for help. In their naïveté, they believed that someone would care for them in their agony. Instead, they were taken to an open field and encouraged for the first time to "test fire" the weapon. Despite the pain they suffered, the results were dramatically successful and unbelievably fast. It also immediately took care of treating these soldiers who had either rejected the implant or had some other medical problem.

Regardless of the minor setbacks, soon they would have an adequate number for their unique army.

THE EDGE OF THE DMZ, DPRK

General Il Jun Sik knew the challenge. The first target would be the force from Camp Casey. Only six thousand strong, they represented the initial and closest US regiment the general would come across. Because the North Korean Army would be entering well south of any of the tunnel openings their southern brethren knew about, the US Forces from the camp would also likely be the first military company the general's army would engage. Any failure in this first effort would destroy morale, cripple strategy, and swing momentum against the NKPA. It was General Sik's job, as the commanding general officer, to worry about every detail, and the US Army was extremely unpredictable. Unlike his highly disciplined fighting machine, the US Forces might have appeared to be a loosely compiled committee of individuals, as they were always described by the political officers, but the general knew better. He had spoken with the North Korean officers who had faced the United States in 1951. He had listened in awestruck horror at the laughable concept that men individually motivated by a flag and a concept called democracy could act both individually and as a team to with devastating success. General Sik would be among the first group through tunnel thirty-three, and he hoped, for his soldiers' sake, that the enemy would be caught off guard.

RECREATION ROOM, NATIONAL INSTITUTES OF HEALTH

As Jack watched Alex and Emiko drop to the floor, he started toward them. It was all Carlos could do to restrain him.

"Cool it, amigo. Nothing you do right now is going to help them."

At that moment, Charles came running into the room wearing an enigmatic smile on his face. Jack looked over at Carlos; he had noticed it too.

"All right, get those two up and take them down to the infirmary," Charles take-charge tone seemed oddly pleasant.

Jack noted that Charles seemed to know there were only two victims even though he hadn't been in the room when it happened.

All at once, four men started toward the fallen doctors, with Charles Stanton, the one they called Jock, in the lead. Just as Jock got close to Emiko and reached down to pick her up, Rock leveled him with an uppercut. To Jack's amazement, the other two cleaners that had rode in with them that morning ripped off their Hectors uniform shirts revealing CIA insignias. Others joined Charles and Jock from the front lobby and the kitchen area, but within seconds the agents had restrained four of the five. Jock and Rock were still in a heated battle, and anytime any others came near them, Rock would throw a chair or table at them to keep them at bay. He seemed determined to fight this out with Jock.

The Eyes

Jack was watching Charles, who had moved into the dark area of the room by the dart tables and seemed to be looking for something. Charles picked up something from the table and held it gingerly in his hands. More agents made their way into the room and approached him.

"Stop!" he screamed. "This dart is filled with sarin. It will kill whomever I scratch with it in seconds. Let my men go and let us leave this facility. You have lost. It is over and you might as well get used to it."

Rock spoke as he held Jock in what would be described in wrestling jargon as a half nelson. "Forget it, Charles. We've been watching you for a very long time; you have some explaining to do. Your henchmen will gladly fill us in on the details. It is you who has lost, so put down the dart and let's do this rationally."

Charles looked about the room at the ever-increasing number of CIA agents arriving and his face sobered. "You'll see," he shouted. "Very soon our work will demonstrate that not all great technological weapons come from the United States. You will see your own blood everywhere; if you need a clue, look at Korea! Soon it will be all one country, and America will not be welcome!" With that, he deliberately scratched his own arm and in one motion flung the dart at Rock, where it embedded itself in Jock's chest. Both men slumped over.

"Oh my God! They're all dead," Jack started. "What the hell is going on?"

Rock carefully picked up Alex and motioned for Jack to pick up Emiko. They walked them over and laid them on the couch, Jack having a little more trouble than Rock did. "They aren't dead, Jack. Thanks to Carlos and the men he brought, they are merely sedated. We switched the darts this morning before the lady came through security. The chemical in the darts is a derivative of the chemical used in the Moscow theater a few years back. It has been refined and perfected, of course, but I wouldn't want to be too close to the young lady when she wakes up. The side effects tend to irritate even calm people, and I've seen her angry side. By the way, my name is Roger, Roger Davidson." He turned to Carlos and said, "Good work, Carlos. Another victory for the good guys." Then he motioned for the agents to pick up Alex and Emiko and get them to the infirmary.

Jack turned to Carlos and said, "Time to come clean, bro. What is this, and who are you?"

"Relax, amigo." Carlos smiled, "I haven't been with the CIA very long, so there's is no long spy story to tell. They knew I had worked at the facility where Dr. Dorman worked, and when I showed up here, they asked if I'd mind keeping my eyes and ears open. After you called, I reported some of what you said to Roger, and things just started falling into place. As to how much I knew was going to happen today, the answer is, absolutely nothing. All these guys ever tell me is where to go, how many people to pick up, and not to ask any questions. As far as I knew, you, the girl, or the other two guys could have been the CIA agents. Speaking of which, where did the young lady go?" Carlos and Jack started looking around.

"She's right here," Lee walked up to Carlos. "Well done, Carlos. We couldn't have pulled this off if too many of us had known what was happening. I didn't know how they were going to keep the two doctors alive; I just had to trust they would."

Yin Hee stood beside Lee looking stunned and more than a little overwhelmed.

"Where are the two doctors now?" she asked sheepishly. "I have to see them with my own eyes or I'll go mad."

"This is Noriko Suzuki," Lee introduced her. "Her story is very long and complicated. I assure you she meant no harm to your friends. Why don't we all go to the infirmary and see them now?"

PROPAGANDA MINISTER'S OFFICE

Propaganda Minister Chon Ul was growing weary of his role as puppet to the brat child of the great leader. *Who does he think he is?* he asked himself. *We created him because it is easier to control the transfer of power if the stupid masses believe it is by divine right. But this idiot has begun to believe the story himself. This plan he has is lunacy. As if we could convince Arabs, Germans, and expatriate US scientists to work with us for the advancement of that Juche drivel he babbles about all the time.*

"Sir, General Il Jun Han is here to see you," the crude metal intercom crackled. Chon Ul didn't even know the name of the person on the other end.

"Then send him in, you idiot. Don't waste my time!" Chon Ul seemed to always be in a foul mood lately, which probably accounted for the greater amount of spaces on his calendar. "Come in, General. What do you want?"

"Sir, I have news from the desert." The general paused. It irked him to no end to have to report to this pathetic old man. Despite never obtaining the great leader's respect, and certainly not the dear leader's approval, it astonished him the power this man had nevertheless corralled.

The Eyes

"What is it? I haven't all day to banter with the likes of you." Chon Ul spat the last part hatefully.

"Sir, with all due respect, do not speak to me that way again." General Han had many friends as well, and was easily twice the size and strength of the minister. "The American scientist has been working for nearly a year in the desert camp removing the eyes. His work has been good enough that the arrogant doctors in Germany now believe their implants are close to 98 percent successful. We should be ready within weeks if we can get the men transported here and inserted into South Korea." The general started to turn and walk out of the room.

"Fine. Get out. And if you are insolent again, I will have you shot!" The minister stood and walked toward the bigger man.

The general stopped in his tracks, turned, and walked directly up to the minister. Leaning forward and down to get right next to the old man's face, he whispered, "I did not choose to report to you. You chose me. I could give these reports to anyone. I will not be insolent again. But if you ever speak to me without fair respect, I will kill you where you stand without a thought; so take heed, Chon Ul. You are not as invincible as you would like to believe." The general stood abruptly, spun around, and walked out of the office.

The minister stood silently. *There is another one that I will be happy to dispense with personally when this is over*, he thought. *For now, I need him to keep me informed, and then I will filter the information I feed to Jong Il. General Han must feel informed but not have enough information to act alone.*

Across the plaza, Kim Jong Il had just received General Han's report and was trying to assess the next step. *Han is a good man*, he thought. *He is fair and does what he must without compromising himself. It must be very difficult to have to pretend to serve Chon Ul. That will end soon enough.*

The discussion between Jong Il and the general had been militarily tactical, but clear. It would be simple enough to move the forces through the tunnels without alerting the puppets to the south. Once in place, these NKPA personnel were a formidable force all on their own. Add in the virtual elimination of Seoul, and with it the South's central communication node, and South Korea and the US Forces would have more than they could handle, especially with Jong Il's new special forces taking out the majority of the aviation assets, both foreign and domestic.

It was almost enough to make Jong Il desire to expand the goal. Could the peninsula be taken in its entirety? If he left it up to General Il Jung Sik, then surely the North Korean Army would be able to make tremendous strides. It was tempting enough. To rule over the united Korean peninsula had been the dear leader's goal all of his adult life.

PYONGYANG

"Welcome, Comrade," Jong Il gushed. "It is so kind of you to make such a long trip on our behalf."

"Never mind all that. Have our plans changed? China has heard little of the progress we had hoped would be made by now. As you know, we have our hands full with these illnesses on the mainland and the insolence of the former British colony. We need to get the attention of the world focused on Asian issues instead of the American global police actions. It is imperative that we work quickly to establish the new economic zone for the DPRK. In addition to our genuine desire to help the people of Korea, it will also be a great market for the products from China's new economic zones. What a relief to establish trade with another socialist nation. The premier is anxious for progress."

"It is to that end that I have asked you to visit. I have managed to set up a lower-level meeting with the warrior in Hawaii. I snubbed the commander of the so-called United Nations Command intentionally to irritate and confuse the Americans. I imagine there is considerable turmoil on their part as to what it is I wish to discuss; yet they cannot refuse. I would ask you, Big Brother, to host the meeting in Beijing. I believe there is considerable hope that we can actually get the Americans to help us in our plan."

The Eyes

"Why would they help us do something they would obviously find detrimental to their allies in South Korea?" Comrade Jui Heisa asked.

"Because they won't know they are helping us. The Americans are still smarting from their loss of diplomatic stature following their illegal invasions of Afghanistan and Iraq. They are still trying to exploit aid to Africa as a means of boosting their international pride, but AIDS is a hopeless cause for them. At the very best, they can only convince the world that the war on AIDS is now being lost more slowly. The American public likes to win, and an election year looms ominously for the incumbent president. We are fortunate they have selected a leader with so little understanding about the world outside America, her oil partners, and the Christian church. We can appeal to his instinct for humanitarian showmanship by asking him to transport our people from China to South Korea on their aircraft for free as a way to help Asia. During the meeting with the admiral, it would be helpful to have China positioned on our side. Your perspective on the outcome of the Korean War with its unfair resolution will help keep the Americans off balance. I will offer to stop our nonexistent nuclear development program at just six weapons, a statement that will serve to disrupt the global thought process once more. The International Atomic Energy Agency will push for inspections. At that point, we will bring forward our documentation of Chinese analysis of our progress. China can claim to have browbeaten us into cooperation, and in making this magnanimous offer, allowed Chinese scientists to destroy four of the weapons. This will give you the opportunity to rid yourselves of those rudimentary early nuclear weapons your program developed early on but never divulged to the world. In doing so, you lend an aura of authenticity to our claims of nuclear development and increase the chances the rest of the world will advance money and oil to us. Naturally, this is also a good time to air all negative thoughts about the US Pacific fleet, Taiwan, South Korean exercises, and so forth. We will need those assets to capitalize the Oijongbu Economic District." Jong Il was pleased. He knew this was a win-win situation for China and the DPRK. It wasn't too often of late that North Korea was in any position to help China, and her age-old goodwill for North Korea's historical support during her time of greatest need was wearing thin from the trials of modern-day problems.

"It is a solid idea. I can speak for Premier Jin Wei, and we approve. The premier not only thinks this is an excellent plan, he is extremely excited about the concept for and execution of an economic zone on the Korean peninsula. He has promised full support and development expertise and assistance. We will inform the United States through the Pacific Command of the meeting."

Kim Jong Il was ecstatic. *The West is already unwittingly participating in my plan. Soon*, he thought, *they will do much more.*

The DIA had arranged the seminar despite the experience of the two commanders. It could have been considered an insult, especially to General Hodge, but he had been approached by the DIA and felt it would be a good refresher for him, enlightening for Admiral Corping, and a chance for both of them to see what new information may have developed in recent weeks. As General Hodge knew the briefer from a previous tour of duty. He introduced him to USCINCPAC.

"Admiral, this is Mr. Paul Dawson. We go back a few years, and he has more knowledge about the geography of the Korean peninsula than any human being I know. I think I'll just shut up now and let him do the talking."

"Thank you, General. Admiral Corping, I've been asked to brief you both on North Korean tunnel operations. In general, North Korea uses tunnel operations as a central part of their overall concept of waging war. The primary purpose of these tunnels is to move, undetected, large numbers of conventional and nonconventional forces with limited fire support behind the United States and ROK's initial line of defense along the DMZ. These forces will act as part of an invasion force. The successful placement of a large number of troops with supporting firepower behind our lines, without our detection at the onset of hostilities, would be a major tactical advantage for them. Our penetration capability is state of the art and highly classified, yet we fear we haven't identified all their tunnels. Clearly, this is the kind of technology oil companies would love to get their hands on, but to give away our sources and means has, to date, been ruled more significant to national security than to finding new oil fields. At this level, I can share that the oil fields in Alaska were not found exclusively through the good work of the folks at Exxon, though the hints were delivered surreptitiously enough that most of their field researchers probably believe it was an independent find.

"We have found and documented four large infiltration tunnels under the DMZ and we suspect there are as many as seventeen others. The detected and mapped tunnels are impressive enough to demonstrate to us the significance of tunnel operations to North Korean military strategy. The first tunnel we detected in November of 1974. It was only three feet below the earth's surface, but measured six feet by six feet, and was constructed utilizing prefabricated concrete slab walls and lines. The size of the tunnel is large enough for the movement of significant supporting firepower for troops. Tunnel one is located a few kilometers east of P'anmunjom. It is interesting to note the tunnel was built the same year North Korea and South Korea began peace talks.

"The second tunnel was detected in March 1975. It was built 196 feet below the earth's surface, also measured six feet by six feet, and it was dug through solid granite. It is significant to note the tunnel had been completed for some time before it was detected, despite satellite surveillance. Tunnel two is barely a kilometer west of P'anmunjom, a location of special surveillance.

"We detected tunnel three in October 1978. This tunnel is 246 feet below the earth's surface, measures six feet by six feet, and it too was dug through solid granite. Tunnel three is half way across the peninsula.

"The fourth tunnel is located strategically along what we consider to be the most likely invasion route in the eastern sector. It is buried some 145 yards below the earth's surface.

"What is most significant about these tunnels, in addition to having been constructed without detection, is the size and capacity. When we Americans think of wartime tunnels, we have a tendency to think in terms of the tunnels we found in Guam and Iwo Jima. Those tunnels served a drastically different purpose and were constructed with little in the way of assets and manpower and in a relatively brief period of time. The tunnels under the DMZ are sophisticated tunnels large enough to allow a battalion of men to pass through every hour. They are also lighted and equipped with rail lines. The former president, Kim Il Sung, believed, if constructed properly, each tunnel would have the equivalent effect in war to ten atomic bombs. North Korean Army doctrine believes strongly that these tunnels are an equalizer. Our assessment is that if North Korea uses even two tunnels that we have not identified and if they achieve the surprise they are designed for, Kim Il Sung might be correct in his estimation. That's pretty much it, unless you have other questions."

"Wow," Admiral Corping managed to say. "I admit that while I knew of the existence of the tunnels, I never really considered the size or value they could hold. There is much more to the peninsula than a regular study would afford. We do tend to think of Korea as the war that was and then dismiss it as a manageable current threat. Thanks for helping me understand it a little better."

The two commanders spent the rest of the day shuffling between offices on the hill, getting the spin on every possible issue between the United States and Korea, and its ramifications on the other powers in the region. For every concept, one had to consider the reaction of the Chinese, Taiwanese, Russians, South Koreans, Japanese, and increasingly the cumulative members of the Association of Southeast Asian Nations, or ASEAN. Both four-stars were familiar with many of the topics, but it was still an exhausting day.

Finally back at the room, General Hodge was met with a message to call his wife back in Hawaii. Admiral Corping left him alone and went to his room.

Some twenty minutes later, the admiral knocked on the door. "Is everything OK, Dave?"

"Yes, thankfully. My daughter, Jillian, was out enjoying the boogie boarding and got a Portuguese man-of-war wrapped around her ankle. She was treated and released at Tripler Army Medical Center, but, man, that must have been a long trip to have to make with acid eating at her flesh. Luckily, one of the folks at the cabins had some Adolph's meat tenderizer, which I guess has something in it to neutralize the acid. Still, it doesn't get it all. What has her most upset though is that she'll miss her next two volleyball games. Naturally, all of this is my fault for setting them up at Bellows. So I blamed you. I knew you'd understand." Both men laughed.

"Our flight is going to leave late tonight, if that's OK with you. We will get into Hickam Air Force Base around noon tomorrow." The admiral didn't like to stay away from his base if he didn't have to. He traveled enough as it was without these extensive trips.

The general made one more phone call to Yongsan. He told his vice that the meeting had been approved and asked if there had been any more information from the North on the details of the meeting. There hadn't been any word at all.

The flight back to Hickam was event free, and his wife was awaiting him at the base. He said his good-byes to Admiral Corping and joined his wife on the other C-135 the admiral graciously authorized him to fly back to Osan. From there, his people would take him by helicopter to Yongsan and home. He would arrive around 2300 hours, get a quick briefing from his vice, and then go to bed. It would be another long day spent traveling.

"General Han, I need your best man on this. No one is to know what you are up to, especially not that conniving worm, Chon Ul. The man you put in charge should have the competence, tenacity, and intelligence to do what he is told, not what he thinks is right."

"Of course, Dear Leader, it will be as you wish. But I must say it seems we have waited so long and now timing has handed us a splendid opportunity to make you ruler of the reunited Korean peninsula. You have decided not to take that route?"

"I have, and I will share with you the reason why. If you observed what happened first in Afghanistan and then in Iraq, you will notice the key ingredient was the existence of a sovereign government hostile to the United States holding assets valuable to the United States. The Democratic People's Republic of Korea has nothing the United States needs or wants. In fact, they need us to stay pretty much just as we are to keep the global economy going, and to continue the logic behind maintaining such a fierce and enormous standing military in the South. The existence of that military is always defined by the existence of an enemy. It is needed to continue to feed the need for an economic outlet for the industrial sector of the United States' economy. What we need, old friend, is just a little more in the way of resources and assets to remain in power indefinitely. If we take too much of South Korea, we first assail an ally of the United States; they are bound by treaty to defend her. Second, we alarm the Japanese, the United States' most important Asian ally, which would certainly drive America to arms. We must avoid a full-scale mobilization of the US military, as they would simply take over the entire peninsula and reinstall the puppets from the South to rule. I have laid the groundwork in many arenas, fomenting support from a variety of sources disaffected by the United States. Also, our ancient allies, the Chinese, have value found in this plan for their economic growth. So you see, it is critical that we make a rapid, decisive first strike, then use diplomacy, the death tool the West fashioned for themselves, against them. With careful preplanning, we have a sequence of actions pre-coordinated to short-circuit their efforts in the United Nations and make it an obvious decision to simply allow us to take the land we want. In addition, they will themselves prepare that land for us and allow much greater assets and aid to flow into our tired country. I too would like to see the peninsula reunited, but I decided long ago that would not happen on my watch; it may never happen. This will be the last we speak of this."

"Yes, Dear Leader. I will have the attack headed up by General Sik. He has all the qualities you have described, and he trusts me implicitly. I will have him make preparations immediately."

USPACOM HEADQUARTERS

A little over two weeks after their trip to Washington, Admiral Corping made a secure call to CINCUNC. The mini-summit was now set for ten days hence in Beijing. Andrews was sending one of its newer jets out to pick up the admiral and would stop at Kimpo International to pick up the general the next day. Both had decided this was not a trip for their respective spouses, a decision that was decidedly unpopular on the home front.

Neither commander could shake the nagging feeling that something was going on here that didn't meet the eye. The North Korean and Chinese diplomatic corps were making convoluted plans for what should have been a very straightforward meeting. Combining relief aid with diplomatic negotiations was very rarely done, and usually went poorly when attempted. Nevertheless, the State Department had jumped at a request over the previous two weeks for three empty C-17s to accompany the US delegation to transport an unknown number of men from China to South Korea, who would then be driven to North Korea. While the military folks were concerned, the purported number of individuals exceeding five thousand, the State Department explained this was a definite win politically. It showed the administration's willingness to assist the North Koreans, while maintaining a hard line on the issues that really mattered to the people of the world. Besides, none of these people would be armed, and they would depart the aircraft in South Korea. What could be less risky for American interests?

Once the State Department sanctioned the missions, it was given one of the highest codes in the Joint Chiefs of Staff priority system for movement. Once again America began to believe its own spin, and that was rarely a good thing. The mission flowed from headquarters through United States Transportation Command (USTRANSCOM) to Tactical Airlift Control Center (TACC) to the wings. Despite the size of the movement, for the men and women of Air Mobility Command, the mission was a straightforward, simple effort.

The missions went off without a hitch. Each aircraft made four trips each day for three days completely full of passengers. With the aircraft configured with palletized seats, they carried 144 per flight for a grand total of 5,100 individuals from China to Cheoung Ju. From there, the men boarded trucks and headed north.

GORAN-PO, NORTH KOREA

Captain Gaul Young Chul was proud of his hard-working men. On average, they labored fifteen- to eighteen-hour days, six days a week, training and practicing in the ways of war. As a unit poised on the DMZ, much of the time was focused on maintaining equipment and guard duty. A considerable amount of time was also expended maintaining the myriad security positions and patrolling for, well, anything. None of them made very much money, but in the world of the NKPA soldier, money wasn't extremely necessary. In addition to adequate food, itself a very big luxury, each was given cigarettes, stationary, and personal comfort and toiletry articles. All in all, even the newest and lowest-ranking soldier was much better off than his civilian counterpart. It made motivation reasonably easy to maintain. The schedule was demanding, but the enemy was in plain sight. The rigorous physical training was hardly limited to daylight hours, especially since nighttime operations were the poor nation's first and most effective obstacle in the effort to even the battlefield, given that almost any nation on earth had technologically superior weaponry.

The captain's soldiers were purposely not allowed to rest after a strenuous night's training. It was his personal intent for every soldier to continue hard physical training until at least noon the next day. This allowed his men to develop into the type of warriors that could withstand the physical and mental fatigue that the next war would bring.

Unlike many of Captain Gaul's compatriots, he was sure the next war, the final war of the peninsula, was close at hand. He planned for his men to be through the tunnels first. Beyond that, he intended his unit to be the first to march down through the heart of South Korea and the first to smell the ocean from the port of Pusan. Seoul may be the heart of Korea, but he knew his history. To possess Seoul was to rule Korea, so the logic went, and he knew it had its rationale. He also knew that the possession of Seoul changed more than one hundred times during the first war. He would let others fight the urban conflict for that monstrous community. He wanted to be the one in command of the force that drove all the way south. He believed no country would have the time or opportunity to mount a foreign counterattack.

The captain was well liked by his men, mostly because his work ethic was every bit as rigorous as what he demanded of his subordinates. He had never asked them to do anything that he wasn't willing to experience. If they had a rough terrain, eighty-kilometer hike with full backpacks, the captain would be humping up the hill right along with them. That was important to the men. Before entering this tour of duty, each soldier believed to one degree or another they would be a distracting group of fire ants whose primary purpose was to sting the giant as much as possible while the politicians fought the inevitable war of words that often spelled the death of men like them. But this captain was different. He made them believe that if they would expend their energy and focus their efforts, they could not only distract but defeat the giant. He beguiled them with his depth of knowledge about the first war and the current capabilities and weaknesses of their enemies to the south. They all knew that US ground forces were a tremendous threat, but that threat had become lesser men with greater weapons. Therein lay the possibility. If they could overcome technology with diligence, preparedness, courage, and surprise, the remaining enemy soldier was not superior and might, in fact, be soft.

Captain Gaul's group of NKPA soldiers was ready, honed to a razor's edge, and as eager as humanly possible for conflict. Give the order, and they'd be halfway to Pusan in twenty-four hours.

BEIJING, CHINA

Admiral Corping and General Hodge had made innumerable trips to foreign lands to meet with high-ranking civilian leaders and heads of states, but this time, it felt different. To be meeting with the world's most mysterious and reclusive leader on behalf of the president of the United States was different.

Both officers were acutely aware of the cameras. Through those lenses, the Chinese State Department and the administration would be watching their arrival and getting periodic feedback.

Admiral Corping flawlessly delivered the speech written and rewritten by the president's speechwriters. Following his lecture, the premier of China gave a similarly short welcoming speech. The Chinese leader made no hint of any subject this meeting was about to address. It was all fluff and political eye candy. The dear leader of North Korea did not appear welcoming toward his guests. This would normally be a major faux pas, but he could get away with it because at least half the world thought he was crazy anyway, so the usual diplomatic standards didn't apply.

The pomp and circumstance of the greeting and the appointments of the hotel belied the nation's overall economic condition. It demonstrated quite clearly that China was rapidly gaining on the rest of the world, though. It was obvious that while the economic strength of

China may be concentrated, it was very real. It was much easier to see both the potential market value of the billion-strong population and the potential economic competitor the country could be if diplomacy wasn't handled well.

General Hodge and Admiral Corping witnessed parades and traditional dance demonstrations, and attended a formal state dinner, a true feast. The next morning began with a helicopter ride out to the Great Wall, a point selected from which one could not see any disrepair in the structure, increasing the impact of the Herculean task the building of such a wall must have been. Finally the sightseeing was winding down. It was time for the mini-summit to begin.

The admiral entered right after the Chinese leader, with General Hodge following. Their positions at the table were side by side to the left of the Chinese premier, and directly across from them sat Kim Jong Il. He stood as the Chinese leader entered the room, but sat as the admiral and general made their way to their seats—another snub, intentional or not. The two sat still, waiting for the host or his counterpart to begin the meeting.

After what seemed forever to the two military men, the Chinese premier turned to Kim Jong Il and said through his interpreter, "This is the meeting you requested; why don't you present your agenda."

"Very well," the Korean interpreter began, "I have asked for this meeting on behalf of the peace-loving population of the Democratic People's Republic of Korea. We have suffered for over fifty years from the unfair separation of our great nation. The people of what you call North Korea were industrious, successful, and growing in number until the Western nations joined together to divide our country. No nation can continue to prosper when it is suddenly and catastrophically sundered across an arbitrarily chosen middle. Naturally, Seoul, the very heart of the united Korea, was taken for the South, leaving those of us north of the imposed perpetual war zone to find a new center for our government.

"Likewise, the access to established seaports was cut off, not to mention access to the fields in the more moderately temperate South. In short, the Democratic People's Republic of Korea was choked off to die. But we did not die. North Korea is still strong and growing stronger. We are, as I have mentioned, a peace-loving people at heart, but for several consecutive years, nature has conspired with the West against us—our crops have been abysmal and people have had a difficult time making a living. My people grow weary of the political banter over whether or not the rest of the world will abide by their legal responsibilities agreed to by your former president, Mr. Jimmy Carter. At that time, with the honest efforts of our people and the United States, the DPRK magnanimously abandoned portions of our right as a sovereign nation to develop defensive systems to protect our population from the American-inspired war machine just to our south. The president had asked us to stop our nuclear research, so critical to our nation as a source of energy for our people. In good faith, we abandoned our peaceful nuclear energy research to prove we had no intent to develop nuclear weapons. The United States–led four-party coalition that was to build light water reactors and provide 250 million barrels of oil per year reneged on their part of the bargain. It is time to make amends." And the interpreter abruptly stopped speaking. Both heads of state turned to look at Admiral Corping and General Hodge.

After what he hoped was the appropriate pause, the admiral said, "We understand your frustration with the four-party talks. What is there to be discussed at this juncture, since none of the other member's party to the talks are present?"

The dear leader snapped his head around to the admiral; as he spoke, the interpreter never missed a beat. "Simply this, Admiral. You will take my message back to your president. We want the accumulated missing oil shipments, which totals 2.32 billion barrels of processed oil, to begin arriving at our ports within two weeks. In addition, we want the light water reactor construction to commence at the same time. Our workers have already begun work at the selected sites. We are now nearly ten years behind schedule. We will wait no more."

"And what shall I tell him will happen if your demands are not met?" Admiral Corping asked calmly, though he desired to reach across the table and slap the arrogant man he faced.

"You should tell him that commencing at the time of our choosing, the interests of the United States in South Korea will come to a catastrophic end."

With that, Kim Jong Il stood and left the room without giving the admiral a chance to respond. With the North Korean leader gone, there was little purpose in remaining. Despite the anger welling up inside, the admiral turned to the Chinese leader and thanked him graciously for hosting the conference and for his hospitality during their brief visit. As they shook hands, General Hodge arranged to have the jet ready by the time they arrived at the airport.

The aircrew had been to many of these meetings and knew better than to let down their guard. They were standing by and ready to go. The aircraft commander could tell by how brief the meeting was and by the sound of General Hodge's voice that this had been something less than a pleasant exchange, and he had no intention of allowing himself or his crew to bear the unwitting brunt of two CINCs' frustrations.

Admiral Corping used the sophisticated communications on board the aircraft and flash precedence to contact the secretary of state. At the same time, General Hodge called the chairman of the Joint Chiefs of Staff (CJCS) General Hillyard; General Carlton Albright; and the secretary of defense, Dr. Ann Hathaway. What they had just heard was clearly a threat of war. While that wasn't new coming from the North Koreans, the fact they had gone so far as to bring the two CINCs to a meeting to convey the threat face to face was.

Both commanders received the instruction to alter the mission they were on and return directly to Washington. The aircraft was air refueling capable, and the eighteenth wing in Kadena had already been contacted to arrange the first air-to-air refueling over the Pacific. They would hit another tanker off the coast of California to make the trip back nonstop. The flight crew was walking around like the floor of the aircraft was constructed of eggshells and they could already see signs of cracking, and General Hodge knew why. They had had a fun flight in with a professional but relaxed and jovial interaction between the crew and their distinguished passengers. Since their return, neither CINC had spoken a word to the crew or to each other. That was a sure way to keep the pucker factor high.

General Hodge decided he would try to break the dismal atmosphere. He watched the admiral hand the phone back wordlessly to the communications specialist, walk back to his seat, and flop down. The general gave him a moment, but from the muscle movement along the admiral's jaw, he could tell the admiral was still seething. He walked up the aisle and sat down across from him. Keeping his face calm and straight, he leaned forward, obviously to say something privately to the admiral.

Although he would rather just be left alone, he knew he needed to know what the secretary of defense and CJCS had to say, so he leaned forward to listen.

The commander of United Nations Command looked him right in the eyes and said, "Well, I thought that went well." And despite himself, the admiral burst into laughter.

"Damn you, Dave. Here we are on the brink of war and you're clowning around. You're not going to have much of a career if you keep that up."

"Yeah, well I've got even graver concerns," the general began. "Look at the men and women around you who are going to be the ones who either kill us or get us back to Washington safe and sound. With the two of us stomping around like wounded elephants, they're too scared to come back to the cabin. If there's a fire on board, they might not even bother to tell us!"

"You're right again, Dave. Let's go thaw the iceberg." And he stood and headed up to the galley. They made a concerted effort to speak to each member of the crew, thanking them for the rapidity with which they got them out of Beijing. Without going into detail, they acknowledged what the crew had already guessed; the meeting had gone south quickly. Both were careful not to use any of the derogatory phrases they'd really like to have called the North Korean leader, but at the same time, it was clear that neither CINC was impressed with his countenance.

Both senior leaders got quiet when the copilot, a major, suddenly said, "Sir, from the look on your faces since we first saw you on the Tarmac at Beijing, I thought we'd just been issued an ultimatum of a second Korean War."

General Hodge fielded the veiled question, "When you are dealing with the leader of a country that has 1.2 million armed forces facing the DMZ, every day is the day you expect war to begin. Our goal is to keep that ever-present possibility from slipping into our comfort zone, lulling us into the subconscious belief that it will never happen." He spoke long enough to reach the initial stages of boredom for the major, which was precisely what he had intended.

The Eyes

Back in the cabin, Admiral Corping turned to General Hodge and said, "Are you thinking what I'm thinking?"

"If you mean that we'd better work on our poker face before we arrive at Andrews, then yes. For now, we had better get plenty of sleep. This is going to be one heck of a trip."

The general stood and walked back up to the galley. "You know, I'm going to get fat if you guys keep feeding me. If it isn't too late to say so, I think I'll skip the next meal and grab a couple of these fine bananas a little later, if you can save them from the admiral." He winked at the chef, who nodded as he turned and went back to his cabin. He wouldn't wake for the next nine hours, and would later reflect that he hadn't slept that long in years.

BEIJING

Once the two commanders had left, Kim Jong Il rejoined Jin Wei. "This is a dangerous gambit, my friend. Did we get the men aboard their C-17 aircraft into South Korea? If not, you can be sure that effort has failed now," Jin Wei stated.

"Don't worry, comrade. That process took only three days and was finished yesterday while the two generals were being entertained. We have people in place in Cheong Ju to take the men north, and we have places to hide them before they get to Kimpo. We'll have plenty of soldiers available for when we move. All of them are highly motivated, and each has been trained on his particular mission. The hardest part is being patient enough for them to get into position. In the meantime, we've sent word through our chain of people inside Japan to ask Mr. Ishikawa to press hard for his plan to move the Iranian men from Japan to South Korea. He has done well, stirring considerable debate and genuinely trying hard to get the trip moving. It will be only a matter of time before the Americans attempt to stop the plan."

"What is the purpose of having Mr. Ishikawa continue his efforts? Surely they will be stopped either by Japan or as a result of growing US concerns, won't they?"

"You have answered your own question. The United States will attempt to stop whatever they think I am planning. It is far better that we help them find something to act on, than to sit back and hope they won't attack a part of the plan I can't afford to lose. If they discover the people they have just transported to South Korea for us are Middle Eastern men, and I'm sure they will, they will be all the more suspect of the injection of more men from that region into South Korea. Stopping the Japanese plan will satisfy their desire to control things, hopefully enough to keep them out of our way as we prepare to attack." Jong Il smiled; his plan was falling into place.

FINAL APPROACH, ANDREWS AFB

"Good morning, Rip Van Winkle." Admiral Corping's spirits seemed to have returned to normal.

"Wow, I've got to get one of those beds for my house," General Hodge responded.

"I'm not so sure Amy would approve of that. Besides, without the four turbine-powered engines pushing you across the sky at almost five hundred miles an hour while gently performing a barely discernible figure-eight corkscrew through the air, it just wouldn't be the same."

"You're probably right. Well, it looks like it's still raining here at Andrews. You'd think we were flying in and out of Seattle in the winter."

"We're just lucky enough to catch the cold fronts. But I do feel sorry for Steve. He is waiting for us at the airport again."

"Yes, boss, I'll be careful." The doors opened and the two commanders stood and walked to the front.

Admiral Corping turned to Dave and said, grinning, "Hey, you want to go out first?"

"Thanks for asking, but no. You get the honors both when we're in the penthouse and when we're in the outhouse, lucky you." And he pushed the admiral in fun toward the door. As they stepped out onto the stair truck, they could see they were going to be herded directly into a vehicle for the trip to the Pentagon.

As they stepped inside the car, the young man driving turned and said, "Welcome, sir. I've been instructed to take you to the White House. I know the plans were to meet at the Pentagon first, but the secretary of defense himself made the call. If you need to make a confirmation call, I can drive you over to the command center."

At that point, Colonel Wilson tapped on the glass window next to General Hodge. He rolled the window down.

"Sir, I'm sorry, I forgot to tell you this, but your plans have changed in the last thirty minutes. You are to be taken directly to the White House."

"Thanks, Steve. Our driver was just telling us the same thing. We're on our way." He rolled the window back up and said, "Let's go, driver. We don't want to keep the important people waiting."

They were escorted directly into the White House Oval office, where the secretaries of state and defense, the directors of the CIA and DIA, the White House chief of staff, and the chairman of the Joint Chiefs of Staff had already gathered. Shortly after, the president of the United States, Roger Fulton, walked into the room. Everyone was still standing as he walked over to the presidential desk and sat down.

"Ladies and gentlemen, please sit. John and Dave, I want to thank you for meeting with the dear leader for me. I also appreciate you taking the rude spear, and handling it so well. There may be a future for you two in politics down the road." The president was always campaigning for good men and women to participate in the wonderful world of government, as he called it. "John, please give us a rundown on what was said and who did the talking so that we all have the same story directly from you."

"Mr. President, I anticipated that would be our starting point, so I had the meeting transcribed after the fact. Dave, I, and the translator put down, as closely as we could remember, the exact words spoken at the summit. Fortunately, for this effort, the meeting was short, and the only person really saying anything significant was Kim Jong Il. I've distributed a copy of the minutes to each of you. Mr. President, yours are in the folder there in front of you." He indicated the folder just to the right of the president's right hand.

"OK," the president said, "let's start there. Everybody read please." He pulled out his reading glasses, opened the folder, and began to review it. When everyone was done, the looks around the room mirrored the same anger and grave concern Admiral Corping and General Hodge had felt in person.

"Did Jin Wei make any other comments before or after the meeting that gave you any indication of what was happening?" The president looked at the admiral, then at General Hodge. General Hodge spoke for the first time.

"Mr. President, the premier didn't say anything verbally, but his mannerisms spoke volumes. Especially the fact that he showed no surprise when Kim Jong Il just stood up and walked out after all he had done to host the meeting. That indicated to me that he knew exactly what was going to happen."

"That, plus his cool acceptance of our immediate departure with no messages from him to you or anyone else, seems to spell a conspiracy of some sort," Admiral Corping added.

"What do you recommend, Admiral?" The president gave him the first shot. He'd been through the tough part and had earned it.

"I think we should start preparing for war, Mr. President, but slowly and quietly. General Hodge, I know we haven't run one for the last ten years, but traditionally isn't this the time of year when we used to run the Team Spirit exercise?" Admiral Corping was true to his word. The Korean Peninsula was Dave's turf, especially if this was about wartime preparations.

General Hodge answered immediately. "Mr. President, though we haven't run the exercise for ten years, we've kept it on the books for saber-rattling purposes; canceling it is easy each year. So far this year, we've made no concession and have asserted our intent to run the exercise as planned."

General William Hillyard, the chairman of the Joint Chiefs of Staff also an army officer, spoke up, "Have we kept the planning current enough to actually execute it?"

General Hodge thought for a moment and said, "We have the archived *TPFDD*, but unless we start in earnest right now, we'll never be able to get our guys to the fight in two weeks."

The Eyes

He was referring to the *Time Phased Forced Deployment Document*. This central planning document accounted for every person and every piece of equipment needed to perform a mission. The purpose of this colossal and extremely detailed document was to also coordinate the means of transportation to and from the deployed location. The development of the *TPFDD* was never really finished. It was a living document all the way through execution. No matter how careful the planning, loads would end up larger or heavier than the planning figures, which, in turn, would affect how many air, ground, or sea sorties would be necessary to move them. In addition, aircraft, ships, and trucks all experienced maintenance delays and cancellations at some time or another. Emergencies, illnesses, and injuries complicated the flow of people, making it often appear completely impossible to get what was needed, where it needed to be, when it needed to be there. Amazingly, the logistical geniuses that did the planning, coordinated the transportation, and monitored, reacted to, and rescheduled the flow were largely unsung heroes. Still, trying to execute the movement of over one hundred thousand Department of Defense (DOD) personnel to Korea with the gear they needed to do their job and the supplies they needed for support would take a considerable amount of time.

"I agree with Dave, Mr. President. We should issue a warning order today that explains this is to be treated as real. I'll get each of the chiefs of staff and the commander of naval operations to run this down the command systems via emergency action message once we break. We'll get to every commander within the next twelve hours via secure phone so that they understand the sensitivity and the urgency. I'd also recommend we start quietly moving as many naval air assets as we can toward Korea. The Middle East is largely a ground problem at this juncture, and while I'm sure the air force will disagree, I think we need to get all our fighters in strike range as quickly as we can. The biggest problem of course is fuel support, but we'll start working that out ASAP." General Hillyard was already drafting the message in his mind.

The secretary of state joined the conversation. "Mr. President, perhaps we can buy some time and help the general with the fuel problem."

Final Approach, Andrews AFB

"How so, Lisa?" the president was rubbing his eyes. He had already been through the fourth major flare up in Iraq, which had just been quieted, and now this.

"Well, with some subtle obfuscation, we can start shipping aviation fuel to Korea under the guise of stockpiling to meet Kim Jong Il's demands for 2.32 billion barrels. Even he'll understand it takes a while to get that much oil together. We'll feed the information to the US ambassador to China to convey to North Korea through Premier Wei. In the meantime, we'll start the rounds with South Korea, Japan, Russia, and Australia. By way of further concerning information, I'd like the general and admiral to take a look at some photos our satellites shot when we took our first look at the dam. One of the DIA folks says there is a new camp, very similar to the old terrorist training camps in Afghanistan, set up in the Gobi desert."

The president rubbed his eyes again and stood. "OK, let's go with that as a plan. Issue the warning order, and check out the camp in China. We don't need to be blindsided right now. I don't see any need for me to officially respond or even acknowledge that the Chinese meeting occurred. Let's keep on this. Bill, can you handle the coordination with Supreme Headquarters Allied Powers, Europe, and NATO? I'll make a few calls to our more jittery allies to let them know we need to tell the world we can fight in more places than one and we'll still be able to meet their needs when it's appropriate. Lisa, get the oil moving; work with the DOD on where it needs to go. You work the cover story. Leak it to the media so it gets full coverage. I'll have a spokesperson confirm it at the next press meeting. It's probably time for you to send your deputy to England as well. I may need him to run some face to faces with some of our allies. Lisa, you need to get to Tokyo. Dave, thanks again, you have your work cut out for you. By the time you get back to Yongsan, the US ambassador will be fully informed and will likely want to meet with you. I'll make it clear to him that as far as these preparations are concerned, you have the stick."

"Thank you, Mr. President."

With that, President Fulton stood and headed off to his next meeting, a Boy Scout photo opportunity. Everyone else headed back to his or her offices, and Admiral Corping and General Hodge to the airport.

The Eyes

This time Andrews supplied each commander with his own jet so that they could return to their own base as quickly as possible.

THE INFIRMARY, NATIONAL INSTITUTES OF HEALTH LABORATORY

"They're both fine. A bit groggy, for sure, and each is nursing a tremendous headache, but other than that, they are fine. You can go in now, but speak quietly," the nurse instructed. All four of them walked through the open door to find Emiko and Alex resting in standard hospital beds. Jack rushed over to Emiko, who veritably glowed when she saw him. She grabbed him and held him in a tight embrace. Neither spoke, so as to cover the awkwardness. Dr. Sanderson turned toward the other two visitors and said, "Hello, I'm Dr. Alex Sanderson. Who are you?"

Jack untangled himself from Emiko and stood up straight, "Oh, sorry, Alex. Perhaps you remember Carlos; you met in the janitor's closet upstairs. These other two are Lee Wong and Noriko Suzuki. I think I'll let them explain from there."

Lee stepped forward and shook Dr. Sanderson's hand. "I work primarily for the Defense Intelligence Agency. On this case, I also worked closely with the Central Intelligence Agency. Ms. Suzuki is rather an unwilling accomplice in some larger scheme that we have yet to work out. This is probably the wrong time to ask, but do you have any idea what research you're engaged in that might be of interest to North Korea?"

Emiko answered first, "Nothing at all. Do you know anything about where Dr. Dorman is?" She was irritated, and the question came across rather more as an accusation than a question.

"No idea at all," Lee replied calmly. "I don't mean to upset you; this can wait."

Alex sat up, "No, it can't." He turned to Emiko, "Just listen, Emiko. I didn't have the opportunity to share this with you earlier. We have been trying to discover what it was that Dr. Dorman had discovered that might account for his disappearance. We watched a video of his laboratory, and it appears he had stumbled across a means to allow living tissue to blend with synthetic material in a way that would allow the synthetic material to become active. The simplest but probably most inaccurate way to describe it is that he seems to have found a way to allow living tissue and synthetic material to combine, with the resulting product responding as living tissue, complete with nerves and systemic circulation. I also found an Internet story about a doctor from the former East Germany, a Dr. Lehnon. The article described a technique for taking the human eye, placing it in a synthetic casing, and then reinserting the eye, which became accepted as a single living organ by the body. It didn't explain how or why, but implied that the synthetic casing could have computer enhancements built into it. But that isn't the strangest thing I found. The Internet search also came up with an article on human eyes—it was a puzzling article indicating significant traffic in human eyes from China to Germany. I hope the two stories are unrelated, but my gut tells me otherwise. I think this needs to be brought up to some authority; perhaps you know who?' Alex left the question hanging.

"I'll do my best to get it to Mr. Bob Cochlen. Although his specialty is Korea, he has contacts in the United States and will know who to get it to. In fact, I am still convinced something about all this has to be tied to Korea because Noriko was assigned to kill the two of you by North Korean handlers."

One look at Emiko's face was enough to let them know the idea of her and her father being a target of assassination didn't sit well. "Why would you want to kill us?" Emiko looked directly at Noriko. Noriko didn't respond but her eyes welled up with tears.

"She only carried out the motions under an absolute guarantee that neither of you would be harmed. The rationale for allowing the attack to go through was to flush out the people here at the lab responsible for or associated with the assassination. I'm sure it is no surprise to you that Charles was involved, but we had no idea how many accomplices he had. The problem is this is the proverbial tip of the iceberg. It's like finding a snake hole and not knowing how deep it is or where it is leading us."

Lee turned to Noriko and said, "OK, I think you can see we held up our end of the bargain. Both of them will be fine."

Finally Noriko spoke to them, "I'm sorry for any pain or discomfort you went through. Perhaps sometime in the future we can meet again and I can explain in detail what has happened. I can assure you I meant you no harm. If it is of any consolation, this event may finally have given me my life back. You see, North Korean agents kidnapped me as a child, and I haven't seen my home or family since then. Now I hope that is all in the past, and I can begin to live a normal life again. I have no ill feelings toward you at all. I don't even know anything about you."

"Then why would you try to kill us?" Emiko glared at her.

"I'll answer that," Lee interjected. "Noriko was abducted as a child from the coast of Japan. She is not unique; there may have been hundreds of others. North Korean intelligence needed to be sure it could keep a flow of young Japanese coming through their military academies, mandatory for every Korean military officer, to be able to penetrate Japan. While Japan represents considerable propaganda hatred, it also has great wealth and technological capability. For North Korean agents to fit in with Japanese society, they would need exposure to many different Japanese people. Noriko was but one. Fortunately or unfortunately, they saw promise in Noriko as more than just a resident teacher. They attempted to brainwash her and then send her into deep cover. Basically that means sending her to the United States and letting her live a somewhat regular life, until they needed her. Relying on the fear they instilled in her as a child, they reasoned, accurately, that she would be too afraid to ask for help, with her own life and her parents'

347

life at risk. Still, when the order came to execute the two of you, she refused, until I convinced her we would not let you be killed, and that she should just play along. I admit now I did not know the means by which the agency would save you, but they did."

"Then it is you who gambled with my father's and my life?" Her anger had found a new target.

"Yes, that is probably a fair assessment. But without the ploy, we'd never really know who was behind it. Now I need to find out the answer to the question we're all asking—why you two? Any ideas?" Lee sat down, hoping the questions would calm the increasingly tense situation.

"I may have some idea," Alex interjected, but I need to get back to my lab and an e-mail connection that may have something more from Dr. Dorman."

"We can arrange that as soon as you feel well enough to travel," Lee smiled. "I hope you won't mind, but as long as she agrees, where I go, Noriko goes."

"I think that will be just fine," Emiko seemed somehow happy. "It's fairly obvious you two are more than professional acquaintances, and that's a good thing. It's nice to know there are still men who know how to treat a lady," involuntarily her head snapped around to Jack.

Carlos decided it was time to lighten the atmosphere at his friend's expense. "Ouch, dude, need help getting that spear out of your chest?" and he made the physical simulation of pulling a spear out of Jack's torso.

Everyone got a laugh out of that, and they decided they would leave the next morning for Alex and Emiko's house and laboratory. For now, it was time for Lee to check in and try to set up the secure call based on the new information Noriko had on the dam at Cho Mya.

"Lee here. Any progress on my request for a secure call?"

"Yes, you are instructed to make the call in the consultation room where you are. That way you can be on speaker and we can conference the call. If you are ready now, we'll have it set up by the time you get there. Our folks will escort you."

"We're on our way now. Lee out." It took Noriko and Lee less than ten minutes to get to the room. The technicians had already placed the call by the time they took their seats. They also had a computer hookup set for a conference—the first time Noriko had ever seen anything like it.

"Lee, are you there? We have you secure at this end. I have Mr. Bob Cochlen here. He runs the North Korean desk."

"Mr. Wong, I'm pleased to finally speak with you. Do you have your source with you?"

"My name is Noriko Suzuki, and I'm here. How can I help you?"

"Agent Wong has informed us you have contact with someone who knows something of the dam at Cho Mya. Is that correct?"

"Yes, sir, it is. I don't know him well, and I can't think of anything he's written to me that would be important, but I'll help anyway I can."

"That is very kind of you. Just to make it clear, we are taping this conference call. Don't worry, no one will ever hear it or know who you are. If you are comfortable with this, it is perhaps best for us to begin with what you remember of his e-mails. Can you give us a general characterization of the information? To keep it simple, let's just stick with his latest assignment, the one at the dam. In general, what has he told you?"

"OK, here goes. My impression is that he is quite disappointed that his government doesn't take his dam more seriously. You have to understand that for Colonel Song, the world itself revolves around the technology embedded in a functioning hydroelectric dam. He is totally convinced that by operating one successfully, enough energy can be created to help the DPRK become financially independent. He's no fool, though; he knows it would take many years, but it was his hope all along to be a part of making it happen for real. Anyway, from his first day on the job at Cho Mya, it became apparent to him that he alone felt the dam's use for the production of electricity was its most important contribution." Noriko looked over at Lee and shrugged.

"Mr. Cochlen, I think that is it for her initial thoughts. Do you have more questions?" Lee asked.

"Not right now. Ms. Suzuki, could we get you to log on and see if there are any new messages from him? If you have personal data you'd rather we not see, we can provide a computer that isn't a part of the conference so you can take care of those first."

"No, that's OK. I lead a rather boring life, at least in cyberspace." At that point, she winked at Lee, who blushed in response. "I haven't checked my e-mail for a week, so it is likely there is a message. What should I do?"

"Well, if it is OK with you, just open it the way you always would. We'll be able to read it from here. It is also important for you to know we will be able to read your password, so if you want to change it to a generic one first, we can arrange that as well." Bob was trying to be as careful as he possibly could. Sitting across from him, Carol was intrigued but said nothing. She had been told not to speak without first raising her hand and then discussing it with Mr. Cochlen. It seemed a bit melodramatic for her, but then it was her first glimpse into this side of espionage.

"Let me make it simple for you, Mr. Cochlen. I set up this e-mail account for the sole purpose of staying in touch with Colonel Song. Right or wrong, I believed he was tracking me in a sense with his boring yet reasonably frequent e-mails. My thought was that he was a part of the system to make sure I remained stable and aware that I was never really alone. It is why I continued to stay in touch with him, even after I met Lee."

"Excellent, Ms. Suzuki. If it will help you, I too will be forthright. There is information we need about the dam he is running."

"Well, what is it you want to know? I'll ask him." Noriko said it with some impatience. *Why did these people always seem to approach the simplest situation with such complexity?*

"Ms. Suzuki, the information I need is very important, and we dare not ask the question outright. As you mentioned, you have never before responded to his e-mails with any serious interest. He would surely find it odd if you changed your way and suddenly had a detailed interest in his work, don't you think?"

"I suppose so. Then what do we do?" She was now genuinely curious about what they wanted from her.

"Well, first of all, we see what, if any, information he has for you. Then we'll see about what we can ask him. Would you please go ahead and log in to your e-mail account?"

Seconds later she was opening the latest e-mail from Colonel Song. Noriko found absolutely nothing interesting in this e-mail. The first three paragraphs spoke in general about the dam not functioning in its hydroelectric capacity due to an oversight in its construction. Why would that be significant? But the silence on the other end of the conference line was poignant.

Bob Cochlen had hit mute just before she opened the e-mail, and was now very grateful he had. Even Stan Wadell had audibly gasped as he read the e-mail.

"My God, Bob, how reliable is this source? This is the exact answer we needed. If we trust this information, we now know absolutely that the dam was constructed without hydroelectric motors. We also know this colonel is unhappy with it. This is every agent's dream come true. Can we ask this individual any questions?"

"Stan, slow down. As I mentioned, neither the e-mail you're reading nor the source of that e-mail has been validated. It is exactly as it appears. It is an e-mail from one friend to another. It just happens that one of the friends is the commander of the dam at Cho Mya, and the recipient is, well, for her safety, I'll just say she is in contact with us for other reasons. Right now, I need to speak to her so she doesn't think we've fallen off the face of the earth."

He, motioned for silence with the universal finger to the lips gesture, and then hit the mute again.

"Ms. Suzuki, I'm sorry to leave you hanging. There is some information in this e-mail that we find very interesting. We won't know if it is important until we get some more answers, but again we must not ask direct questions. If it is all right with you, I'd like to think about this e-mail for a while and then develop some questions for you to ask your friend. It is important, however, for you to rephrase any questions we suggest in your own words. Everything must appear unchanged, or this Colonel Song may grow suspicious and stop e-mailing you."

"Are you implying he has been sending me this information not to keep track of me, but to provide me data to give to America? I don't believe it!"

"Not at all, Ms. Suzuki. I strongly doubt if he has been trying to keep track of you. That just isn't how it's done. I believe he has simply been sending you e-mails, one friend to another, and it is important to us that you preserve that relationship. I don't mean to be intentionally cryptic, but it is probably best if you actually don't know the precise answers we are looking for when you correspond with him. What we don't need is to alarm him, or make him think he has told you too much. It might also be dangerous for him; I notice he sent the e-mail to another person as well, someone named Hae-Jung. Do you know her?"

"Yes, Hae-Jung Nim was a student of mine at the same time as Colonel Song. She is now, as I understand it, a reporter for a television news program in South Korea."

Bob had hit the mute button just in time again. "She is probably a plant and forwards all his e-mail to the North," Stan said with authority. The glare he got from Bob reminded him he wasn't supposed to be talking during this call.

"Oh, sorry about that," Stan said trying hard to shrink up a little. Bob hit the button again.

Bob restarted the phone conversation, "I have to ask you this question, Ms. Suzuki."

She cut him off, "Please, just call me Noriko."

"Thank you, Noriko. I go by Bob. The two people here with me are Carol and Stan. Both of them are what civilians refer to as spooks. Their job is to gather and analyze information. Sometimes their questions can be a little hard to figure out, and some are just weird, but please bear with us—they don't get out much."

Noriko laughed, but Stan and Carol were holding Bob in a look of feigned insult. It was too much for Bob, and they all disintegrated into laughter. It was a good thing, as far as he was concerned.

"OK," he said as he tried to regain control. In that brief time, he had made the decision to let Noriko farther in than he had ever let someone before. *She deserves it*, he thought. "Noriko, your source in North Korea could hold information exceptionally vital to the United States, Japan, and most of the so-called free world. The question I was going to ask you is this: Is Colonel Song a dedicated North Korean officer, or in your opinion, does he hold beliefs more compatible with the West? Remember, I'm only asking your opinion."

"He is as dedicated to Kim Jong Il as anyone else I met in my stay in North Korea. I believe he feels strongly that his country was wronged in the Korean War. Beyond that, his central focus is on the peaceful resurrection of North Korea. He wants the North to regain its prewar superiority over South Korea, and he genuinely believes they can do it. In my opinion, he would never knowingly betray his country. As for Hae-Jung, she was, if I may be so bold, a truly catty female who desperately tried to attract Colonel Song, though not out of love, but out of her natural desire to improve her own lot by manipulating others who are in a position to help her. We were not friends, as I'm sure you can tell by now. She info-copies me when she responds to Colonel Song, but it is so sporadic that I get the impression that she doesn't answer most of his messages, or that I'm included on only some of them. I never really cared, so I didn't keep track. If I'd known it was important, I…"

"Never mind," Lee broke in. "If I'd been more professional, we'd have had this conversation long ago. I just wasn't paying attention."

"Nonsense," Carol allowed herself to enter the conversation. "If I have learned one thing in this business it is this: nobody is ever aware of how important a piece of information is when they first hear it. That is why there is this huge, complex, bureaucratic system for analyzing this kind of data. It is too complex for just one person. Besides, had you known, you might have said something that would have scared off this source. Certainly, if you had listened to me and asked the questions I'm dying to ask, this would have been the last e-mail he would have sent you. We're going to have to move carefully with this."

Bob spoke up again, "Absolutely right. This is going to be tough. We have to try to get more information from him, but, Noriko, you have to know what Stan said a few minutes ago. At the time, I thought you would be better off not hearing this, but we're all going to have to work together to get this right, and you might as well know the dangers facing Colonel Song up front. Go ahead, Stan. Tell her what you said earlier about Hae-Jung."

"Well," Stan began, once again uncomfortable as he felt himself enter the spotlight, "from what I've heard so far, and this is just speculative, you understand, this other woman, Hae-Jung, is likely an agent of the North Korean intelligence service. Otherwise, she would never be in South Korea. She is probably forwarding every e-mail Colonel Song sends to the two of you directly back to the government in the North."

"That is why we don't want to ask him specific questions, Noriko," Bob began. "Not just to keep from spooking him, but also to prevent him from answering bluntly in a fashion that would likely cost him his life. It is possible that he has developed a pattern of response that no longer alarms the intelligence analysts in the North, but we don't know that for sure. It is better that he gives us all he can under his terms. With luck, it will be all we need. If we're extremely lucky, he may say something that would give us an opportunity to approach him openly, in which case we might be able to afford him some level of protection, but that is unlikely. Are you comfortable with proceeding?"

Noriko settled back in her chair and closed her eyes. What did she really feel about Colonel Song? While she didn't want to have anything to do with causing his death, she concluded she really had nothing to do with him other than knowing him as a student.

After an uncomfortably long pause, she responded. "I don't want to do anything that will cause his death, but I'm not opposed to trying to get the information you need, especially if you are willing to do it in the safest way possible for him."

Bob let out a sigh of relief, "Thank you. I promise we will do all we can to get the information we need without unduly jeopardizing Colonel Song. Let us think on this e-mail for a while. Why don't we start with you responding to it? I'd like you to rephrase the following question in your own words. 'If the dam has no hydroelectric motors, what was the point in building it in the first place?'"

"That sounds like something I would ask without changing a thing. I'll put in some cursory flowery information about my work in the hardware store first, as I always do, then I'll ask the question. Is that alright?"

"It's perfect. We don't need to see any of this, so go ahead with your e-mail after we hang up. Can we contact you through Agent Wong?"

She started to say anytime day or night, but decided to let Lee off the hook, "Yes, I will probably stay in touch with Lee, so that's a good way to contact me." Then she mouthed the silent words "You owe me" to Lee, who used all his self-control to keep from laughing out loud again.

With that, the conference call ended, leaving Bob, Carol, and Stan with much work to do, and Lee and Noriko feeling safe and content.

DR. SANDERSON'S LABORATORY
AND HOUSE

The trip back was considerably less tense for Noriko, Lee, Jack, Alex, and Emiko. Carlos returned to Washington to continue, as he described it, the long march up to the most important toilets in the world. Jack was quite certain his friend would be changing directions out of the janitorial service arena altogether, but he made no comment other than to implore Carlos to stay in touch. With Lee and Noriko entertaining each other, and Jack and Emiko acting like lovesick high-school students, Alex decided he would sleep through the flight home; it was obvious who'd be doing the research back at the lab anyway. He awoke with an increasing sinus pressure that always heralded descent into a landing area. Looking around, he saw that Emiko was practically wrapped around Jack, and Noriko was in the same position with Lee. Both of the younger men were awake, and the expressions on their faces indicated they weren't the slightest bit inconvenienced by someone laying on them.

The agency had sent a seven-passenger bus to pick them up at the airport. The trip home couldn't go by fast enough for any of them. It seemed that everyone's first priority after they arrived at Alex and Emiko's home and laboratory was to take a shower or a bath. Alex wondered if he was truly the only one who was hungry. Betting that

The Eyes

wasn't the case, he had the young man who drove them pick up Mexican takeout from Senior Pepe's, a popular local restaurant. Since things were looking pretty good and his companions all seemed to be in a good mood, he added a couple of liters of margaritas to the order and decided the research could wait until the morning. Everyone deserved an evening to get to know each other and relax.

Later that evening, as they consumed their dinner with all the gusto Alex had hoped they would, they began to share their stories. After a few hours of jovial conversation, Alex finally decided it might be time to wrap things up, "I think we should all retire early and get ready for tomorrow. We have a lot of things to try to decipher, but I'm just too tired to start now." He didn't expect any argument and got none.

Lee and Noriko moved quietly into one room—Alex didn't bother suggesting otherwise—and Jack and Emiko did the same.

Alone in the hallway, Alex turned and headed toward his room. *Kids*, he thought, as he went into his bedroom. *If I could harness the human energy about to be expended tonight, I wouldn't have an electric bill to worry about anymore.*

The next morning Lee, Noriko, Jack, Emiko, and Alex made their way into the reefer room to open out Alex's archaic computer so that they could check for any new e-mails from Dr. Dorman. Once on-line, they found that, indeed, there was a new e-mail from the doctor. The sending address came across as unreadable characters; even looking at the properties didn't help them to unravel the sending location. The body of the message was intact, however.

Alex,

May this message find you at peace with yourself and your family. I am at peace, the peace of the traditional lands. Though I was unaware through most of my travels, I find myself with my original peoples, and have need of your help. If it is within your capability, I need information on the neural jump capacity of polyvinyl in the presence of neonatal solution with excitatory stimuli. Previous results grew dramatically, though the end was near. It is apparent that the presence of neonatal fluid alone is inadequate to stimulate growth. Following logic, some form of excitatory stimu-

Dr. Sanderson's Laboratory and House

lus must also be present, lest the growth become uncontrolled in the nature of cancerous tumors. It is almost like a movie. It would be a vital link to find the methodology of such stimulus; it would allow for the development of growth in otherwise-inanimate tissue. My efforts follow the Japanese research of a similar nature regarding light transmission through neural excitation. It is such with the eyes.

May Allah keep you in his light.—Gene

"Well," Dr. Sanderson began, "I think there are enough inferences here to conclude that Gene is in a precarious situation, probably somewhere back in the Middle East. His reference to Japanese research clearly indicates that vision is the subject. What I found through the Internet search, added to my knowledge of Gene being an incredibly talented eye surgeon, leads to some disquieting conclusions. The missing piece is any sort of Chinese connection through Germany. If Gene is removing eyes, and they are being modified and computer upgraded in Germany, and then reinserted into humans, there is the potential for a very dangerous weapon that could be used anywhere at any time, virtually undetected. Mr. Wong, do your sources have any ideas?"

"Well, I have an appointment with Mr. Bob Cochlen the day after tomorrow in the morning. In fact, we all have an appointment with him. We each have specific pieces of information that I could never put together for him the way a presentation by all of us would."

"Ugh, not another cross-country flight," Emiko whined. "I think I've had enough of traveling for now."

"Me too," Noriko chimed in. "But if you think our information might help get this doctor back and find out what Korea has to do with human eye donations, I'm willing to go. C'mon, Emiko-san, we've gone through all of this; let's finish it."

"Oh, I guess you're right. But don't you think we should review the information we finally got out of Dr. Dorman's stuff, Dad? With Jack here to help us recreate it, we might be able to get a picture of what this stuff is capable of. There might just be something worthwhile that hasn't been built into a weapon."

"I think that is a great idea. It will take several days for the results, so if we set it up now, we might have some answers by the time we get

357

back. What do you think, Jack?" Dr. Sanderson was clearly eager to set it up. It was the closest thing to getting back to what he really liked to do.

"I can certainly help set it up as Dr. Dorman and I did, but if I read his e-mail correctly, something else happened to affect the parameters of the experiments. It was something unintentional, which yielded surprising results of some sort. I have no idea what that was." Jack looked at Alex and Emiko and said, "OK, Alex, this is where I say you're holding out on me. What did you find that I have yet to hear about?"

"Well," Alex began, "before we get into all of that, we have our guests to tend to. Lee, what will you and Noriko do? You are certainly welcome to watch the experiments, but I'm afraid they aren't very exciting."

"Don't worry about us. If there is a vehicle we can use, Noriko and I can set up everyone's travel arrangements. I presume no one will complain if we spend an extra day or so after the meeting?"

"No, I will not stay one day longer than I have to," Emiko said with some finality. "I am beginning to hate Washington, D.C.!"

"Actually," Jack put in, "it might be best for you to check with your contacts and see what they think. If they want us to make additional presentations to others on the East Coast, I'd rather get it all done and over with on the same trip." Jack turned to Emiko, "I know you are tired of all this Emi-chan, but it is unlikely we could refuse additional requests, and I too tire of the cross-country flights."

"Oh, I just hate it when you're right," Emiko laughed. "We're in your hands, Lee. Take good care of us."

"I will. And you might all be somewhat happier to know that the meeting is in Hawaii, not Washington. I would also request that Noriko and I stay with you three to the end of this if you don't mind. I can make sure that we are not a financial burden on anyone, and it will make it easier on me as I have to find a place to hide her for a while. Also, I have a second agenda. Noriko and I have to go through a rather lengthy debriefing regarding pretty much everything she can remember about her life since she was stolen from her parents. We can do that in Hawaii."

"Speaking of which," Emiko sat up straight. "When will Noriko-san get to see her parents again? I'm surprised she's been so patient."

Dr. Sanderson's Laboratory and House

Lee looked at Noriko to answer, "Noriko's parents are being protected at a location neither she nor I know of, which is how it must stay until we are sure the chain of handlers trying to get to her is taken care of. Usually in a situation like hers, once the mission has been carried out, the agent in the field is abandoned. Since the agent usually does something that results in an investigation, it is pretty close to an execution just to strand them. That's another reason we wanted to let her do what she was instructed. It may seem like 'honor among thieves,' but there is a protocol and she did accomplish her mission. There are still several missing links in her case. First, there is the Korean police detective, Ohl Suk Chee, who seems to have disappeared, and then there is the mysterious Middle Eastern man who came to the farmhouse and gave Noriko her final instructions and the equipment. Also, there are bound to be some serious repercussions concerning the problems with the contracted security at all the labs. That final piece will include your laboratory, Dr. Sanderson."

"I understand, but at least we don't have any live-in hooligans like the other two places. Here are the keys to my Honda Accord."

SEINE'S FACTORY,
THE FORMER EAST GERMANY

Ibin-Il Raheed had suffered for days on end with the burning pain that racked him day and night. The eye wasn't the problem. It was the implants in his arm and chest that had simply become unbearable. The tissue just above his elbow on the back side of his arm was swollen and turning black. His chest and abdomen throbbed with his every breath. Finally he reported it to the nurse who came by once a day to see if anyone had died. Although the nurse seemed completely unconcerned, she escorted him to a waiting room away from the others. He assumed he would see a doctor and things would get better, and knowing that comforted him a little. He sat in the room alone for several hours, but patience was something he had grown very used to displaying. It seemed his whole life had been one long demonstration of patient suffering for the reward that would come in time.

He thought back to the day he had decided it was time to join the jihad, the fight to free his people. Sometimes, when he was honest with himself, he admitted that to a certain extent, he just had to do something to escape the hopelessness of his village. But his ultimate decision to join the experiments had been a true one; knowing full well the possibility that he might not survive, he went without hesitation. He still did not know exactly what he was training to do, but he understood

The Eyes

he was now equipped with a very powerful weapon. It had only to be activated, and he could destroy a target by merely thinking about it. Finally the doctor arrived.

Through the translator, he asked Raheed where it hurt and to show him how much movement he had in the arm. Raheed did as he was told, bravely aggravating the injured arm and suffering the agony in the demonstration. The doctor gave him an injection directly into the tissue of his arm, and within seconds the pain subsided. Raheed was ecstatic. He was not in pain any more. Then the doctor told him that since he had suffered so, he would be one of the few allowed to test fire the weapon inside, if he cared to. Raheed could hardly believe his ears. Of course he would; that is what every man here wanted to do—to see just how powerful the weapon was and to know it would perform perfectly.

The doctor and translator escorted him to what looked like a target range. Sitting about a hundred yards away in the sandy field was a standard army truck with camouflaged paint.

"I will now activate your weapon," the doctor said through the translator. "When you are ready, point at the truck and destroy it."

Raheed stood erect despite the discomfort. *I will do this flawlessly*, he thought to himself. He raised his arm slowly and began to focus on the truck.

"No!" the doctor shouted at him. "You must do this as quickly as you possibly can. The attack must be nearly instantaneous. You cannot allow anyone the time to stop you. Feel the attack; don't think about it."

Slightly confused and a bit embarrassed, Raheed began again. He stood stiffly with his hands at his side. Then in one swift motion, he bent his elbow, pointed at the truck, and thought, *Kill!* Instantaneously he could smell a strange odor, like cooked meat. He recognized a severe burning sensation from mid-forearm to his fingertip, and only seconds after the explosion of the truck, he dropped dead.

Dr. Lehnon was pleased with this trial. The specimen had destroyed an armored vehicle one hundred meters away by thought in nanoseconds, and was left unable to be interrogated—a definite win-win experiment.

UNC HEADQUARTERS, YONGSAN, SOUTH KOREA

The SIPRNET was humming. Since the warning order and chain of phone calls had flowed from the Pentagon down through every echelon of the Department of Defense, battle staffs had been activated at every military facility touched by Team Spirit. Dave thought to himself that it was a shame that no matter how hard the military tried, there was always a difference between exercises and the real thing. With every commander now aware that this was a Team Spirit that actually might be preparing for combat, the attention level had become intense yet efficient. The usual whining about swap outs for personnel, equipment shortfalls, and choice locations were absent. The State Department had done its job in likewise efficiency, and the fuel the Pacific theater had been complaining about for decades was already sourced and on its way to strategic locations. For the aircraft, Elmendorf AFB, Hawaii, Guam, and Japan were being augmented with fuel and tankers. Behind the scenes, leaders were quietly discussing possibilities with former allies in Thailand and the Philippines, and even Vietnam, to add some irony to the new global relationships. The preparation would still take a considerable amount of time, with the personnel being the last to move into place, only because they were the most visible component. Ships and aviation wings were moving closer to their targets, but that too would take several more weeks. One didn't just pick up an aircraft carrier battle group and ship them out in a few days; the logistics were complex and time consuming. *But progress is being made*, Dave thought to himself, *and within another month, the United States and South Korea will be ready*. Now all he could do was hope nothing precipitated preemptive action from the DPRK. He had heard absolutely nothing, and PACOM assets confirmed that everything in the North looked normal, down to their scheduled training maneuvers designed to help the saber-rattling protest of the Team Spirit exercise.

HONOLULU, HAWAII

The flight into Honolulu from Seattle was uneventful. Noriko had been thrilled with Lee's proposal to take a quick break from the events in their lives with what she decided would include some rest and relaxation on the island chain. Emiko echoed the idea.

The weather never ceased to amaze Lee when he stepped out of the terminal in Hawaii. For those not acclimated to it, it felt like stepping into a sauna. But wasn't that what everyone expected of a tropical island? The ever-present Hawaiian music, the lei stands, and the palm trees all announced a return to "paradise." He picked up the keys to the rental caravan and walked over to pick up the vehicle. The air was hot and sticky; he was already beginning to sweat. He got in the car and drove the circuitous route back to the terminal where Noriko and the others were standing with their luggage. After loading their gear, they got in and he drove off down Highway 3 toward Honolulu.

They would be staying at the Hale Koa. The name meant "house of the warrior" in Hawaiian, and under an arrangement with the Department of Defense, the other agencies of the government were occasionally supported at this hotel, which was usually reserved for active duty and retired military members. The trip from the airport took only twenty minutes. Lee was glad he had decided there was no longer any real reason to continue with the pretext that he and Noriko each needed

The Eyes

a room of their own and had reserved only one. Noriko wasn't surprised when Lee told her she didn't need to register herself this time. She flushed slightly but said nothing as they finished the paperwork and went up to their room.

Lee was acting a little funny, going back down to "check on something" as they arrived at the room. He barely set his carry on baggage on the counter before retreating to the hallway.

Well, perhaps the overtly obvious room arrangement has actually embarrassed him; guys can be weird that way, Noriko thought to herself. She opened the refrigerator and checked out the beverages. Though this wasn't the typical time of day to try a drink, the trip from Washington to San Francisco to Honolulu had made her feel a bit strange. After all, the trip had included over fourteen hours of travel covering six time zones. She grabbed a wine cooler, twisted off the top, and served herself in the standard hotel room glass, then settled in on the couch and thumbed the TV to life with the remote. Simultaneously tired, bored, and apathetic, she just let it drone on.

"I see you're getting comfortable," Lee said as he walked in the room unexpectedly. "When you're finished, there is one thing I need to show you before we grab dinner and settle in."

"Whatever," Noriko yawned. "I'm not sure what time it is, and I'm almost sure I can handle drinking my dinner, which probably won't take any more effort than trying to finish this glass." She shadow toasted Lee, and then patted the couch next to her. "Sure you don't want to just curl up here and start the tourist thing tomorrow?" she purred. "I doubt if any of the others will miss us at dinner."

Lee hesitated; *I hate it when she does this*, he thought. *Here I am trying to do the truly noble thing, and she's doing everything she can to make it impossible. Well, I'm a trained professional, and I will win this battle.* He smiled at his own pathetic joke, but he knew what awaited her would stop her cold. "No, I think we should do this right now," he intoned wistfully. "Some things can't wait. The good news is we won't even leave the hotel. Besides, if you still feel the same way later…" He let it hang in the air, knowing full well he would likely spend tonight alone.

"OK, killjoy. Let's get this over with. What can be so exciting that it beats a night of special quiet moments?"

Honolulu, Hawaii

"You'll see," he said as he opened the door.

Noriko took a swig of the wine cooler and set it carefully on the end table. She strode to the door, slipped on her sandals, and walked into the hallway. Lee really hadn't been able to figure out if it was perfume, body soap, or shampoo, but whatever the smell was, she was absolutely intoxicating. Cursing himself for having so little insight on timing, Lee shut the door and led the way to the elevator. Instead of heading for the lobby, as she expected, Lee hit the button for the top floor.

Oh, men, she thought. *With all the signals I've sent, he still has to take me up to the top floor for the romantic view of the ocean. Doesn't he realize we just spent the last three hours staring down at that ocean? Oh well, being part of the fairer sex also means putting up with the stupid sex.*

The elevator door opened and they strolled down the hall hand in hand. They walked up to one of the "named" doors, obviously a suite of some sort. *Well*, she thought, *this is a step up. Although*, her practical side said to her, *if he had a suite, we should have just checked into it.*

The door was slightly ajar, held open with a metal slide bar used for security. Lee turned to Noriko and said, "You first Nori-chan."

As she walked into the open suite, she turned to grab Lee's hand to pull him in, but the look on his face stopped her. He gestured into the room with a jerk of his head, and she followed the direction of his nod inside. Through the door was a fairly spacious foyer. She walked cautiously into the living room with its opulently appointed couch, armchair, and big-screen TV. To her left, a light was on in another room, which turned out to be a small kitchen area. She looked back at Lee, who kept up his maddening silence and motioned her inside. Now her defenses were coming on. Her heart rate increased, and her senses sharpened as once again as she began the decent into fear that had become far too prevalent in her life of late. Bravely, she stepped into the kitchen, not knowing what to expect.

There, sitting at the table, also unaware of what was happening, sat Noriko's mother and father. All recognized one another in an instant. The fifteen years of fear, frustration, anger, and hate gave way to spontaneous weeping and irrepressible shudders, which culminated in uncontrollable emotion. Lee stood uncomfortably at the entrance to the kitchen, unending tears flowing down his face and dripping unceremo-

The Eyes

niously onto the floor. There was little room for thought and zero opportunity for words. His supervisor had been wise to insist that Lee write down the instructions he must provide the three. He took the envelope from his pocket and placed it gently on the kitchen counter.

He could barely see as he made his way to the suite door. As he closed it behind him and headed back to the other room, he thought how much more respectful this was than the tragic public reunions he'd seen on television.

Inside the suite, Noriko and her parents clung to each other in a ball of emotion. She had been a child when she was stolen from them. For her, it had been the ultimate nightmare a child could face—alone, abducted by people without regard for her safety, not understanding what or why it had happened. For her parents, not much could be worse than having your daughter taken from you without a hint of where she had gone. It would be a long while before any of them could speak. Catching up, in the normal sense of the words, was quite impossible. None of them were the same. None saw the world the way normal family members saw it. What they knew and what they felt all dissolved into the basic instinct to hold and comfort one another. They had no desire except to savor the longed for feeling of parent and child, clinging to each other in the most honest expression of love. Despite all their gratitude for what he had done for them, none would even think of Lee until the next morning.

For his part, Lee barely managed to make it back to the room before breaking down in a most unmanly expression of emotion. Embarrassed at his reaction, and grateful to experience it completely alone, he recovered slowly, whereupon he approached the stocked refrigerator with a vengeance. He tried to focus on the mysterious meeting Mr. Cochlen had arranged for the next day, without much success. The instructions he had left for Noriko and her parents now seemed cruel in their coldness. The hastily written letter told them in unfairly unemotional terms that they would have just this one night to be together, with Noriko's mother and father flying back to Japan the next morning.

They had spent over a week here in Honolulu, not knowing why they had been brought here. They were told they had an important meeting, which usually meant with someone from the CIA. Sometimes it was Lee; lately it had been another agent. They felt fortunate, though, as they had met many other parents from the same area around Niigata whose children had gone missing. At least they knew they were being told the truth, where their precious Noriko was, and how she was doing. Replacing what fear dissipated with that knowledge was the guilt they felt, much as the sole survivor of any catastrophe inevitably faces—the questions, Why us? Why are we alone able to know the fact of our loved one, when so many others have no information, no relief from the unending pain of loss without knowing?

All suspected North Korea and most had been vociferous in letting their own government know what they felt, only to come face to face with the stony impotence of their government in international affairs. Some blamed the United States and MacArthur for stripping the spine from Japan. Others acquiesced that Japan's own violent past with Korea prevented a more forceful effort to recover its own citizens, but for grieving parents of missing children, for spouses who lost spouses, and for communities who lost citizens, leaving everyone suspicious and afraid, the inaction was intolerable. For most people, the conduct of governments was the subject of conversations, occasionally excited, over tea and rice crackers, or during intermissions between innings of baseball games consumed with enthusiasm. But for the people of the fishing villages along the coast of Japan facing the yellow sea nearest North Korea, every interaction with North Korea, Kita Chōsen, as they called the DPRK, was a personal event felt intimately. The betrayal, as they saw it, was more than just unacceptable; it was unconscionable. With the surprise admission of senior leadership within the DPRK that it held Japanese nationals against their will, the families had hoped for action and resolution. Once again they were witness to the subjugation of the few for the perceived needs of the many, as the world continued to deal with North Korea and their loved ones continued to go unaccounted for and unreturned. A small number of Japanese citizens were allowed to come back to Japan, but all had new ties to North Korea that would make staying in Japan exceedingly difficult. All had new families in North Korea that were held as ransom for their return. All had been re-selected for torment as pawns in a government-to-government game that wasn't theirs and that they had little possibility to influence.

THE CHENGIS KAHN HOTEL

Dr. Dorman checked in to the Chengis Kahn, the primary hotel for foreign visitors to Ulaanbaatar, the capitol of Mongolia. Entering his room, he was excited to see the familiar Western setting: the queen-sized bed, the standard chair and desk, and, of course, the television with remote. Absently, he turned on the television to welcome the first electronic imagery he'd seen in a very long time. As an Asian sports channel showing a playoff game between two Japanese professional soccer teams played in the background, he walked over to the window to look out over the city. He smiled at the thought of the Russian architect designing the place. He could just imagine him saying, "We put big square concrete building here and here and here and here," until what Dr. Dorman saw from his window emerged—a huge series of what looked like concrete dominos.

As the game droned on, the doctor decided what he really wanted was a hot bath, which he started, and then sleep. He wasn't really hungry, and he was too tired to deal with whatever course of action he would have to take to get a meal. The bath turned out to be exactly what he needed, and when he finally dragged himself out of the tub, he barely made it to the bed before falling fast asleep.

The Eyes

The next morning, a sharp-looking Colonel Hester from the embassy was waiting for him in the lobby. "Good morning, Dr. Dorman. On behalf of the government of the United States…"

"Please, spare me the formalities," Dr. Dorman interrupted. "Let's get to the important stuff. How did you find me and why did you get me out of there? There has to be some significant reason to have expended that much energy on a reasonably unknown researcher."

"OK, Doctor, you deserve that much. To be brutally honest, I don't know why. I got a call from the State Department asking us to check for camps in the desert. The general here was happy to oblige as he isn't a big fan of foreigners camping in his land uninvited. Once we found the camp, he was ready to take it out and asked if we wanted you extricated. Washington said yes; otherwise, I suspect you wouldn't be here right now. Once the Mongolians found out about the camp, its fate was a foregone conclusion. I hope there weren't any of your compatriots with you." It was more of a question than a statement.

"I'm not really sure how to feel. I spent over a year there, so certainly there was an attachment to some of them, but the nature and depth of those relationships hasn't really set in my mind. I will probably be thinking about that for some time to come, but I don't feel traumatized about it yet. I've seen a lot of things I don't quite know how to take, but I don't feel comfortable discussing it now, if that's OK."

"Perfectly all right, Dr. Dorman. My current desire and task is to meet your needs and get you on this morning's flight headed for Hawaii. There are only two aircraft in the Mongolian Airlines fleet, so we don't want to miss this one. On the other hand, I know you didn't eat last night, and I want to offer you the opportunity to have breakfast."

"I'm not terribly hungry, so I think I will just get on the plane and head back to the United States, as long as that is OK with you. The sooner I get back, the sooner I can resume a normal life."

"Well then, let's go. I know you don't have any luggage, and we'll be handling the paperwork to get you through customs on this end." Colonel Hester escorted the doctor to the waiting van and then drove him to the main airport, where he was whisked through the customs checkpoints and issued a ticket. From Ulaanbaatar, the embassy flew him to Kansai International Airport, and after a very brief stop, on to Hawaii. Once in Hawaii, he was given a night off in the hotel. He'd also been given a new wallet with five hundred dollars and the instructions that anything he charged to his room and the room itself would be taken care of by the State Department. All in all, he reflected he hadn't been treated this well at anytime in entire his life, though going through what he had in the past year was hardly worth it.

He hadn't eaten for some time, a feat easily accomplished after the spartan conditions of the camp. Now, he seemed to be regaining his appetite, or perhaps it was the advertisements for shrimp and steak adorning the hotel elevator. *Perhaps*, he thought a bit sheepishly, *it might be the knowledge that I can order whatever I want for free.* Whatever the reason, he decided the chef's special would be fine and placed the order over the phone.

"Yes, sir, we'll have that up to your room in about forty minutes," the young lady said politely. Now he could just sit back and relax while someone else not only prepared a virtual feast, but also delivered and served it to him. He decided he could get very used to this lifestyle.

A little less than thirty minutes later, there was a knock at the door and a male voiced called out, "Room service." Dr. Dorman stood and walked to the door. When he opened it, he found himself face to face with Jack Armstead.

"Jack! How did you get here? What are you doing here?" And then he grabbed Jack in a mutual bear hug.

"Dr. Dorman, you have no idea how great it is to see you. When you disappeared, my life changed dramatically, though not in as dangerous a way as I hear yours did. I can't wait to hear all about it. But for tonight, none of that. I'm not alone, and we can all hear about your adventures tomorrow," Jack responded. "Dr. Sanderson and others are waiting to see you. We thought I should be the welcome wagon and see if you were up to some company."

"I certainly am, especially Alex and Emiko," he responded emphatically. "I'm afraid I didn't order enough food for everyone, but you are all welcome. I've been given a very nice room here. It'd be a shame for it to go to waste on little old me."

"Don't worry about the food. I took the liberty of increasing your order, so it should be fine. I've also ordered some wine for the occasion. Naturally, we'll take care of the expenses."

The Eyes

"Don't worry about that. They told me anything I needed or wanted I could charge to my room and it would be taken care of like magic. So far, I haven't bought a thing, so I think they're getting off fairly easy. I'm scheduled for some 'personal time shopping' tomorrow morning, when I'll buy some new clothes and such. I've been a little reluctant to do much of anything but sleep so far."

"Then I'll go get everyone, and I'll be right back." Jack left the large cart, still covered, and retreated down the hallway. Gene decided to take a look at the food and get the glasses ready. He found the cork-screw by the refrigerator and started working on the three bottles Jack had ordered. By the time he successfully opened the second bottle, Emiko had strode into the room with her father and Lee right behind her.

"Dr. Dorman, how wonderful to see you again," she gushed and gave him a polite hug.

"My how you've grown up," Gene responded. "And now that it is Dr. Sanderson and Dr. Sanderson, how about if we dispense with all the formality. I'm Gene, and it is absolutely wonderful to be with company that can call me by that name again."

"Gene it is," Emiko repeated. "I think the only person you don't know is Mr. Lee Wong. He is our resident spook. That is to say, he works for one or more of our nation's intelligence agencies. He is reluctant to explain all of it, and we haven't pressed him. All we know is he's one of the good guys, and he's been helping us all along, when he's not trying to kill us." Her laughter let Lee off the hook, and he was grateful.

"I'm very pleased to meet you, sir," Lee said as he shook Dr. Dorman's hand. "My association with your plight is somewhat tangential, or at least I think it is. This whole event has been strange, even for me. I'm pleased that you were found."

"Are you the source of the information that led authorities to the camp?"

"Not exactly. I think it was a combination of disparate facts that led them to look in the deserts of Mongolia. Everyone seemed to think you were in the Middle East somewhere."

"That makes sense. I also thought I was somewhere in the Middle East, but a lot of the world's deserts look the same, and unless you've been in the exact same spot before, there's no real way to know. In my case, everyone in the camp really was from the Middle East, mostly from Afghanistan. I'm not sure how many of them knew where we were. It isn't something we discussed very often, since none of us ever left the camp. The ones who came and went were undergoing such trauma that where they were or where they were going was about the last thing on their mind. But as Jack said, we can speak of this and many other things tomorrow. Tonight I just want to hear about mundane things, like the baseball and football seasons, what the funniest commercials are on the air now, and who the president is. I haven't been getting out much lately." The laughter was genuine and the beginning of a comfortable evening of camaraderie.

The next morning, Gene was brought to USPACOM headquarters, where he was taken into a standard briefing room. Bob Cochlen from the DIA met him at the door.

"Dr. Dorman, it is truly an honor." His firm handshake and warm smile let Gene know he was still among friendly people. He found himself almost anticipating this debriefing, mostly to try and piece together what had happened with a larger perspective that might make more sense.

"Let me get this started," Bob began. "In order for this to make any sense, we'll need to start with your abduction and move forward through the time you spent at the camp. I'm sure there will be a lot you don't know, so we'll try to fill in the blanks as best we can. For our part," he said as he gestured towards Jack, Emiko, Alex, Noriko and Lee, "we'll try to hold all our questions until your narrative is over. If anything in Dr. Dorman's description brings up something that has happened to anyone else, please chime in. It'll help bring the whole picture together for us."

Gene coughed nervously and looked around the room. Once he began his story, he soon warmed to the attentive audience. He explained what he had been doing at the lab in North Dakota, and how he had discovered, quite by accident, a means of using the combination of neonatal fluids and vibration at a slightly increased temperature to induce neural growth into plastic. He explained about the two men who abducted him, including the similarity between his abduction and his father's death; Bob assured him they knew of no connection, but that they would certainly check for one. Gene also pointed out that he remembered very little of the trip to the camp, save the fear, discomfort, thirst, and hunger he experienced. He gave a detailed explanation of his purpose in the surgical procedures for the removal of the eyes from young men in the desert. Then he startled everyone with information he had gotten from one of the young men after the surgery.

"I asked him how he was doing, always careful not to pry into any details that might be dangerous for me to have. Sometimes it's better to not know what is going on. Clearly this was the standard in the camp, at least as far as I could tell. Few seemed to have much information about what became of the men who passed through. This young man seemed particularly touched that I would try to be as gentle as possible and that I actually cared for his well-being. He began to talk to me about his role in removing evil from the earth. I listened patiently to what I thought was simply more propaganda fed to an impressionable young man. But then he explained he would become a living weapon and would be traveling to Europe and then the Far East, beyond the Silk Road's distant end. I asked him carefully how he thought he could be a living weapon, and he said 'they' would install a weapon in his arm that would be guided by a device that would replace his eye. I really don't know what that means, but I wouldn't disregard it. The young man had no reason to fabricate a story for me."

"Well, I think I speak for everyone when I say that's pretty fascinating. Do you have any idea who might have the technology to accomplish what he was talking about?" Bob was concerned, but tried successfully not to show it.

"I think I do," Alex chimed in. "I think that is exactly what Dr. Lehnon in Germany was working toward. If it is true, we may have a real problem here.

TUNNEL THIRTY-THREE

The North Korean Army was ready to go. The men had already checked the prepositioned armor near the opening of the tunnel, some 450 meters below the earth's surface. It wasn't difficult to get the men to check them on a regular basis, once they had concluded that they were virtually invisible and their presence was unknown to the enemy above. They would start the engines approximately two hours before they expected to move, so now was the time to ensure fluid levels were right and the exteriors of the vehicles were all in working order. If things went according to plan, this would take another ten hours to accomplish. All around the men were the vast stockpiles of munitions. This would be a bad place to be if an errant or enemy explosion began.

The charges were ready to go. It would be a singular explosion that removed the final fifty meters of rock and dirt separating the North Korean Army from the South Korean landscape. They had already seen it accomplished in the distant northern sector, where they practiced their munitions. It was quite clever really. They built a test tunnel ending underneath their normal munitions impact area. That way, when they tested the exit strategy, anyone watching would see exactly what they expected to see—munitions exploding in the munitions impact area. The test had been a success, and to the participants, amazingly quieter than expected. Afterward, they thought it through and realized the movement of the earth had absorbed most of the energy and the noise. It gave the men a large measure of comfort that their presence would not be announced to any creature within five kilometers. They didn't expect their attack to be a complete surprise, but they didn't want a welcome team either.

With everything in order, the men now sat quietly. The explosion would be the only "Go" signal they needed. Their first order of business was to establish a secure area just outside the tunnel for the rest of the brigade to marshal. That would be accomplished by layered fire if needed. They were prepared for either a hostile or quiet reception; like most soldiers, they hoped for the latter.

IN ENGLAND

All the trappings of power were kept intact aboard the Andrews aircraft. This included the stately reception at Heathrow, complete with the British prime minister and his wife receiving their American friends on the Tarmac. Everyone was quickly herded into the bulletproof limousines for the trip to 10 Downing Street. On arrival, the entourage was ushered through the Pillared Drawing Room, complete with the famous Persian carpet, copied from a sixteenth-century original in the Victoria and Albert Museum containing the inscription, "I have no refuge in the world other than thy threshold. My head has no protection other than this porch way. The work of a slave of the Holy Place, Maqsud of Kashan in the year 926." Finally everyone settled around the boat-shaped conference table of the Cabinet Room. The history of the room notwithstanding, they paused only briefly to take in the ambiance.

The deputy US secretary of state began, "Prime Minister McNairy, we have a crisis on our hands on the Korean peninsula. War may be breaking out anew. We have to deal with what we have now. President Fulton has asked for your help. Likely we'll need to station more of our long-range aircraft on English soil to start."

"Well, that'll keep us out of a bit of a rub over here," Lord Vitmount was beaming, "Our assumption was that the United States would take on this hooligan head to head. Consequently, we've been rather hard nosed in our public statements. Not inconsequentially, the British public would like nothing more than to see this brought to an end, and the bloodier the better!" he proclaimed with some rancor.

"That may well be true, and the US public would probably find a bludgeoning of one of the 'Axis of Evil' a good thing as well, but the truth of the matter is that they could have the drop on us. They could conceivably drive the US Forces off the peninsula by the time we have significant enough forces in range to engage."

"But how is that possible? You Yanks have some thirty-six thousand troops in Korea and a boatload of fighter aircraft to boot. Nevertheless, we'll stand shoulder to shoulder with you through this." Prime Minster McNairy stood and extended his hand. "I'll not drag this out. You have our cooperation; just let us know what you need."

"Thank you, sir. There is one area where we could use your help. Do you have any information on a terrorist cell in China that may be working with the Koreans? It seems the Democratic People's Republic has harnessed support from terrorists and other discontent sources, some of which may have impressive technological capabilities. I don't suppose MI5 has anything?" The prime minister stood, and in the direct British way, turned to Britain's home secretary, Sir Charles Brigans, and spoke plainly, "I want any and all information on this issue on the table here within the hour, and I don't give a hang about the propriety. We need this information now." Turning to the US deputy secretary, he continued, "What do you have that we can begin with?"

They settled in as the story of the satellite imagery and how it all came to the surface was retold in some detail.

TOKYO, JAPAN

The US secretary of state was a little woozy after the aerial refuel flight in from Washington. She had spent the majority of the flight reading, passing on the exquisitely prepared meal, much to the chagrin of the aircrew. It was a little difficult to anticipate the needs of the new secretary. At just five feet nothing and ninety-nine pounds, one really never knew what she would or would not like to eat. The primarily male aircrew found her quite the "babe," though all were smart enough to keep that piece of information firmly inside their minds. At thirty-six years of age, she was decidedly younger than most in her profession, which was a two-edged sword to say the least. She had been dismissed out of hand more than once for being too young, and plenty of times for being female. She had made it through, and now had a reputation as a fair yet firm negotiator with an insightful view of the world's political landscape. An ardent student of Professor Kissinger, she was a force to be reckoned with.

Today she would be meeting with Mr. Hideo Ishikawa. She had been well briefed on his reputation as a ladies' man, real or imagined, and after the long flight, she wasn't looking forward to a sophomoric encounter with another larger-than-life, testosterone-charged diplomat, but that was her lot. She had no more than alighted the car when he appeared at her side.

The Eyes

"Madam Secretary," he began in good English, "welcome to Japan. I trust your flight was not too difficult."

"International flying is never fun, but the flight was as good as any I've ever had. You must be Mr. Ishikawa. Thank you for meeting me. Shall we get the photo opportunity over and get to work?"

"Of course." The two shook hands and held it for the myriad photographers and camera crews. Despite the numerous questions, neither responded to any inquiries; they just smiled, shook hands, and then entered the building.

"Well, here we are, Madam Secretary. The prime minister will be with us momentarily. Please make yourself comfortable, and perhaps we can get to know each other a little."

Here we go, she thought, and instead said, "How gracious of you. If it is alright, I'd like a moment to confer with my staff before the prime minister arrives." She turned and walked over to her senior staff member before Mr. Ishikawa had the opportunity to say anything that would annoy or distract her, leaving him standing alone and not just a little miffed.

Ms. Sandra Quillen, a no-nonsense professional staff member, had already found an Internet connection and checked her e-mail for any late-breaking dispatches. Naturally, there were many. Most could wait; one was marked, "Read before meeting with prime minister of Japan." She had printed it and held the copy out for the secretary. "This just in…" she deadpanned.

"Thanks, Sandra. Do me a favor and try to make sure someone sits between the Neanderthal and me over there. It wouldn't do for the US secretary of state to have to slap a Japanese congressman during a formal meeting."

"No problem, ma'am. I'll have Joe sit between you two. That should resolve any physical intimidation problems. Then we'll just have to deal with Joe's inflated ego the rest of the trip, but I can handle that." Joe was actually Joseph Quillen, Sandra's husband. They had met at a political rally and worked together ever since, turning their passion for political activism into matching careers. Joe was just over six feet seven inches and, according to him, a compact 280 pounds. While his real talents lay in devising creative compromises, he was very often used to play the big oaf role, which he had no problem with.

PYONGYANG

"General Han, we must act now. I don't know how, but the United States must have some information that we have made a decision to move forward. They are not only saying they will run their Team Spirit exercise, I've been told by our Chinese friends that the United States is preparing to do exactly that at this very moment. We can't afford for them to get their assets in place before we move. I hope General Sik is ready; he is cleared to begin operations in forty-eight hours."

"Thank you, Comrade General. We will succeed. As I expected, General Sik has spent much of his life planning just such an operation, and his plan is considerably creative. I will give him the go-ahead immediately." The general stood, bowed, and turned to leave.

"General, you may also begin collecting the individuals we previously discussed from my staff in forty-eight hours. When I reset in Oijambu, I want none of their dead weight dragging us down."

"With great pleasure, Dear Leader." And with that, the general left with a genuine smile on his face.

DIA HEADQUARTERS, WASHINGTON

The continuous satellite coverage of the area near the DMZ seemed to have paid off. Right at the end of the third known tunnel from the north, a significant heat signature had blossomed over the past few hours. The image had been collected, confirmed, analyzed, and transmitted to Washington within minutes. Less than ten minutes later, the Pentagon had issued the order for a B-2, Crusher 63, stationed at Whiteman Air Force Base, to prepare for a mission. They were to load two bunker-penetrating two-thousand-pound bombs, which were laser guided with heat capability; one should have been enough, but when the target had to be taken out, more was better. The coordinates were loaded into the on-board computer, and the crew was placed in crew rest—that required period of time preflight for crews to have the opportunity for uninterrupted rest. It also formally indicated to the crew that they were tasked to fly a mission and therefore had the responsibility to be ready to fly. In twelve hours, they would report for duty to find their mission had changed from a training mission to an actual one. The tunnel they would hit was located in a live fire area with no local civilians to gum up the attack. It looked like the DPRK was about to get a bloody nose before they fired their first shot.

Sadly, that would not be the case this time.

SITUATION ROOM, THE WHITE HOUSE

President Fulton watched the screen intently. He'd just been told the mission would begin within the next fifteen minutes. The screens were set up with a conference call including General Hodge in Korea, Admiral Corping in Hawaii, and what appeared to be a blank screen. "What is on the third screen?" the president asked.

"Well, if the technology people are right, Mr. President, you'll be seeing exactly what our missile sees as it flies to its target," General Hillyard explained. "It's just like watching CNN only, perhaps as a first, you'll be seeing it before the news media. This appears to have been handled correctly for once. The target is a nondescript piece of land in a target area in South Korea, as far as the public arena is concerned. Most people in Korea don't know about this mission. Certainly, warnings have been posted over the Airman's Advisories (AIRADs) and Notices to Airmen (NOTAMs) systems, both used to make sure flyers know something is happening that they should avoid. There were no other missions set in that area, thanks to Dave's work de-conflicting training missions. With any luck, sir, you're going to see the DPRK get smacked hard first, and all with plausible deniability if anything goes wrong, which it won't."

The Eyes

"You'll forgive me if I wait and see before applauding," the president responded.

"Here we go, sir." The third screen came alive, and within seconds, the green glow of static was replaced with the green shaded contours of the earth as seen from two thousand feet above ground level or AGL. The missile dropped rapidly to five hundred feet, then accelerated as a circle with crosshairs appeared and locked onto a glowing spot in the distance. The missile had already locked on to the heat signature, and in less than fifteen seconds, the screen went completely white, then blank. Four thousand miles away, an enormous explosion engulfed over five hundred heaters set up in tunnel number three to imitate the heat signature of a waiting brigade. The unmanned tunnel collapsed in on itself, and had there really been a brigade there, few would have survived.

Cheers erupted simultaneously from the two other screens and all around the president in the situation room.

General Hillyard was the first to speak, "Mr. President, they'll be dropping a second bomb just to be sure, but we won't be able to see that one from here. It's really just a formality. This one has done the necessary damage, and we're monitoring from space to see if it all goes quiet. I think we can get back to our business, and wait to see what the dear leader has to say in the morning." As they left the room, the communication specialists shut down the connections, the screens, and the projectors.

ABOARD CRUSHER 63

"Way to go, guys," the aircraft commander, Captain Jerry Himmel, said over the intercom. "Let's turn back and drop the second one."

"No can do, boss," the copilot confirmed. "I'm getting a no go on the inertial navigation system for the second weapon. Let's just fly back over for the battle damage assessment and return to base. We'll let the ground crew figure out what's wrong with the second bird." Capturing the battle damage assessment before returning to base was a fairly standard procedure for training runs, and that is what this was supposed to be, so the AC cranked the aircraft into a forty-degree bank and pulled back into a tight but unexciting turn toward the target.

DIA HEADQUARTERS

Satellite imagery showed the unmistakable explosion clearly, and all around the monitors, high fives were exchanged. A few seconds later, the explosion from what they all expected to be the second bomb went off.

"Oops, looks like somebody is going to have some 'splaining to do,'" First Lieutenant Cindy Radner commented. "That second bomb is easily five miles off target."

"They're flyboys; they'll survive this. They've got hero written all over 'em already," her compatriot, Staff Sergeant Garvin, replied. "Who's going to bust their chops for missing on the second run when the first one took out the target?"

"Yeah, you're right. It must be nice to fly—everyone wants you to succeed." Lieutenant Radner switched the monitor over to the next satellite that would come up over Korea in about three hours. As they stood in unison and headed for the coffee pot, neither realized they had just missed an opportunity to help stop the first invasion of South Korea in over fifty years.

GENERAL IL JUN HAN'S OFFICE

General Il Jun Han now understood how Admiral Yamamoto must have felt on December 8, 1941. In the end, all he could do was run through the plan he had developed in his mind, which had preserved the traditional triple triangle approach to ground warfare his men knew so well. Change could be important in battle, but better to start with what everyone was trained to do.

The army would approach the battle configured into three firing platoons in each firing battery. That would roll into three firing batteries per artillery battalion, and finally three firing battalions in each artillery regiment. The emphasis would be on the concentration of fire to influence the course of battle. As it appeared on the battlefield, that doctrinal note meant the virtual annihilation of everything in the path of the fire to provide a corridor for the army to advance. A universal truth in the military was that the doctrinal notes found euphemistic ways to explain death and destruction, but it wasn't that complicated in execution. Someone had to think up the strategy, but when you were a grunt in the field advancing into the teeth of a firefight where the source seemed to be everywhere at once, even the newest warrior understood putting all the firepower at one's disposal on the opposing group. Mass on the battlefield was comforting to a soldier and, despite technological advance, the surest means to success.

The Eyes

The answer the general arrived at was to have reserve forces amass and start toward the tunnels the South already knew about. As they approached these tunnels, they would take the high ground and wait. In the meantime, the real assault forces would head toward the newest tunnels. The location of the entrances to these tunnels had been carefully selected along the natural movement pathway between the garrison positions and the tunnels already known, so it would appear from the air or space that there was a long line headed for the infiltration tunnels. Beneath the surface, these new tunnels turned and headed in drastically different directions. To further assist in the deception, General Han would order heating units be taken forward in yet other tunnels, those he wasn't sure the South knew of, and start them running at least twelve hours in advance. Prior to the actual infiltration, his troops would blow the opening with explosives and leave the heating units running. Thermal imaging would reveal the locations and, hopefully, result in the first round of bombs hitting these decoy tunnels. With the confusion of the rest of the assault, there was a reasonable expectation they would gain a window of opportunity to bring in significant forces through the new tunnels. It was a plan, he told himself, and perhaps it would work—only actual operations would reveal success or failure.

ONE KILOMETER
NORTH OF CAMP CASEY

Lieutenant Colonel Drierdan was tired but happy. It had been a great night. The march was long and bitterly cold, but his men were getting in extremely good condition. He'd start increasing their pack weights next week, slowly working them up to fighting trim. They handled their packs and weapons well enough, but for a real mission, they would also be carrying significantly more armament and ammunition. He had already sent the proper paperwork to USFK for approval to make a forced march from Camp Casey to the gunner range in P-518. The men would be able to prove to themselves that they could handle the rigors of the march, and then be rewarded with a live fire exercise of a size they hadn't experienced before. P-518, or prohibited area, was a buffer zone designed for aircraft flying near the demilitarized zone. It required coordination and special permission, fully functioning IFF/SIF (Identification Friend or Foe/Selective Identification Feature), and radar contact with frequent check-ins to fly into the area south of the actual demilitarized zone. This increased restriction was set in place to help prevent the violation of the airspace and a resulting international incident or actual aircraft shoot-down following an inadvertent incursion.

The Eyes

On the ground, however, it was just a convenient designation that they were approaching the DMZ. Regardless of world political events, being this near the DMZ meant staying more vigilant than in the training camps of Southern California or Georgia.

Tonight, though, all they were thinking about was a warm, dry cot. Most of the men would forgo their showers until the next morning, and Lieutenant Drierdan wouldn't begrudge them a slow start the next day. They had been on one heck of a training regimen of late, and the men were in great spirits. The upcoming Team Spirit had also helped make the men feel good. More soldiers meant more goodies, from better goods in the mess halls to more things to buy in the exchanges. The lieutenant couldn't remember when his men had started calling cadence again, but it was a sign the team was pulling together very well.

From inside the tunnel, the sound was near deafening. Though the North Korean Army had been waiting for over two hours with engines running, most of them were startled to the core by the noise, the wind, and the sudden rush of cold. When the dirt and dust settled, the stars began to appear overhead. The opening was twice what they had expected; perhaps the explosives ordnance folks had overdone it just a bit. As adrenaline and training kicked in, the armored vehicles lurched forward almost as one, climbing out of the hole like so many giant insects.

The sight was beautiful; no human beings in sight anywhere. The North Korean men were elated, everyone but General Sik, that is. That wasn't unusual, though; he was always in a foul mood lately. He rode up front, which gave his men a feeling of pride. Perhaps there was more to this man than they gave him credit for. Somehow they had all expected him to be sitting back in Pyongyang sipping sake with the dear leader while they went south wreaking havoc and taking their natural share of fatalities. But here he was; for some men, it was the first time they'd seen him in person. He looked fit and determined, another surprise. They had presumed he was a lazy, fat, bureaucratic peon, not a real soldier.

The army formed up on the command vehicle with its farm of antennae, watching intently as their leader stood in the opening of the tunnel essentially directing traffic by visual signal. It took three-quarters of an hour for all the vehicles to emerge and take their positions. Simultaneously, ground personnel made their way into and through the tunnel. They could move one and one-half brigades through the tunnel each hour, so in about three hours, the first NKPA fighting increment in fifty years was ten kilometers deep into South Korea. They turned and headed directly for Camp Casey.

The march was very short compared with their usual training regimen, but that was nothing new; the training was harder than the actual event by design. The general watched with increasing trepidation as they approached the camp. They saw virtually no activity where there should have been plenty. Even in the dead of night, a military camp had considerable movement, the more so seeing as this was a surprise attack. The general pulled his forces to a stop on the ridgeline overlooking the Tongduchon valley. He called for his captain and directed a scouting mission move forward to probe the camp. While it was unusual to remain stationary, his men would idle in position until the scouts returned.

Something was out of kilter here, and General Sik wasn't about to walk into a trap if he could help it. At times like this, he envied the rich nations with their intelligence and satellite capabilities. Still, he would have to send his men in to verify the intelligence regardless of the source, so this wasn't such a tremendous deficit. While they waited, he looked off to the east and saw lights. He signaled for all engines to be stopped, an order quickly and silently passed through the brigade. It seemed an intolerably long time, but finally all fell silent. In its place, came an increasing cacophony of sound. Unidentifiable at first, slowly it dawned on the general that the men of Camp Casey were returning from a training of their own, chanting as marching men do to keep spirits up and the pace steady. In keeping with Hollywood, some talented voice began and the rest chimed in on beat. Drifting in on the light breeze came the double-time marching lyrics:

> *C-130 rolling down the strip.*
> *Airborne Daddy gonna take a little trip.*
> *Stand up. Buckle up. Shuffle to the door.*
> *Jump right out and count to four.*
> *If my main don't open wide,*
> *I've got a reserve by my side.*

The Eyes

If that one don't open too,
Look out ground, I'm a comin' through!
Pin my medals upon my chest,
and bury me in the front leaning rest.
When I get to heaven,
St. Peter's gonna say,
How'd you earn your livin'?
How'd you earn your pay?
And I will reply with a little bit of anger:
Earned my pay as an airborne ranger.
Sound off! One. Two.
Say it again!! Three. Four.
Bring it on down now!
One, Two, Three, Four! One, Two, THREE, FOUR!

General Sik did not believe in luck, nor did he believe in divinity, but something was most certainly working in his favor on this night. The horseshoe-shaped formation he had selected at the top of the ridge had placed his army in the perfect position for what would now be an easy ambush. The men returning to Camp Casey would march right down the center of the valley he had virtually surrounded. In addition, this was clearly the return trip from a long night's strenuous forced march. The men were likely tired and ill equipped for a real firefight. The general knew all armies acted the same during training; they preserved all the surface issues regarding the simulation of wartime efforts, but left behind real ammunition and functioning equipment. They were both too dangerous and too expensive to risk on training forays. Now the North Korean Army stood directly between the tired American forces and their equipment, ammunition, and C3—command, control and communications capabilities.

General Sik knew immediately that he would need to speak with General Han—how to best use this windfall would be his decision. In addition to his high-ranking position, he was a good friend who had taken many spears for Il Jun Sik. Such debts were repaid whenever possible.

General Han was more than pleased. The initial movement into South Korea had exceeded all expectations, and now his star commander and close personal friend had the good fortune of having trapped a sizeable US force. General Sik was instructed to order his commanding officer to contact United Nations Command and demand the United States, as head of the United Nations Command, sign a full peace treaty with North Korea and that they include South Korea, Japan, China, and Russia as co-signatories recognizing the border between North and South Korea to include the land currently occupied by DPRK forces as North Korean territory, and allow global aid into North Korea. In addition, global aid to the DPRK would be held at last year's level, and the "four plus two" negotiations would be resumed. If they refused or could not agree to these terms immediately, General Sik was to execute fifty US soldiers and ensure the event was filmed. Then his commanding officer was to inform the US commander that the film would be transmitted to Al Jazeera for dissemination on the Web and that another five hundred men would be executed every hour until the United Nations complied.

General Sik ordered his men into position to await his command. As the hapless American soldiers marched on, he had but to give the order and their lives would take a remarkable turn. This would be the first volley in the new Korean War. He wanted its impact to be perfect. He had ordered his men to arrange a pattern of overlaying firepower that would immediately make it clear to the Americans that they were surrounded, outnumbered, outgunned, and out of options.

The attack came quickly—simultaneous mortar fire, cannons, and tank rounds crossed just over the heads of the marching troops, from all sides. By firing from the high ground with depressed angles, the rounds impacted across the canyon below their compatriots on the other ridge.

The effect on the men marching through the valley below was instantaneous. They dropped to the ground and began maneuvering to form firing positions. It was the correct thing to do, but also desperately futile. All they had with them were their M-16s with possibly two clips each.

Sadly, General Sik thought, *they will use every round they have unless their leader understands the predicament he is in.* With another signal came an equally deafening roar, and the earth on both sides of the canyon erupted, this time another one hundred meters closer to the US troops.

The Eyes

The Americans were not firing back because there were no targets close enough to them, and they knew that wasting what precious ammunition they had would be foolish.

Still, the general was impressed with the discipline needed for that kind of restraint, given the size of the force the Americans faced and the nearness of the attack. He motioned for a third round of firing that would hit the edges of the forces below, perhaps killing some, but he needed to let them know he meant business here.

Now the North Korean Army would wait. Snipers and infantry forces watched intently for movement on the flanks and both ahead and behind, lest the enemy try, as they should, to get someone out of the formation to make contact with the rear guard at Camp Casey and hopefully bring in supporting air fire and reinforcements. The general's instructions to his men were simple: try to capture these men, but if you are in danger or if they are uncooperative, kill them.

It took only ten minutes for the Americans to send their men for help, and all of them were captured. They had their instructions too, but were cooperative when captured, surrounded as they were; shots fired in their departing direction would tell their comrades in arms they had failed anyway.

Captain Kim, Joo-Hyung, strode up to the general and saluted. "General, we have taken five of their men. They have been searched, their weapons confiscated, and they are restrained. One among them speaks Korean."

"That will be very helpful. Bring him to me." The general thought for the few minutes it took to escort the soldier over to the general's command vehicle. The American soldier stood and saluted, though the look in his eyes was definitely not respectful; instead, it was filled with a burning rage, internal and external.

"I am O, Song-bon, private first class." His Korean was passable but not truly native.

"Relax," the general soothed. "This is a tenuous situation that, I'm sure you see, you have lost. Many lives hang in the balance of your actions now. I wish to meet with your field commander immediately. You may tell him I am General Il Jun Sik, commander of the Democratic People's Republic of Korea Army. We will give you twenty minutes to return to your formation and bring him here. After twenty minutes, we will finish what we have started. It makes little difference to me. Do you understand your mission?"

"Yes, General. Sir, what about the rest of the men?"

At this, the general astonished the others by saying, "Take them with you; just make sure you are quick and return unarmed." He turned and walked away. The five American soldiers were released and double-timed back down the hillside toward their command.

"General. If I may be so bold as to ask…"

He did not let his captain finish the inquiry, cutting him off with an answer. "Because they are all our prisoners, separating five only makes our task more difficult. They will either all die or all surrender. By releasing them, I ensure they understand I mean what I say."

OSAN AIR BASE, ROK

"Osan Tower, Dragon Flight ready for takeoff, fifteen-second intervals."

"Dragon Flight, taxi into position and hold for hard release on the hour."

"Tower, Dragon Flight on to hold." The six F-16s taxied one by one onto the runway. The first aircraft lined up on the left side, and then the second aircraft on the right side with its nose about one hundred yards behind the first aircraft. The rest of the formation stacked left and right so that the third aircraft was behind the first and the fourth aircraft was behind the second.

"Dragon Flight, check in when ready."

"Two."

"Three."

"Four."

"Five."

"Six."

"Tower, Dragon Flight ready for takeoff, standing by your hack."

"Dragon Flight, you are cleared for takeoff in forty seconds on my hack."

"Dragon Flight cleared for takeoff."

"Ten seconds. Five seconds." The lead aircraft pushed the power all the way up.

The Eyes

"Hack!"

The lead released the brakes and started down the runway. Number two hit the timer and waited. After five seconds, he started pushing up the power. At ten seconds, he pushed it all the way up, as the second hand hit fifteen seconds, he released the brakes and number three began his timer.

In the tower, the two airmen were watching the aircraft with joy. Though seeing fighters take off was routine from the tower, six ship night launches didn't happen that often. Just as the lead aircraft's nose lifted and they expected to hear the roar from the afterburner, the plane exploded into a ball of flame.

The tower airmen couldn't believe their eyes.

Then numbers four exploded then two, three, and five and finally number six. Every aircraft in the formation had exploded into a fireball.

Completely numb, the two airmen turned to each other; then one grabbed the crash phone, and the other hit the hotline to the wing commander's home.

INSIDE A TUNNEL
BENEATH THE DMZ

Private Lee hated these shifts. Yes, it was true you could go to sleep if you chose, but you had to sleep lightly enough to hear someone coming toward you. That was the story told in the barracks, but everyone knew it was someone coming up from behind that was the real threat. Leadership was not a big fan of one sleeping at one's post. No, it would be better to just adhere to the usual callisthenic regimen throughout his time here. Still, in the three-hundred-odd shifts he had pulled in these tunnels, he'd heard something only one time, when the South Koreans made their quarterly tunnel check on his shift. They made so much noise, he heard them before they got near the tunnel, so he just kept moving backward until they stopped coming forward, turned, and left the tunnel. It was a little exciting, and certainly made that shift go by a little faster, but for the most part, this job was sheer boredom. This was a completely new tunnel and had only been open a few weeks, but in Private Lee's opinion, they were all exactly the same. This one seemed a little cleaner, and it was unusual to have concrete walls, but it was still a tunnel. His job, for which he got fed and was provided clothes, shoes, and a place to sleep, was to guard this tunnel.

He must have zoned out a little. A noise had startled him. It wasn't a scary noise, but it was definitely coming from inside the tunnel. The

The Eyes

private's senses prickled; he could feel his heartbeat quicken and his breathing becoming more rapid and shallow. Of the many problems a soldier had in these tunnels, the worst was the difficulty of being able to see in both directions. Noises were virtually impossible to locate until whatever caused them was clearly in sight. In the case of South Korean soldiers, what they said identified them, and then one could assume they were in front of you. You knew which direction to move in. This was different. It sounded, for lack of a better description, like a toilet flushing.

By the time he had managed that much analysis, he found himself under water, being rapidly pushed forward. His body careened off the concrete sides of the tunnel, losing chunks of flesh with every impact. He held his hands over his head instinctively in an attempt to protect his face. The rushing water twisted and turned him like a wave tosses a body surfer when it breaks. His back impacted the side of the tunnel, and the wind was knocked out of his lungs. *It won't take long now*, he thought.

Private Lee held out as long as he could; then his body took over and he inhaled the water, filling his lungs. He thrashed in his panic, but to no avail. He began to lose consciousness. He couldn't see or feel anything anymore. And then it was over, his body hurtling through the concrete tunnel, just a piece of debris.

SEOUL

Lee Jun worked on the eighteenth floor of the bank building, and it was now quitting time. It was already dark as he made his way through the lobby on his way out into the street. He had a pretty good walk back to his third-floor apartment, but he never minded. If he kept it up, he'd have enough money for a car in the not-too-distant future. He looked forward to the additional mobility, not to mention the status. Sure, most people used the buses and subways here in the city, but if you wanted to take your girl out into the countryside, you needed a car.

Yeah, like I've got to worry about that, he thought.

A little over twenty minutes later, he was reaching the outskirts of the business district. The buildings were a little shorter, and the glitz and glitter of the plasma screen advertisements were gone. Things were transitioning from the heart of the big city to the suburbs.

At first he thought he heard another big military jet rumbling over-head, but he looked up into clear blue skies and found no flashing lights. Besides, the noise was continuous. It was a low, deep, growling sound, too unsettling to ignore. He stopped walking and started looking around to find the source. The more he tried to figure it out, the more nervous he got. He started looking at the buildings and hanging signs for any indication of movement, but nothing seemed out of place, and still the noise was growing. Now he felt it as well as heard it. *It has to be an earthquake,* he thought. He started to run down the street, to get away from the power lines and light poles. He found a spot that was relatively clear of structures and wires and poles, so he stopped to catch his breath. A concrete box next to him had a huge steel circular cover on it with the characters for the words "sewer line" engraved on it.

He climbed up on top and waited. The noise was steady but growing. Now he was becoming more interested than scared. *What on earth could be causing this?* he thought. Then, suddenly, off in the distance, he heard what sounded like a gunshot. Just a sharp popping sound, and it was over. Then he heard it again and realized it was happening every few seconds. With each crack, it got a little louder, felt a little closer. He listened carefully, trying to decide which direction the noises were coming from. Again it seemed to be coming from directly in front of him in the city. Crack, crack—it was getting closer, but he still couldn't see anything. The rumbling was growing in intensity as well. His body knew something was wrong. He was getting that feeling like when you think you're going to get into a fight, and you don't want to, but you can't run—heart racing, pulse screaming. CRACK, CRACK—it was coming. Then he realized why he couldn't see anything. He was hearing the echo off the building closest to him. He turned just in time for the hundred pound steel cover to erupt from its bolted position, severing his arm and head as it careened fifty feet in the air with an enormous cracking sound.

TAEGU, SOUTH KOREA

The three-ship of A-10s had just landed and was taxiing in. "Three, Lead."

"Go ahead, Lead."

"Nice run back there. Beer's on me."

"Roger that, Lead. Thanks."

They shut the machines down and climbed out. The crew bus was waiting for them.

"Looks like my luck meter is pegged tonight," Captain Mike Strong joked. "I haven't been doing all that smoothly with these targets lately, but tonight they looked three times as big, and the crew bus is here waiting for us!"

"I told you it would come around—you just have to relax a little," Major Chris Reed was nodding his head. "You were taking it too seriously. You have to feel the machine. This is still more art than science." As an evaluator and one of the highest-time flyers in the squadron, the younger guys tried to really listen to Chris and incorporate his advice into their flying skills.

Just as the crew bus was turning to leave the ramp, they heard an explosion that they knew could only mean one thing. Before they could react, they heard, and then felt two more explosions. The blast knocked the crew bus into a ditch. Mike came to his senses with the strong smell of burning fuel seeping into his body, burning his eyes and lungs. He looked forward toward the driver, but the cab had been smashed and he could see blood and the crushed body of the driver impaled on the steering wheel. He turned to his two flight mates. Neither was moving. He tried to help Chris up, but his back was burned to the side of the crew bus and he was unresponsive. He looked at his classmate, Alex Steward, another captain two months from finishing his tour and heading home to his fiancée, and saw a piece of steel protruding from his forehead. He was dead. Mike knew he had to get out of the van. He tried to stand, but he couldn't feel his legs. Looking down, he could see both legs were severely lacerated at mid-shin. The blast had forced the tool chest under the seat across from him through his legs. He elected not to examine them too closely, for fear he would discover they had been cut off and that he would not be able to make himself get out of the van.

His upper body seemed unscathed, so he started pulling himself along the wall of the van using holes and bent pieces of metal to pull against. At least he had his NOMEX flight gloves on—that would help some. It took him five minutes to crawl out of the van. Safely away from the still-burning vehicle, he reached down and discovered to his great delight that his legs were still attached. They might have to be amputated later, but for now, they were still there. He looked around and saw exactly what he had feared. All three A-10s had been destroyed and were burning in three separate JP-8 fuel-fed fires. He could hear the fire engines screaming and heading his way. There was little more he could do but save his strength and wait.

USFK COMMAND CENTER

"General Bradley, this is Captain Erlitz from the command center. Sir, we don't have any details on this yet, but I couldn't wait any longer to report it. Our phones are ringing off the hook from every command post in Korea reporting aircraft destroyed on the ramp. I haven't been able to collate all the reports, but I have personally taken the phone calls of more than twenty fighter aircraft destroyed. At your instruction, we will activate the Battle Staff and prepare flash messages for transmission with the best information we can get."

"Do that, Captain. I want all my commanders in now. Do you have speaker phone on this line?" the general inquired.

"Yes, sir."

"Tell all your controllers to ignore the phones for one minute and listen to me."

"Go ahead, sir. There are five male controllers here tonight."

"Gentlemen, your area is about to be immersed in an incredibly confusing nightmare. It could take us days to wade through it all. There will be panic on the other end of each phone call you take. I want you to take a moment to make a simple chart with six columns; label them People, Injured, Dead, Aircraft, Damaged, and Destroyed. One of you will be responsible for recording. As a call comes in, each of you write down the time and from where the call is being placed. Be patient and calm with the caller, but get those six pieces of information from each one. When you get a second call from the same location, make sure the person is clear you need total numbers; let that person do the math. As you finish each call, raise your hand, and the one person recording the data will get the sheet and keep track of what is happening. You will all be yelled at tonight, sometimes by high-ranking individuals. I believe in each of you, and I will back you to the end, so do not fear the calls. Try to remember they are living with death and destruction. Any questions?"

There was a unanimous, "No, sir."

"Then get back to work. And try to handle as much as you can by yourself. I need Captain Erlitz to do some things for me."

"Yes, sir." And the five young airmen set out to tackle the night, confident they now had an approach that would work.

"It's Paul, isn't it?" General Bradley asked.

"Yes, sir."

"OK, Paul," hook me up with General Hodge.

While he waited, he looked up and said a silent prayer, thankful that he had sent his wife back to her Mom's place in Phoenix to get her out of the cold for a few weeks. *Timing is everything*, he thought.

"Sir, General Hodge is coming on the line."

"Nick, what are you getting this old man out of bed for at this hour?"

"General, I don't know what is happening exactly, but from the sounds of the reports we're getting here at USFK, the entire peninsula is under attack at this time. Captain Erlitz will brief you on what we know so far. General, I've told him to give you numbers, even though their validity is practically impossible to verify at this time, but I want you to get a sense of the scale of this."

Captain Erlitz motioned for the recorder to bring him the tally sheet, and he began.

"Sir, this is Captain Erlitz from the USFK Command Center. So far, we have had sketchy reports from fifteen air bases in Korea. Some we have no aircraft stationed at, but apparently even transitioning aircraft were attacked. In total, we have reports of sixty-three aircraft destroyed and another twenty damaged. We have reports of more than eighty people dead and nearly one hundred injured. Almost all aircraft appear to have exploded in place, but so far there are no reports of what caused the explosions—no hand grenades, missiles, or rocket launches have been reported. I'm sorry, sir. That is all I have right now."

"Captain, given the chaos you must be living in right now, that was remarkably well done. Nick, I see you have the A-team on again. Keep up the good work and go ahead and send the reports to the NMCC, the NCA, and so forth from your level. I'm calling the president and USCINCPAC. Nick, when you get your CAT set up, get your communications guys to work with mine and set up a direct line so we can stay in touch. Out."

"Wilco, General. Good luck to us all."

DIA HEADQUARTERS

At the DIA, more disturbing news was filtering in from the DPRK and South Korea. Two patriot missile batteries were reported destroyed by a directed energy impulse weapon of some kind. Witnesses described that a Caucasian man in his mid-twenties to early thirties had pointed at the battery as if indicating something about it to a friend, and the missile battery burst into flame, and then exploded. The three-man crew of the mobile engagement control station, from where the missiles were targeted and fired, was lost in the explosion. This high-altitude, all-weather, antimissile battery had merely set up and switched power on for calibration. Only two of the eight firing tubes were hit, but one had a patriot advance capability 3, or PAC3, warhead loaded. When it went up, it took out the other thirty-two warheads. Local investigators found no weapons in the area reported to have been the location of the Caucasian suspect, but they did discover what appeared to be charred human flesh. DSRJ intercepts were negative for oral instructions within a two-hour window surrounding the reported attack time. This was now the third scorpion battery destroyed in less than thirteen hours.

The number of reported aircraft destroyed was growing by the hour. Somehow, virtually every US aircraft on the ground was severely damaged or destroyed overnight. Those that were flying were directed to bases in Japan, but Iwakuni Marine Corps Air Station (MCAS) was the closest, and it was filling up exceedingly fast. Furthermore, the fuel system at Iwakuni was undergoing repairs, and the aging R-9 refueling trucks were hard pressed to refuel the fighters and get them back in the air to Yokota Air Base or Atsugi. The Japanese were gracious and helpful, but the only real field that was within reach was Fukuoka, which had precious little support of any kind.

The patriot missile battery destruction, combined with the destroyed aircraft, made it obvious it was time to do something, but no one had any idea what they were trying to protect their assets from.

THE SITUATION ROOM

"Mr. President, General Hodge secure. He has an offer from Kim Jong Il." The national security advisor handed the phone to the president.

"Hodge, what in blazes is going on?" The president's demeanor was steadily degrading. "I haven't heard anything from any of you in six hours. How the hell am I supposed to run this? We have word that some four thousand American soldiers have been captured—what are you doing about it?"

"Forgive me, Mr. President. It's been a rather hectic day."

"Forget it, Dave. I know it has been, and I know you are running this, not me. What do you have from the madman?"

"Well, sir, Kim Jong Il contacted me through his senior army general. He demands that the United States, as head of the United Nations Command, sign a full peace treaty with North Korea, that we include South Korea, Japan, China, and Russia as co-signatories recognizing the border between North and South Korea to include the land the North Korean armies currently occupy as North Korean territory, and that we allow global aid into North Korea. He also wants US aid to the DPRK held at last year's level, and the re-initiation of the "four plus two" negotiations. In exchange, he will release all the Americans unconditionally and immediately cease all hostility."

The Eyes

"And if we don't, Dave?" The president held his breath silently.

"They will execute all the soldiers, launch the four target Taep'o Dong II missiles at Japan and South Korea, which he assures me are nuclear laden, re-flood from the Cho Mya Dam, and pursue reunification of the peninsula with great vigor. He said the new targets of the flooding would be Taegu and P'ohang, with Pusan as a secondary target. Mr. President, are we on speaker phone?" General Hodge's voice was set and disturbed.

"Yes we are, Dave. Anything you need to tell me the rest of the folks in the room need to hear as well—what else?"

"They executed fifty men when I didn't agree to his plan right away, and they will execute fifty more in one hour unless we change our minds. In addition, the executions were done in front of the remaining prisoners and filmed. Al Jazeera is planning to simulcast it over satellite, cable, and the Internet fifteen minutes from now. I don't see much room to maneuver here, Mr. President. I don't wish to be insolent or rude, but there are a number of things I need to take care of over here. I will call you back in ten minutes, sir. My parting thoughts as always are for all of your health, and I beg you to continue to keep the men on the ground here in your thoughts as you contemplate the free world's next move. Hodge out, hooah."

"God be with you, Dave." The president of the United States handed the phone back to his national security advisor, who noted the president's eyes were tearing up a bit.

"Ladies and gentlemen, we have no time. I need to know our options. First get somebody to stop those broadcasts; I don't care if we shut the Web down completely. I know it'll be tough dealing with all the implications of stopping free speech, but I don't want sons, daughters, wives, husbands, mothers, and fathers watching their loved ones be executed before we even tell them they have been captured. If we have to, get those technology geniuses at Microsoft on it. Next I want an immediate assessment of his threats, reality or fiction? I want to know where our patriot missile battery teams are and the percentage chance they have of stopping those Taep'o Dong missiles. Can the North really re-flood from Cho Mya, and can they target Taegu and P'ohang, for that matter, and how many Americans and others are there?

The Situation Room

"He wants to sue for peace from where he is now, so I need to know where that is. I'll be on the line with Russia, China, South Korea, and Japan, so let's reconvene in fifteen minutes. Now, before any of you say it, let me first acknowledge that to make a rational decision will take longer than the time we have been given. When Dave calls back in ten minutes, Al, you tell him the truth, and then tell him he is cleared to tell Jong Il we agree unconditionally. We have to get some breathing room for the next fifty victims of this insanity. Now let's move people. This is an insane amount of work to do in very little time. I need the big chunks—don't get bogged down in details. I'll even take gut feels for this one." He stood and walked out of the situation room and headed for the oval office, surrounded by his media and Department of State advisors. Unusually, no one stood. They were already on the phone trying desperately to track down some answers.

SEOUL, REPUBLIC OF KOREA

The news desk was flooded with calls. Half were asking what was happening, the other half were reporting death and devastation. Hae-Jung had just gone on the air with a piece about the appointment of a new leader to head the charge for the next attempt to bring the Winter Olympics to South Korea. She heard and felt the rumbling just as her off-camera assistant held up a hand-written cue card. With practiced professionalism, she read the card directly into the camera.

"This just in: There is some type of serious geological disturbance affecting all of Seoul at this time. We have no indication as to the cause of this disturbance. The US geological service has not recorded a major earthquake in the region, yet there are reports of damage, flooding, buildings collapsing, and some deaths. We urge our viewers to exercise care and judgment in their activities, avoid large buildings, and take the same precautions one might for an earthquake. We'll have more on this breaking story after these messages."

The on-air light went dead and she asked, "Well, what the heck is it?"

At that moment, the entire forty-story building the studio was housed in lurched sharply to the left, and all the electricity went out. Everyone who had been standing was sent sprawling to the ground. After a pause of less than a second, it continued its movement, and as it tilted farther, it increased in speed. The external facade began to break up, and pieces of the structure fell to the street below.

Those unfortunate enough to be sitting at a desk near a window were launched into the night air amidst a shower of broken glass. Those farther inside the building grabbed hold of anything they could—doors, walls, support columns. The screaming was deafening.

Hae-Jung thought to herself that an earthquake wouldn't feel like this; the building was inexplicably falling over.

It would be her last thought. She lost her grip on the door and fell. Seconds later she was impaled on a steel girder that only moments before had been hidden inside the structural concrete of the building.

The same scene was playing out all over Seoul. As the water rushed through the underground sewers and communications lines, it tore open their fifty-year-old sides and began eroding the earth that housed the lines. Most of these sewer lines were either under or right beside the main infrastructure of the city. Roads began developing sinkholes, swallowing up cars and trucks. Making matters worse, these vehicles fell into a developing sinkhole but remained protruding from the ground. Within minutes, traffic was at a dead stop due to literally thousands of accidents. With complete gridlock and almost no communication, the city descended into complete blackness, which was compounded by rising flood waters that engulfed packed commuter subways that sat dark and motionless on their underground tracks. Later they would find that not one person in a subway train beneath the road surface had survived.

The president of Korea had left the Blue House early in the morning for a trip to Cheju a popular recreation area on an island south of the southernmost tip of the peninsula, with the visiting ambassador from Brunei. They were out hunting pheasants all day and were relaxing in a very hot bath when an aid interrupted them.

"Mr. President, we are under attack from North Korea. The US military reports portions of their aircraft have been destroyed at almost every air base in the ROK. Our aircraft have been similarly targeted. We have lost communication with the Blue House, and there are reports of fighting across the DMZ. We have your helicopter ready and we have requested and been granted permission to fly you and the ambassador to Japan."

Seoul, Republic of Korea

As the president rose from the bath and reached for his robe, he was already thinking about defensive counterstrike capabilities.

"You will take the ambassador to Japan. I will be flown back to the Blue House. What is our military capability? I need some information now," he barked and ran to the locker room.

His clothes had already been laid out, and he was fully dressed in minutes, as was the ambassador. His aid was now pleading with him to maintain a cool head.

"Mr. President, with all due respect, sir, we have no idea if the Blue House is still standing. All communications north of Cheoung Ju are out. From Japan, you will be better able to communicate. Then you can get in touch with US Forces, Japan, and even the president of the United States. Sir, there is very little you can do here now. We need you safe and informed."

EAST OF CAMP CASEY, ROK

BOOM! The US regiment stopped in their tracks, stunned into silence, awed and confused. All around them the land exploded. They were under attack. They immediately dropped to the ground and began maneuvering into defensive positions. The big question was at whom and where to fire.

Lieutenant Colonel Drierdan turned toward his ops officer, "Where is Hammer? I need comm. right now!"

Airman Charles Frederick, nicknamed Hammer for his prowess in the boxing ring, was already making his way forward. He'd lugged the radios up and down the hill all night, silently cursing his selection of military occupational specialty (MOS) with every step. Sure, communications is critical to the combat soldier; the commander without communication would be dead in the water, as they always say. On a day-to-day basis, however, it meant Hammer had to carry the stupid thing wherever his regiment went, along with all the other stuff his buddies carried. Luckily, he was a pretty strong guy, but it was small consolation heading uphill in the later hours of the numerous marches they had taken that day.

In the instant the explosions sounded, the radio set became much lighter, and a truly great honor to bear. He crawled to the front of the formation and in a hoarse whisper reported to his commander.

The Eyes

"Sir, Airman Frederick, Charles J., reporting."

"Hammer, get USFK Command Center on the radio now!"

"Working, sir. Here you go."

"USFK, Captain Erlitz speaking."

"Captain, listen carefully. This is Lieutenant Colonel Drierdan from Camp Casey. We are approximately two kilometers east of Camp Casey, and we have come under full military attack. Repeat, military attack. This is not a civilian event. We need immediate air and ground support."

"We'll keep this line open. Can you authenticate Whiskey Charlie?"

Colonel Drierdan looked around him. He wasn't sure if they had their authentication codes with them. For a fleeting moment, he entertained the idea of guessing, but decided better.

"Captain, we are returning from an overnight training march and I'm not sure anyone brought any authentication secrets. You can verify all this through headquarters US Eighth Army. I don't blame you for exercising protocol, but just how many regiments have this kind of radio? I need your help, so do what you must to verify who I am and what I've requested, but do it as quickly as humanly possible. The lives of half my command are riding on your actions right now. Drierdan out." He turned to his operations officer and asked the question anyway. "I don't suppose you brought the secrets, did you?"

"Of course, we did, Colonel. Or, I should say, I told them to. To be honest, I didn't really think it was all that important. Sorry, sir."

Major Klude turned and headed back down the column to his men. He found his lieutenant, and together they scurried to get back to the commander. As they approached, Hammer took the cue and rang up USFK. By the time the colonel had the authentication table in sight, Hammer was holding the receiver out for whoever needed it.

"Sir, USFK on the line—our initiation."

Lieutenant Colonel Drierdan smiled and took the phone. "Thanks," and his smile gave away the return of his usual countenance.

He spoke into the mouthpiece, "Captain Erlitz, this is Lieutenant Colonel Drierdan. I'm putting my communications officer on, ready to authenticate."

The formality took only seconds, but it was truly critical, considering the colonel was requesting United Nations Command to employ

426

combat forces absent of any declaration of war, or even verification of a conflict. This would severely test the system in conducting international operations. Authority to employ arms would require authorization from a high level. Certainly Lieutenant Colonel Drierdan had the implicit authority to use his own forces in self-defense, and there would be no second-guessing in this circumstance. The problem was, as with so many conflicts on the ground, one of reality versus strategy. He was truly outgunned. If he chose to fight back absent support, it would be a fight to the last man standing, with an unfortunate and predictable outcome for his men. Contrary to media hype, ordering one's men to fight to their death was not an easy decision and certainly not one to be arrived at hastily without exhausting all other possibilities. Certainly these men were here to do just that, to fight, to the death, if necessary. And it was that caveat, if necessary, that was Lieutenant Colonel Roland Drierdan's decision to make. The decision of a lifetime—the decision he'd spent all his time studying strategy, wars won and lost, conflicts, theories, even psychology to prepare for, to be ready to make. And with all that preparation, he loathed the decision not one iota less than any of the leaders who had gone before him. Now that the authentication was complete, all he could do was wait and pray. His mind wandered as he spoke the words he knew the men needed to hear.

"Alright, everybody, remain calm. I'm no surer of what is going on than you are. So keep your minds on what has really happened, and away from what the enemy's thoughts might be. Let's keep our guard up, post security watches, and use this to practice our response to an ambush. Get yourselves ready for a firefight. Clean and load your weapon, and assess how much live ammunition you have. If we are to have a firefight, we'll need to know how much we have so that we can use it to maximum effect. I want each element to prepare and then report up through the chain of command to me. After you are as ready as you can be, take a load off and rest; this could be a very long night."

"Hooah," was the unanimous but less-than-thunderous response. The men headed back to their positions as the deepening quiet ate at the colonel's mind. He ran through the scenarios he'd previously contemplated for battle. None of them ever started with an expert combat team he had intentionally tired out, a lack of ammunition, and in the bottom of a valley at night, and yet here they were.

The Eyes

"Colonel Drierdan! The scouts are back, and it doesn't look good. They need to talk to you ASAP."

"What the heck are they doing back here? They're supposed to be at camp by now. Well, where are they?"

As he spoke, the five men approached. One look told the colonel everything he needed to know.

"OK, guys. Relax. You didn't fail; sending you guys was a desperate long shot. Frankly, it was a risk of your lives, so I'm very happy to see you. Who are they and what do they want?"

"Sir, their commander is a General Il Jun Sik. He's given me twenty minutes to come and get you and bring you to him. Otherwise, they plan to finish this right here and now. We managed to see some of what they brought. Colonel, they are easily six times our number and armed to the teeth."

"I know they sent you because you speak Korean. How did you arrange for the release of the others?"

"I didn't really do anything, sir. I just asked," Private Song-bon O said as he lowered his eyes and head.

"Stand proud, Private. Major, make a note of this. Private O has saved the life of four men tonight. Private O, you are now Sergeant O, and you will accompany me back to this general immediately." The stentorian voice Lieutenant Colonel Drierdan adopted for this speech was meant to bolster the men as well as reinvigorate this soldier, on whose shoulders so much would rest in the immediate future. The young man's stunned look of despair was slowly replaced by just a hint of a smile, and the firm handshake from his commander brought him back to full strength.

"Thank you, sir! We are to go unarmed, which I strongly recommend we do. Nothing we could carry would likely help our situation anyway."

"I agree. We'd better get started." He took off his 9 mm pistol and handed it to his operations officer. "Major Klude, if I'm not back in twenty-four hours, you are in command."

"Yes, sir!"

Sergeant O led the way through the grass, and in just a short while, the colonel could hear men talking in Korean. Living in the "Rock" as long as he had, the sounds were not so unusual. Still, as they ap-

428

proached in the slowly lifting mist of dawn, Lieutenant Colonel Drierdan had a severe cold feeling in his gut. He knew it was fear, but not
the kind of fear one gets from concern for personal safety. This was
from a feeling of loss of control over himself and his men. He reached
out and grabbed Sergeant O by the shoulder. Quietly, he leaned down
and whispered to him.

"We will not raise our hands in surrender, Sergeant, but neither
must we be belligerent or aggressive. They have the upper hand; remember, we need to make it through this conflict so we can survive to
fight again. Don't give him any information without asking me first,
and be sure there will be some among them who can at least *understand* English. Whatever happens, soldier, you have served well. Now
let's do this!"

Subconsciously, the colonel reached up and placed his right hand
over the left pocket of his battle dress uniform. His men had seen him
do this so often they had decided it was of some religious nature, as it
appeared that he was placing his hand over his heart. He did this every
time there was any stress in a situation, and he obviously gained some
measure of strength and comfort in the action. This time, though, he
followed the movement by removing a photograph from his pocket. It
was a picture of his wife and their two daughters in front of their
Christmas tree. He took one long last look at it, and then knelt and laid
it carefully in the mud. He had kept the photo with him in that pocket
of his uniform throughout his career, but he knew that when he went on
real missions, he was supposed to be "sanitized." It was a procedure the
US Army learned about through the hard lessons of the prisoners of
war from the Vietnam conflict. Interrogators took great pleasure in using photographs of loved ones to torment their captors.

"Hooah!" Sergeant O stood and walked confidently into the clear-
ing.

Immediately, they were surrounded and searched. Despite the large
number of NKPA soldiers pointing rifles at them, they were treated
with respect, not too roughly, and they were not handcuffed or restrained. An NKPA soldier escorted them on each side toward a tall,
stern-looking man.

The Eyes

General Il Jun Sik stepped toward Lieutenant Colonel Drierdan. He held the colonel's gaze, never looking away, and spoke directly to him, though he was well aware the colonel did not speak Hongul.

"Colonel, you were wise to take our offer to discuss your predicament. As you can see from the men here with me, our forces are many times larger than yours. In addition, as we have shown you, we also have considerable armament with us. By now you have undoubtedly contacted you headquarters for assistance. That will not save your men. If there is to be a battle here, your men will all die quickly and we will turn our forces toward whoever comes to your aid. You must surrender your command to me now."

After listening to Sergeant O's translation, Lieutenant Colonel continued staring down the general. Speaking directly to him, the colonel was deliberate with his words, knowing his men's fate lay in the balance. His first thought was to reject the demand, spit on this officer, and go down fighting. As he collected his thoughts, amazingly clarity of purpose struck him. He would fashion a means to delay this force. If he could convince them he needed to speak with escalating levels of command, something the NKPA was famous for, he could fight a delaying game.

"General, if I am to surrender my command to you, it must be done at Camp Casey, and in front of my men." He continued, watching the general as Sergeant O translated. The general had no visible reaction. Instead, he turned to his men and motioned for them to move forward. At once, the command vehicle lurched to life and crawled forward to where the men stood.

"No. You will surrender in front of your men in the field. If we return to your camp, it will be to destroy it. As of this moment, you are not in charge of anything, Colonel. I will not restrain you at this time. But make no mistake, this is not a negotiable situation. Your forces are mine. Whether they remain alive or not is up to you."

Colonel Drierdan and Sergeant O mounted the command vehicle and stood beside the general. None of them spoke; they knew where they were going. The trip, which lasted less than five minutes, seemed like hours to Colonel Drierdan. His greatest fear was that his men wouldn't see him standing there and would initiate hostilities. He stood tall, hoping beyond hope that they would see him instead of just the general and the DPRK flag they had all learned to think of as the enemy's. They approached slowly, and while Colonel Drierdan could see some of the men, most were in defensive fighting positions. Then, just as the colonel was close enough to start making out the faces of his men, a single round was fired.

Colonel Drierdan felt the blood spatter on his face and watched in horror as the general beside him collapsed to the deck of the vehicle. At once, there came a cacophony of deafening firepower. The bushes from whence the first shot was fired virtually exploded, and the first US casualty of the new war was physically sawed in half. A brief and unchoreographed pause in the firing was the break Colonel Drierdan needed.

"Cease fire!" he bellowed in a thunderous voice.

Shooters on both sides stopped, not so much from understanding his words, but because the obvious command nature of the colonel's voice meant something important, and the normal response would be to stop whatever one is doing. To his great surprise and relief, the general had made it back to his feet and, though obviously in pain, passed the word to his second in command who, as instructed, also screamed the cease-fire command, in Hongul. Colonel Drierdan turned to the general. He could see the bullet wound was in his upper thigh, which was now wrapped in a blood-stained cloth. The general motioned the colonel to face his men.

"Tell them to stack their weapons and step away from them."

Lieutenant Colonel Drierdan faced his men and bellowed, "Stack rifles!"

Wordlessly and incredulously, his men followed the order, and then formed up on their platoon leaders.

"First Sergeant, present the formation!" The men formed up in parade fashion in front of their commander. Their expressions told him he was not alone in the disbelief that they had fallen into this predicament. What hurt most were their wistful looks, the hope in their eyes that he had the answer to this situation and could, as his daughters so often said, make it go away. He pulled himself inward and addressed his command for what he thought was surely the last time.

"At ease! Men, as you have discerned, we have been captured in total by forces of the North Korean People's Army. I have decided our lives should not be forfeited in vain. This is the most difficult decision I have ever had to make in my career, and I do not make it lightly. As of this moment, we are now prisoners of war. Our chain of command does not change with this decision. You are still under my command, and I am ordering all of you to surrender peacefully. Each of us will abide by our code of conduct. There will be no heroics. We will abide by the international laws of war, and I hold the general responsible for ensuring his men abide by international law and the Geneva convention."

General Sik allowed a smile to cross his face as Colonel Drierdan's address was translated. Immediately, he stepped forward and addressed his men.

"Collect their weapons and restrain them with handcuffs. I want each man treated with respect, but do not allow yourselves to be victimized by the occasional cowboy you may encounter. These men are our prisoners, and as such may be very valuable to the dear leader."

The Korean soldiers could not contain their joy at having captured such a large force of Americans in the first few hours of this liberating war to reunite their homeland. They were professional if not gentle in handling the Americans; the process would take several hours.

The general turned to Colonel Drierdan, and the look on his face told the story: it was time to take this to the second level. "You will now strike your colors, Colonel."

"No, sir, I will not." This was the moment he had been expecting. He would most likely die now, he assumed, and tried to brace for it.

"Put me in contact with the United Nations commander." It was spoken in neutral terms, but Colonel Drierdan knew it was not a request.

"Hammer, get USFK on the horn!" Now he would have to bring his humiliation home, but he had no alternative.

"General Hodge here."

"General, I am Lieutenant Colonel Roland Drierdan of the Eighth US Army, First Brigade, Second Infantry Division. We have been taken captive, all 2,300 of us at once. We are prisoners of war, and General Il Jun Sik wishes to speak with you now."

"Put him on, Colonel." General Hodge had no intention of jeopardizing lives with diplomatic doublespeak.

East of Camp Casey, ROK

"General Hodge, so nice to speak with you again," the translator spoke into the receiver. "I will make this short. We are both busy men. You will, as head of the United Nations Command, sign a full peace treaty with the Democratic People's Republic of Korea. You will include South Korea, Japan, China, and Russia as co-signatories recognizing the new border between North and South Korea, which will include the land we currently occupy as North Korean territory, and you will allow global aid into North Korea. You will agree to hold US aid to the DPRK at last year's level, and you will reinitiate the "four plus two" negotiations.

In exchange, I will release all the Americans currently under my control unconditionally, and we will immediately cease all hostility. If you do not agree, I will execute all the soldiers, and give the command to launch our four nuclear-laden Taep'o Dong II missiles at Japan and South Korea. We will also re-flood from the Cho Mya Dam and pursue reunification of the peninsula with great vigor. The new targets of the flooding are Taegu and P'ohang, with Pusan as a secondary target."

"I do not have the unilateral authority to do anything on behalf of the United Nations without consultation with the security council, as I'm sure you are aware, General Sik. I will immediately contact headquarters and get an answer back to you as soon as practicable. I do, however, evoke the authority of the United Nations in insisting the men you have taken prisoner are held under conditions agreed to under the covenants of the Geneva convention."

"Stand by one moment, General Hodge," General Sik cut him off and turned. He raised his right hand and then dropped it sharply.

At once a barrage of gunfire pierced the still night, cutting Lieutenant Colonel Drierdan to his soul. The colonel found he had to hold the railing to keep from crumpling to the ground in front of his men. He held his jaw resolute, though he felt he was disintegrating inside. He could see his men pass through the predictable stages of disbelief, despair, and then anger.

"General, America has the first fifty casualties of this war. We have recorded the event and will provide it to our compatriots from Al Jazeera for transmission over the Web in fifteen minutes. In one hour, we will execute another fifty American soldiers. In two hours, your time is up and they will all perish. I have much to do, and traveling with prisoners is much more difficult than advancing alone. Provide your response to Colonel Drierdan when it is convenient for you."

The general dismounted the command vehicle, leaving Colonel Drierdan to come to grips with the event and comfort his men as best he could.

THE SITUATION ROOM, WHITE HOUSE

"Mr. President, we may not be able to completely stop the broadcasts, but we have the capability to disrupt most of the transmissions from Al Jazeera, and our people are standing by with orders to do so. Our folks in communications command are working to firewall all Internet transmissions from Korea and Al Jazeera. It's only a temporary fix, sir. With every kid in college capable of transmitting over the World Wide Web, it just isn't feasible to stop them. Shutting down the whole Web would hurt us as much as them—it would prevent the flow of information our commanders and you need here.

"As for our patriot missile batteries, every battery in the country has been attacked. All have sustained damage and three have been completely destroyed. Our capability to intercept missiles at Taep'o Dong before they hit South Korea or Japan is 15 percent or less, and that is with good luck. I'll turn it over to the CIA for the estimate on the dam."

Darren Marks, the CIA director, stood. "Mr. President, it is our estimate that they can use the dam to flood the plains and valleys downstream of the dam, which will render the DMZ unusable for fighting. While doing so will affect his troops before ours, if they are briefed and ready, they may be willing to gamble that their forces, with their much greater numbers, will gain the advantage. If they have the equipment to help their forces, they could be right. Unfortunately, we just don't know if they have anything that would give them that assistance. We have seen no signs of the development of channels to route the water anywhere specifically, and imagery shows no built-in mechanism from which to release the water in sufficiently large quantities to do anything productive. Our estimate is that they plan to blow the dam and hope for the best. As for your question concerning Taegu and P'ohang, they are cities located nearly 160 miles southeast of Seoul, P'ohang being a port city. We don't believe they could target either of those two cities for flooding. Mr. President, that's pretty much all we could come up with for now." The CIA director paused for a moment, and then took his seat when it appeared there were no questions.

General Albright thought deeply for a moment. "Mr. President, based on this information, I'd recommend we tell General Hodge to back his forces up farther than they are now and have the ROK forces back down and away from the DMZ as quickly as possible, holing up in pockets wherever the highest terrain will allow."

"Approved. Go ahead, Carlton. Give General Hodge all the information we've got so far; he needs it the most."

Ms. Hunter spoke up before the room could disintegrate into chaos, "Mr. President, we have President Cho Myun Roo on the line, from Japan. His translator is being patched through the United States Forces Japan (USFJ) command center. If you hit the button on the speaker phone, we can all hear. I can also have a Korean language specialist brought in here, but it could take a while."

"Make the call for the linguist. We'll probably need him later. Quiet everyone. We need to hear this. President Roo, this is President Fulton. Please go ahead."

"I'm sorry, sir, my English not too good. I am helicopter pilot. President Roo is evacuating to Japan. We hear North Korea attack many areas. Seoul has no, how you say, telephone, lights, that sort of thing. They say maybe earthquake causing flood. Do you know?"

Throughout the conversation, the president of South Korea, an obviously agitated man, kept a constant barrage of sentences going to the pilot doubling as a translator. The US president turned to the room with his hands upturned in the universal, did anybody get that? gesture.

The Situation Room, White House

He got nothing but silence in return, so he responded, "Mr. President, we do not know about Seoul. We cannot confirm that North Korea has begun an attack on South Korea, but someone has."

At that moment, Technical Sergeant Oh was escorted into the room.

"Sir, Sergeant Oh reporting." With this much leadership in one room, he wasn't really sure who he was reporting to, so he just sort of faced the president and saluted.

"At ease, Sergeant," General Albright spoke calmly. "Do you speak Korean?"

"Yes, sir." The young man was still pretty stiff.

"Come up here and sit next to the president. Something is happening in South Korea, and we need to talk with President Roo. The man on the line right now is a helicopter pilot trying to help out. I'm sure he is going to be very relieved when you start talking to him. So relax, tell him who you are, and ask him to put his president on the line." General Albright sat down to listen.

After Sergeant Oh introduced himself, the phone was obviously passed to the South Korean president, who began a rapid string of questions. The sergeant had to break in and explain that while he spoke Korean, he was not a simultaneous translator. Then they began again.

"President Fulton, the Republic of Korea has come under attack by forces of the Democratic People's Republic. In addition to your losses, our aircraft and our bases have also been targeted. Most distressing, all of Seoul seems to be without any power or communications. Due to the location of the Blue House, my people thought it best I come here to Japan, but I am requesting assistance in returning to South Korea as soon as possible. Has the United Nations Command begun any type of counteroffensive?"

"Mr. President, the people of the United States join you in your concern and loss. Unfortunately, we have yet to confirm Kim Jong Il's forces initiated any of these attacks. Our military has been put at the highest state of readiness, however." President Fulton then turned to General Albright and asked, "General Albright, what assets do we have in Japan that can get the president back to Korea?"

"We have one of the Andrews aircraft at Yokota right now. They were supposed to pick up the four senators visiting Thailand tomorrow. Perhaps we could coordinate another means to bring the senators home

437

and use this aircraft to get President Roo back to South Korea. Of course, we don't actually know where it would be safe to take him at this point."

"Carlton," the president caught him as he was leaving for the communication room, "ask General Hodge to give us his best guess on how to get President Roo back home. Also, see if there is any way for him to check on the Blue House and the status of the president's family."

"Yes, Mr. President."

As the president headed out the door, the chairman of the Joint Chiefs of Staff hit the now-established hotline to Korea.

"Hodge here." The situation in Korea had taken the last step toward a wartime footing.

"Dave, it's Carlton. What do you need?" The irony of being the senior military officer in the United States was that you were no longer a war fighter. Your job was to fight for what the war fighters needed to do their job.

"A few fighter wings would be helpful, and I don't give a damn if they're air force or navy, as long as they can fire air-to-ground weapons." He still maintained a level of control demonstrated through humor.

"I'll get Admiral Corping to work on getting you the fighters from Iwakuni Naval Air Station, Kadena Air Base's F-16s, and Misawa Air Base's F-16s. The question of course is, should we move them to Korea or stage them from Japan?"

"I'd like some of both. I don't need any political hamstringing about launching from Japanese soil right now. What has the CIA learned about the people attacking our forces? Every one of them seems a clean kill on an aircraft. Every witness who's seen anything swears the only people in the area are Caucasian, and no one has seen any weapon, carried or left behind. No one has been apprehended to date. Do we have any flattops in the area?"

"One at Yokosuka Naval Air Station—they're recalling and launching now. They should be in position this time tomorrow, though the fighters could launch much sooner, if we know what to attack. Dave, we need to help get President Roo back into the country. Where should we put him?"

The Situation Room, White House

"I thought he was down in the South. We have been unable to contact him or anyone at the Blue House. For that matter, we can't reach Ambassador Evans either. I've dispatched two teams to find out what is going on, and I expect to hear from them at any time. Mr. Chairman, what I need most is information, satellite imagery if possible. We are blind here. Some kind of earthquake has taken out most of the regular communication. We are using the field gear in the interim, which is pretty good, by the way. "

"OK, the answer to your question about President Roo is to have him flown into Osan Air Base. But I need two things more from you. First, we need to override their process of shutting down all flights while the president is airborne, and I think we should have him fly with a heavy escort. Osan has bulldozed the burning fighters off the runway, and is in the process of trying to repair the few fighter aircraft not completely destroyed, which my numbers indicate are only five jets. I need to get them in the air, because we grunts, despite all our talk, feel a lot better with our fighter's overhead. So get me some firepower in here, and I'll see what we can do to find them some targets."

"I'll work on it, Dave. Good luck!"

"Hodge out, hooah!"

DIA HEADQUARTERS

"Bob Cochlen here." He switched the phone to his right hand.

"Hi Bob, this is Director Marks. What did the imagery show?"

"Sir, it shows the dam standing just as she was, no visible damage."

"That's a relief."

"Maybe not, sir. All the water is gone. It is practically a dry dam at this point. And we have more. We may have pieced together a very unsettling scenario. As usual, there is no real proof, but it fits all the data we have so far."

"Bob, I can't just pass this on to the president and his staff. Bring the imagery and your thoughts up here ASAP. I hope the logic is compelling."

"Yes, sir. I'll be there right away." He didn't have to ask; he knew a car would be waiting downstairs by the time he reached the front door. This was his first police-escorted trip to the White House, and he couldn't help but wish all his trips could be expedited this way. Upon arrival, he was escorted to the situation room.

"Mr. President, this is Mr. Bob Cochlen. He is our senior analyst for Korea. Bob is going to show the satellite imagery and then share his thoughts on what is happening." The CIA director turned to Mr. Cochlen, "The floor is yours, Bob."

The Eyes

"Thank you, sir. As you can see, this first shot from about three months ago shows the dam is full and everything looks pretty normal except for this area over on the side here." He used the laser pointer to indicate a flat field to the southwest of the dam and water. "This huge slab of concrete, which we estimate became some forty feet thick, was to serve as a protective cover to this important water supply. Naturally, the DPRK has implied they are protecting it from us. If you look at the lake formed by the dam, you'll see these rails located all around the circumference. These are the attachment points for the concrete cover."

"Here is an image from about a month ago. As you can see, the slab of concrete has been mounted on the rails and is in position above the water. This final image, taken within the last forty-eight hours, shows the concrete slab lying on the floor of a now-empty lake. Gentlemen, it is obvious the water went somewhere, and now we have reports of inexplicable flooding in Seoul. Mr. President, I believe North Korea has used their dam at Cho Mya as a weapon to attack the South."

The president looked around the room. "Anyone care to guess how that was done?"

CIA Director Marks stood, "Mr. President, I think the explanation for all the extra concrete is becoming clearer. They must have used it to first connect to existing tunnels, to extend those tunnels south, and perhaps to strengthen them."

"Well, I believe you'd better have your folks take another look at our intelligence estimate and see what else we missed. Also, I want some information on these Caucasian assassins reported to have wrought havoc all over South Korea undetected. I thought we stopped the Japanese plan to export their Middle Eastern undesirables under the guise of helping South Korea."

Lisa Hunter rose, "We did, Mr. President, and we are still dealing with the political repercussions. Mr. Ishikawa is a very vocal dissenter in the diet over all things American, and our interfering with their legislation offended him personally. Add to it that this is his bill, and you can imagine the drumbeat he's fomenting now."

Bob Cochlen rose again, "Mr. President, I believe we already have these answers—we just don't like them. First, the concrete is enough to assume they have flooded Seoul from Cho Mya. Second, it is unlikely that they could reach all the way to Taegu and P'ohang. As for the

Caucasian attackers, I believe we flew them to South Korea ourselves in conjunction with the so-called mini-summit in Beijing. What is important now is to assess what comes next, in my humble opinion. I believe we will find that Kim Jong Il has no intention of reunifying the peninsula at this time and no delusions that he can defeat the United States in an all-out conflict of any duration. I believe he wants to gain land. This was a quick thrust south. Its overwhelming success is the result of having no logistical preparation for sustenance. It took the psychologically significant city of Seoul entirely by surprise, but there has been no indication of forces in place or moving to hold the area. I strongly believe he has once again duped the world. He has allies in China and Russia who will press the issue to stop the fighting now, and he will then gain the land much as Israel did in the seven-day war."

"So he is totally mad," the president scoffed.

"Mr. President, nothing could be further from the truth. We in the West continue to be manipulated by a ruthless but cunning political success story. His nation is without significant industry; his people are destitute, yet his political clout equals that of most modern nation states. He cannot be ignored, yet he manages enough friendly overtures toward his historical partners to remain aloof but not a complete outcast. In my estimation, with the help of countless intelligence analysts, I see two possible outcomes. We allow him to take the land he currently occupies, or we take him out in an effort twice as difficult as Iraq was. We lack the luxury of defining the timeline ourselves, and we don't know exactly what weapons he has or how accurately he can use them. He has, however, already demonstrated a capacity to reach to and beyond Japan. An attack on Tokyo, even with conventional weapons, would be devastating to an already-struggling world economy. While this has yet to be briefed to or blessed by senior DIA officials, we at the working end of the stick think we should allow him to take the land, and respond to it after the bloodshed has stopped. Forgive me if I've overstepped my bounds here." Mr. Cochlen sat down, believing this would be his last day of government service.

"What does China say about this, Lisa? The Russian president is convinced that we started something, and the Japanese and South Koreans simply want it stopped without further bloodshed." The president looked directly at her.

The Eyes

"Mr. President, the Chinese premier is following along the same lines his country did in the last Korean War. China is supporting North Korea. It has already started lobbying the nonaligned nations within the United Nations to support the development of a new economic zone where the DMZ stood. The plan would require all land mines, concertina wire, and other military-related hazards to be removed. It has a lot of support from smaller nations that have themselves experienced land mines. Mr. President, it is significant that a plan of this complexity was ready for delivery to the United Nations this soon into this conflict. We believe they were planning this with the North Koreans all along."

"Darren, what is your assessment on their willingness to let the US soldiers go free if they get their demands?"

"I believe they'll let them go, if we promise to let their forces retreat unharmed." The CIA director didn't like the obvious conclusion at all.

The secretary of state stood and motioned to the speakerphone. "Mr. President, I have General Hodge, Admiral Corping, and Ambassador Evans on the line."

The president was resigned but angry.

"Gentlemen, I need more time. At this point, it appears we have lost the initial battle in this conflict. Certainly, I am aware this is a temporary military setback. We can bring to bear significant armament on the North, or we could annihilate all the forces in or near the DMZ. The problem with this rationale is what we lose in the short term. We also have some significant weapons technology here that we don't know much about. I want a plan for what we should do next. Dave, you are the closest to the fire. I need you and Ambassador Evans to be hand in hand as we bring our South Korean allies into this loop. The decision to allow Kim Jong Il to have the DMZ and a small portion of the ROK will be unpalatable to President Roo, so he needs to understand clearly that it is a tactical decision."

"Mr. President, Ambassador Evans here. This will be, as you know, a very tough sell to our South Korean allies, and I suspect Japan isn't going to be ecstatic about it either. I'll need to share our end game with them. What should I tell them?"

"Tell them we plan on letting the North set up shop near the DMZ for now, and then take them out when we have our assets positioned. What more can we do?"

DIA Headquarters

"If I may, sir. One idea would be to have the headquarters for the dear leader preselected and, how shall I say, prepared for his arrival. Then we allow them to set up a functioning economic zone. All the while, we slowly ring the area and, when we're ready, take it back. Or more correctly, let the ROK take it back. It will allow us to prevent the mass exodus from North to South while boosting the economic recovery of the North."

"OK. Hold that thought." The president looked around the room and continued, "I like the idea on first brush, but we have to do something right now."

"Mr. President," the vice president spoke for the first time, "the American people, especially some of our staunchest backers, are not going to take even the hint of the United States laying down arms very well. This could be political suicide."

"Nolan, I appreciate your input, and I won't deny that the thought has entered my mind as well. Bottom line, though, is that we were caught with all our toys in the wrong sandbox. That being the case, we are probably dead in the water anyway, so we have the rare opportunity to try and do things the right way because it is what we should do. With all the technology we have, coercion is an easily attainable goal, but again at what price? If we work this out without the massive loss of life we anticipate with full engagement, we take the moral high ground back. Ambassador Evans has the start of an intriguing plan brewing. Let's get him all the help we can and get a realistic plan down on paper. It is going to be tough and we have little time. See if we can get an advance copy of the Chinese initiative and get that to the ambassador as well.

"Dave, I know that what I am about to say is anathema to everything you've ever thought, so bear with me. I want you to tell General Il Jun Sik that his demands are accepted." The room froze. All conversation, even sidebar whispering, stopped. "Before anyone speaks, hear me out. I will not stand by while the North Korean Army slaughters every man and woman from Camp Casey. In the meantime, I want power projection. I want B-2s moved to Guam. I want no less than two carrier battle groups moved, one through the straights of Taiwan, the other to Yokosuka. The USS Independence flotilla will move into the Sea of Japan. Every ship will remain at the loaded and cocked position.

If they don't let our men go, then there will be little left of the DMZ and surrounding areas for them to covet. I also want to know where they crossed the DMZ and how. Now, I am ready to hear your thoughts."

After nearly a minute of uncomfortable silence, General Hodge spoke. "Mr. President, I will convey these instructions to the NKPA, and I'll get their answer back to you as fast as I can. I'll need some satellite support to determine the extent of their current deployment, but even that is going to be difficult since we are socked in weather wise. I'd say they did a great job of selecting the timing of their push."

"Go to it, Dave. We'll keep the lines open." President Fulton hung up the phone.

YONGSAN, SOUTH KOREA

General Hodge picked up the phone and hit speed dial. "Tell General Sik I need to speak to him immediately."

"This is General Sik. Has your president come to understand your situation?"

"Yes, General, he has. I am authorized to tell you we will meet all your demands, effective immediately. The appropriate personnel to execute the political requirements are traveling to this theater as we speak. Your other demands have also been addressed. Now I need to know what your plans are to release the men you hold prisoner."

"As I explained, once I have verified your message, they will be released. We have little desire to drag them along with us."

General Hodge closed his eyes in thanks. The implication of this last sentence was dramatic; he now knew for sure that if the United States had not complied, all Colonel Drierdan's men would have been killed.

TAEGU, ROK

Drs. Dorman and Sanderson checked in and picked up their room keys from the front desk while Emiko, Jack, Lee, and Noriko looked around the lobby, checking out the small concession room, seemingly killing time.

Finally Dr. Dorman turned to Alex and said, "Perhaps if we fossils head upstairs, the remainder of our party might find checking in a bit less stressful."

Noriko and Emiko blushed, while Jack and Lee beamed. The two older doctors took Bob Cochlen in tow and headed upstairs with their suitcases. Bob requested the two meet him in the lobby in half an hour for a discussion of the next day's events.

Alex turned to him and asked, "Shouldn't we include the others?"

Gene shook his head in mock disbelief and put his hand on Alex's shoulder.

"Earth to Dr. Sanderson," he intoned in a simulated radio call, "the others are way more interested in enjoying their own company than this trip. I realize Emiko is your daughter, but she is also old enough to go unchaperoned, and they are beyond that anyway, if my feeble eyes still see clearly enough. I believe the three of us should have enough intellectual power to scope out tomorrow's agenda alone. Also, let's not try to plan too early a start; even I remember what it was like to be young."

The Eyes

Now laughing aloud, Alex was also turning a bit red as he mustered his response, "Yes, Gene, I too remember, and I have noticed a rather poignant interest between your protégé and my daughter. You, on the other hand, have yet to feel the wrath of excluding Emiko from something she feels professionally qualified to participate in—this is a sticky wicket any way you look at it."

Bob Cochlen grinned and said, "I have a solution. I will simply place a note on their doors via the front desk stating the three of us will handle it, and I'll take the heat later, after a few peach Oscars."

Downstairs, the two new couples finally checked in and headed off to their rooms. The hotel was fine by Korean standards, but not particularly well appointed. It was probably the prominently displayed "Nonpotable Water" signs in the bathrooms that gave both Emiko and Noriko their biggest concern. They made it through the first evening eating bulgogi in their rooms. They wouldn't notice the notes on their doors until it was much too late. In the morning, all were awakened by the unusual sounding telephone. Each couple was surprised to find a real human being making the call; no automated systems here.

They met downstairs and elected to pass on breakfast, hoping they would find a recognizable restaurant somewhere en route. Bob Cochlen addressed them first.

"OK, we're here to see if the men gathering downtown are the same men Dr. Dorman treated at his camp in Mongolia. For all of you, I ask that you remain calm, speak very little, and focus hard on these men. We need to know all we can about their conditions and their capabilities, if that is something we can ascertain without detailed examinations. Don't worry if you are not a doctor by trade. I've learned in my business that any observation, by anyone, can be critical, so keep your eyes open and please don't keep anything you see to yourselves."

When they arrived at the simple, white, square building, Noriko grabbed Lee's arm and whispered, "I have a very bad feeling about this. We don't have any real security with us. What will we do if this isn't a friendly meeting?"

"Don't worry. With Bob here, we can muster some assistance pretty quickly. Besides, unless I miss my mark, Dr. Dorman has the respect of these men. That's probably a lot more valuable than weapons right now."

They entered the building from a side door and suddenly realized they were walking into an assembled mass of some three hundred men. All were seated on small woven blankets with their legs crossed. None were speaking, and every member of the new group could feel their collective eyes upon them.

Mohammed, Gene recognized his first patient, stood and addressed the disheveled group of men in Arabic. They looked at him with forlorn eyes, the passion with which they had voluntarily endured so much clearly waning in their minds and hearts.

"All of you listen to me," he spoke evenly. "We have been used, that is true. But it is also not the first time this has happened. To give up now would be tantamount to giving them what they want, control over all of us. We must not let that happen. Here again with us is the doctor; each of you knows him, and you know that what he did was under duress. His life was in jeopardy as well as his extended family. We all know what that means. Despite that, he treated us with respect, care, and, at least in my case, with compassion I have rarely received. It is because of that that I agreed to meet here with him. Let us hear his words; each of you is free to make your own decisions afterward."

He turned toward Gene and motioned him forward. Gene approached the stage and stood looking at the men for a time. Finally he addressed them.

"To each of you, please accept my apologies. My part in this will haunt me all the days of my life. I feel ashamed that I did not refuse; though, in my heart I know that would not have spared any of you anyway. I assure you I had no knowledge of what lay ahead for you, only that I must do all that was possible for your survival, and that I did to the best of my ability. I will share with you now what I have learned about your experiences since I was liberated from the camps. Then I would like to hear the answers to some critical questions from you.

I know that after leaving the camp, you were transported to Germany where you underwent surgery to have a new ocular system installed in your vacant eye sockets. I also know you endured further surgery to your arms, where a device was implanted. What I do not know is how you were trained to use that device, and the ramifications of its use on you. I do not care what the weapon does, only what it does to you. Does anyone care to speak?"

The Eyes

A long silence followed. Jack scanned the room not really sure what he should be looking for, but he felt an encompassing wave of sorrow for these men. Suddenly, he realized why the first question in biotechnical research should never be to discover what we can do, but instead what we should do.

Slowly a frail, young man near the back of the room stood, "I will speak," he said. "You were kind to me, and I did not suffer as I had imagined."

Alex, Bob, Jack, Emiko, Lee, and Noriko watched in amazement as each young man in turn stood and spoke. They observed the depth of the connection these men had with Dr. Eugene Dorman, and when his friends finally turned to look at him, Dr. Dorman wept openly and began to walk out among the men. They parted as he moved to the center of the room and all faced him. What ensued over the next four hours was a nearly magical transformation as the men, one by one, came to Dr. Dorman, showing him their arms and willingly submitting to his physical examination. Each spoke at length with a calm tone, as the rest of the entourage just sat quietly. When he had seen the last of them, Gene stood and spoke to them again.

"I have brought with me friends of varying specialties. Some are scientists. Some are United States government agents. You must trust them, despite your teachings. Together, we will discuss a plan of action. I will not make hollow promises; I intend to see what we can do for you, and I'm sure there will be things we must ask of you. In the meantime, I will arrange for you to be sheltered, cared for, and fed." He turned to Bob who was already nodding in agreement. "We must take our leave for now. May Allah keep you in his light."

He motioned for the others, and the team left in silence, leaving the men sitting in a circle facing each other. Noriko was crying as she left the building. She turned to Lee and asked, "What was done to those men? Will they all die?"

"I don't know the answer to either question," Lee admitted quietly.

Dr. Dorman waited until they were in the van to speak, and then he addressed Bob Cochlen directly. "It is imperative we get these men medical attention soon. There is little that can be done here, and the treatment can wait a few weeks, but all that has befallen them must be reversed, save the eye implants. If you will give me your word they will get whatever treatment they need, and that they will be treated with respect and given their choice of final destinations, I believe I have a plan. With their assistance, we may be able to significantly impact the current conflict."

"You have my word, Doctor. They will get what they need and, to the extent possible, what they want." Bob told the driver to head back to the hotel.

As they drove, Dr. Dorman gave a synopsis of the conversations he had had with the men. Alex noted with silence but intense interest the use of Dr. Dorman's and his own work to engender living tissue and inorganic matter. They had been right, and, as he had feared, they had now unleashed a nightmare.

The van fell completely silent when Gene described the effect of the weapon on the men who had used it. Jack was the first to reach the correct conclusion as to why the men would suddenly die afterward.

"They have added to the sequence of weapon activation the injection of a fast-acting poison into the bloodstream of the user. That way there is no witness to the event afterward."

"I fear you are exactly correct," Gene responded sadly. "Each of these brave men was sentenced to death, and I believe they all know it now. Each of them will need surgery to remove the poison, probably a cyanide derivative, when they are taken to a suitable facility. We won't know until we begin the first surgery what else we can do for them. Alex, when the time comes, will you assist me?"

"Absolutely, Gene, I would be honored. I recommend Jack and Emiko assist as well. They aren't medical doctors yet, but their assistance will be of great help."

"I agree, if they are available that is." Everyone turned to look at the pair; Jack found himself stammering his response.

"Well, sure, we'll be there. Why wouldn't we be?"

Emiko answered him promptly, "Because we just might be too busy somewhere else, but I think that can wait a while. You all might as well know, Jack and I have decided to marry!" It wasn't the time or place they had wanted for the announcement, but it couldn't have come at a better time for the rest of the team. Then Lee decided he should speak too, probably because Noriko had jabbed her elbow into his rib cage.

The Eyes

"We haven't really discussed it with you two, but perhaps we could just make this a double wedding, time and place to be determined later." Jack and Emiko nodded in agreement, and the entire group exited the vehicle much happier than when they had entered it earlier in the day.

EAST OF CAMP CASEY, ROK

General Sik made his call to General Han. "It has gone well, sir. We have many of their men, and now we have their president's agreement to our demands. What are your instructions? We could easily advance to the south. We have used very little ammunition, and the men are eager and ready."

"That is well, comrade, but the dear leader has a plan in place. I disagreed at first, but now I see the logic of his decision. Stay where you are for now, and when we are sure the Americans are acting on our demands, retreat back to the DMZ."

"It shall be as you say, Comrade General." He handed the field phone back to his subordinate and walked silently off to the side. This was frustrating for him. It would be morale crushing to his men. They could easily take this peninsula. They had already defeated the lead unit. They could carve a path from Seoul to Pusan in less than three days.

"Gather the officers," he told his adjutant. "I have news they must hear immediately."

"Yes, General."

He walked over to the command vehicle and waited for the officers to gather. He addressed them without emotion. "We have our orders. We are to hold this position and these men until we get word from

The Eyes

General Han. If things develop as we expect, we will then likely release these soldiers and retreat back through the tunnel to the homeland. I know that is not what you wanted to hear. Likewise, I am well aware of the quality and ferocity of your men. All will be duly noted and re-warded, but I will have no grousing or complaining about these orders. Sometimes the most difficult duty to perform is to refrain from doing what you want to do. Such is our mission. You must be assured that we are the only force to have engaged in battle, and we may very well have succeeded in achieving the dear leader's vision all by ourselves. This is a historic event that will be celebrated for all time. Let your men know how proud you and I are of their readiness and accomplishment."

"General, you have an urgent phone call from General Han."

The private handed the phone to General Sik as the assembled officers stood in silent anticipation. He took the handset and listened.

"Yes, General Han, as you say." He handed the handset back to the private and turned toward his men. "Our orders are to release these men and return to the Democratic People's Republic of Korea. Dismissed!"

As he turned to walk away, he stopped short. Directly in front of him stood a man clad in white, a turban wound around his head. The expressionless apparition raised his arm and pointed at the command vehicle. From behind him, Lieutenant Colonel Roland Drierdan stepped forward.

"General Sik, it would seem the tide has turned. If you are as informed as I believe you are, you will recognize the power this man standing next to me represents. I would have you order your men to surrender their weapons, and then they will be released to go north, all except for your officers and you, who will be held for trial. Your summary execution of my men is a violation of the laws of armed conflict, and I intend to make sure you are held accountable. You will be accorded the rights and protections due you as a prisoner of war."

Stunned, General Sik held his hand up to indicate for none of his men to act rashly. He turned slowly, his face now ashen and enraged.

"Officers, you will do nothing to disrupt this event. I believe we have already prevailed in this conflict. The men dressed in white have a special weapons capability that can destroy tanks and mechanized vehicles instantly. They are the advantage army the dear leader created to make our advance possible. Unfortunately, they are obviously loyal to the highest bidder, and that is now the forces here in the South. They have already done what we needed, but I will not allow our forces to be decimated by them. Leave your weapons and vehicles where they are, and return to the tunnel immediately. Move!"

The officers dropped their weapons to the ground and went about the task of forming up their men under the watchful eyes of the now-rearmed American forces. The grins and remarks, though not understood by the DPRK forces, were unmistakably derisive. In less than three hours, the engagement was over. Had it not been for the fifty men executed and the fourteen officers now in US custody at Camp Casey, one might never have known it had happened at all. The prisoners were held in confinement with an abundance of armed guards.

A few hours later, a helicopter motored in and touched down, from which a group of men and two women emerged.

"Mr. Cochlen?" the colonel asked.

"Bob Cochlen, DIA," he began. "These are the other members of my team. We are all here to maintain team integrity as we travel. As you can imagine, there is a lot of confusion right now, and we don't want to lose anyone. My first question concerns the group of men who aided in your rescue. Are they all OK and did any of them have to fire their unique weapons?"

"They are very quiet, calm, and seem fine, though they do not eat or drink. We saw no weapons, though there is clearly something they possess that the North Korean Army respects very much. What is it they can do?"

"Colonel, there will be time for explanations later. For now, I would ask you to allow one of my team, Dr. Dorman here, access to these men and to make preparations for their safe transport to Osan Air Base as soon as possible, and with a high priority. These men need our help, and as they have given theirs to us, we should not delay."

"We shall have transportation ready within the hour, sir."

Dr. Dorman walked into the fenced-off compound to find all his men sitting in quiet contemplation. Although they had all been given bright yellow packages of meals ready to eat, or MREs, none had made any attempt to open them, much less consume them. As he walked in with the others in tow, the men bowed in his direction. He walked up to Mohammed and embraced him.

The Eyes

In Arabic, he whispered, "You have honored yourself, your people, and me with your actions. Now we will begin the journey back to normalcy. We will do everything we can to reverse what has been done to you. Is the pain great?"

"It can be tolerated, wise one. We will wait here for what comes next."

A sudden commotion from behind startled the two men. Dr. Dorman felt a familiar grip on his left arm as he was spun to his left. Hassim stood facing him, the ever-present knife in his right hand. Before Gene could react, he saw in slow motion the muscles in Hassim's arm tighten and begin the arc up and toward his head. *After all I have been through, it will end here*, he thought. *How ironic.*

Suddenly, the expression on Hassim's face changed from concentration and hate to surprise and then, unmistakably, pain. He collapsed backward as his feet were literally swept out from under him by Mohammed. In an instant, the young men leapt forward as a group, burying Hassim in a mass of bodies. After a brief struggle, the young men forced Hassim to his feet.

Hassim spit at the doctor and growled, "You seem to have many lives, Doctor, but I believe your time will be coming soon. This struggle has just begun."

While he spoke, an older man gently pulled the knife from the martyr who had saved the doctor's life and then quietly walked up behind Hassim. He did not speak, but simply and efficiently reached around the restrained prisoner and slit his throat from right to left. Everyone watched in horror as Hassim's blood spurted out on the ground and on everyone holding him. They released him involuntarily, and he fell to the ground, another victim to his own knife.

"You! You are the assistant from the surgeries. How..." Dr. Dorman stammered. "I thought you died in the camp the night I was liberated. How did...how could you have survived?"

"We are a strong breed, Ibn Il Hosni Muhammad. We are also occasionally very lucky. For the first time since I entered the camp, I went to check on the conditions our brothers were transported in, and so it was that I ended up with these brave men in another country. I traveled with them, overlooked by the wicked men who cut them and used them for their own purposes. I tended to them as best I could and decided to stay with them until the end. We heard about the raid on the camp, but until I saw you a few days ago, I thought you were dead. Now I have avenged my brother's death, and your father's. You have made him proud and me as well."

"Your brother? I don't understand."

"I am your uncle, though you did not know me as a youth. I was taken the same night your father was killed. I have waited all this time to make amends."

"But, why didn't you tell me in the camp? We were alone many times. No one would have heard."

"You would have heard, my nephew. And that knowledge would have affected your actions and probably would have cost us our lives. You have acted heroically, and I am proud to have assisted you. Your skill is great."

The guards had heard the commotion and rushed in with weapons drawn. Alex addressed the officer with them.

"Sir, it is over now. I can't quite explain what happened, but the danger is over."

Dr. Dorman explained to the security forces everything that had happened, and the officer told him he would make the appropriate reports. He also informed the group that the trucks were ready and they could go to Osan now, where they would be picked up in a heavy C-5 and flown to Ramstein AB, Germany.

Gene turned to Alex and asked, "What is your plan, old friend?"

"If it pleases you, Gene, I will go with you."

Bob Cochlen had returned and began to address them all.

"I believe it is time for us to part ways, gentlemen. Gene, your team will be flown to Osan Air Base in the helicopter. You should all, with the exceptions of Lee and Noriko, go with these men to Germany. I'll arrange for your trip back to the United States. Lee, you and Noriko have an evening flight to Niigata, where I understand some very happy people are anxiously awaiting to meet you."

At hearing this, Emiko turned to her father, her eyes filled with excitement and confusion, "Dad, what should I do?"

"Mr. Cochlen, if it is alright with you, can my daughter accompany them to Niigata? Her mother is there, and we haven't seen her for some time now."

The Eyes

"Certainly, the aircraft can take five more people. Anyone else?"

Alex looked at his daughter and spoke before she could, "Make the reservation for two." In the silence following, Emiko, Jack, Gene, Lee, and Noriko all stood staring at Alex. "I'm sure Jack will want to make the trip with you, Emiko," he said as he smiled. She threw her arms around him and whispered to him, "I love you, Dad. Don't take too long in Germany. We all need to get this behind us, and we have a wedding to plan!"

OIJONGBU, NORTH KOREA

General Il Jun Han briefed the dear leader on the execution of the former information minister, Chon Ul, with some satisfaction. He looked up suddenly and stated, "We have failed once again to unite the Korean people under your leadership. I do not ask for forgiveness, but I pledge I will continue working to that aim the rest of my life."

Kim Jong Il sat back in his mahogany chair behind his new presidential-style desk and thought for a moment. Then he looked at his new supreme military commander and said with a wry smile, "Why, yes, we lost this war too, didn't we? General, we are a small and impoverished nation, unable to care even for ourselves. The best we can do, given the hand we've been dealt, is to capitalize on the squeamishness of nations like Japan. They are economically powerful and so do not lack for natural resources, since they can buy them. But by being tied to economics, they may be vulnerable to actions that would disrupt the Asian and the world economy. Our only strength is to play spoiler and madman of the North against the world's desire for calm. Asia and the world are content for Korea to remain separated permanently; otherwise, someone would have to cough up the money to deal with the humanitarian crisis of mopping up North Korea. No one wants to. So we have just carved out another swath of South Korea for ourselves and convinced the rest of the world to clean it up so it will be safe for our children, and in doing so, they will bring in hundreds of millions of dollars worth of goods for our people. This is the best loss we have had so far. Call in your new deputy, General. I'd like to meet him. What is his name?"

"His name is Ohl Suk Chee, and he comes very highly recommended for the position by both surviving and executed members of your former staff."

A-306, REPUBLIC OF KOREA

Captain Frederick Davidson, the aircraft commander, had just maneuvered the C-130 for takeoff from A-306, a 3,500-foot runway just south of the demilitarized zone. They dropped off some ammunition to a small contingent of air force personnel manning the tactical airlift control element.

"Before-takeoff checklist," he intoned professionally.

The crew ran through the well-practiced steps and readied to check back in the prescribed order when queried by the copilot, First Lieutenant Kimberly Atkins.

"Before-takeoff checklist," she called over the interphone.

"Pilot."

"Copilot."

"Navigator."

"Engineer."

"Loadmaster."

Each crewmember responded in turn. Fred advanced the throttles to 937-turbine inlet temperature.

Just as the engines stabilized, the engineer spoke, "We have an intermittent essential AC light on number one."

"Great," the pilot responded and retarded the throttles to neutral. "What is the load reading?"

"She looks stable enough. Why don't you advance the throttles again, and we'll see if it happens again. It was just a flash anyway."

"Co, get on the radio with tower and tell them we'll be a minute here."

"Roger." Kim switched her wafer switch to select the tower frequency and called, "Tower, Tacky sixty-two has experienced a maintenance problem, and we'll be just a couple more minutes on the runway."

The Korean air traffic controller responded in passable English, "No, you must takeoff immediately."

"That is not possible; requesting three minutes on the runway."

"Tacky aircraft, you must take off now." The urgency in his voice was both apparent and baffling. This takeoff wasn't that important, and the visual pattern was empty of other aircraft.

"Geez, I wonder what's eating him," the copilot spoke over the intercom. "Pilot, Co. How close to going are we?"

"Crew, Pilot. It looks like a temporary problem; I've decided to take the aircraft airborne. Conditions are Visual Flight Rules from here to Osan, which is the only place we're going to get any help anyway. Does anybody have a safety-of-flight concern with this decision?"

He didn't have to ask. The decision was his to make, but a crew aircraft meant there were other skills available, and Fred had enough war stories of other crewmembers pointing out important things he'd overlooked himself. There were no objections. Who would want to stay here anyway? was on everyone's mind. Besides, this aging hero had enough write-ups that could never be duplicated to fill a large binder. This was probably just another gremlin. It would be thoroughly checked out, but probably nothing would be found.

"Copilot, call Tower. Let's get out of here."

"Tower, Tacky sixty-two ready for takeoff."

"Tacky sixty-two, hold your position."

"Well, that's certainly a change of heart," Kim said to the crew. The controller's mindset became clear seconds later when fifteen Apache helicopters emerged from under the tree canopy and slid to simultaneous landings. From within, charged a force of soldiers racing to all parts of the runway complex in what could only be an exercise to train for the seizing of facilities. Their swift appearance and unbelievably rapid movement belied the size and firepower of the unit. This was a specialized team, and they had obviously done this before.

"Impressive," was all Kim could manage to say. "I wonder what they are training for. I understood we had ceased hostilities."

"Well, we'll probably never know. In the meantime, let's run the after-landing checklist. We will probably be here for a while. We may as well enjoy the show."

Lieutenant Colonel Roland Drierdan was satisfied; the men and women had trained hard, and it wasn't that often one gets a second chance in this business. Once they had been released from their POW status, the men and women were understandably depressed. All wanted nothing more than to leave the service and go home, but Drierdan knew better. It had taken a lot of cajoling and even begging to get his way, but he had won. Not one single soldier had been released; all would remain with their unit to complete its new mission. They would take out the newly reestablished capital of North Korea in Oijongbu, as soon as the Department of State was ready.

ACKNOWLEDGMENTS

I extend my warmest thanks to my lovely wife, Akiko, for putting up with me throughout the long process of putting this book together, and to my two beautiful daughters, Eriko and Mariko. A special thanks to Mariko for actually reading the entire manuscript and helping me get through the earliest, ugliest versions. Thanks to Col George (Skinman) Wagasky (Ret) for your editorial assistance and inspiration. Thanks to SMSgt Jessie Gillette (Ret) for your instrumental assistance in putting this story together. Col James Fellows (Ret), thanks for your time reading the manuscript and in helping rename the characters to more palatable forms. To TSgt Michael Scruggs, your assistance in the flow, tempo, and direction of the story were essential to the book's completion and for helping me maintain my sanity. To MSgt Michael McClendon (Ret), for you assistance and support through this process. To Lt Col Jim Lewis (Ret), the book wouldn't exist without your help. Lt Col John Schmedake, thanks for taking the time out of your incredibly busy schedule.

Anyone who has experienced this process knows there are no great writers, only great editors, and Ms. Brandi Cameron was the ultimate professional. She was the key to taking a very raw manuscript and turning it into a polished product—thanks Brandi!

ABOUT THE AUTHOR

Don Rosenberry graduated from the United States Air Force Academy. His military career spanned twenty-five years, with eighteen years in the Pacific theater of operations. Don is also a graduate of the Asia-Pacific Center for Security Studies and its College of Security Strategy. He flew as a C-130 navigator on airdrop and air-land missions throughout the Pacific theater, and participated in every Joint Chiefs of Staff combat exercise in Korea and the Philippines. A former chief of combat plans for an airlift wing, a chief of the consolidated command center for US Forces, Japan; US Air Forces, Japan; Fifth Air Force; and the 374th Airlift Wing; he served as the senior airlift officer for a time on the Pacific Air Force (PACAF) and Pacific Command (PACOM) staffs, representing PACOM with the US embassy in an airlift assessment of the nation of Mongolia.

He also served a tour as an editor for the military airlift command's safety publication, following his stints as a flight safety officer and then a wing chief of safety. He has had a number of original articles reprinted in other countries and other US safety periodicals. He holds a master's degree from Webster University (management and business administration), and is a graduate of the University of Southern California's Flight Safety (graduated second in class) and Chief of Safety Courses, and the Military Airlift Command's Contingency Wartime Planning Course and Airlift Operations Course. His professional military education includes USAF Squadron Officers School (selected as outstanding contributor and excelled in briefing), the USAF Air Command and Staff College, and the USMC Command and General Staff Course.

He lives with Akiko, his wife of twenty-six years, in Tacoma, Washington. Aki is Japanese, and Don has a rudimentary knowledge of the Japanese language.

Donald L. Rosenberry
Nome de guerre: DONAKI
2912 Galleon CT N.E.
Tacoma WA 98422
donaki78@harbornet.com